Janet Laurence began her career in advertising and public relations. In 1978 she moved to Somerset with her husband, and started Mrs Laurence's Cookery Courses, beginning with basic cookery techniques for teenagers and later introducing courses for the more advanced. She combined this with writing for the *Daily Telegraph*, eventually taking over Bon Viveur's weekly cookery column. Janet Laurence now divides her time between writing crime fiction and cookery books.

Janet Laurence's previous culinary whodunnits are also available from Headline, and have been widely praised:

'Exuberant tale of gastronomic homicide, full of intriguing inside-knowledge . . . Engaging chefette, Darina Lisle, sleuths zestfully and there are even some helpful culinary hints along the way' *The Times*

'Filled with mouth-watering recipes as well as mystery' *Sunday Express*

'Food and detective stories are both providers of comfort and Laurence has had the shrewd idea of combining them in a series' *Observer*

Diet for Death

Janet Laurence

HEADLINE

First published in 1996
by Macmillan

First published in paperback in 1997
by HEADLINE BOOK PUBLISHING

10 9 8 7 6 5 4 3 2 1

ISBN 0 7472 5523 7

Printed and bound in Great Britain by
Cox & Wyman Ltd, Reading, Berks

HEADLINE BOOK PUBLISHING
A division of Hodder Headline PLC
338 Euston Road
London NW1 3BH

To Serena
with much love

Acknowledgements

As usual, many people have helped with this book. I want to thank 'The Group' who during our regular meetings discussed many points and helped improve the writing in all sorts of ways. I particularly want to thank Shelley Bovey, whose excellent book, *The Forbidden Body*, provided so much background information and opened my eyes to prejudices I hadn't even realised existed. Other sources are far too numerous to mention. Conifers Spa health farm does not, of course, exist but I have very much enjoyed several visits to Cedars Fall in Somerset. Once again, all my thanks to Keith, my husband, for his endless patience with my writing. None of the characters or events in this book bears any resemblance to any actual event or person except by coincidence.

Chapter One

'A delicious salad is a contradiction in terms,' declared Lady Stocks.

'You sound just like William,' observed her daughter, Darina Lisle.

'Your husband does have his good points.'

'It's just a knee-jerk reaction with both of you. Come on, loosen up your prejudices. Anything that looks this beautiful just has to taste good.'

'I've never noticed you eating a Renoir or nibbling on a frock from Armani!' Lady Stocks poked petulantly at the outer circle of crisp little lettuce leaves that surrounded an arrangement of mango slices, slivers of peeled tomato, cucumber batons and pineapple cubes. Tiny, dark eau de Cologne mint leaves decorated the salad and it was accompanied by a lemon and mint dressing. 'Anyway, there's no substance to all this. The body needs something to work on.'

'Well, you must be feeling better!' Darina said cheerfully. 'I knew this place would do you good.'

Lady Stocks looked about the large dining room of the Conifers Spa health farm. The country house decor offered the substance their food lacked, garden flowers were generously arranged and the sun poured through long sash windows. 'I suppose one can say it's pleasant,' Lady Stocks said grudgingly.

'And after a week here we're both going to be ready for anything.'

'I thought the idea was for you to lose some weight. I

don't know what's happened since your honeymoon!' Darina's mother looked pointedly at the loose-fitting top that was knotted at the hips over cream linen trousers. The trousers were hidden by the table but Darina was only too conscious that their fit could no longer be called loose.

'A few less pounds wouldn't do me any harm.' Darina tried to sound relaxed about it; getting irritated with her mother was no part of the plan. 'But mainly we're here to get away from everything, tone up our bodies and enjoy being pampered. This dressing is delicious; do try it,' she said persuasively, wielding her fork with enthusiasm.

'Gerry always said,' her mother started, then her eyes widened. She blinked hard and pressed her thin lips together until her mouth disappeared, but nothing stopped two tears slowly sliding down the carefully made-up cheeks.

Darina unobtrusively passed a Kleenex across the table.

An elegant hand only slightly marred with the liver spots of age quickly dabbed away the tears. 'I'm sorry, darling, take no notice. I'm a fool.'

'No, you're not.'

'I had enough practice being a widow after your father died. What was it, twelve years? And Gerry and I were married less than a year.'

'Time has nothing to do with it,' Darina said gently.

'Yes,' her mother agreed. She pushed at her food with a fork absentmindedly, ruining the circular pattern. 'It was so sudden,' she added, blinking hard again. 'Gerry was only seventy-three. One minute he was sitting there, telling me just what he thought about all the latest army cuts and who he was going to write to about them, the next he'd slumped back.' The hand holding the Kleenex clutched convulsively until the knuckles were white. 'He promised me he came from a long-lived family!' The outrage was almost comical.

'I know, it's not fair,' Darina said gently.

'As if you haven't heard all this before. I tell you, I'm getting senile.' Lady Stocks stuffed the crumpled tissue into her gold-chained Chanel handbag and picked up her fork again.

Darina muttered an automatic denial. All her life she had been used to listening to her mother chatter. A social animal, Ann Stocks's preferred diet was people. But ever since the sudden death a few months ago of her second husband, General Sir Gerald Stocks, she had declared she couldn't face society and that Darina and her son-in-law William were the only ones who understood.

It had been William's idea that Darina should bring her mother to Conifers Spa.

'Didn't you say that friend of yours was running a health farm?' he'd asked Darina after she'd mentioned how much she was worried by her mother's depression. 'Carolyn Pierce, isn't that her name? And weren't you saying you'd like to see what the place was like? Well, why don't you take your mother there for a week. Getting away from everything that reminds her of Gerry could be the answer.'

'You know how I irritate Ma,' Darina had objected. And how she gets under my skin, she had added silently to herself.

'Not at the moment you don't,' William reminded her. 'Come on, I know you want to visit this place and it seems an ideal scheme to me. I'll pay; a company I've got shares in has just been taken over and I'm due for a cash handout.'

Darina was beginning to get used to odd treats as a result of lucky share deals organised by her husband's stockbroker. William didn't have a large portfolio but it did help augment his salary as an inspector in the Avon and Somerset police, criminal investigation division.

'Darling, I hope Ma appreciates what a splendid son-in-law she has.'

He had given a rueful shake to his head. 'She's never really got over you marrying a policeman.'

'Any more than your mother accepts having to settle for a cook as daughter-in-law!' They had looked at each other affectionately. 'But you're right, I've got to do something with Ma, I've never seen her quite so lost. Gerry was such a dear and he knew just how to handle her. It's a devastating blow. Perhaps a stay at a health farm will give her a boost. It shouldn't cost too much, Carolyn's bound to give me a good rate; one of the perks of writing a newspaper cookery column.'

It hadn't been easy to get her mother to come. Declaring on the one hand that she was so lonely and on the other that she couldn't cope with people, Lady Stocks had required a combination of coaxing and gentle bullying.

Half listening to an often repeated account of how impossible her mother was finding life, Darina found her attention wandering. They'd arrived early for lunch and people were still coming into the dining room. A large woman entered followed by a tall, whipcord-thin man. They did not appear to be a couple but the man waved an arm towards a table not far from where Darina and her mother were sitting and appeared to suggest that the woman join him. Almost it seemed as if she'd agree, then she gave a decisive shake to her head and went to join another large woman already sitting at a table for two. This other woman had looked up as the two of them entered and had given a deprecating little smile that suggested she was there, waiting, but didn't necessarily expect company. Now she leaned forward in welcome as the woman sat down.

The little incident was over in a moment but Darina found herself regarding the players with interest. Had the first woman felt obliged to join a friend? Or was there something about the man that had decided her not to accept his invitation? Then her mother's voice reclaimed her attention.

'I shan't be a burden to you, I promise.'

Darina stifled a quick sigh. 'You're only sixty-five, you're in excellent health, are independent, with lots of friends and live in a delightful house. How can you be a burden? And would I have suggested we come away together like this if I thought you were?' she added decisively.

Her mother looked across the table pensively, then gave her daughter a smile full of charm. 'I'm a wicked old woman and you're right to take me to task. We're going to have a lovely time together.' After a moment she added impulsively, 'I can't tell you what it means to me to be here with you.'

Darina took another look at her mother and decided that their trip had already produced an improvement in her looks, for there was the faintest hint of colour in the pale skin that was set off by the silver of hair that had gone white early. And the porcelain blue eyes seemed a deeper shade, or was that the effect of the blue silk knitted two-piece she was wearing? Darina wondered for the thousandth time in her life why she'd had to inherit her father's height and big bones instead of her mother's dainty figure.

A girl only a couple of inches shorter than Darina's shade-under-six-foot approached their table, energy sparking off a well-disciplined body dressed in the Conifers Spa uniform, a turquoise linen suit, nicely cut, with the health farm logo embroidered in navy blue on the left breast pocket. It wasn't only the uniform, though, that set her apart from the clients. Her air of purpose, the way she glanced around the dining room as though checking what everyone was eating, picked her out as part of the management. Blunt-featured and angular she couldn't be called pretty and her expression was severe enough to be off-putting. Then she stopped beside Darina and a smile opened up her face making her suddenly approachable.

'Miss Lisle, Lady Stocks, I do hope you are being properly looked after? Mrs Pierce was so sorry not to be here when you arrived, she had to go up to London to a meeting. But she should be back quite soon. I'm Maria Russell, the health manager.'

Darina returned the smile, 'We've settled in beautifully. Our room is lovely and this salad is delicious.'

Maria Russell's smile grew even warmer. 'Our chef is first-rate. I'm sure you're going to enjoy the food here.'

'When we're allowed to eat a proper meal!' Lady Stocks gave her hardly touched plate a slight push away.

The health manager looked concerned. 'You don't have to eat salad if you prefer not. It's just that we recommend a couple of days detoxifying the system with salad at lunch and brown rice with steamed vegetables in the evening.'

Lady Stocks looked horrified. 'Brown rice! And vegetables! That's supposed to do us good?'

'It will, I promise you, and Rick, that's our chef, Rick Harris, manages to make it taste very good. Now, I think you have an appointment with me at two thirty? So we can sort out which treatments you'd like? The basic fee includes four a day, but of course we can always fit in more. We have some excellent slimming aids.' The health manager's rather small hazel eyes lingered on Darina's figure with an X-ray quality that seemed to identify all the excess flesh. 'And Mrs Pierce will be talking to you about diet.'

To suggest a special diet to a food writer was like asking an MP to cut down on politics. The only way for a cookery expert to follow a particular regime was to write a book on it. Darina toyed briefly with the idea of a rival to the various diet books already on the market, looked thoughtfully at what was left of her salad and said nothing.

Maria Russell gave them another smile and turned to leave the dining room. On her way out she paused at the table of the two large women. The earlier arrival was sitting in front of a plate of salad but the other woman had helped herself liberally to the buffet table. Maria Russell looked disapprovingly at the loaded plate and pursed her lips. She said nothing, however, but continued on her way until stopped just inside the dining room door for a chat by an incoming couple.

'Now there's someone with an uncomfortable relationship with food,' Lady Stocks said, picking up her fork again and jabbing at her salad.

Darina looked at her mother in surprise. 'What makes you say that?'

'Didn't you see how shifty her eyes looked when you said how delicious the food was? And the determined satisfaction in her voice as she mentioned the diet they're forcing on us?'

'She did say you didn't have to eat it.'

'But the *way* she said it! As though hell and perdition awaited us if we dared to ask for a piece of real meat or even a fillet of fish.'

Darina smiled at her mother. 'I shall have to tell William you're becoming quite a detective.' But Lady Stocks had always been perceptive about people. It was only recently her attention had focused entirely on herself.

Darina looked towards the door where the health manager was now disengaging herself from the couple who had stopped her: a middle-aged, medium-sized man with silver hair accompanied by a short, very overweight wife. Maria Russell certainly couldn't be called overweight but she did have a large frame; and was there, perhaps, just a hint of solidity in the hips and around the waist?

'I'm surprised she didn't have a word with that woman over there.' Lady Stocks nodded towards the table with the two large ladies. 'If anyone needs salads, it's her. Look at the size of them both and that woman who's just come in. It's quite disgraceful what some people allow themselves to become.'

Darina felt the tightness of her trousers and a surge of irritation with her mother rose. What did she know about the overweight ladies? Perhaps they had metabolic problems; perhaps they were already losing weight here. Anyway, what did it matter? Weren't there more important things to worry about?

'They look very cheerful,' Darina stated firmly. 'And I don't know why Maria Russell looked at that plate like that. Everything on that buffet table is extremely healthy.'

'A question of quantity?' suggested her mother acidly. 'But I shall be there tomorrow, I'm not having another of these salads, however good they may be for me.'

Darina was longing to be allowed to attack the buffet herself. Spicy-looking chicken breasts, fish dressed with grilled red peppers and garlic, Puy lentils with pickled lemons and capers, large prawns with a bowl of lemon-flavoured low-fat yoghurt and various imaginative salad combinations had caught her eye as they passed by the display on their way to their table. She waited for her stomach to suggest just a quick trip to help it keep going until dinner. Her gastric juices, however, appeared satisfied with the admittedly generous portion of salad she was eating.

The buffet, however, did look exciting. Darina thought again about the possibility of writing a slimming cookbook. What, though, did she know about dieting? And cream and butter and eggs were so good. Surely a small amount didn't harm one?

Then Darina had a guilty mental picture of a procession of rich puddings, gateaux and chocolates; since her French honeymoon her eating had definitely got out of control. No longer could she rely on her height to disguise the extra pounds, and love grips were all very well but hers were becoming bolsters. She needed this stay at Conifers Spa just as much as her mother.

Lady Stocks picked up her bag and the spectacles she refused to wear unless she needed to read something. 'If you don't mind, darling, I think I'll go and have a small rest. It's what the doctor recommended.'

'What a good idea. I'll have coffee and come and wake you in time for our appointment with the health manager. There's a brochure in our room telling you all about the different treatments: massage, aromatherapy, reflexology, slendertone, sauna, sunlamp . . .'

'Oh, I know exactly what I'm going to choose,' Lady Stocks said blithely and left the table.

Darina watched her mother move lightly through the dining room and saw how the knitted silk jacket hung loosely from her shoulders and that her legs now looked gaunt rather than slender. She felt an unaccustomed rush of tenderness for her mother and blessed her thoughtful husband. Then she returned to finishing her salad, enjoying the combination of flavours and textures and the comforting knowledge that it was both healthy and non-fattening. While she ate, she reinforced her determination to revise her eating patterns and discreetly surveyed the other tables.

The dining room was about half full, the other guests a varied mix, mostly middle-aged or older. Apart from the three women they'd already noticed, only a fashion fanatic could class most of them as overweight.

Darina unobtrusively studied the three who were. The girl who'd come in with her husband – she supposed it must be her husband, they were hardly talking as they sat at their table – had been given one of the salads Darina and her mother had been served. Like Lady Stocks, she didn't seem to find it to her taste. She had a round, chubby, open face that looked made for smiles instead of the dragged-down mouth and sulky eyes she currently displayed. Sandy hair erupted in a tangle of tight curls and a sand-coloured velour tracksuit strained to cover her ample curves. A number of others in the dining room were wearing similar tracksuits, all with the Conifers Spa logo embroidered in navy blue over the left breast. She gave a small wave to the table of two, a sign of camaraderie amongst members of a club no one wanted to join?

Once again Darina felt that surge of irritation her mother's thoughtless comment had raised. What, after all, did being fat matter to anyone but oneself? She looked at the two large women eating together. Apart from their size, they couldn't have looked more different. The woman who'd joined the table was taller than her companion, had a more commanding presence. Her long dark hair was pulled back into a chignon emphasising a heavy face that was fiercely attractive in a vivid, almost pagan way with dark eyes that compelled attention. She was dressed in a tracksuit that miraculously managed to minimise her size, accessorised with large gold earrings and a chunky gold bracelet that glowed in the same way as her tanned skin.

The other woman was wearing a turquoise version of the health farm's tracksuit. Not nearly as well cut as her companion's, it emphasised a fleshy body that a second glance said was actually no larger than the first woman's. Fair hair hung too long around a pleasant face with an uncertain expression. There was an air of deference about her, a suggestion that her sense of self-worth wasn't as secure as her companion's.

Their chatter together was lively but Darina noticed the dark-haired woman glancing every now and then towards the table where the man who'd invited her to join him now sat alone.

His attention was concentrated on a plate of large prawns in their shells, strong fingers efficiently releasing the flesh and dipping it into the yoghurt dressing then popping each into a long, rather thin-lipped mouth.

Darina thought he didn't look the type to come to a health farm. It wasn't just because of his lean body; after all, she knew many businessmen who regarded this as a way to relax and tone tired bodies. She continued to study him, wondering exactly what it was that set him apart. Like the rest, he wore a tracksuit, a dark navy one with a Ralph Lauren Polo logo. But it was the only note of fashion about him. His face with its pared boniness and slicked back dark hair brought to mind images of East End gangsters, an impression aided by the presence of a heavy gold signet ring on the little finger of his left hand. The slim watch on his wrist, though, was anonymous and his face had an alert air of sophistication, looked too intelligent for such a stereotype assessment. Darina was intrigued. Here was someone who gave off a number of conflicting signals, someone she found it impossible to categorise. She smiled to herself, he was probably a quite ordinary businessman.

Then, for a moment, their eyes met. It was only the briefest of contacts, but she thought that if he was a businessman he was no ordinary one. This was someone who could exude charisma. There was something about the observant interest in his eyes as he looked at her which had nothing to do with sexual challenge. It wasn't the macho stare of a man who had to assert his attractiveness, but it left her with the certain knowledge that she interested him.

The contact was broken as his attention was caught by a new arrival in the dining room. One who instantly drew most eyes.

Perhaps middle to late twenties, the girl had a cloud of dark hair and the sort of tan that took steady work to achieve, set off by a dazzling white tracksuit. Darina couldn't help wondering how hard she found it to maintain her model girl's size. Her eyes, large and round, were a startling green, the green of newly opened leaves in spring, and her pretty face bore a sweet smile. This was someone who appeared to like the world and hoped it liked her back.

The girl paused in the doorway for a split second. If she surveyed the room, it must have been with the speed of a computer scanning a text before she picked her way between the tables, heading it seemed for an empty one on the far side.

Then she passed the table of the single man and gave a little nod of acknowledgement. He made some comment, she paused – and a moment later had seated herself opposite him.

Darina caught the merest flick of the man's eyes towards the table with the two large women, then he gave the girl a smile of open charm.

Darina couldn't help glancing herself towards the dark-haired woman. Sure enough, she was looking at the man and the girl and for a moment the classically cut nostrils widened and the expression in her eyes seemed to harden. But it was only for a moment, then she was once again talking to her companion in a particularly lively way.

Well, well! Darina looked thoughtfully back at the man and the girl. There was something about their ease with each other that suggested to her they knew each other well, hadn't just met. He hadn't gestured to her to join him, though, and there'd been no overt invitation in the way he'd spoken to her. Then Darina wondered just how much you could read into body language. She told herself she had to stamp on the detecting instinct that kept surfacing. It was threatening to take over her life.

A waitress came up to the newcomer. After a brief chat the girl went and helped herself to the buffet. She came back with a sliver of chicken and two lettuce leaves and proceeded to dissect these with the care of a surgeon while maintaining a steady flow of conversation. Her companion went back to the buffet for a large plate of choice items. Darina looked at his whipcord body and envied the metabolism that could cope so well with food. Every now and then the girl raised her fork to her mouth but there never appeared to be much on it. Anorexic, decided Darina.

She had long finished her own salad and now looked about for the waitress so she could order coffee. Then forgot about that as Carolyn Pierce came into the dining room and hurried towards her.

On the way, she paused at other tables, exchanging a brief word or two. Her neat figure, dressed in a smart black linen suit sparked with a vivid scarf, gave the impression of a whirlwind of activity, her hands gesturing, her dark head bobbing to emphasise some point or other, her body dancing rather than walking. She appeared on easy terms with everyone and the atmosphere in the room had risen with her entrance.

'Darling, I'm so sorry I wasn't here when you arrived.' She bent and kissed Darina's cheek then flung herself into the other chair. 'Just had the most dreadful meeting!'

Chapter Two

Darina smiled at her. 'It couldn't have produced anything you can't handle.'

Carolyn gave a small groan. 'You just don't know!' She looked around. 'But where's your mother?'

'Gone to lie down. Have you had lunch?' Carolyn nodded. 'Can you have coffee with me and fill me in on everything?'

Carolyn raised a finger at the waitress. 'I must warn you, Darina, we don't allow coffee here.'

'Withdrawal symptoms will set in. What do you offer as an alternative?'

'My usual tipple is peppermint tea.'

Darina mentally compared chewing-gum blandness with complex flavours that packed an adrenalin-raising punch and sighed. 'OK, I'll join you.'

Carolyn gave her a sympathetic grin, 'Good girl! Two peppermint teas, Judy, please, in the conservatory.' The girl gave a quick nod of her head, removed Darina's empty plate and left.

Carolyn rose with a lithe movement that seemed designed to display the slimness of her hips, the neatness of her waist.

Darina's attempt to rise with the same elegance and grace was ruined by her heel catching in the chair leg. Both the waitress and Carolyn moved to pick up the chair that clattered to the floor, tangling with Darina. She gave up any attempt to help and stood, apologising for her clumsiness, feeling gauche and overweight. Then she felt eyes following her as Carolyn led the way from the dining room and was sure they were noticing the tightness of her trousers.

'The conservatory should be quiet.' Carolyn threw the words over her shoulder as she led the way across the reception hall to a door marked Drawing Room.

'Carolyn!' The statuesque health manager's voice rang with an imperious note as she appeared through a large arch at the rear of the hall.

'Yes, Maria?' Carolyn stood poised, one hand grasping the door handle. Be quick, her attitude said, I haven't much time for you.

Maria Russell advanced with authoritative steps. 'I need to talk to you about rotas, we're in trouble over next week.'

'I'm sure you don't need my help to sort it out, Maria. Art of management and all that, you know?' A steely smile, then she'd opened the door and whisked through.

As Darina followed, she caught an expression of chagrin and something more on the health manager's face. 'Staff troubles?' she murmured to Carolyn as they crossed a luxuriously appointed room towards the french windows that opened into a large conservatory.

Carolyn's small shoulders tensed. 'Aren't people always the worst of one's problems?' Her face wore an expression of controlled determination. 'Come and sit down and bring me up to date with your world.' She patted a white wrought-iron chair comfortably cushioned in navy and sand striped canvas.

Darina seated herself. All around, strong-leaved green plants reared up from moist soil in an atmosphere that was fecund, rich and touched with a primaeval force. Bright sun filtered palely through a whitewashed glass roof and the leaves of two huge palm trees; somewhere water splashed busily. Compared with the clean sparkle of the air outside, the humid atmosphere seemed overpowering and faintly sinister.

'Tell me,' Carolyn urged, 'how is married life? I'm so sorry I couldn't come to the wedding, there was a crisis here and I just couldn't get away.'

'I'm just as sorry I was in Hong Kong when Robert died.'

Carolyn's husband had been killed in a multi-car pile-up on the M4 the previous summer. Darina had heard the news on her return from the Far East. She'd rung immediately and they'd talked about meeting but, somehow, they had never managed to get together.

Once Carolyn and Darina had giggled at school together, had gossiped and exchanged recipes; later they had agonised over boyfriends, or their lack, as they struggled to establish themselves in different careers. When Carolyn had first married, Darina had often been asked down for weekends. But it had been many years now since they had seen each other regularly.

Carolyn smoothed the black linen of her skirt, her face set. 'Yes, well, that's all behind me now,' she said, then looked up at Darina again. 'Come on, tell, tell. He's a policeman isn't he, your William? Or is it Bill?'

'Yes, an inspector now, and no, it's William, he hates Bill, despite, or perhaps because of, the fact that he gets called it all the time.'

'So, tell me more, what's he like – apart, of course, from marvellous?'

Darina eyed Carolyn. She remembered her husband. A difficult, complex man always involved in business yet jealous of his wife's career as a nutritionist. She'd had to give up working for a commercial food company on marriage but had then managed to build a reputation as a freelance journalist writing on food and health, juggling the demands of deadlines with those of running her home, husband and small son, Michael.

'William's tall and dark and handsome.' Darina giggled, all at once back in her teenage days. 'Bit old-fashioned in a way.' Then she caught her breath as sudden longing flooded her. For the last ten days William had been working under cover with a neighbouring force and she hadn't seen him.

'Old-fashioned? You mean he likes his wife to be at home, is that it?' Carolyn looked at her with bright eyes.

Darina shook her head. 'Far from it, he's always very supportive about my career.'

'Lucky you!' The words were heartfelt.

'Except when I trespass on his territory,' Darina continued. 'Then he goes rather silent and becomes a little difficult. But only a little,' she added quickly.

The waitress appeared and set a tray on the small table between them. Carolyn thanked her and poured two cups of steaming, lightly golden liquid.

Darina took a sip. 'Oh, that's refreshing,' she said, surprised.

'I know, I can't tell you what a difference giving up coffee has made. It was getting me so wound up!' Carolyn ran a hand through her short dark hair.

'Wound up' was precisely the phrase Darina would have used to describe her friend's current state. Carolyn's eyes were never still, she seemed to have a constant need to check everything around her. One of her feet was beating time to an invisible rhythm, there were dark smudges under the almond-shaped brown eyes and her white, even teeth bit into her lower lip as she replaced her cup on the table.

'What's up?'

'Nothing.' Carolyn darted up and broke off a couple of dead heads from some pots of geraniums standing underneath a soaring fern.

'What happened at that meeting? I can't believe it had anything to do with this place, it seems humming with success.'

Carolyn brought the withered stems back to the table and tossed them onto the tray, her mouth straight and tense. 'We've got several empty rooms and we could handle many more day clients. And this is high season. Soon everyone will be hiding bumps and bulges in winter clothes and shivering at the thought of swimming. My meeting was with the directors and, well, they're not sure how long they're prepared to go on running at a loss.'

'Someone's made a considerable investment,' said Darina, glancing back into the drawing room with its deeply cushioned sofas and chairs. 'They must know it takes time to get a new place properly launched.'

'That's what I keep telling them,' Carolyn wailed in frustration. 'But there's so much well established competition.' Then her face brightened a little. 'However, there was one piece of good news. Apparently someone's interested in providing more capital. If they do, we could hang on a bit longer. Our reputation will soon spread.'

'Of course it will,' Darina said robustly. 'What about your staff, though?' she suggested more hesitantly. 'Didn't you say you had problems with your health manager?'

'Maria? Oh, we have our little differences,' said Carolyn carelessly, 'but she runs the treatment side brilliantly. This place should be a first-class investment. They've got to see that!' There was a fierce light of determination in Carolyn's eyes and her hand closed convulsively over the flower heads she'd tossed on the tray.

'When will you know if the extra capital's coming through?'

'The directors said whoever it is will be coming to a decision within a few days.' Carolyn opened her fingers and a shower of tiny dry fragments fell to the table. She started absentmindedly fraying more off the main stalk. 'The thing is, we need publicity. I was thrilled when you rang. You can write us up, can't you?' There was unashamed pleading in her voice and she looked Darina full in the face.

'Should be able to. I had a chat with my editor and we decided some healthy recipes from your chef could work well. How to keep summer energy running into winter, that sort of thing. All introduced with a bit about my stay here.'

Carolyn's face cleared. 'Perfect! I'll introduce you to Rick as soon as you've finished your tea. That's Rick Harris, our chef,' she said with a touch of complacent ownership. 'He's got wonderful ideas, you'll find him an inspiration. Not that you need inspiration, of course,' she added hastily. 'But Rick, well, he is rather special.'

'Special, eh?' Darina looked quizzically at Carolyn. 'Tell me more,' she invited.

Carolyn's eyes softened and Darina recognised something of her old friend. 'Oh, Darina, I've been so lucky to find him. He was running his own restaurant in London, l'Auberge, in Knightsbridge.'

'L'Auberge? I went there once,' Darina exclaimed. 'French food, really good. It disappeared a few months ago. What happened?'

'Rick decided to extend, the work went way over budget and there wasn't enough new business so he lost it all.' Carolyn's glow dimmed. 'I think that restaurant meant everything to him. But then he heard we were looking for a chef with something special, our first one was a sad disappointment, and he got in touch.' The soft light returned to her eyes. 'We hit it off immediately. He's such fun and a wonderful chef. Food is so important, isn't it? People have to enjoy what they eat.'

'I suppose you've taught him about calories and all that? You must spend a lot of time together.'

'Don't look so worried, Darina, Rick's not like Robert, I won't be throwing anything at him!'

'Glad to hear it!' The last weekend Darina had spent with Carolyn had ended in a spectacular row after a local party when Robert had accused her of flirting with one of their neighbours. Darina, who'd gone to make coffee, had rushed into the lounge as she heard Carolyn scream and found Robert on the floor with blood pouring from a wound in his head. A frantic Carolyn had said he'd made her so mad she'd thrown the first thing at him that had come to hand. The weapon had been a heavy glass ashtray.

While Carolyn had driven Robert to the nearest casualty department, he clutching a tea towel to his bloody wound, Darina had babysat for their seven-year-old son, Michael, and cleared up the blood and broken glass from the carpet.

'You know, things were never the same after that.' Carolyn's mouth drooped and she played again with the dead flower heads. 'I could never do anything right for Robert and he was so jealous. Then when he died I found everything was in a terrible mess. He always had this terrific front of being a successful businessman but, you know, he owed money everywhere! I should have known things weren't going so well when he allowed me to take that job.'

Nearly three years ago Carolyn had been offered the position of assistant manageress with an old-established health farm in Surrey. At the time Darina had wondered how she'd been able to persuade her husband to let her go out to work.

'I'm so sorry, Caro. Is everything straightened out yet?'

'Just about. Robert's accountant has worked as though the hounds of hell were after him, and perhaps they were. He must have been responsible for at least some of the mess. He saved me from bankruptcy but there's absolutely no money left. If this place collapses, I don't know what Michael and I will do.'

'Is Michael around? I've been looking forward to catching up with him.'

A light switched on inside Carolyn. 'He's getting on so well, Darina! He's at summer camp at the moment. His best friend was going, and it was so funny! Michael thought I'd be upset he wanted to go too. When I'd been worrying about how to make the holidays fun for him

20

with me so occupied here. This school I found for him has made all the difference. He never had any confidence with Robert always telling him he had to face up to things and not be a mummy's boy! That's another reason why I have to make this place a success. It could take me ages to find another job and those school fees keep coming around.' Carolyn's mobile face darkened for a moment, then, impulsively, she leant across the table, smiled and squeezed Darina's hand. 'Oh, it's so good to see you again. Remember what fun we had in the sixth form together?'

'Dreadful home economics, yuk!' Darina pulled a face. 'All those nutritional values! All I was interested in was learning how to cook. But you enjoyed it, didn't you?'

'It was always what food meant to people rather than what it tasted like that interested me. It's taken Rick to show me how food can be a delight as well as essential.'

Back to the chef! Darina looked forward to meeting someone who could turn salad into a gastronomic adventure and Carolyn from a hypertense superwoman into something approaching a teenager in the throes of first love.

'What sort of emphasis do you place on food at Conifers Spa?' Darina asked, wanting to hear how her thunder thighs could be transformed into something she wouldn't mind displaying in a leotard and tights.

Carolyn leaned forward earnestly. 'We don't go in for slimming diets as such. Most of people's troubles with food come from a bad self-image. Society has forced a totally false idea of bodily beauty on us.'

Darina stared at her in disbelief. 'How am I going to lose all this flesh?' She patted one well-covered hip defensively.

'Exercise will soon tone you up. You're tall, well-built and looking quite marvellous.'

'Well-built! You mean fat! It's all the eating we did on our honeymoon, and since.'

'And why not? Look, don't worry about it. I guarantee

within a month or so your eating will settle down again and with it your weight. You're never going to be reed thin and if you try you'll only create problems for yourself.' Easy enough for Carolyn to say, thought Darina a touch resentfully. If you looked like her, you could afford to recommend not worrying about your eating.

Carolyn edged a little closer. 'If only you could see the number of really large women I meet who've yo-yoed between being what they consider an acceptable size and ballooning out of control, all because at some stage, usually far too young, they've gone on some ridiculous diet.'

'But surely you get too fat because you eat too much?'

Carolyn waved her hands in a despairing gesture. Darina was reminded of one of the more enthusiastic teachers at school, always trying to fire her pupils with her own love for her subject. What had it been – history, geography?

'Some people are just meant to be rounder and heavier than other people. They can force their bodies to be thinner but then they are doomed either to a life of incredible control, watching every single thing they eat, or nature pushes them back and they end up fatter than before they started dieting.' The brown eyes were fixed on Darina; she could feel a messianic fervour in the message. 'So they go on another diet, get desperate for what they call a really sinful chocolate or a sweet biscuit, even bread and butter, can't stop at one or two and binge themselves stupid. And once again they end up fatter than they were before. Then they feel even guiltier and start hating themselves. And the bad feelings invade their lives, ruining everything for them.'

Darina suddenly remembered what the teacher's subject had been as a vision of Rubens's fleshy nudes flashed across her mind and she heard the voice of the schoolmistress: 'Remember, girls, ideals of feminine beauty have altered down the ages. In those days you didn't have to worry about a couple of Mars bars.'

Darina thought of all the slimming regimes she'd tried: grapefruit diets, calorie-controlled diets, low-fat diets, low-carbohydrate diets, high-protein diets, high-fibre diets, she'd lost weight on all of them – and, yes, put it back on again afterwards! But surely the body beautiful couldn't rely on anything so simple as sensible eating?

'What do you do about women who really need to lose weight?' she asked, thinking of the three she'd seen at luncheon.

'Encourage them to lose it very, very gradually by changing to a sensible diet, not just while they are here but for ever. And I'm not talking about concentrating on calorie counts, low fats such as highly processed margarines, or sugar substitutes; just fresh, unprocessed foods with lots of fruit and vegetables, fish and white meats, olive oil rather than butter. And we emphasise the importance of exercise. We've got lots of machines here that can help tone and shape you. As far as you're concerned, my advice is to get in touch with your body, learn what it feels good on, not what the scales tell you every day. Do you know the difference between actual hunger and what I call mouth hunger?'

'Hunger is hunger,' said Darina. 'Controlling appetite is surely what it's all about.'

'Yes and no. We can be hungry for tastes, for food sensations, even though our bodies don't need feeding. Identify those hungers, learn if certain foods intensify them. I refer to them as trigger foods. For instance, I know if I start eating cheese, I can't stop. It has nothing to do with being actually hungry. So I only touch cheese as a special treat.' Carolyn lost a little of her intensity and smiled at Darina. 'Here's a cheerful thought for you. Studies have been done that suggest people with the longest life expectancy are thirty per cent over the ideal weight tables. So don't worry about enjoying the odd luscious pudding or rich sauce. You'll probably notice that we serve dishes here you'd think wouldn't be allowed near a health farm,' she added.

'Yet I've been put on brown rice and vegetables!' Darina exclaimed.

Carolyn's expression became earnest again. 'That's because it helps clean out your system, gets rid of toxic waste. You'll be amazed at how much better you feel after a couple of days. You don't have to stick to it if you don't want to but it'll probably make you lose weight as well!'

'In that case, I'll certainly stick to it. Your health manager said that the chef actually made it taste good,' she added slyly.

Carolyn jumped up. 'Let's go and find Rick. He's dying to meet you.'

They went back through the deserted drawing room, cool under its high, beautifully plastered ceiling, to the kitchen area at the back of the building.

At first sight the kitchens appeared to be deserted. Then, in a corner, stacking a large dishwasher, Darina saw a lad with greasy hair and a long, lugubrious face.

'Chef's outside.' He waved a hand towards the back door. 'Said he wanted a quick fag.' There was innuendo in his voice and a curious smile split the sulky mouth.

Carolyn didn't seem to notice. 'Thanks, Pete,' she said.

Darina followed as she opened the door to the yard and saw a flurry of movement as the slim girl from the dining room pulled away from a young man lolling against a parked van. He wore a white chef's jacket over smartly cut blue and white checked trousers and a pair of spotless white clogs. His long dark hair was worn in a ponytail, and a beaky nose dominating a square, open face turned ordinary good looks into an interesting individuality. Darina could see immediately how he might have captivated Carolyn.

It was impossible to tell how close the girl and the young man had been. A confidential chat – or an embrace? The chef, at least, seemed not at all discomposed at being interrupted. He levered himself away from the side of the van and said cheerfully, 'Hi, Carolyn, you met Jessica yet?' He waved a negligent hand at the girl, now hovering a good two yards away from him, looking a good deal more flustered than he was. 'Used to come to my restaurant in London, nice surprise to see her here!'

Jessica gave a small, uncertain smile. 'L'Auberge was quite a home from home to us, we ate there so often.' She spoke rapidly, as though she couldn't quite control the words. 'It was just round the corner from our flat and Rick was such a friend to us both, me and Paul, my husband. He used to advise me on cooking. I was never any great shakes in the kitchen but I learned such a lot from him.' You could see confidence returning to her as she spoke till she ended on a note that was almost triumphant and gave them one of her lovely smiles.

'Indeed!' said Carolyn.

The girl glanced at her watch. 'Have to run, time for my massage. See you, Rick!' She flashed him a smile that could have successfully advertised toothpaste and disappeared.

'I'll see you in my office, Rick,' said Carolyn with a voice like ice, then she suddenly seemed to remember Darina. 'Maria will be wanting to go through your programme now, I'll introduce you to our chef later.' She swung on her heel and went back inside.

Rick Harris gave a quick lift of eyes so dark they were almost black, like coals, except that coals were incapable of suggesting that depth of mischief. 'In the pig 'ouse again!' he said with a grin at Darina.

'Darina!' called Carolyn from the kitchen.

Darina hurried after her friend. What, just what, had Carolyn involved herself in? Rick Harris might be a genius with food but as far as women were concerned, Darina doubted if he could control his appetites any more than could a dog in the vicinity of a meaty bone. And had he any idea what he had taken on with Carolyn?

Chapter Three

'So there I am in this little-bitty dress that didn't come down further than here,' the speaker drew a line at the top of her thighs. 'And I'm singing my heart out with all the swoops and groans and Perry is making it on the trombone, you know, reaching all the way down to Hades and then right up to Paradise, when all of a sudden that son of a bitch catches the hem of my skirt and it's sailing way, way above my waist! And the crowd, they don't know if it's part of the act or what! I tell you, we got more applause that night than ever.'

There were four of them in the sauna and all were laughing. The speaker was the woman who'd come into the dining room with her husband. In her early forties, she would be unlikely to contemplate wearing a mini these days, not with the cellulite dimpling her upper thighs and the way their flesh bulged over her knees.

Gina Cazalet was her name. Some thirteen years ago, just on twenty, Darina had attended a lavish Oxford ball where Perry Cazalet's jazz band had provided part of the entertainment and Gina had sung. She'd worn some sort of patio pants outfit that time, with a backless top, on a figure that had been ripe but firm, her tomboy face framed by a mass of copper curls. Now the sharp planes had been blurred, as though the soft skin covered marshmallow rather than bone. Everything about Gina Cazalet now was soft; soft and sagging. But the grey eyes were still large and bright, the hair, clinging damply to her forehead, was only a little less colourful, freckles still powdered her face and the gap in her front teeth still added a boyish charm.

At that Oxford college Darina had listened to her voice, low with that blues timbre that can touch the heart, and applauded as wildly as the rest. Though no jazz fan, she had watched out for the Cazalet name over the following years. Now she realised that the last time she'd listened to a Gina Cazalet record had to have been at least five years ago.

The atmosphere in the pale Scandinavian pine sauna was cosy and confidential. No one had dashed water over the electric coals yet so the air shimmered with a dry heat that caught the hairs on the inside of one's nose. It was a heat that both stimulated the mind and relaxed the body and encouraged confessions and exchanges that offered short cuts to intimacy. After all, no one could remain formal when stripped to the buff, and none of the four women in there that afternoon had been prissy enough to wear a swimsuit.

Darina, long blonde hair tucked under a towel, reclined on the lowest of the slatted wooden shelves. For once she felt no embarrassment about displaying her large frame. Beside the others she looked positively svelte.

Sitting next to Darina, towel wrapped modestly around a body that was as out of control as Gina's, the ends securely fastened over her pillowy breasts, was Maureen Channing, the older of the two large women Darina had seen lunching together. Even without the aid of water on the coals, sweat poured down her face and bound together the ends of her shoulder-length fair hair into rat tails. She was helpless with laughter.

'God, Gina, you're a card. You got to tell me when you're coming again so I can book as well, you make the starvation worthwhile.'

'Tush, Maureen, you're just a captive to other people's standards. I keep telling you to be proud of your body!'

Seen naked, it was clear that Esme Lee was actually even larger than either Maureen or Gina. Stripped of her stylish tracksuit, her size burst upon the eye with the force of a Wagner overture played at full blast. Her hips overflowed the upper shelf where she sat. Her belly wasn't a pot, it was as huge as a catering kettle and her breasts embodied exuberant plenitude. Her pagan face was full of generous curves out of which her dark eyes sparkled with fun and intelligence. Yet, despite the fact that she must be in her middle forties, there was nothing uncontrolled about her flesh; it was firm and glowed with muscle tone. 'We don't all have to be Twiggys or Kate Mosses. Remember the Cretan goddesses, go to Fiji and glory in cultures that worship an ample body.' She reached for a ladle of water and flung it onto the coals. There was a hellish sizzle and steam filled the cabinet.

Maureen giggled. 'I'd like to hear Len if I suggested Fiji for our holiday. He likes the golf in Portugal. That's why we have a villa there. And he says it helps him meet the right people.'

'Do you always have to do what your husband wants? Really, Maureen, shape up your act or we'll throw you out of the sisterhood.'

'The sisterhood?' Maureen's pale blue eyes with their short stubby lashes looked puzzled. Gina remained relaxed against the back of the panelled cubicle, her eyes closed and a blissful expression on her face as sweat started to pour down her face.

'Today's women, the women who don't allow men to crawl all over them.'

'Ohhhh!' it was an exhalation of breath that expressed comprehension and denial in equal measure.

'Don't bully us, Esme,' Gina said firmly, opening her eyes and using a finger to scrape away beads of moisture from her forehead. 'We can't all be rootin' tootin' flash lawyers like you.'

'You mean you're going to let Perry make you cut

your weight to what he thinks it should be?' Esme's tone was disgusted.

'Come on, Darina, explain to this single lady that once you throw your lot in with a man, you've lost some of your independence. You learn to love it and lump it.'

'Like Britain and the European Union, you mean?' Esme swapped the disgust for acidity. 'But the Treaty of Rome means we all fight on an equal basis for what we feel is best for us.'

'Surely it's a matter of compromise?' Darina hauled herself into a sitting position and used a corner of the towel she'd been lying on to wipe her sweaty face. 'Perhaps we should negotiate our weight with our husbands, just like who does the washing up and who cuts the lawn?'

'Oho! Don't tell me you've got one of the new men! Someone who even knows where the hoover is and doesn't mind a bit of cooking and ironing?'

'Esme, he's the newest of the new.'

'Remarkable!'

'You'll think it even more so when I tell you he's a policeman!'

'Never! I deal with them day in and day out and I've yet to meet one who knows which end of the iron is up.'

'You're a criminal lawyer?' asked Darina curiously. She found it difficult to imagine this vast woman in wig and gown dealing with the flotsam and jetsam of life in the crime courts.

'That's where the interesting cases are.' Esme looked at Darina derisively. 'I've done my time with dock briefs but these days I'm in there with the big boys. Nothing less than major fraud or murder for Ms Lee.'

'You should have been here the other night, Darina.' Gina lay down on the topmost shelf and ran a lazy hand over her wet flesh. 'She was telling us tales you'd never believe. About the murderers she's got off and the fraud cases that went on for months.'

'Defendants accused of murder who were acquitted,' corrected Esme sardonically.

'You mean you've never got a guilty man off?'

'Cut the scepticism, Darina. It's not my business to ask if a man is guilty or innocent. I use the law to get him, or her, the best deal I can. And the other side does their best to see they end in jail.' She raised a quizzical eyebrow. 'No doubt your husband – just what is he, by the way?'

'CID, an inspector,' Darina said proudly, 'Avon and Somerset police.'

'Ah, the lot who don't believe in calling them detectives. Well, I bet he whinges on and on to you about how the dice are loaded against the forces of law and order these days.'

'I've heard something of the sort,' murmured Darina, always hopelessly honest.

'The police have a sense of justice,' continued Esme. 'They want the wicked to get their deserts.'

'Don't you?' Gina asked quizzically. 'You're law and order incarnate.'

'That's not necessarily anything to do with justice.'

'Oh come on, Esme, even for you that's going too far,' Maureen murmured, leaning back against the wooden wall, her eyes half closed.

'Think of it as a game, with an elaborate set of rules. You play it taking into account all your opponent's strengths and weaknesses, using both against him. All you care about, all you can care about, is winning.' Esme gave a sudden, rich laugh. 'You can tell your husband that I sometimes envy him the opportunity to care about justice.'

'That'll make him feel much better,' said Darina ironically.

Gina stepped down from the shelf, dragging her towel with her. 'I'm for the shower,' she announced, opened the door to the sauna and skittered with tiny dancing steps across the tiled floor to the shower cabinets.

'Are you hoping to lose weight, Darina?' asked Maureen, opening one of her eyes wide enough to survey the ample frame that sat next to her.

'I wouldn't mind losing a few pounds,' Darina said cheerfully. 'I ate far too much on our honeymoon in the South of France five months ago. I said I was going to lose everything I'd gained as soon as we got back but, I don't know, we've been asked to so many dinner parties . . .' she allowed the sentence to remain open-ended. No point in going into the recipes she'd had to develop, and try.

'Ah, food!' said Esme with gusto.

'Ah, food!' said Maureen in despair.

'What about food?' asked Gina, skipping back into the sauna dripping with cold water that started to steam as soon as she sat down again.

'It's just too delicious,' groaned Maureen.

'It's one of the things that makes life worthwhile,' asserted Esme. 'How any of you can confine yourselves to salad and brown rice when you can sample Rick's divine dishes is past my comprehension. Carolyn's picked herself a gem there.'

'What was the previous chef like?' Darina asked curiously.

'Oh, mundane I think is the word. Knew the fat rating of everything and the taste of very little,' Esme said crisply. Then her expression melted into one of a woman contemplating an evening with her lover. 'Now, I think tonight I will have tournedos of beef with the wild mushroom and burgundy sauce followed by tarte tatin. I saw the tarte on someone else's plate last night and the apple pieces were almost translucent, they were so rich with caramelised butter and sugar, while the pastry looked so light and crisp it could float.' She broke off and gave another of her full-bodied laughs. 'If you could only see your faces!'

'I wouldn't care to be a witness in front of you,' declared Gina. 'You're a sadist.'

'Come on, indulge yourself, just for once. What would you have if the calories didn't count?'

Gina leant back and closed her eyes as delight stole over her face. 'That really up-market battered fish.'

'Tempura,' murmured Darina.

'That's it, all crisp on the outside with succulent white juicy flesh inside, accompanied by the best chips, cracker crisp on the outside with not a trace of oil, and all soft and floury in the middle. Oh, sheer heaven! Followed by Haagen Daz fudge and vanilla ice cream.'

'I'd start with lots of smoked salmon,' said Maureen, her round face a delicious combination of earnestness and enthusiasm. 'Or perhaps that heavenly gravadlax, the flesh so cool and smooth, packed with those wonderfully subtle flavours and dripping with mustard and dill sauce. Then breast of chicken in a white wine sauce with asparagus tips, tiny new potatoes smothered in butter with chopped dill and mangetout. And for dessert, wild strawberries loaded with rich Guernsey cream.'

'Oh, don't,' Gina groaned while Esme gave a quick yelp of laughter. 'I'm just starving and it's hours to dinner!'

The door to the sauna opened. 'Room for another?' asked Jessica with a pretty hesitation.

'Of course,' said Darina, shifting slightly along the bench in a welcoming gesture. Nobody else moved.

The girl didn't seem to recognise Darina. Naked, her hair wrapped in a towel, her height not apparent as she lounged on the shelf, perhaps it wasn't surprising. 'I'm Jessica Barry,' she said as she settled onto the shelf next to Darina. 'Lady Barry actually, but now Paul's dead it seems a little silly to keep telling people that.' She slipped off her towel and laid it on the bench. She was wearing an electric blue swimsuit cut high in the thighs and low in the bust. She glanced around at the others. Gina had pulled her towel self-consciously around her body until she was as modest as Maureen but Esme made no move to cover herself, nor did Darina. 'Oh, how silly of me! Yesterday there were some older women in here and they were all wearing swimsuits. I thought maybe that's what the form was.' She pulled hers off with a graceful gesture, placed it neatly on the bench and settled herself on her towel.

In the swimsuit Jessica had looked enviably slim. Without it, she looked half starved; the bones of her hips and ribs pressed uncomfortably against the skin and at close quarters Darina could see she was a good ten years older than she'd first thought. Without the cloud of dark hair, now wet and clinging to her skull, the face looked ordinary, apart from the mesmerisingly large green eyes, from which fine lines radiated out. More were beginning to etch themselves into the smooth throat, and a few broken veins marred the fair skin that was also beginning to suffer enlarged pores round the nose and mouth. Well past thirty and heading for forty, decided Darina.

'Isn't all this just too wonderful?' exclaimed Jessica, stretching out two slim legs and eyeing the perfect ankles. 'I wish I could come here every few months or so.'

'You hardly look as though you need it,' said Maureen sourly.

'Well, I do keep myself in shape,' Jessica acknowledged, just avoiding smugness. 'What were you talking about as I came in? You sounded as though you were having such fun.' The wistfulness was obvious.

'Dream meals,' Gina explained. 'What we'd have for dinner tonight if we weren't worried about counting the calories. Come on, tell us what yours would be.'

It was an invitation to join the sisterhood, to confess, to reveal the most secret of one's dietary desires.

'I always watch what I eat,' Jessica said earnestly. 'I

mean, weight creeps on so, bit by bit, doesn't it? You can't really afford ever to let go.'

There was a small silence.

'There you are, girls,' Esme said, deadpan. 'Discipline, that's all it takes. Deny your appetites, bury your desires, forget the chips, the butter, the cream and you too can face yourself in the mirror. But I can have all that *and* enjoy the sight of myself. Just change your perception of what is desirable.'

She glanced at the clock on the wall and picked up her towel. 'I'm about done; just time for a few lengths in the pool before a session on the sunbed. See you later, girls.' Her monumental figure marched firmly out of the sauna and strode across the tiles towards the showers.

'Me too,' said Gina.

'And I've got a massage in a few minutes.' Maureen followed the other two out, leaving Darina alone with Jessica.

Chapter Four

'Well, that leaves just us,' said Jessica. She made it sound as though it was exactly what she would prefer. 'You arrived today, didn't you? I saw you in the reception hall with, is it your mother?'

Darina nodded.

'She looks lovely. I'd love to be able to come here with a mother. I'm sort of all alone in the world now.' She said it with a curious little dip of her head, as though she knew she was fishing for sympathy and didn't like herself for it.

'Your parents are both dead?'

Jessica flushed. 'I haven't seen my father since I announced my engagement. Anyway, he left us when I was young. He may as well be dead as far as I am concerned.' Her mouth drooped.

'And you haven't any other family?'

She shook her head. 'I had a sister but we were,' there was a small hesitation before she brought out a word to fit the circumstances, 'estranged. That was years ago. I did try and get us together again; well, I mean, blood relations are just that, aren't they? But she wasn't interested.' She gave an elaborate sigh then turned her small face up towards Darina and said with determined camaraderie, 'But tell me about you. You and your mother looked so, so cosy together somehow.'

Darina couldn't help thinking Jessica's powers of observation were limited. She and her mother had never been cosy together. What a curious little thing Jessica Barry, *Lady* Barry, was.

'My mother was recently widowed. William, my husband, and I thought it would do her good to get away, have a complete change, and I wanted to see this place. So here we are. Did you say you'd lost your husband as well?'

Jessica closed her eyes and nodded. She leant against the upper shelf, sweat beginning to run down her face in well-behaved little rivulets. 'Just a few months ago. It, it was a terrible shock. I had no idea anything was wrong with him.'

'Was it heart?' asked Darina sympathetically. It was time for her to take a shower, cool herself off, help the sauna to have a greater effect, but somehow it seemed unfriendly to leave Jessica. 'Gerry, my stepfather, he died of a heart attack; he must have been much older than your husband but it was such a shock for my mother.'

Jessica's eyes opened wide. 'Actually, Paul was quite a bit older than me.' The earnest look came back. 'We were very much in love, he was so sophisticated, so debonair, I thought he was wonderful.' Something shifted in Jessica's face and genuine emotion shone through. 'I never realised how much I would miss him.' She sounded almost surprised.

'It must be difficult,' murmured Darina, feeling the heat beginning to overpower her.

'He'd bring us tea in bed every morning. Earl Grey, Paul said Earl Grey was the only tea worth drinking. And he'd climb back in with the paper and read me the political news.' Jessica gave a tiny, bleak smile. 'I never understood much about it but he was always so funny about everyone.' She sighed. 'I think he was really sorry he gave up being a member of parliament.'

'Why did he?'

Jessica drew a little pattern on the wet wood beside

her thigh. 'He said he wanted to spend more time with me,' she said without conviction.

'What a wonderful compliment!'

Jessica looked at Darina. Her face was flushed. 'He really did love me,' she said in a soft voice. 'And, and I really miss my morning tea.' Her eyes blinked rapidly. 'Being left alone has devastated me.' Her social voice was back and Darina remembered the way Jessica had so casually made it possible to be invited to join the table of the single man in the restaurant at lunch, and how Carolyn had found her with Rick Harris outside the kitchen.

'You need friends to help cheer you up,' she suggested.

Jessica immediately brightened. 'Oh, yes. It was such a good idea to come here. All thanks to Frank. Frank Borden, an old friend. He's here too, I had lunch with him.'

Her very naturalness stripped the encounter of innuendo but Darina felt she had to add, 'And of course you know the chef, too, don't you?'

Jessica's eyes were guileless as she said, 'Oh, Rick, yes! Paul and I used to eat so often at his restaurant, it was darling. "*Sympa*," Paul used to say. He spoke French fluently, you know. Then one day it was all closed up and when it opened again it was a sort of brasserie. I never tried it because that was when Paul died.' Jessica's face clouded again and, almost despite her instincts, Darina felt her distress was sincere.

The heat was now overpowering. 'It's time for a quick shower,' she said as she got up. 'I'll be back in a minute,' she added as she caught Jessica's look of disappointment.

Darina slipped across the tiled floor and into the shower, turned on the powerful jet of cold water and braced her overheated body. But the sensation was wonderful, it seemed to cleanse her mind as well as her body. As she turned under the needle-sharp spray, Darina couldn't help wondering about Jessica Barry. What was she? Classic bimbo or just a girl who needed a constant supply of affection?

She did sound very alone and the others hadn't been friendly to her. Who had Sir Paul Barry been and how long had they been married? That clumsy introduction of her title suggested she'd hardly got used to using it. Despite her age, she seemed naive.

'What do you do?' Darina asked as she settled herself again on her shelf. Then she thought what a stupid question that was. Girls like Jessica Barry didn't work.

'Oh, nothing very much. I was an air hostess before Paul and I married but of course I gave it up then. He needed a hostess and someone to be there for him. Now I shall have to start looking for another job.'

So, not such a stupid question. Why the urge to work? Not left nicely off financially after all, or boredom? 'Back with the airlines?'

'I don't think so,' the grave little voice said. 'I mean, one has to move on, doesn't one? Done that, read the book, seen the film, got the T-shirt!'

'So have you anything in mind?' Darina didn't think she'd ever met anyone quite like Jessica Barry before. Despite the initial impression of a manhunter, when you talked to her, she came over as someone rather lost, unsure of herself, almost desperate for human contact. Darina wondered how many real friends she had. Any?

'Well, yes.' There came the sound of Jessica shifting her position. Darina opened one eye and saw she was sitting up, clutching a towel. 'Promise you won't laugh if I tell you?'

Slightly intrigued, Darina assured her she wouldn't.

'Well, I want to be a singer!' Jessica said breathlessly.

'Like Gina?' It seemed the obvious comment to make. 'Right!'

Darina raised herself on an elbow. 'Isn't it rather difficult to break into that world?' This didn't seem to be financial necessity, more the fulfilment of some sort of dream.

Jessica leant back against an upper shelf, hugging her knees; she looked like a small animal curling itself into a tight space. 'I've been taking lessons. I've always wanted to sing but I've never really had the opportunity before.' She gave a secretive little smile that lifted her cheeks like a hamster's. 'There's someone I know who might be able to get me a spot in a nightclub but he says I've got to get really professional. Well, Perry Cazalet is here, isn't he? He's ever such a big name and if he took me on then I'd be able to make it, wouldn't I?'

'I'm afraid I know nothing about the music world,' Darina said, thinking that Jessica was making it all sound too easy. 'Have you discussed it with him yet?' she added, remembering the hostility Jessica had raised in Gina Cazalet.

Jessica shook her head but there was a mischievous smile in the green eyes that looked even larger with her wet hair slicked back from her face. 'But I've made sure he's noticed me. Only a matter of nailing him down now.' There was a wealth of confidence in her voice.

Darina decided Jessica Barry reminded her of a fox creeping up on unsuspecting chickens, her plan of campaign all worked out. It seemed life at Conifers Spa might not be the restful time she had thought.

Chapter Five

Being massaged has to be one of the most pleasantly physical experiences there is: totally sybaritic without overtones of lust, thought Darina, submitting to the long, firm strokes of a small girl with a pug face and short fair hair who'd welcomed her with a big smile and announced her name was Sally.

'You've got a good body,' Sally said, running her oiled hands up the back of Darina's thigh.

'Too much weight,' groaned her patient.

'You don't want to be too skinny. What matters is muscle tone. Tiny bit flabby here,' the expert hands manipulated the right buttock, 'but exercise will soon put that right.'

'Running?' Darina was alarmed.

'Cycling or swimming is better. Been in the pool yet?'

'We only arrived today. I've come with my mother. She had a massage straight after our appointment with the health manager and I had a sauna. Now she's having a mudbath and I'm here.'

'Lady Stocks, is she your mother? I was the one did her and she was telling me she'd come with her daughter!' Sally sounded delighted. 'She was sweet, but so tense! I spent for ever on her shoulder muscles. But you're staying a week?' Darina nodded, feeling contentment beginning to seep through her body. 'We should be able to work out all the knots by then.' A little later Sally worked her way up to Darina's shoulders and exclaimed at the tension she found there. 'What do you do?'

'I'm a cook really but I write cookery books and articles so I spend a lot of time at the word processor.'

'Oh, they're the worst for the shoulders. You have a husband or a partner or something?'

Darina said she did.

'Then teach him to work out the tension. Make all the difference!'

Darina tried for a quick mental picture of William kneading her shoulder muscles like a neophyte baker, but couldn't quite get it into focus. Oh, he'd try all right, William was always willing to try anything he thought would help Darina, but good with his hands he was not. Except in certain ways she could think of. Once again she missed him badly.

'He's picking me up here on Saturday night,' she told Sally. 'One of his mates has just been promoted and there's a big party. It's not far from here.' That had been another reason for coming this particular week. The local force William was working with on a case that spanned the two counties of Wiltshire and Somerset was not far from Conifers Spa and staying here was going to save Darina an hour and a half's drive. 'He'll be picking me up; perhaps you can give him a lesson.'

'Saturday's my day off,' Sally said regretfully. 'It should be Sunday but one of the other girls wanted to go to a cricket match with her boyfriend and I swapped with her.'

'You only get one day off a week?'

Sally moved the towel down Darina's back and started smooth strokes up her waist. 'One and a half.'

When you worked for yourself as Darina did, often you didn't get any days off, but then there were other times you could please yourself. To be tied to only one and a half days off a week seemed to her rather hard. 'Do you like working here?'

'It's OK. The girls are all friendly and there's a good

42

atmosphere. The pay's not very good but then it isn't anywhere.'

'So why do you do it?'

'Well, pay isn't everything, is it? It's good experience. I want to open my own salon one of these days. First, though, I need to have a job like Ms Russell's, learn all the ropes.'

'She run the treatment side well?' Darina thought about that 'Ms'. Well, the health manager did seem a little daunting, not someone to accept junior staff calling her by her Christian name.

'Boy!' Sally started slapping into Darina's sides with the edges of her hands, keeping up a rhythm a drummer would envy. 'The army could use her!' But her tone was admiring.

Darina couldn't fault the way Maria Russell had sorted out her and her mother's requirements. She had delved into their reasons for coming to the Spa, gone through how much exercise they usually took, assessed their expectations of the stay, then explained the various choices available to them, what was included in the basic fee and some of the extras that were offered.

As Darina had listened to the quiet, reassuring voice talking about the benefits of exercise and waited for the dreaded words 'regular jogging' to appear, she wondered what it would take to upset that calm. Then found that the manager had stopped talking and was looking at Darina with a questioning lift of her finely arched eyebrow and a gleam of amusement in the hazel eyes that were almost green at their outer corona. 'I'm sorry,' Darina said, 'I didn't quite catch that.'

The wide mouth tilted a little at the corners but the calm never varied. 'I was explaining we have an aerobics class every day except Sunday, and pool exercises. Do you work out regularly?'

Here it came! 'No,' Darina had said, refusing to add excuses such as lack of time, good intentions that were constantly frustrated or anything like that. The fact was, exercise bored her and there were always better ways of spending time. William and she sometimes managed the odd game of tennis or squash but it couldn't qualify as regular exercise.

'You cook?' Maria Russell had glanced again at the cards she'd been filling out. 'That's a lot of standing around on your feet. Varicose veins have to be a danger.' She'd looked down at Darina's long legs but there were no unsightly veins sticking out of the lightly tanned skin. 'Exercise would help keep them away. And you say you spend several hours a day at the word processor; that won't help your upper thighs and bottom.' She didn't have to move her gaze this time, they both knew these were problem areas with Darina. 'Give the aerobics class a try.'

Darina had heaved a small sigh and nodded. If you put yourself in the hands of experts, it was foolish not to take their advice.

She had also been impressed by the atmosphere in the treatment centre. Carolyn had no doubt been responsible for the tasteful decor, a soothing peach and light turquoise with lots of pale, satiny pinewood. But the cheerful efficiency of the staff, the way no guest was left hanging around for an appointment, the fact that all the areas were spotless, towels removed as soon as discarded, equipment neatly replaced when used: that must be due to Maria Russell. And the fact that Sally didn't seem to resent the discipline imposed on her said a lot for the manager's people-handling abilities.

Sally moved on to Darina's upper arms. 'This is one of the places where the older women have trouble,' she said. Even though Darina knew her muscles there were firm, a terrifying sense of flab seeped into her. She fought it off by reminding herself of the exercise a cook gets, all the beating and stirring and kneading. Though, she thought suddenly, machines now did most of that. Perhaps an aerobics class wouldn't be such a bad idea.

'Do you take regular exercise?' she asked Sally.

There was an explosive laugh as Sally pushed hard at Darina's flesh. 'What do you think this is?'

'I suppose it must be hard work.'

'You can say that again! Three thousand calories a day, that's what someone worked out we spend.'

'You don't have weight problems, then?'

'It takes some eating to make that up,' Sally agreed. 'That's you done, now just lie there and let it all hang out. No need to get up for a bit.' She covered Darina with the towel and disappeared out of the louvred pine booth.

A delicious feeling of total relaxation spread through Darina. She hoped her mother had enjoyed a similar feeling after her massage. She lay with eyes closed and drifted away.

Through her pleasant haze came the sound of a man's voice from the next door cubicle.

'Theresa, isn't it? You did me earlier in the week.'

'That's right, Mr Borden.' The girl sounded pleased to have been remembered. 'I've had a couple of days off.' There came the sound of hands being applied to flesh. Frank Borden had olive skin, Darina remembered, and his body looked tough and wiry. Quite hard work to massage, she would imagine.

'And what have you been doing with your days off, Theresa?' It was a warm voice, full of friendly interest. Frank Borden managed to sound as though he really cared what Theresa had been up to.

'Oh, me and Jeff, that's my boyfriend, went to see a garage just outside Birmingham, Walsall way. He's been offered a job there by a friend of his dad's. But Jeff doesn't know. It's more money than he's getting and Mr Weeks, that's the owner, says he can maybe be service manager next year if he handles himself right.'

'But it means moving, is that it?'

'You got it! There's me mum, you see. She doesn't

want me to go so far away. And Jeff's got all his mates here.'

'Probably wouldn't take him long to find some more in – Walsall, was it? Of course you'd miss your mother; didn't you tell me you lived at home? And weren't you thrilled at this place opening because then you didn't have to move away?'

'Right!' Again there was delight in Theresa's voice at her client remembering what she'd said.

'Is it the job you don't want to leave or your mum?'

'Oh, the job's OK but it's nothing special.'

'You don't like it here?'

'I like the other girls, and the clients, of course,' Theresa put in hastily. 'But, well, Ms Russell's a bit of a tartar!' the words came out in short, sharp bursts, testifying to the effort she was putting into her work.

'So it's really your mum.' Frank Borden's voice remained sincerely interested but Darina heard a slight hint of amusement as well. 'There's the telephone, you know. And you could get down here to visit in a couple of hours.'

'I suppose.' Theresa didn't sound any too certain. There was a faint rustle as though she'd moved her position. 'My, our shoulder muscles are much better, Mr Borden. The knots are almost gone. You never told me what you did. It must build up lots of tension to get your shoulders like they were.'

'Business, Theresa, that's what I do. A bit of this and a bit of that. Mostly boring things with money. And I don't notice the tension. I think I handle it pretty well. But you're absolutely right, that's where it all goes.'

'We get a lot of businessmen here. They seem to like getting away for a few days. Sometimes the men's sauna is like a club, Jim says. Jim looks after the men's side, you've met him I expect.'

'Yes, he's most helpful.'

'Well.' The effort Theresa was putting into her massage came through in her voice. 'Well, Jim says they're hardly ever talking about girls, you know, like you'd expect? No, they're talking money.'

'You'd hardly think that'd be more important than girls.' Amusement oozed out of the light, flexible voice and Darina smiled involuntarily.

'Mr Borden, you're a tease, that's what you are!'

'And you love every minute of it, Theresa.'

'Now, if you'd just turn over, I'll work on your thighs.'

There was the ring of a telephone and Theresa's scandalised tones said, 'Mr Borden! You know you're not supposed to bring your mobile in here!'

'Sorry, but it'll be something important, won't take a moment.' The sound of his voice and another rustle indicated he was sitting up. Where had he hidden the phone, Darina wondered; the pocket of his dressing gown or under the towel? 'Yes? Frank here.' There was a small silence.

'I'll be back in two seconds,' Theresa said threateningly. There came the slight click of a cubicle door closing.

'Yes?' Frank Borden said again, his voice lower, confidential.

There was a pause. Darina wondered whether she should say something, make him aware she was in the next cubicle. She gave a cough but the sound was drowned by his voice speaking at the same moment. 'The whole shipment, you said? And Archimedes did nothing?' he exploded, then controlled himself. 'What the hell does he think we pay him for? What's happening now?' A pause, and Darina could imagine a frantic subordinate on the other end of the phone trying to explain. If he hadn't realised by now that he could be overheard, perhaps it was better to keep quiet. It was only some business call, after all. 'Can we distance ourselves?' Another pause. 'I see. Well, you'd better get it sorted out, hadn't you?' Was Darina imagining undertones of threat in the pleasant voice? 'Ring me back as soon as you have.' There was no sort of goodbye, just a cut-off sound.

The door to Darina's cubicle opened and a cheerful voice said, 'I think you're down for a slendertone now, Miss Lisle, but no need to rush.'

Darina got reluctantly down from the bench and slipped on her towelling wrap. Had Frank Borden realised now he could have been overheard? Well, it hadn't been her fault, and after all, apart from that one moment when he'd sounded threatening, there'd been nothing very private about the call, had there?

She followed the girl into another cubicle, one with a narrow bed and a machine sprouting a fine collection of wires, submitted to the process of having cold wet pads attached to her waist and thighs and wondered if the way to a perfect figure could be so easy. No hard exercising, no strict dieting. A small gurgle from her stomach reminded her it was not too long now till supper. What, she wondered, would the brown rice and vegetables taste like, and would her mother agree to continue with the detoxifying regime?

Ann Stocks hadn't said a word as Carolyn Pierce had gone through the advantages of the diet during their nutritional discussion but her smile had become as enigmatic as the Mona Lisa's. Darina had asked if everyone followed this regime when they first arrived at Conifers Spa. Carolyn had given her a regretful smile. 'We try to recommend they do but some people refuse to realise how much good it can do them.'

As she felt the first convulsive jerks of the pads on her waist and thighs, Darina thought she was willing to place a small bet that Frank Borden had not submitted to brown rice and vegetables for dinner.

Chapter Six

'Darling, I've decided it's not such a good idea for me to have the rice and veggie thing,' Ann Stocks said as Darina lowered herself onto a lounger beside the outdoor swimming pool. It was late afternoon but the heat of the glorious summer day had been absorbed by the paving stones round the pool and the air was still soft and warm. Ann Stocks was reclining dressed in one of the Conifers Spa tracksuits, its soft turquoise eminently flattering to her fair skin. Darina wondered if she'd bought anything else in the dress shop and took this renewed interest in clothes as another good sign.

'You know Baz and Molly are coming to eat with us tomorrow and it wouldn't be polite. They'd feel awful eating a proper meal while we toyed with brown rice.'

General Sir Basil Creighton had been something of a protégé of Darina's stepfather, Lieutenant-General Sir Gerald Stocks. One of the most senior officers in Her Majesty's army, the general and his wife lived in official style not far from Conifers Spa. Ann and Gerry Stocks had stayed with them shortly before Gerry died and the Creightons had attended his funeral.

As soon as the health farm stay had been organised, Lady Stocks had been on the telephone insisting that Basil and Molly came and ate with them.

'So if I can't complete this detoxification thing, whatever it is, there's no point in starting it,' her mother ended triumphantly. 'And anyway, it's not as though I need to diet. I need feeding up!'

Darina arranged the flap of her dressing gown neatly over her legs, lay back in the last of the sun and decided a lecture on nutrition was not what her mother needed. 'Have you enjoyed your treatments this afternoon?'

'The mudbath was definitely *not* me! Far too debilitating, I can't think what they were doing recommending it.' Darina forbore to point out that Maria Russell had warned her she might find it draining but her mother had insisted it was what she wanted. 'The massage was sheer heaven, though, and I've so enjoyed myself sitting in this lovely sun. I've met a charming couple who live in the Cotswolds. He's in merchant banking . . .' Darina let her mother's words float over her. It was enough that Ann Stocks had found people she could connect with. The words 'love to play bridge' drifted by her and Darina knew it wouldn't be long before a fourth had been found. Nothing else could have shown more clearly that a corner had been turned for her mother.

The garden of Conifers Spa was really lovely. All around them was the late August blaze of yellows and oranges that said, take our warmth while you can, soon autumn will be here and frosts will kill us off. And beyond the flowerbeds were gracious trees, offering a backdrop of differing greens to the colourful flowers.

A few people were walking gently round the grounds but most of the guests appeared to have gone inside. Apart from Darina and her mother, there were only two others sitting round the pool. On a lounger on the other side of the bright blue water was Jessica Barry, wearing a white one-piece bathing suit that showed off her golden tan. She was talking in her earnest way to Perry Cazalet.

His head of silver hair glittered in the late sun above an outfit of dark glasses plus a small pair of swimming trunks. He had one of the hairiest bodies Darina had ever seen, greying hair fluffing his chest, arms and legs. It didn't seem to put Jessica Barry off. She was leaning towards him in a confidential manner, smiling up at him, waiting for him to respond to whatever she'd been saying.

'And I've been telling them all about my clever daughter,' Ann Stocks patted Darina's arm. 'They are looking forward so much to meeting you. What a pity it is you don't play bridge, darling.'

'I'm sure you'll find someone else, Ma,' said Darina absentmindedly, watching as Gina Cazalet in a floating wrap came up to the couple on the other side of the pool, sat down and put a hand on the man's hairy arm in a way that could only be termed possessive. Then she shed her wrap, revealing a navy blue swimsuit that had 'control' written all over it. She lowered herself carefully into the pool, followed by her husband, his neat figure cleaving the water. Jessica was left to watch them swimming powerfully up and down the length of the pool. For a moment it looked as though she might join them, then her shoulders drooped, she picked up a towelling wrap and went inside.

That evening Darina's mother indulged in what the waiter described as 'a watercress soup made with chicken stock and finished with a little cream' and 'a chicken breast stuffed with apricots and pistachio nuts and served with a lemon grass beurre blanc.' 'An excellent choice,' he added, 'if I may say so. And can I suggest, my lady, fresh tagliatelle and broccoli florets to accompany?' Lady Stocks agreed that that sounded delicious and threw a triumphant look at Darina as a plate of brown rice and vegetables was placed in front of her.

'I really feel sorry for you, darling, having to cope with that lot,' she said complacently, dipping in her soup spoon and briefly closing her eyes in delight as she sipped at it.

'In fact it tastes very good!' Darina said in surprise. Beautifully diced carrots, celery, French beans, onions and courgettes had been mixed with fresh corn on the cob and mushrooms, all steamed and mixed with brown rice and chopped fresh herbs. A sauce of Puy lentils accompanied the dish. The clean taste of the steamed vegetables, the pungency of the herbs, the contrast of the different textures, the comforting simplicity of the dish, all made it a delight to eat.

'I'm sure it's delicious, darling, and if it helps there to be rather less of you when you return to William, it will all have been worth while.'

'I'm not *fat*, Ma,' said Darina tartly.

'No, but you can't afford to put on any more weight. Such a pity you had to decide on food as a career. With your height you could have been a model.'

'Mother, I'd never have been skinny enough for that!'

'If you hadn't eaten so much you might have been.'

'Anyway I'd never have wanted to be a clothes horse. I haven't your dress sense,' she added craftily.

The compliment fell on stony ground. 'Nonsense, all it needs is a little thought. That's your trouble, darling, you don't pay enough attention to what you wear. Look at you this evening, for instance.'

Darina had put on a pair of black linen trousers with a silky jersey top in cinnamon. She'd thought it set off her long blonde hair, caught back from her face tonight with a pair of tortoiseshell combs, and diminished her size.

'Such an ordinary look! Now, over there is that very large woman,' a touch of disapproval entered Lady Stocks's voice. 'She may have let her figure go but she certainly knows how to dress.'

Esme Lee was sitting in a corner of the dining room with Maureen. She wore a brightly patterned, bat-winged, full-length silk wrap and her dark hair had been pushed into a matching silk turban. Her eyes were faultlessly made up with two shades of grey eyeshadow and a white highlighter that emphasised their size and minimised

their heavy lids, and she was using a singing coral lipstick. Otherwise, though, her skin was bare except for a
faint gloss of oil that played up her tan. Maureen, in
a lilac knitted number, looked colourless beside her.

Darina agreed that Esme Lee looked great.

'You know, darling, I've often wondered if the way
you took to food wasn't a subtle way of getting back at
me,' added Ann Stocks, helping herself to another milk
roll from the basket of home-made bread that had been
placed on their table and liberally spreading a piece of it
with butter.

'What do you mean?' Darina's heart sank.

'I mean I was never particularly interested in cooking; I think your poor father often wished for something
like steak and kidney pie or a hearty casserole instead of
the grilled chops I gave him.'

A fleeting vision of the overcooked chops
accompanied by reconstituted powdered potatoes and
frozen vegetables passed through Darina's mind. Plus the
resigned look on her father's face as the plate was placed
in front of him. The only time Ann Stocks really tried
was when they had people to dinner. Then she achieved
good food by paying someone else to cook it, usually
passing it off as her own handiwork.

'You were always so devoted to your father. I remember the first meal you cooked for us was steak and kidney
pudding followed by treacle tart.' Lady Stocks gave a brief
shudder. 'I'm sure you'd agree now that the combination
has to be dire but we were so proud of you!' She gave
Darina a brilliant smile.

'Looking back,' said Darina carefully, 'I think Digby
was the major influence.'

'Oh, your poor cousin! Of course, he was a towering
figure in the food world. You aren't doing badly, darling,
but you could never hope to emulate him!'

A familiar feeling of panic invaded Darina. No, she
would never approach Digby Cary's reputation. She didn't

expect to; he had been a household name, someone recognised even by those not interested in food. But she had thought she was beginning to make her own mark. Now the television programme she'd been involved with had collapsed and the high profile she'd been on the point of achieving had taken a dive back to obscurity. Writing a newspaper column wasn't the same. Some people didn't even notice her name on the articles. Then Darina wondered if that was important. Surely what mattered was that she had an outlet for her work? Readers valued her articles even if they didn't know who she was; that was what counted.

Lady Stock's main dish had arrived and Darina tried not to wish she could also taste the succulent-looking chicken breast in its light and glossy sauce.

'I suppose you could say that Digby has shaped my entire life so far, from encouraging me when he stayed with us and taught me so much about cooking, to being the means of introducing me to William,' said Darina, refusing to think about chicken breasts.

Lady Stocks gave a discreet shudder. 'That dreadful murder! I can't think that was any help at all.'

Darina left the question of whether her mother meant it would have been better if she and William hadn't met or was merely regretting poor Digby's awful end. 'But even if Digby hadn't been there, I'm sure I'd have ended up a cook.'

'You had a vocation, you mean? Well, I suppose if I was born uninterested in cooking you came into the world with a metaphorical wooden spoon in your hand. The question is, my darling, when are you going to settle down and start a family?'

'Heavens, Ma, William and I have only just married!'

'Darina, you are heading for thirty-five.'

'Ma, I'm thirty-two; I don't think we need worry too much about my biological clock yet.'

'After all, I don't want to be so old I can't enjoy my

grandchildren when they come along. You know how tiring small children are!'

Darina finished her brown rice and suggested to her mother she go and choose herself a dessert from the buffet table.

Lady Stocks eyed it from her seat. 'They all look most delicious but I think I've had quite enough for this evening, darling. I haven't eaten so much in a long time. Perhaps tomorrow, when we have Baz and Molly with us. He does so love sweet things.'

'You'd like some tea, perhaps, in the drawing room?' suggested the waiter.

'You have jasmine tea? I gather coffee is forbidden but that would be an acceptable substitute. Come along, Darina, we'll go and find two comfortable chairs before everyone else gets there.'

Getting 'two comfortable chairs' amounted to choosing a corner where Ann Stocks could survey everyone entering the drawing room and imperiously summon to join them the couple she'd told Darina about earlier.

Opportunity for conversation with Peter and Rose Rochester proved limited, though, for no sooner had the tea arrived than Perry Cazalet approached the piano that stood near the big windows leading into the conservatory.

'I remember promising you last night that Gina would sing,' he announced, opening up the instrument and summoning his wife with a quick wave of his hand. For an instant it looked as though she might refuse, then she gave a small, resigned smile and stood in the curve of the baby grand, leaning across with some difficulty for a small discussion with her husband. They spoke for a moment, then Perry sat and played a chord or two and Gina turned to face a drawing room that was by now filled with people.

Perry Cazalet went into the introduction to one of the jazz songs Darina had heard Gina sing all those years ago at the Oxford ball. It was sad and hungry and Gina's throaty, edgy voice sent a small shiver down Darina's spine.

There was loud applause after it. 'Now here's a new number that Gina includes on her forthcoming record,' said Perry. There was a flutter of interest, then Gina started another song that to Darina didn't sound much different from the first. Nor did the third that followed which, Perry announced, was also new. The applause after that was more polite than enthusiastic.

Gina smiled at them all. 'You're very sweet and I'd love to try your patience just one more time, if Perry will forgive me.' She moved behind her husband and whispered in his ear.

A dark look crossed his face. For a moment it seemed he would disagree with whatever she was suggesting, but then he rose from the piano seat and stood by the door to the conservatory, fished a pair of dark glasses out of his mustard linen jacket, put them on, crossed his arms over his chest and leant against the open door.

Gina sat down and started to play a few notes. She wasn't the pianist her husband was and the accompaniment to her song was sketchy. It didn't matter. What she sang was completely different from her previous numbers. It was witty and light, the timbre of her voice somehow counterpointing the song. 'When the man in my head is the man in my bed,' she sang to a rich little melody. At the end the applause was even more enthusiastic than it had been for her first song.

Gina smiled at them with a touch of shyness. 'That was the first public performance of one of my own songs,' she said simply.

'Let's have some more,' someone shouted out.

Gina touched a key, played a small riff and for a moment it looked as though she'd agree. Then she got up from the piano. 'You know what they say, leave them wanting more,' she said gaily. Darina saw her throw a small look at the impassive figure of her husband, then move across the room to where Frank Borden was sitting with Jessica Barry. Frank stood up, took Gina's hand and kissed it. 'Superb,' he said. 'Let me buy you a drink, you deserve it.'

They moved out of the drawing room and Jessica Barry was left once again looking disconsolate. Not for long, though. It didn't take a moment for Perry Cazalet to move into the seat that Frank Borden had vacated.

'Nice voice that girl has,' said Ann Stocks. 'Have I heard of her?'

'Got quite a reputation in jazz circles,' said Peter Rochester, the merchant banker. 'Her husband, the one who played the piano, writes all her songs and she used to sing with his band. He'd made something of a name for himself before she came along, but they say it's her voice that took him to the high spots.'

'I preferred that song she sang at the end,' said his wife. Then she looked round the room and waved at a woman sitting on the far side. 'She plays bridge,' Rose Rochester hissed at Ann Stocks as the woman moved towards them. 'I knew you'd want to meet her.'

Chapter Seven

By the following evening, Darina felt she and her mother were caught in a bubble, an insulating screen that protected them from the real world. She felt pampered and cosseted, all concerns floating away from her.

Once again that day she shared a session in the sauna with Gina, Maureen and Esme.

Gina had accepted their compliments on her singing with poise. Only over the praise for her own song had she allowed a wide grin to spread over her face. 'Really? You really, truly liked it, more than the others?'

'Madly, truly and deeply,' announced Esme. 'It was different and it suited you.' Maureen and Darina murmured agreement with this.

'Perry can't see it,' Gina said bitterly. 'I've written umpteen songs, and I think several are as good as "The Man in my Head". They sort of make a story. I want to put them together for a record but he's dead against it.'

'So do your own thing,' advised Esme.

'That's easy enough for you to say,' Gina said with a touch of bitterness. 'Single women never understand what being married means.'

'I've been married,' Esme said briefly. 'He couldn't stand it that I was more successful than he was and I couldn't take the way he tried to tell me what my duty was as a wife.'

'You didn't love him,' Gina said simply.

Esme looked at her keenly. 'No, I suppose I didn't, or

not enough. You're telling me you love Perry, I suppose, and that you'll put up with whatever shit he hands out.'

Gina shrugged her shoulders. 'Not everything, no. But I know, infuriating as he can be, life is better with him than without.' She scratched nervously at her thigh, raising a red weal on the pale flesh. 'I have nightmares sometimes that he's left me. That he's got fed up with my size and found some other honeypot. I couldn't stand that, I really couldn't.' The scratching increased until tiny drops of blood appeared and she seemed in danger of tearing her skin apart.

'I make Len too comfortable,' said Maureen, gently removing Gina's hand from her thigh and holding it for a moment in hers. 'And I pretend not to notice his stupid excuses when he's got a little something on the side. I know they're not really important. And if he's happy to pay for me to come here, what does it matter if he goes off for a couple of nights with some bimbo who'll bore the socks off him once he's spent two nights running with her? And don't look at me like that, Esme! I haven't got a successful career to take to bed with me.'

'There are better things to take to bed,' Esme said with a lewd chuckle. 'You're hopeless, both of you.'

As Darina was going upstairs to change for lunch from her dressing gown into her tracksuit, she heard someone playing the introduction to one of the songs Gina had sung the previous evening. But the voice that came in with the melody had none of Gina's jazz timbre. It was sweet and true, though, and sounded trained. Darina paused on the stairs to listen. As she did so, the piano broke off and she heard Perry's voice. He appeared to be coaching the singer. A moment later the accompaniment began again and the singer repeated the last phrase with a different emphasis. Darina listened for a little longer, then continued on her way upstairs.

As she negotiated the turn, she saw Gina standing on the landing, her hand grasping the banisters so tightly her knuckles were white. Then she saw Darina, gave a small toss to her head and moved away, the flip-flop of her sandals making an irritated counterpoint against her heels to the beat of the music rising up the stairs.

That afternoon Darina forced herself to attend an aerobics class, and was pleasantly surprised at how much fun it was and how energized she felt at the end of it. She decided to fit in a class each day she was at Conifers Spa and then see if she couldn't maintain the discipline of at least a weekly session back home.

Changing for dinner that evening, Darina found her pleated silk tobacco brown trousers were definitely looser on her than the last time she'd worn them. As she added the cinnamon top she'd worn the previous evening, she imagined the scornful comment Esme Lee would make if she mentioned this and smiled to herself. She liked the scathing lawyer, there was something so refreshingly direct about her. Darina was sure Esme would go after everything she wanted in that direct way, whether it was personal or professional.

'It looks positively monastic.' Molly Creighton eyed Darina's plate with fascination. 'I'm so glad you're not eating that as well.' She looked at Ann Stocks's plate of veal escalope with chive and cucumber sauce. 'I'm sure it's doing Darina an immense amount of good but I like to enjoy my food.'

Molly Creighton was the sort of woman who made you feel comfortable, thought Darina. She, like her husband, was in her mid-fifties. She dressed smartly without being threatening, her kind, far from beautiful face was well made up, her pepper and salt hair nicely styled.

'And what Baz would say if I ever dared to place a plate like that in front of him, I dread to think!'

'You know I eat anything you give me,' her husband grinned at her.

'That's because I know what you like,' retorted his wife.

Baz Creighton had a charisma his wife lacked. Though he was by no means tall, there was a sense of power about him, a magnetism that deflected your attention from his slight paunch and the fact that his abundant hair was white. He looked round the dining room. 'I came here once when old Toler Wyatt had it. Very different it was then.'

'Do tell us what it looked like. I've been wondering ever since we arrived,' Ann Stocks pleaded.

'Great barn of a place. Toler's father built it at the turn of the century. He was Canadian, made a fortune out of railway stock then came over here determined to move into politics. Never made it, I'm afraid, and the fortune gradually petered out. But the time I got to know Toler, there was dry rot and wet rot and rats and cockroaches and God knows what else.' He gave them an amused grin. 'The place was falling down around him. But you could see what tremendous style it had once had.'

'Must have cost a lot to restore it,' Darina commented, looking around again at the panelled dining room.

'A bomb,' Baz Creighton agreed promptly. 'They've done a good job and the place seems well run too.'

'You would know all about that, of course,' Ann Stocks said. 'I remember Gerry saying that the army taught you how to run things.'

'Discipline in everything,' Baz said briefly.

'You should see his office at home, Ann, never a piece of paper out of place! Everything dealt with immediately, he even handwrites his own thank-you letters.'

'Only common courtesy,' her husband said. 'What sort of people come to a place like this?'

Darina could see how Baz Creighton had made such a success of his career. He was interested in everything, amusing and not at all pompous. Gerry Stocks had said Baz was brilliant, but he didn't flaunt it. He and his wife had arrived in time for a tour of the health farm before dinner and he'd shown a lively interest in every aspect of the treatment areas and exercise facilities. He listened to her mother chatting happily about the people she'd met as though he actually cared to hear about them. He really was very attractive with his strong, heavy-boned face and piercing blue eyes – and he had charm.

Darina caught Molly Creighton looking at her with a quizzical expression. 'I'm really impressed to be sitting here with a real live general, and to realise that he's actually human,' she whispered to her.

'No man's a hero to his valet or his wife,' Molly smiled at her.

After the meal they went across to the drawing room for their tea. 'Sorry about the coffee,' Lady Stocks mourned, 'I haven't been able to persuade them to allow us even a little cup.'

'I never drink it,' said Molly, 'but Baz will no doubt complain.' She glanced fondly at her husband, who appeared not to hear her comment.

'We had such a nice little concert last night,' said Ann Stocks. 'Quite a famous jazz singer entertained us – Gina Cazalet.'

'Really! Gina Cazalet? We met her once, you remember, Baz?'

'What?'

'That's her over there, isn't it? With Perry Cazalet.' Molly managed to indicate where Gina and her husband were sitting without making it obvious.

'Ah, I remember, had them once for a ball, didn't we?

Quite a success they were, too. Can't say I'm much of a one for jazz, though.'

'I loved her voice,' Molly said gently.

Ann Stocks went across to the Cazalets and brought them back to where Darina and the Creightons were sitting, making smooth introductions. The general seemed somewhat taken aback by her move; for the first time Darina saw him not completely in control. But he soon recovered his aplomb and asked if there was any chance of a repetition of the previous night's concert.

Lady Creighton looked expectant.

'I'm so sorry,' Gina said before her husband could respond, 'I've got a sore throat.' She said it with a firmness that made it impossible to suggest she might manage just one song.

Perry Cazalet looked at his wife and Darina saw a little pulse twitch beside his left eye. His mouth tightened, then he got up and went back to the other side of the room. Frank Borden and Jessica Barry had come in a few moments earlier. Darina hadn't seen them in the dining room; perhaps they'd gone out for a quiet meal on their own. Frank had on a dark jacket and an open-necked light blue shirt in what looked like knitted silk, plus elegantly cut cream trousers. Jessica was wearing an ultra-short dress in shimmering silver. She beamed up at Perry, rose and allowed herself to be led to the piano.

'Ladies and gentlemen, unfortunately my wife doesn't feel up to performing this evening, but I know you're going to enjoy hearing little Jessica here sing instead.'

A small, sibilant sound escaped Gina's mouth, then she clamped her lips firmly together and sat back in her chair. Only the rapid beat of her foot betrayed her dislike of the turn events had taken.

Jessica looked pale and slightly frightened. Her wide eyes glanced desperately around the room, then she took a deep breath and looked back at Perry, who gave her an encouraging smile and a brief nod then started the introduction. Jessica opened her mouth and sang.

Off key.

She stopped and flushed deeply. Perry smiled at her reassuringly and went back to the beginning of the introduction. This time she hit the note accurately if slightly breathlessly and continued, gradually gaining confidence.

It was, of course, the voice Darina had heard that morning. The applause at the end of the song was sufficiently enthusiastic for Perry to start playing another one. By now Jessica was completely relaxed and Darina thought she gave a polished performance. But beside her, out of the corner of her eye, she could see the general tapping irritably on the arm of his chair, until Molly reached across and gently placed her hand on top of his. He gave her a brief glance and forced a smile.

On Darina's other side, Gina sat rigid and appeared hardly able to keep her seat. As soon as the applause broke out after the second song, she rose to her feet and left the room, her face set and grim. Darina saw Frank Borden's eyes watching her. For a moment she thought he was going to follow, then he relaxed back into his seat and applauded Jessica instead.

Jessica bowed demurely. Perry came and stood beside her, lifted her hand and gave it a kiss. 'Ladies and gentlemen,' he said, 'I give you Jessica Barry, a new star.'

Jessica looked thrilled and as though she hardly believed anything that had happened.

'Sweet looking girl,' said Ann Stocks. 'I've noticed her at the pool, always friendly and quiet, never pushes herself forward.'

'And such a nice voice,' added Molly. 'I should think she'll be quite a success.'

'If Cazalet's behind her, she should be all right,' said the general. 'Remember him when I was organising that regimental ball, he was quite a businessman.' He sounded grudging, as though he resented Perry Cazalet's business sense. Yes; despite his charm, Darina didn't think Baz would think too kindly of anyone who challenged him on any front. 'Time for us to go, my dear.'

Molly bent down and picked up her handbag. 'Ann, I'm sorry, it's been a delightful evening but Baz is off to Scotland at crack of dawn tomorrow.'

Darina and her mother walked their guests out to their car, parked in front of the house. There the general slapped the breast pocket of his jacket. 'Damnation, I think I left my diary on the table in the dining room. I had it out when we were discussing your visit to us, Ann. Excuse me.' He strode off back to the house, his big body tense with irritation.

'Baz does so hate screwing up in any way,' murmured Molly. 'Oh, look, isn't that the jazz singer, Gina?'

Coming towards them over the lawn, ghostly in the evening light, was, indeed, Gina, her low-backed white dress swirling round her legs. Molly stepped forward. 'I'm so sorry you couldn't sing for us,' she said.

'Yeah, I'm sorry too, but you know how it is.' Gina stood awkwardly, her weight on one leg, one hip thrust out; her underlip was thrust out too, not in a sulky way, more defiant, as though she was determined the world wasn't going to come tumbling down.

'I've never forgotten how you sounded when you came to the regiment,' Molly said enthusiastically. 'I went and bought two of your records. If I'd known you were going to be here tonight I'd have brought them and asked if you wouldn't mind autographing them.'

Gina gave Molly a big grin. 'Someone only has to drop a hat for me to sign a record. The trouble with cassettes and CDs is there's so little room for my sprawling signature.' She hesitated and gave the three women a bright, shrewd look from underneath half-closed eyes. 'What was your opinion of Perry's latest little find?'

'Very pleasant,' Ann Stocks rushed in with, 'but ordinary compared with you last night.'

'Yeah, well, by the time he's finished with her, you can reckon she'll have learnt all the tricks.'

'You mean he's really going to launch her?' Darina asked in amazement. Jessica hadn't sounded anything special to her.

'Add her sweet little eyes to her sweet little voice and a touching faith in his clapped-out abilities and she's a hard act to resist,' Gina said bitterly. 'Once I was like that.'

'My dear, whoever that girl is, she'll never sound half as good as you.' Molly put a hand on Gina's arm.

'Hell, if she's got what it takes, who am I to grudge her a bit of success?' Gina's voice was hard. 'And I've got a few irons in the fire myself.'

'Well, best of luck,' Ann Stocks said.

'Ladies, you'll excuse me? It really is time I took myself off to beddybyes.' Gina in her white dress swayed towards the house.

'Ah, here's Baz now,' said Molly with a note of relief in her voice.

The general came round the back of the house waving his diary. 'Sorry about that, I had to go through to the kitchens and find a waiter.'

'Well, as long you've got it back.'

More kisses and farewells.

'You know, darling,' said Darina's mother as they went back inside the house, 'I missed Gerry more than ever this evening. Every time Baz spoke, I could hear him. Is there some military rhythm that all officers have, do you think? Oh well, it's nice that they want to see me again, even though Gerry has gone, don't you think?'

Darina couldn't ever remember seeing her mother so triste, or remember when she had felt more sympathetic towards her. 'Will you be all right tomorrow night? Or would you like me to ring William and say I can't go with him to this party?' she said as they climbed the stairs.

'Of course I'll be all right, dear. I've got a date for bridge with those nice people we were talking to. I shall be fine.' Lady Stocks paused, a hand on her daughter's arm. 'You're very kind to your old ma. I really appreciate being here with you.'

Darina gave her mother a brief hug. As she straightened, she could hear furious voices from within the room they had paused outside. Gina was tearing a strip off Perry. As Darina and her mother moved off again down the corridor, she could hear, 'You just leave that little tramp alone, do you hear me? Or I'll do something that'll make her sorry she ever met you.'

Chapter Eight

The party was one of those noisy, boozy, smoke-injected evenings that Darina wished would come to a speedy end. William was at the bar, with the newly promoted Superintendent Roger Marks and a group of other police officers. They were laughing, exchanging stories, a group of macho men wrapped in a camaraderie that was a female exclusion zone.

When they'd arrived, William had introduced Darina to Roger with that delightful note of pride in his voice that always did things to her.

Roger had taken Darina's hand and given her a long, long look that said he found her height excessive but the rest of her a more than cosy armful. She wished she'd worn something a bit more, well, effacing than the cream Armani patio pants outfit. The sleeveless vest top was too revealing but the night was too hot for the long cardigan that went with it. There'd been a heavy downfall of rain that afternoon but it hadn't seemed to clear the air.

'Congratulations,' she'd said, easing back her hand.

'No wonder old Bill was so keen to get you here,' Roger said with a smile she could only class as lewd. 'Still the lovelorn honeymooner, he is. And now we know why!' He was a huge man with a beer gut that bulged over a pair of lightweight trousers tailored for a smaller figure. A pale blue shirt strained at the fleshy neck and the floral tie was at odds with his suit jacket. Small, round brown eyes were set into rolls of flesh out of which emerged a triumphantly crooked nose, a wide mouth and a pugnacious chin.

Darina had been seated between her husband and Roger Marks for the meal. The menu of prawn cocktail, steak and chips followed by Mississippi mud pie confirmed Darina in a set of prejudices that had instantly formed on meeting William's pal.

After the meal apartheid had set in and now Darina sat at a table with some of the wives. Others were dancing, some with men but more with each other.

'You must be delighted with Roger's promotion,' Darina said to the blonde on her left.

Tracy Marks stubbed out her cigarette and lit another. 'About time too. I was beginning to think he'd never make super.' She took a deep drag, throwing her head back, inhaling the smoke into her lungs with a practised greed. Her medium-length platinum fair hair was carefully set and she wore a black dress in some shiny material that was just the wrong length, neither short enough to display her good legs nor long enough to be stylish. 'And he was beginning to take it out on me and the kids.'

'That was tough,' Darina commented in a neutral voice.

'Ah well, if it hadn't been that, it'd have been something else, they're all the same,' Tracy said, glancing over at the noisy group of men. She sounded resigned rather than bitter. 'You'll find that with your Bill if he doesn't get along as fast as he thinks he should. Still inspector, isn't he?'

'He was pretty pleased with the promotion from sergeant,' protested Darina. 'He only joined a few years ago and he's not expecting another promotion just yet.'

Tracy eyed her sceptically. 'Entered late, did he? Seem to remember Rog saying he'd done something before the police.'

'The Foreign Office,' Darina said.

'Really? Accounts for the way he talks, I suppose.'

Tracy seemed to lose interest in William Pigram. 'God, do you think they're going to be at it all night? The babysitter charges extra after midnight.'

'Don't be such a wet blanket, Trace,' urged one of the other girls. 'Come on, have another drink.'

'Yes, my turn for a round,' said Darina, resigned to several more hours of trying to make conversation with these women she was locked into strange fellowship with. She went to the bar with orders for gin and orange, lager and lime, a babycham and two sweet white wines. She ordered a tonic water with a touch of angostura bitters and a slice of lemon for herself. One of them had to keep sober. While she waited to be served, Darina watched William sink the last of his bitter and order another round. Thank heavens Carolyn had promised him a room for the night.

They'd had a drink with Carolyn at her cottage in the grounds before leaving for the party. The cottage was one of a terrace of three, standing nearly at the end of the half-mile drive that led up to the main house.

'Quite small,' said Carolyn, showing them around. 'But ideal for Michael and me.'

There were two bedrooms and a bathroom upstairs plus a slip of a room that Carolyn had fitted out as a study with a narrow bed in case Michael wanted a friend to stay.

Darina remembered the huge house Carolyn and Robert had had in Surrey, its plush furnishings, the swimming pool, the games room with full-size billiard table, the guest suites with private bathrooms, the huge kitchen with eating area plus separate utility, storeroom and ironing areas. She asked if it had been sold after Robert died.

Carolyn shook her head. 'Negative equity. Still, I managed to rent it for a tidy sum that more than takes care of the mortgage. If I can hang on in there, perhaps I'll be able to sell at a profit one of these days.'

She opened the door into her room. Simple and

uncluttered, not a spare piece of furniture, the only orna-
ment a stunning glass figure that Darina remembered
Robert had brought back from some trip to Sweden.

'Really, I've quite enjoyed doing this place up,' said
Carolyn as she took them back downstairs. 'I thought
Conifers Spa was going to take off, be the success I need.'
There was a defeated note in her voice.

'Has something happened?' Darina asked as Carolyn
took them into the compact room that occupied most of
the ground floor, incorporating kitchen and eating area
as well as seating for four people.

Carolyn shrugged, tossing her head, the shiny curls
settling back into place round the neat head as she
opened the fridge door and got out a bottle of white wine.
'Nothing, I suppose. It's just that I heard this evening that
the investor everyone had been hoping would come up
with the extra capital we need is now having second
thoughts. Shows you can't ever count on anything!'

She handed glasses of wine to Darina and William.
Through the wall came music; Darina recognised the
Marriage of Figaro overture.

'That must be a blow,' Darina said sympathetically,
noticing the new lines of strain in Carolyn's face. 'But he
hasn't definitely said he won't invest?'

'No, just that he's now considering an alternative prospect.' Carolyn sighed and flopped down into a chair. 'But
I think I've worked out who it is, and maybe I can persuade him that Conifers truly is a good bet.'

'Really, who is it? Someone here now?'

Carolyn shook her head and gave a secretive smile,
'Can't say. I could be wrong, anyway.'

William had taken his glass of wine over to the
window and stood looking out over the sweep of grass
that led up to the health farm. 'Who lives in the other
cottages?'

'Maria, that's Maria Russell, the manager of the treatment side, has the one next to mine and Jim Hughes,

manager of the men's side, has the end one. It's a great advantage to be able to offer accommodation with the job.'

'Also means that you can't really get away from each other,' observed William, sitting down in a small armchair and crossing one long leg over the other.

Darina was content to let him and Carolyn do the talking. It was so good to see William again. He'd said the job should be finished by the end of the following week but Darina put no trust in that. Police work never carried any guarantees about free time.

So now she feasted on the sight of his tall figure, the dark curly hair cut crisply against his well-shaped head, the dark flecked grey eyes and cleancut features. An old-time matinee idol, as someone had once referred to him. But that was unfair, his face was more interesting than that, the cheekbones too broad, the chin too determined, the mouth too tightly tucked away to have met Hollywood standards. Nevertheless he stirred her in a way few other men had managed.

However, initially it had been his personality that had attracted her more than his looks. Never before had she met someone who could be lively and interesting without being threatening and who could involve himself with people without being judgemental. The fact that he really seemed to enjoy her company had been immensely seductive. The boost he gave to her self-confidence was of rocket-like proportions. With him on her side, she could do anything. She hoped now, looking at him, she managed to do just a little of the same for him.

'I've built pretty much of a team here,' Carolyn was saying casually. 'We have our differences of course but we manage to rub along pretty well. And we work too hard to have energy left over for much of a social life.'

Was there an unspoken message there? That there wasn't anything intimate to overhear through those thin walls, through which came the sound of Count Almaviva paying court to his wife's maid, Susanna?

'Rick seemed to have quite a lot of energy after lunch the other afternoon,' Darina couldn't resist saying.

Carolyn put down her glass of wine and there was the merest hint of a pause before she said smoothly, 'Rick likes to think he's a bit of a ladykiller but he isn't really any trouble.'

A slight hint of over-confidence, perhaps?

'Doesn't sound as though you have much opportunity for fun,' observed William quietly.

A little smile curved round Carolyn's full mouth. 'Oh, we manage a pretty full life. At least,' she added hastily, 'I do, I mustn't speak for the others.'

And what part did Rick play in that full life? wondered Darina.

Then Carolyn asked William about the case he was working on and the conversation moved to police work. 'It's what you would probably call undercover work. Armed with a dodgy con man record, I've managed to get myself recruited into an outfit we believe is responsible for fleecing senior citizens of their life savings by selling them fraudulent unit trusts.'

'I reckon you could sell me a fraudulent unit trust,' said Carolyn with a frank smile at him.

Soon after that, William was driving them on their way to the party. 'I'm sorry,' he'd said as they approached the hotel where it was being held. 'This is going to be a boring evening for you, but Roger was really keen for you to come as well.'

'I'm looking forward to meeting him. Your friends are always fun.'

There was the slightest hesitation before William said, 'Roger is, well, I suppose I have to say slightly different.'

'Different? In what way?'

'Sometimes I think all he's really interested in is police work. He's totally dedicated.'

'So are you.'

'But I make time for other things.' Darina tried to think of the last time they'd managed to go to the theatre or a concert, visit William's parents, take a walk in the country or go out to dinner.

'Where did you say you met?'

'He was the inspector I worked with when I first moved onto the detection side. We're more or less the same age but he joined the police straight out of university and I, as you know, tried other things first.'

Tried the Foreign Office but hadn't found the work sufficiently involving.

Darina wondered about this friendship with someone William had made no attempt to ask home. He'd tried to have most of his chums back for a meal since they'd started living together; he enjoyed showing off both her and her cooking. 'It must have been a blow when he was transferred to Wiltshire.'

'Well, relationships come and go, just as in any other force, but I jumped at the chance to work with him again. My God!' William braked sharply as another motorist cut in front of his car. 'Look at that! I've half a mind to stop him.'

Darina put a hand on his thigh. 'Relax, you're off duty this evening.'

Now, looking at the tight-knit little group of police who'd switched from beer to shorts and had a seemingly inexhaustible fund of stories that raised louder and louder laughs of appreciation, Darina thought that they might be off duty but they all seemed totally oblivious of anything outside their little world. She hoped the hotel hadn't applied for an extended licence.

It hadn't, but after last orders had been called for, it appeared that another of Roger's mates was staying there and had laid on a supply of booze in his room. 'Come on, darling,' said William, his face shining with good fellowship and alcohol. 'We've time for a quick one.'

Darina couldn't plead exhaustion, not with two and a half days of healthy living behind her; nor work tomorrow, when all she had waiting was another hard day being massaged, exercised and titivated. So she trailed up to the small room and crowded in with a dozen others.

By the time William finally announced they were leaving, it was past one o'clock.

'Just as well Carolyn has given you a double room for the night,' whispered Darina as she used the key she'd been supplied with to let them into Conifers Spa. 'I'd hate to wake Mother up at this hour.' And she couldn't wait to get her husband into bed. It seemed weeks since they had spent a night together.

'Hey,' said William, opening the drawing-room door, 'nice room!' He walked over to the piano, lifted the keyboard lid and struck a few notes. 'In tune!'

'Shush, you'll wake people up!'

William crossed the hall and looked into another room. 'Hmm, you dine in some style, I see!'

Darina tugged at his arm and he allowed her to pull him back into the hall.

'Now, show me where all the flesh is slapped and you sweat away the excess pounds.'

'Darling, it's nearly two o'clock in the morning!'

'Just the right time. No one will be around. I'd be embarrassed if it was full of scantily clad ladies!'

'That'll be the day!' Darina said caustically. 'I thought you wanted to go to bed!'

'I do, oh, how I do, with you, but first I want to see where it all goes on.'

Darina remembered that he was footing the bill for their stay. A short tour seemed only fair. With a deep sigh she led the way through the back of the hall to the purpose-built treatment annexe.

'This is the reception desk, here are the treatment rooms for the slendertone and the sunlamp and reflexology. Back here are the cubicles for massage and aromatherapy. Here are the sauna and the Turkish steamers and the showers.'

William poked about, opening doors, testing couches with a press of his hand, switching on showers and watching the cascading water with an expression that Darina recognised with a sinking heart.

William half-drunk developed an unpredictability that could be unnerving.

'Is this mixed farming?' he asked, switching off a shower and shaking a wet hand.

'No, the men have their own section the other side of the indoor swimming pool.'

'Well, come on, lead me to it, I want to see everything.'

'I think it's just the same as here,' objected Darina.

'You've been in there?' Darina shook her head. 'So how do you know? I want to see everything and I mean everything.'

There was no arguing with William in this mood. But, 'I think the pool area is locked at night time, we're not supposed to use it without a member of staff on hand, you see.'

William strode towards the large, heavy sliding door that was part of the wall of glass between reception and the pool area and gave it an assertive push. It glided back without a hitch. Stifling a groan, Darina followed him into the echoing turquoise space.

The night had been dark. Stormy clouds lingering from the afternoon's rain had obscured the almost full moon. Now the wind chased the last of them away and silver light flooded in through the high windows. The huge, kidney-shaped pool reflected it back in eerie moving flashes from the gently quivering water. Bushy plants arranged around the roughcast walls threw strange-shaped shadows, and loungers with striped cushions seemed waiting for ghostly occupants. At the far side of the pool, on a raised platform, was the spa tub.

Darina loved it. She loved sitting on the tiled shelf

that ran around its inside, feeling the action of the turbulent water attacking her thighs and hips, letting its gentle warmth relax her body, while she enjoyed chatting to the others sharing the pool with her.

But it was the swimming pool that William was interested in. He squatted down and felt the water. 'Nice temperature.' He sat down and pulled off his shoes and socks then rolled up his trousers and dangled his legs in the water. 'Lovely!' He looked round at Darina, 'Come and join me. In fact,' he got up, removed his jacket and started to undo his trousers, 'let's strip off and have a swim.'

'William, behave yourself! This is no way for a respectable member of the police force to carry on.'

'But I'm off duty, as you reminded me earlier!'

'If you take a swim after all that alcohol, you're stupider than I thought.'

He gave her a slow, lazy grin. 'Glad to see I can still wind you up, you old married woman, you.'

Darina cast a glance up to the ceiling, high above them. 'Come on, I thought you said you wanted to see where the men's treatment area was. It's over here.'

On the other side of the pool area was a set of changing rooms, used by the local members of the Conifers Spa health club. Beside them a door led into an area equipped exactly as the other, female side, but about half the size.

'Nothing really different, you see,' said Darina, switching on the light and hurriedly opening doors into couch-furnished cubicles, a sauna and showers. 'Now will you come to bed?'

William gave her a sweet smile and wandered back into the pool area, stopping by a small tub-like machine. 'What's this for?'

'Wringing the water out of wet bathing suits. Don't touch that switch, it makes an awful noise . . .'

It was too late. A rapid whirring and clunking echoed

through the pool area. William guiltily switched off the machine and wandered away. 'And what's on this huge throne, here?'

'That's the spa pool.' Knowing now that she hadn't a hope of getting William to bed until he'd seen everything, Darina climbed up the steps and reached for the rubber-covered switch that was set into the pool surround, looking behind her to see that he was paying attention. 'This activates the water, it only keeps going for about ten minutes or so, then you have to switch it on again.' She pressed the switch and, as the motor started up, turned to look at the bubbles that appeared round the edges of the small round pool.

She screamed.

The water wasn't a clear blue, it was muddy purple, like a child's paintbox when scarlet has been mixed with azure. And floating up to the surface was a painted kimono rippling with the motion of the water like a giant butterfly fluttering above a choice flower. Inside the kimono, resting on the bottom of the pool, was a body.

Chapter Nine

William was beside Darina in an instant, some extra-ordinary chemical process managing to achieve an instant sobriety. 'How do you switch that damn thing off?' he asked as he threw away the jacket he'd picked up earlier from beside the swimming pool. A moment later he was in the water, hauling at the body.

'I don't know!' confessed Darina. She swallowed her screams, fought nausea and forced herself into the pool to help William.

The water churned around them; the wet silk wrap-ped itself around Darina's hands as she attempted to grasp stiff legs. William had the shoulders. Making her mind a blank, refusing to think about what she was doing, Darina finally managed to get hold of the thighs. It wasn't the weight that was so awkward as the unyielding nature of the collection of bones and flesh they were trying to rescue. Plus the dripping, clinging material that rippled with the motion of the water as though alive. So much more alive than the figure.

Finally, wet through, they managed to get her out of the bubbling water and onto the tiled surround. By then Darina was panting; small, harsh breaths that echoed through the cavernous area. She knelt back on her heels, flicked the chlorinated water from her hands and watched her husband.

He laid the body on her front, the wet kimono cling-ing to the naked buttocks, riding obscenely up the back of the legs, the bright flowers leaching their colour across sodden silk. William straddled the figure, moved the head to one side, opened the mouth and pumped down on the back, over the lungs. A trickle of water issued from the stiff, blue lips and ran pathetically across the tiles.

Darina couldn't stop looking at the staring eyes. They looked back at her, through her, beyond her. How could they be so open and yet look so, so *dead*?

William lifted himself off the body, urgently moved it over, forced the head back and started mouth-to-mouth resuscitation, alternating breathing into the lungs with pumping down on the sternum.

Darina knew it was hopeless. It must have been hopeless for long before they entered the pool room. All that time they'd been messing about in the treatment area, all the time that William had been horsing around, this poor body had been waiting for them. If they'd come to the pool first, might there have been a chance? But they'd heard nothing. No splash, no noise of the spa motor. Anyway, what had she been doing in the pool with her kimono on? And wearing nothing underneath? No bathing suit, no underclothes, nothing. What had she been doing in here?

Darina couldn't bring herself to look at the spa pool again but the colour of the water filled her mind's eye until all she could see was a rising red that increased in intensity every second. She closed her eyes and put her head in her hands, pressing her palms against her eyeballs until the red gave way first to darkness then shooting firecrackers of gold. She lifted her head, opened her eyes and waited for her vision to clear.

Finally she could see William feeling for a pulse, trying round each wrist and behind the ears. Darina wondered if she should find her bag and the little mirror she kept in there. Wasn't that the classic test for the breath of life? But this was a useless exercise and she couldn't bring herself to get up on legs that felt like cotton wool.

William gave up searching for a pulse and started

carefully inspected the staring eyes, forcing up the already open eyelids still further, looking at first one then the other eyeball. Finally he sat back on his heels and drew the back of his hand across his forehead. He looked very, very tired. 'I'm afraid she's dead; completely, utterly, no shadow of a doubt dead.' He drew in a deep breath, bent over the body again and started examining the neck, gently turning the lifeless head from one side to another, lifting the strands of dripping hair and exploring the scalp.

Darina started shivering. Deep chill was seeping into her bones. It wasn't only because she was wet and totally exhausted. It was because once again she appeared to be confronted with murder. For surely the silk kimono and the blood that darkened the water meant this could be no ghastly accident. For a crazy moment she wondered if she should call the police then stifled an hysterical bubble of laughter. The police were already here!

Darina rose, eased out aching leg muscles and started to move restlessly around the pool area, her eyes automatically taking in every detail, searching for anything that could deflect her mind from that poor body.

All seemed normal enough. The Greek key pattern of dark turquoise tiles around the edges of the swimming pool gleamed through the shimmering water with a sinister chic. The slender, arching ficus trees drooped their graceful leaves around the outer reaches of the pool area, a green backdrop to the loungers silently, emptily waiting for the morning and normal activity. A slight movement caught Darina's eye. In one corner there was a stirring of leaves, not enough for a rustle, merely a light lifting of green beside the huge sliding patio door that looked out onto the terrace. Darina moved over to the corner and stood for a long time looking at the corner without touching the window.

Then she returned to where William was still kneeling on the floor.

He appeared to have finished his inspection of the body. 'Well?' she asked, hunkering down beside him, placing a hand on his shoulder, feeling his warmth beneath the damp shirt.

'Look,' he said, moving the head so she could see. There, on the pale skin, were livid marks the shape of fingers. 'And see the eyes.' Darina forced herself to examine the bulging eyeballs and realised there were pinpoints of red staining the white parts. 'Haemorrhaging,' said William.

It doesn't take long for a detective's wife to learn something of what can be deduced from the appearance of murder victims. 'You mean she was strangled?' Darina's voice seemed to her to come from far away. She grabbed harder at William's shoulder. He didn't seem to notice; all his attention was concentrated on the still figure spreadeagled on the tiling.

'It mayn't have been the cause of death. There's a nasty wound under the hair.' He parted wet strands and Darina could see broken skin.

'Is that where the blood came from?' Involuntarily, she glanced across at the spa pool, still bubbling away.

'Most likely.'

'You mean someone hit her with something?'

'Perhaps, or maybe there was a struggle. She could have stumbled and hit her head on that edging. The tiles are curved but only slightly and if you caught them at the right angle, that's to say, the wrong one, they could be dangerous.' Darina lurched as he rose, removing his supporting shoulder.

William examined the tiled edging to the still burbling and churning pool. It felt as though hours had passed since Darina had first hit that starter button but it could not have been more than ten minutes or it would have gone silent. 'Pity you had to switch on the water.'

Darina swallowed the injustice of that remark, rose and joined him at the edge of the pool. At that moment the motor cut out and the water gradually went quiet. Still a nasty pink, it was clear enough to see through to the bottom. It was Darina who noticed the alien object.

She dropped to her knees, reached down and fished out a piece of pink ribbon. She handed it to her husband. 'Do you think it was always that colour?' she asked, her voice catching.

He nodded. 'The colour's too deep to . . .' he let his voice trail away and Darina was glad. 'Probably came off her hair,' he said. 'Do you know who she is?'

Darina glanced back at the body. Looking at the staring eyes, the expression of congested alarm, the purple lips, the swollen skin, the dark rats' tails of hair, it was hard to imagine the dead woman could ever have been pretty. The skin on the too-slender body seemed to have shrunk, her bones pushed against it, threatened to break through. She looked pathetically thin, half starved.

'She's called Jessica Barry.' A vivid memory of that first session in the sauna came back, together with how the atmosphere had changed on Jessica's entry. 'Lady Barry, in fact. She said her husband was an MP but he'd died.'

William's face as he looked at Jessica's remains was closed and impassive. He'd once told Darina that dealing with a dead body was a battle between emotion and reason. 'What I really want to do is flee, remove myself so I can spew up my guts in private; what I know I have to do is stay there and use every ounce of my powers of observation, intelligence and training.'

He'd certainly gone into action that night without hesitation. Now his expression was defeated. 'Whatever happened, I'm afraid what we've got here is murder.'

'You're never going to be able to live this down, Bill, trashing a murder scene before the SOCO boys had a chance to get at it!' Roger Marks gave an evil little chuckle then winced. 'Anybody got coffee going yet?' he asked.

He looked as though he was nursing a hangover of outsize proportions.

Several hours had passed since Darina and William had discovered Jessica Barry's body. Hours in which first a police constable and then a detective had arrived. Followed by a doctor and a team of scenes-of-crime officers and, finally, the superintendent with a small team of his own. Nobody looked particularly happy to be called out at that time of night. Darina recognised several people who had been at Roger Marks's promotion party and they were even stonier faced than the others. But the scene was being photographed and video-recorded, the body examined, the pool area minutely inspected for evidence with what, under the circumstances, seemed remarkable efficiency.

William had found time to change out of his wet clothes into the jeans and sweatshirt he'd brought for Sunday wear and Darina was now in her tracksuit. She'd taken a hot shower as well and some of the chill had gone from her bones. But not all.

'Conifer Spa clients aren't allowed coffee,' Darina said.

Roger Marks groaned.

She took pity on him. 'But I'll go and see if there isn't a supply lurking around somewhere. Failing that, I'll make tea.'

'That's a good girl,' Roger Marks said abstractedly and went back to observing the forensic experts' examination of the scene.

'Before that, though, there's something I noticed while William was working on the body.' Darina wondered how she could have forgotten it until now.

'Hmm?' Roger hardly seemed to have heard what she said. Darina looked around but William was nowhere to be seen.

She cleared her throat and spoke deliberately and clearly. 'That big sliding door leading onto the terrace was slightly open.'

84

Roger didn't seem impressed. 'Yes, well, we'll be checking into all that.' He smiled briefly at her; there was a touch of indulgence about it but also impatience.

'We didn't touch the windows at all,' Darina persisted, annoyed now.

Roger made a gesture as though batting away an irritating fly. 'Right,' he said. 'Coffee coming up soon?'

Darina bit back an acid comment about willingly showing someone where the kitchen was.

Then Carolyn Pierce was shown back into the reception area. Summoned by a constable immediately Roger Marks had arrived on the scene with his team, she had looked shocked and haunted. Even now, after a session sitting quietly with one of the sergeants while he took a preliminary statement, she didn't look as though she had come to terms with the situation at all.

'I understand the pool area is always locked at night. Are you responsible for that?' asked Roger Marks.

'No, that's Maria, Maria Russell, the health centre manager.' Carolyn's gaze averted itself from the sight of Jessica's body being organised into a rubberised bag and then onto a trolley. Darina, in no hurry to put kettles on, watched it being carefully wheeled across plastic sheeting placed at the opposite end of the pool area from where she had noticed the window that slight bit open. So, no doubt the forensic team had already registered that fact. She felt slightly foolish.

Carolyn was saying, 'I mean Maria is responsible, but of course she isn't always the last one to leave.'

'Where can this Maria Russell be found?' Roger Marks asked, gesturing to a sergeant to take down details. In the process his eye caught Darina's and she decided perhaps, on balance, it wouldn't be a bad idea to produce the hot drink she'd promised.

Emerging into the main hall, Darina realised that the noise of vehicles arriving and equipment being brought in had woken several of the guests. A constable was shooing them up the stairs. 'Please, go back to your rooms,' he said. 'A statement will be made in the morning. Until then no one is to leave.' If he thought anyone was going to sleep after that, he was more optimistic than police college should have left him. Darina edged her way unobtrusively towards the kitchen after a quick glance had reassured her that her mother was not among those crowding the stairs. Esme Lee's authoritative voice followed her down the corridor. 'All right, folks, why don't we try and get some rest for what's left of the night.'

The kitchen was blessedly quiet. Everything was clean and tidy, surfaces spotless, rubbish buckets empty and scoured out, the only food on show an array of breakfast cereal packets waiting on a trolley. At some stage a member of staff would fill large bowls and put them out for clients to help themselves. The Conifers Spa way to start the day was with lots of fibre and fresh fruit. It helped the digestive system to get going and staved off pangs of hunger for more fatty and detrimental foods, Carolyn had explained.

Darina glanced at her watch. Five o'clock. Over three hours had passed since they'd discovered Jessica Barry's body. At one stage William had tried to persuade her to go to bed, saying her statement would be taken later in the day, there was no need for her to hang around. But Darina could no more have left him to it than she could leave a cake burning in the oven.

As she started opening cupboards and looking for coffee, little scenes kept playing themselves through her mind.

Jessica joining Frank Borden's table for lunch the day she and her mother had arrived at Conifers Spa, and the way the atmosphere in the sauna had changed so dramatically after Jessica had entered that afternoon. Jessica earnestly talking to Perry Cazalet beside the outdoor pool then grabbing the spotlight with her singing on the Friday evening.

And on the Saturday morning – had it really been less than twenty-four hours ago? – Darina had once again heard Jessica and Perry practising in the drawing room. She'd been on her way for a swim in the pool, leaving her mother writing a letter in their room.

The song was one she hadn't heard. As before, the singing was continually interrupted as the pianist made suggestions on phrasing and interpretation.

As Darina reached the bottom of the stairs, she realised she wasn't the only one listening. Sitting in one of the reception hall armchairs was Frank Borden.

'Got something, hasn't she?' he said as Jessica's clear little voice repeated a phrase with an added depth. A newspaper lay unattended on his knees.

'I was impressed when I heard her last night,' Darina agreed.

'Wants to make it as a professional singer. I thought she didn't have a hope in hell but now, well, maybe she can make it after all.'

'Perry Cazalet seems to agree with you.'

Frank Borden lifted a quizzical eyebrow. 'She's certainly an attractive girl.'

Darina wondered again just what his relationship with Jessica was.

Then he held up his newspaper. 'But I've been wanting to ask, is it you that writes the excellent cookery column in this every week?'

'Yes, yes it is.' Darina was surprised. Frank Borden didn't seem the sort of man to be interested in cooking.

'I thought it must be, Darina is such an unusual name.' He smiled up at her, the dark eyes friendly and less watchful than usual. 'Can I ask you something?'

Any query from a reader received top priority. Darina mentally shelved her swim and took the chair next to his. 'Ask away, I only hope I can answer.'

'A few weeks ago you had a recipe for barbecued

87

spiced prawns and said they should be raw. Can you really not do it with the ready cooked?'

Darina had anticipated something much more searching. But the most intelligent people were extraordinarily ignorant about basic cooking techniques.

'I'm afraid not.'

'You see,' he leaned forward confidentially, 'I loved the idea of the marinade, all those spicy flavours, but it's so difficult to get hold of raw prawns.'

'You strike me as a resourceful chap, Mr Borden.' Darina gave him a big grin; there was no way he was going to come the simple little fellow over her.

He echoed her grin. 'Frank, please. But you see, they're so expensive!'

'You're saying you're a cheapskate?'

He looked slightly sheepish.

'Did you try it with ready cooked prawns?'

He nodded.

'And they were dry and tough?'

Another nod.

'There's your answer. Prawns are easily overcooked, that's why you should use fresh.'

He gave a deep sigh. 'I should have known I should trust you!'

'Do you do a lot of cooking?' Darina asked curiously.

'I find it a great relaxation.'

'What from?'

'Business, Darina, business,' he said airily.

'And you like food?'

'Have this love affair with it.' The dark eyes sparkled at her.

'Yet you don't seem to have a weight problem.' She looked at the trim figure in its smart tracksuit.

'It's possible to love food that doesn't put on weight.'

'I wish I found that!' Darina sighed deeply.

Frank Borden looked amused. 'More difficult for you,

I can see that. You can't pick and choose the way I can. Me, I only cook what I want to eat.'

'It's not just that,' protested Darina. 'I adore so many fattening things.'

'Ah,' Frank Borden sat back in his chair. 'I've trained myself to forget tastes that aren't good for me.'

Darina couldn't detect a trace of smugness. 'I think you watch yourself in every part of your life,' she said.

One of his eyebrows raised itself again. 'I think you are a smart girl,' he said.

Jessica Barry came out of the drawing room and Darina realised the music had stopped a little time before.

Jessica's face was both exhilarated and expectant.

'Frank, were you listening?'

'Yes, sweetheart, I was. You sounded good.'

'So, what about it?'

'Still thinking about everything. But maybe, just maybe I might be able to fix something.'

Jessica flung herself onto the arm of his chair and hugged him. 'Frank, you're an angel!'

His expression was kindly but serious. 'Listen, sweetheart, I'm not promising anything. Things is complicated.'

She drew back with a confident grin. 'I know, I know. But your half promise is better than most people's bible oath.'

'Frank, you ready for that game?' Unnoticed, Esme Lee, dressed in a scarlet tracksuit that made her look like an oversized strawberry, had come down the stairs and now stood swishing a tennis racket. She came nearer, the racket coming perilously close to Jessica's trim little behind as she remained perched on the chair arm with her own around Frank Borden's neck.

'Right with you, Esme.' Frank rose, disentangling himself from Jessica with an easy movement. 'See you later, sweetheart,' he said and gave her thigh a pat.

Nothing changed in Esme Lee's expression, but the

racket stopped its swishing. 'Right, let's go.' She walked firmly out of the hall without glancing back.

Jessica bit her lip as Frank followed.

'You coming back to work, Jess?' said Perry Cazalet in a tight voice. 'I thought all you wanted was to get a Kleenex.' He stood in the doorway of the drawing room, his face still and angry. Darina wondered just how long he'd been standing there.

Jessica rose from the chair arm, gave him a brilliant smile and walked back into the drawing room, sliding her hand up his chest in an intimate little gesture as she passed him. Darina might not have been there at all.

Perry shut the door behind them both with a decisive click.

Darina opened another set of kitchen cupboards and wondered just how explosive a situation Jessica had engendered there. How interested had Perry Cazalet been in her and her singing? Was it her voice or herself he had been more interested in? And just what role had Frank Borden played in her life?

Tucked behind two large bags of dried pulses, Darina found a coffee filter machine and a packet of ground coffee. Hidden by Rick Harris, perhaps? For his personal use? Darina took them down and filled the machine with water.

As she opened the packet of coffee, Darina remembered the scene Carolyn had interrupted between Jessica and Rick that first afternoon. Now there was another relationship that would require investigating. She realised there was quite a lot she should tell the police. Would Roger Marks be any more interested in these details than he had been in her comment on the open patio window? Maybe she could tell William; he didn't treat her in that patronising way.

Chapter Ten

Maria Russell woke early. She knew it was early because the sky was hardly light against the thin curtains of her bedroom windows.

Memory flooded back, together with the sense of panic that had been consuming her for the last few days. Inside her head the brandy she'd consumed late last night was pounding a relentless rhythm. Her mouth was stale and dry and one of her eyes itched.

She flung back the bedclothes and went into the small bathroom, slipped out of her silk nightdress, climbed into the bath, drew the plastic curtain decorated with corn-flowers and turned on the shower. She slowly rotated in the bath, feeling cold water pulsing against her body.

When she'd moved into the cottage there had only been the bath. Maria liked showers. She liked the swift-ness of them, their cleanness, all that water pouring down her body, instant washing. Carolyn had said she was wel-come to install a shower head but the health farm couldn't meet the cost.

It had been worth the expense.

Maria felt the force of the water waking up every part of her body. She slicked back her shoulder-length hair and let the water slide over that as well.

But the pressure inside her skull never lifted.

All because of Jessica!

She'd thought she'd managed to forget her, until the other day. Self-centred little bitch, how dared she assume

Maria would be there for her? Would give up the biggest dream she'd ever had?

Blood vessels swelled and pressed against Maria's skull; if it hadn't been for the effect of the shower, she really felt they might burst. She stood quite still and tried to make her mind a blank, experience nothing but the wonderful chilly water beating against her skin, her bones reverberating to its pulsing beat. She closed her eyes and imagined she was under a tropical waterfall with dark, mysterious depths; exotically fragrant flowers blossoming amongst mosses and hugely tall trees. Only a little way away was a golden beach and there, waiting for her . . .

Above the noise of the shower and the pounding inside her head she hadn't been able to still, Maria gradually became aware that someone was beating on her front door.

She turned off the water, hastily towelled herself off, found her dressing gown and went barefooted down the steep stairs, trying to dry her hair as she went.

On the doorstep were a policeman and a policewoman. Maria stared at them.

'Mrs Russell?' the policewoman asked.

'Ms Russell,' Maria said automatically.

'We need you to come to the health farm.'

The pit of Maria's stomach started to churn. 'Why?' she stammered. 'What's happened?'

'Please, just dress and come with us,' said the policeman.

She stared at the two of them and they stared stolidly back.

Ten minutes later, dressed in the first tracksuit she could lay hands on, towel-dried hair combed into place, a splash of fresh toilet water giving her courage, Maria was driven up to the health farm. She sat in the back of the police car and tried to remain calm.

As the car drew away, she looked at Carolyn's house. There was a light on outside the door. What did that mean? That Carolyn hadn't got back last night? Or that she'd been woken up as well? Maria's sense of panic increased.

The sight of all the cars and vans outside the health farm jolted her. But she got out of the car and walked up to the front door with steady steps, psyching herself up with a sense of purpose.

Her escorts took her inside to the treatment area.

Her little kingdom. It had helped her climb out of the dreadful pit she'd found herself in when her marriage had gone sour. But, if she was honest with herself, it was the sense of failure that had hurt more than the way Jeremy had walked out. Had she ever really loved him? Or had it just been gratitude? Gratitude for his loving her?

The police had taken over her kingdom. The pool room swarmed with them and so did the treatment area. Maria tried to make out what they were doing; so far no one had said why they were there. The strength of purpose that had filled her as she stepped out of the car started to drain away. This looked as though it was going to be more than she could handle. 'What's happened?' she blurted out to no one in particular.

'Maria Russell?' A large man with the sort of figure Maria spent much of her time trying to discipline into something approaching acceptability stepped forward. He was dressed in a crumpled lightweight suit and had a tired, rubbery face that he was massaging with a hand as though that would remove the strain. The hand dropped down as he spoke. 'Superintendent Roger Marks. I understand you are responsible for the pool being locked up each evening.' It wasn't a question.

Numbly Maria nodded.

'Did you lock it last evening?'

The panic took over and her mind couldn't think straight. 'I, yes, I did.' She gathered up her strength and tried once again. 'I must know what's happened, why won't you tell me?'

It was no use. The superintendent continued to pursue his own enquiries. 'And what time would this have been?'

Maria rubbed at her eyes and tried to concentrate her mind. Beside the big policeman was a much thinner but taller man with dark hair and another tired face. His eyes had an edge to them that seemed to penetrate beneath her skin.

She thrust trembling hands into her tracksuit pockets and forced herself to concentrate. 'The last client left at, I think it was about six o'clock. Most of the girls had finished by then. Theresa was the last, she was doing a massage.'

'Who was the client?'

'Mr Borden.'

'Was that in this area or in the men's area?'

Maria nodded towards the women's cubicles at the far end of where they were standing. 'Over there. It's often more convenient to massage the men here, there's complete privacy.' She heard the steadiness in her voice with satisfaction. She had herself under control now. 'Theresa cleared up and left. I checked everything was in order, then locked the pool door.' She removed a hand from her pocket and gestured towards the huge spread of plate glass that divorced them from the activity on the other side. Almost, she could believe it was happening in another world, nothing to do with her at all.

'And that would have been when?'

Maria ran a hand through her still wet hair. 'About quarter past six, I think. What is all this about? What's happened?' Her voice sounded sharp and edgy.

'And did you check the patio doors out onto the terrace before you locked the pool door?' the big policeman asked impassively.

Maria nodded and thrust her hands back into her trouser pockets. 'That's part of the routine. As well as checking that the outside door to the men's area has been locked.'

'So when you left – at six fifteen you said? – when you left, the pool area was secure?'

'That's what I said.' Again Maria heard the note of edgy panic in her voice.

'And who else has keys to the pool area?'

'Carolyn, that's Mrs Pierce, and there's a spare set kept behind the reception desk.'

'Would you show me, please?'

The small courtesy gave Maria heart. She opened an almost invisible cupboard in the panelled wall and revealed a set of keys hanging on a brass hook.

'Hardly secure!' The superintendent was heavily sarcastic.

'As long as the outside door is locked, the equipment is safe. Here we're just concerned to protect clients. So they don't come and swim in the middle of the night. In case they get into difficulties.' She swallowed hard. 'Is that what's happened? Has someone drowned?' It came out with a small gasp and she couldn't bring herself to look again at the pool area.

'We'll ask the questions, if you don't mind.' That was the superintendent again.

'Do you have your keys with you now?' asked the taller man.

White faced, Maria took out the slim bunch of keys she always carried. They were taken away from her and given to another officer with instructions that they be checked.

'And what were your movements last night?'

'Look—'

'Just answer the question.'

'I went home, had supper, watched television and went to bed.'

'On a Saturday evening?' The superintendent sounded sceptical.

'Not all of us have to pair off or beat up the town,' Maria snapped back. 'I've answered all your questions, now you answer mine. What the hell's been going on?'

'Going on?' The question was slipped in smoothly by the taller man.

'Well there sure as hell has been something going on.' She was sarcastic now, adrenalin surging through her, taking over from the panic, giving courage. 'You don't have half a police force crawling over a place without something to investigate. I think you should tell me what it is.' She looked around. 'Where's Carolyn, Mrs Pierce? She's all right, isn't she?' It was half a question, half a plea.

'What makes you think she mightn't be?' That was the taller officer again.

'Just tell me what's happened, damn you!' Maria demanded.

She stood there, hands jammed deep in her pockets, determined she would say nothing more until they told her exactly what had happened.

The two men looked silently at her.

At last the superintendent said, 'There's been a murder, Mrs Russell.'

'Murder?' she heard her voice croak on the word. 'Who . . .' her voice dried up. She swallowed hard and tried again. 'Who's been murdered?'

'One of your clients, I'm afraid; a Lady Barry,' said the taller man sounding almost kindly.

Maria heard herself make a brief sound and some detached area of her brain registered the noise with disgust, it sounded like a kitten whose tail she had once stepped on, then someone produced a chair for her. She sat and bent over, leant her head on her hands, arms supported on her knees. Damp hair swung forward, hiding her face. One thought dominated the confusion in her head. Jessica was dead.

Her nightmare was over.

Chapter Eleven

William watched one of the sergeants take Maria Russell off to make a statement. He supposed he should feel exhausted but from somewhere had come a fresh surge of energy. Roger, too, he noted, had thrown off the effects both of the party and being woken after no more than a couple of hours of sleep.

Carolyn Pierce produced a print-out on Jessica Barry that she had extracted from her computer record system. Roger took it and announced that he would be using her office until further notice. Ignoring her look of blank fury, he led the way, indicating that William should follow.

He sat down heavily in the comfortable-looking swivel chair behind the antique desk. It creaked ominously beneath his weight but Roger didn't seem to notice. He leant back and placed his hands behind his head. 'I suppose you want in on this one, Bill?' he said curtly.

'I think you could find me useful, Roger.' William kept it low key. Roger wasn't the easygoing slob so many took him for and he could get very prickly if he thought anyone was taking liberties. But churning away in the back of William's mind was a memory of the girl he'd hauled from the spa pool. In death she'd looked so vulnerable. The dripping rats' tails of dark hair, the staring eyes so mesmerisingly green, the pitifully thin body: this was someone who'd been violated and now had no hope of redress.

Five months ago he and Darina had found another corpse, in France. There he'd been denied any part in the official investigation. Here again he was off his patch, but this time he was determined not to be sidelined.

'Useful?'

'Apart from anything else, Roger, Darina's staying at Conifers Spa with her mother. They've been here since Thursday. She met the dead woman.'

'Why do I need you in order to plug into her knowledge?' Roger Marks's button-round brown eyes looked cold. 'What about the undercover work you were seconded to us for?'

There were times when William found it hard to remember why he'd been such friends with him. 'Come on, Rog, we should be able to wrap this one up in a couple of days. The unit trust scam can wait that long.'

'If it wasn't for the fact that you and your wife have such an unbreakable alibi for the time of murder, your behaviour could be viewed as highly suspicious!' Roger said tartly and William realised he wasn't joking. Why the hell had he wanted to explore the treatment areas when they'd got back instead of going to bed as anybody sensible would have done? But if he hadn't, the body wouldn't have been found until morning. He might at least be given credit for that.

The office door opened and his wife entered with a tray of coffee.

'At last! We may find the strength to crack this case after all.' Roger Marks took a cup with hardly a glance at Darina.

William took his and gave her a smile. Her face was tired, with light bruising under the grey eyes that now had hazel tints, always a sign of strain or strong emotion. 'Darling, go to bed. I know it's nearly morning but you could get a couple of hours' sleep.'

'Sit down, Darina, tell us what you know about the victim,' Roger Marks ordered, taking his notebook out of his breast pocket. His voice was brisk, official, unfriendly.

Darina's left eyebrow rose microscopically but she sat

down in front of the desk, in a matching armchair to William's.

William watched Darina's eyes scan the desk. She leant forward and picked out a rubber band from a jumble of odd items sitting in a small porcelain tray. With a swift gesture she caught back the long, creamy-coloured hair that had been allowed to wave enticingly around her face for the party. When they had wrestled with Jessica Barry's body in the pool, it had become almost as drenched as the victim's. As it slowly dried, it had regained its buoyancy, billowing around her face in a way he found enticingly attractive. Now she twisted the band round the thick handful of hair, fastening it back in a ponytail. The effect highlighted the tension in her eyes and the tilt of her chin that said she was ready for action.

Roger Marks waited, one hand drumming lightly at the desk, a pencil poised in the other.

Darina smoothed back stray hairs from her forehead then dropped her hands into her lap. She looked calm, reserved and in control. 'What did the doctor say about time of death?' she asked abruptly.

Roger stiffened. For a moment William thought he wasn't going to answer the question. Then he said, 'As usual, the medical profession won't commit themselves. Anything halfway accurate, he claims, will depend on the temperature of the spa pool and when the heater was turned off. However, it looks as though the latest she could have been killed was twelve thirty.'

'And we got back at one-thirty!'

William recognised Darina's relief. Jessica had been dead long before they arrived back at the health farm. Even if they had gone straight to the pool, it would have been too late to rescue her. As a minor consideration, it also meant they were well out of the murder timeframe.

'And the earliest?'

Roger tapped at the notebook with his pencil. He'd hardly looked at Darina. 'That's the really tricky one.

Could be as early as nine o'clock.' He lifted his eyes. 'Now, what about Jessica Barry? Bill says you knew her.'

Roger's attitude was not helping to enlist Darina's full co-operation, William thought. Amateur meddling, Roger had said when he'd told him something of the amazing talent Darina had for winkling out details from people.

William had asked her once how she did it. 'I just listen,' she'd said. 'People like to talk, especially about themselves, and I find them interesting.'

Now they needed to know everything she'd found out about Jessica Barry, and now wasn't the time for Roger to indulge one of his hates – members of the public thinking they could do better than the police.

Mind you, there were times William himself wished Darina would stifle the irritating urge she seemed to have to enquire into murder investigations.

'I can't say I knew Jessica Barry,' Darina said with a hard stare at Roger Marks. 'The only time we were alone together was for a few minutes in the sauna.'

'Don't you girls spill all the moment you take off your clothes?'

If Roger was trying to jolt Darina with his coarseness, he didn't succeed. She returned his aggressive stare calmly. 'The afternoon I arrived, I was in the sauna with three other women: Gina Cazalet, Maureen Channing and Esme Lee. We got on very well and there was a lot of laughter. Then Jessica came in and the atmosphere changed. It was as if a thunderstorm had come up on a picnic. The others left quite quickly and there was just the two of us.'

Roger looked impatient. 'You mean Barry had antagonised them in some way? How?'

Again Darina refused to be nettled. 'As far as Gina Cazalet was concerned, I think it could have been jealousy. Jessica told me she was going to try and persuade Gina's husband, Perry Cazalet, to give her voice lessons; she wanted to become a singer. She seemed to succeed, too. After Gina refused to sing on Friday night, Perry asked Jessica to entertain us instead. Perry's a musician and he manages his wife's singing career. I don't think Gina took very kindly to Jessica's ambitions.'

William wondered if Roger realised how threatening he could look when he leaned forward to someone the way he was doing now. 'Just a minute, let's take one thing at a time. According to what you've just said, when Barry joined you in the sauna she was only intending to persuade this Cazalet to take an interest in her. Yet already his wife was antagonistic towards her?'

'Some women have antennae for that sort of thing that would put ultrasonic scanning to shame,' Darina said robustly. 'As far as Esme Lee was concerned, I think she could also have been jealous. Maureen Channing told me later that she was quite close to another of the clients here, Frank Borden. I saw myself that he seemed very friendly with Jessica Barry. She hoped he was going to arrange a nightclub spot for her as a singer and she acted as though he was her personal property.'

Roger's face had scepticism written all over it but he was making notes. 'And the other woman, Maureen Channing?'

Darina shook her head, 'I think she was following Esme's lead. They share a table at mealtimes. All I know about her is that she is here without her husband.'

'Bored housewife, perhaps? What about the Lee woman; she another bored housewife hoping to enliven her escape from the sink with an affair?'

Darina gave him a sardonic smile. 'Wait till you meet her! She's a powerful lady, a leading criminal barrister.'

Roger Marks stared at her. '*That* Ms Lee?'

'You know her?' Darina was amused and William wondered just what it was about this Esme Lee.

'I'll say!' Roger flung his pencil down on the table in disgust. 'She only got that bastard Marston off. He'd been running a major drug syndicate for years, thumbing his nose at us. I was on the Drugs Squad then and it took three years of careful graft before we could arrest him. Three years amassing evidence, squeezing snouts, cajoling terrified witnesses. At last we managed to get a case together the Public Prosecution Office would take on. Then she comes along, throws every trick in the book, ties up the witnesses till they don't know what day it is and the jury acquit him! Talk about perversion of justice!'

Darina said nothing.

After a moment Roger looked at her with narrowed eyes. 'Are you telling me this woman reckoned she was going to have it off with someone?'

Darina returned his glance just as keenly. They could have been two dogs squaring up before a fight. 'I wouldn't put it as strongly as that,' she said carefully. 'Just that she seemed very friendly with Frank Borden and resented Jessica's proprietary attitude towards him. Are you saying the possibility's unlikely?' Why the note of belligerence, William wondered?

Roger gave a ribald shout of laughter. 'Bill, you've got to see this woman. Unless she's joined weight watchers, she's the size of a house! Talk about intimidation – when she starts throwing her weight around in court, you can only duck.' He gave another throaty chuckle. 'If she thinks she's got a chance with any man, her judgement's gone doolally!'

Darina's face stiffened and little white patches appeared beside her nostrils. 'She's actually a very attractive woman and Frank Borden seems more than happy to spend time with her. A bit of flesh doesn't put some people off, thank heavens.'

Darina looked pointedly at Roger's beer gut, where buttons strained to keep the sides of his shirt together. He'd loosened his tie and undone the top two buttons several hours ago, giving his massive neck room to breathe. Now his stomach seemed to be demanding the same freedom, threatening to burst through the pale blue cotton.

The brown eyes narrowed and lost the slight warmth they'd had for the last few minutes, and William knew Darina had blown any chance she might have had of being accepted as part of the team. He wondered just what had got into her. Usually she was so adept with people.

Roger picked up his pencil. 'Right, so we've got two jealous women who could have believed this Barry girl was after their men.' He made it sound trivial at best. 'What else can you tell us about her?'

Not an eyelash flickered as Darina spoke but one hand clenched itself in her lap. 'According to Jessica Barry, she was more or less alone in the world. Her husband had died recently and she was estranged from her family. I think her mother's dead and she said she hadn't seen her father since her marriage. I gather he didn't approve. There was something else—'

But Roger broke in, 'Did you find anything out about the husband?' he asked.

'Sir Paul Barry? She said he'd been an MP and was rather older than her. Actually, I think she was older than she looked. I thought she was in her mid-twenties when I saw her first but in the sauna, without make-up and her hair all wet, she looked well over thirty.'

Women's ages were definitely tricky, thought William. It was only when they passed a certain stage that you could pick up on the little things. Face lifts could take away years but no one ever had a hand lift. Even after the bloom of youth had gone, though, there was a long period when, with a bit of care, a woman could fool you by a good ten or fifteen years. No wonder the French referred to females *'d'un certain âge'*. It wasn't a graceful compliment, it was an admission of defeat; they just didn't know!

'Paul Barry!' Roger exclaimed and William cursed his tiredness. The name had slipped right past him while he was studying Darina and admiring her ability to assess women's ages.

'You know who he is?' Darina asked.

A pleased smile lit Roger's face, as though he relished his superior knowledge. 'MP who resigned from parliament shortly after they were married, said he wanted to spend more time with his wife. He'd been in the cabinet at one time, got dropped during some reshuffle, was knighted, a sure sign his high-flying career was over, and retired to the back benches, sounding off from there at every opportunity. Lots of rumours of more sinister reasons for his standing down, lots of digging into the divorce proceedings a couple of years earlier but nothing definite ever emerged.' He smiled, the big mouth baring his teeth in a peculiarly unattractive way. 'Don't you remember the publicity, both when he was married and then when he resigned?'

'It was all over the tabloids,' William said. 'You know, bimbo air stewardess marries knighted MP twice her age.'

Darina looked thoughtful. 'I'd forgotten the name. Stupid of me! Yet, I don't know, Jessica somehow added up to more than a mere fortune-hunter. She sounded genuinely fond of her husband.'

Roger's expression said he'd have difficulty agreeing with her.

William felt everything Darina had said showed this case was not going to be a difficult one to crack. Jessica Barry sounded like a girl with a distinct talent for setting the world against her, and emotional murderers always made mistakes.

Roger picked up the computer print-out on Jessica Barry he'd placed on the desk. 'Her next of kin's noted as one Oliver Barry. Know who he is?'

Darina shook her head.

'Brother-in-law? Stepson? Father-in-law even?' suggested William.

Roger let the paper fall back on the desk. 'We should

know soon enough. I've asked the Met to send someone over to break the news.' He looked up at Darina. 'Thank you, Mrs Pigram, all that's most helpful. We'll take a formal statement later today. Now I repeat your husband's suggestion that you get some rest.'

For a long moment Darina remained sitting where she was, and the way Roger had used her married name seemed to reverberate in the air.

'You've been wonderful, darling,' said William. He reached across and patted her hand, she was too far away for anything more demonstrative. 'Do go and try and catch up on your sleep now. We'll need your observant eye later today.'

There was an impatient gesture from behind the desk that he ignored. Roger Marks was not going to interfere between him and his wife.

Darina looked at him and William's heart sank. He heard again in his mind's ear what he'd said and realised how patronising it had sounded. But he couldn't think of anything to say that would mend the damage.

Chapter Twelve

Detective Sergeant Crawford stood on the steps of an early Victorian villa in St John's Wood, London, and rang the doorbell gingerly. Half past eight on a Sunday morning was early in his book and he was doubtful if his reception would be warm.

Not that he expected a particularly warm reception anyway. Breaking the news of a death was the worst aspect of police work. When he'd been a constable on the beat, he'd several times had to convey news of a fatal accident to the victim's family. It had never been easy.

This time, however, there could be compensations. Opportunities. Sergeant Crawford had only just been promoted. He was young and ambitious and anything to do with a murder investigation could be important. Now he reckoned his job involved more than just being the bearer of bad tidings. There could be important things to be learned: reactions, details of the relationship, background of all sorts. Any little fact might be the clue that could eventually break the case. It was up to him to be alert.

Inside, all seemed silent. Phil Crawford studied the outside of the villa, trying to get an impression of the owner before he tried the bell again. He backed down the steps of the pillared porch and looked at the freshly painted front, peered down the iron staircase that led from the pavement railings to a lower ground floor. But venetian blinds closed off his view through the window. Then he bounded up the steps again and leaned across from the porch to try and look into the room beside the front door. All he could see were heavy curtains tied back by tasselled silken cords and a table supporting an oddly shaped, shiny black vase out of which blossomed an arrangement of white lilies with drooping, lancelike leaves.

Then he had to spring back to attention as there came the sounds of bolts being drawn and a chain being undone followed by the unfastening of a security lock.

'Yes?'

The man standing in the doorway was, Sergeant Crawford reckoned, in his mid-thirties. Phil was ambitious but he found it difficult to imagine that by the time he reached that age he would be able to afford so magnificent a maroon dressing gown with silk facings. He decided, though, that next time he had to change his glasses he'd go for heavyweight tortoiseshell frames that would give him that look of sophistication; plus he'd change his barber immediately. His short crop had none of the style of the slicked back fair hair on the man in front of him.

'Detective Sergeant Crawford of the Metropolitan Police, sir,' he said smartly, showing his warrant card. 'Mr Oliver Barry?'

The man held out his hand for the warrant card and scrutinised it.

Only the dressing gown suggested he had just got out of bed. The fair hair was carefully combed back from the high forehead. The dark navy eyes behind the thick glasses were clear of sleep; despite their lazy lids, they looked uncommonly alert. The heavy face with its thin mouth had been shaved, looked as though it had been anointed with some toiletry, and exuded an expensive aroma. The dressing-gown sash was neatly tied and he wore socks as well as classy leather slippers. Sergeant Crawford concluded that Mr Barry had already bathed and been in the process of dressing when the doorbell had rung.

'You'd better come inside. I assume something has happened and I'd rather whatever it is isn't blurted out for all the neighbours to hear.' Oliver Barry stepped back and held open the door for the sergeant.

Phil Crawford didn't think residents in such an up-market neighbourhood would deign to snoop, but his news was not the sort you imparted on the doorstep.

He was led to a room at the back of the ground floor, a cross between a library and a study, with shelves of books plus a computer, monitor and printer in one corner.

Oliver Barry sat down behind a well-polished mahogany desk, bare except for a small pile of papers in the right-hand top corner, a leather blotter and an ornate silver set of desk accessories centred above the blotter.

He waved a hand towards a wing chair covered in dark green leather and decorated all round the arms and seat with brass studs.

Phil Crawford sat down, pulling up the trouser legs of the dark suit he'd considered the most suitable wear when the call had come through to his home that morning, waking him up. He was fascinated by Oliver Barry's aplomb. Most people faced with a member of the CID on their doorstep, especially on a Sunday morning, tended to lose their cool, demanded to know immediately what had happened, asked to be reassured someone near and dear hadn't suffered a terrible accident. But Oliver Barry just steepled his hands, elbows resting on the arms of the swivel chair, and waited. Only a gentle, almost imperceptible sway of the chair from side to side betrayed anything but polite interest in what the sergeant had to say. A cool customer, Phil decided.

'I'm sorry, sir, I have some tragic news.'

For the first time Oliver Barry showed emotion. He leant forward, one hand reaching across the desk, a pleading gesture. 'Not my mother?'

For an instant Phil hesitated, wondering himself, then

remembered the whole of his information with a certain relief. 'No, sir.'

Oliver Barry remained quite still for a moment, then leant back easily in the chair, once again in complete command. 'Thank God for that. When you said tragedy it was my first thought; I hadn't worried before because you weren't in uniform so I didn't think you could have called about an accident of any sort.' He spoke easily, man to man.

Phil admired his approach. Intelligent the way he'd assessed his non-uniformed status as well. 'A Lady Barry has died, but I understand she is too young to be your mother.'

The eyes snapped wide open. 'Jessica?'

Phil nodded.

'Jessica, dead?' The heavy-set face showed nothing but disbelief. 'How?'

Before Phil could say anything more, the door to the study opened and a blonde head appeared. 'Oliver? Would you like coffee?'

It was a welcome suggestion to Phil.

'Veronica, come in. This is Detective Sergeant Crawford.'

This must be Mrs Oliver Barry. Quite a dish! Neat figure, sweet face with an air of fragility, perhaps because the nose and chin were so small but also because of the fine golden hair that wisped around the high forehead, the pale blue eyes and pale pink lips. She was dressed in narrow navy trousers and a billowy white top. Phil's own wife was dark, her sturdy body the very antithesis of fragility. She had a great sense of humour and Phil reckoned they would never bore each other, but he had to admit it would be easy to be overwhelmed by Veronica Barry.

'Sergeant, this is my wife.'

Phil Crawford scrambled to his feet. 'Mrs Barry, I'm

sorry to disturb you this way.' He hoped the offer of coffee would be repeated. He was doomed to disappointment.

'Veronica, the sergeant says Jessica is dead.' Again there was that note of disbelief.

'No! How?' Veronica's fair face visibly paled and she sank into another of the leather-covered wing chairs.

The sergeant cleared his throat nervously. 'I'm afraid she's been murdered.'

'Murdered?' Shock gave way to incredulity.

Then Oliver Barry raised a hand and brought it crashing down on the desk. 'That stupid bitch, wouldn't you know it!'

'Darling!' Veronica said sharply.

'Now we'll have the press digging over the past, asking all the old questions again. God, I just hope mother can take it.'

'Your mother is much stronger than you think, darling.' Was there just a touch of acid in Veronica Barry's quiet voice?

'How was she murdered?'

'I'm afraid I have no details, Mrs Barry.' Phil Crawford found himself speaking gently.

'And where?'

'That I can tell you, sir.' Phil brought out his notebook. 'Conifers Spa health farm in Wiltshire.'

'A health farm. Just the sort of place Jessica would choose to go to.'

'Darling, she's dead!'

Oliver Barry threw himself back in the swivel chair, picked up a long pen from the silver stand and started turning it over and over in his fingers. 'Do you know any more details?'

'I'm afraid not, sir.' Phil Crawford sat solidly and waited.

Oliver Barry dropped the pen back on his desk, shoved back the chair, got up and stood with his back to the room, looking out of the window. A tree obscured much of the view; all that could be seen were green leaves and a glimpse of lawn.

After a moment he said, 'I should have to be informed of Jessica Barry's death at some stage, but why send a CID officer round at this hour on a Sunday morning?'

Phil Crawford eyed the rigid back. 'I understand the health farm had you noted as next of kin, sir.'

That brought Oliver Barry round again, his face distorted with anger. 'She's no kin of ours, by God!'

'Oliver!' protested Veronica Barry. 'After your father's death, we're the nearest thing poor Jessica had to family.'

' "Poor Jessica," ' her husband repeated savagely. 'How you can even bring yourself to speak of that bitch beggars me.'

'Oliver, you're prejudiced, you know that! I've always said you treat her far too harshly.' Veronica looked distressed, her hands knotting themselves together.

Phil Crawford forgot all about coffee.

Oliver Barry flung a look of contempt at his wife and sat down again. 'So, Jessica's dead. Murdered. What's next?'

'When did you last see her, sir?' Phil got out his pen and flipped over a page in his notebook.

Oliver Barry paused just too long.

'She came here about ten days ago, don't you remember, darling? I'd gone to get Araminta from her party and when I came back she was just leaving.'

'Exactly what day was that, Mrs Barry?'

She rose hastily. 'Just a minute, I'll get my calendar.' She left the room.

Oliver Barry sat biting the side of one finger and said nothing.

His wife was back almost immediately, carrying a monthly calendar with daily spaces. Most of the spaces seemed to have something scribbled in them. Veronica studied it, frowning. 'Let's see, yes, it was a week ago last Tuesday. Here it is, Sarah's birthday party, see?' She held out the calendar so that the sergeant could read the scrawl: 3.00 at Sarah's with present.

'And you got back here at what time, Mrs Barry?'

She thought for a moment. 'Must have been around six thirty.'

'And Jessica Barry was just leaving?'

She nodded. 'She was coming down the steps as Araminta and I came from parking the car.'

'Did you talk to her?'

The fair skin flushed slightly. 'Yes. She, she seemed upset, almost brushed past us without saying anything. But Araminta was so excited to see her, Jessica used to give her lovely presents, and pulled at her skirt. Then she stopped, kissed Araminta and said how nice it was to see us. We . . .' She hesitated, then continued, 'We hadn't seen her for some time. I asked her how she was, you know, talk like that.' She glanced towards her husband but Oliver Barry said nothing, just watched his wife from under the lazy lids.

'And how was she?' asked Phil, making notes of everything.

'She said she was fine.' Veronica was almost falling over her words she was speaking so quickly. 'But I didn't think she was. She tried to talk normally but I think she was very upset. Oliver,' she glanced at her husband, 'Oliver always upset her. She just said she was sorry, she had to go and she'd give me a ring some day.' Again the flush stained the fair skin.

'What time did the deceased arrive here that Tuesday, sir?'

Oliver Barry stared at Phil as though considering not answering the question. For a moment the sergeant thought he might even insist on calling his lawyer. 'Half past five,' he said finally, the words made as short as possible.

'Are you usually home then?'

Again that considering look before Oliver Barry

sighed deeply and seemed to decide there was no point in not giving all the details. 'No, I work in the City, stockbroker. Jessica phoned me that morning and said she wanted to talk to me. Well, I knew what that meant, she wanted money. I wasn't prepared for her to make a scene in the office so I suggested she came here.'

Did he know his wife would be out, collecting their daughter? Were there other people in the house? The questions raced through Phil's mind as he made his notes. A very private man, Mr Barry; didn't want neighbours overhearing, didn't want his office knowing anything of his personal business with, Phil Crawford realised with a start, with his stepmother.

'She turned up late, of course. It was nearly six by the time she arrived. Never worried that I'd had to cut my working day short to see her.' Oliver Barry picked up the pen and started once again to twist it around and around. 'I asked her what was so urgent and she said, as I knew she would, she needed money.' He looked across the desk at Phil and his eyes were angry. 'Jessica married my father for money, plain and simple, and when she found out he hadn't got any, she made his life a misery until he died.'

'Oliver!'

'Veronica, keep quiet! You know nothing about it. You let Jessica charm you with those soft little ways, you've never understood what she's really like, I mean, was like.' He took off his glasses and drew a hand across his eyes, pulling the skin down, revealing a tiny maze of blood vessels under the lower lids. 'God, it's so hard to realise she's dead, that we'll never have to worry about her again.'

'Worry, sir?'

Oliver Barry sent him a long, assessing glance. 'Look, Sergeant, I can't pretend I'm at all sorry I'll never have to see her again. She tried to blackmail me and I don't take kindly to that.'

Phil felt a long frisson of excitement. 'Blackmail, sir?'

'Oliver, you didn't tell me that!' Veronica looked shocked.

'She said she needed money, a lot of money, and if I wouldn't give it to her she was going to sell her story to the newspapers.'

'Oliver, no!'

'What story would that be?'

'Her life with my father.'

'It was sensational, sir?'

Oliver Barry clamped his mouth shut, the thin lips pressed so close together they almost disappeared. He shook his head. 'The old, old story. An elderly man besotted with a much younger girl, marrying her and finding out she didn't love him and wasn't going to take care of him in his old age.' He gave a grim laugh. 'I can't think any newspaper would pay much for it but my father was at one stage a prominent politician so it would no doubt be worth something.'

'And what did you say to her, sir?'

'I told her I'd think about it. That I couldn't give her an answer right away.'

He said it firmly, with conviction.

'Why was that, sir?'

'Why? Why?' Oliver Barry gave him a contemptuous stare. 'I don't know why I should have to tell you but I will. I have a sister and I needed to talk to her. If we agreed that we should try and keep the story out of the papers, then she would have to contribute.'

'And have you talked to her?'

Oliver Barry gave a long, slow nod. 'Yes.'

'And?'

'She was against giving Jessica anything.'

'And did you ring your stepmother and tell her this?'

The navy eyes were wide open, brutally dark. 'I was waiting for Jessica to contact me again. I didn't see any reason to put her out of her suspense.'

'And she hadn't contacted you?'

A slow shake of the head. 'It made me think the newspaper story was a try-on. I don't think she had any intention of going to any of them. After all, she'd end up looking exactly what she was, a fortune-seeking bimbo. Now, I hope you don't need anything else. Time is getting on.' He looked deliberately at his watch.

'I'm afraid we do, sir.' Phil Crawford held his gaze steady. 'We need official identification of the body.'

There was a long pause. Then Oliver Barry sighed and threw down the pen he'd been playing with. 'What the hell, the day's ruined anyway. Do I have to go to Wiltshire?'

'I'm afraid so, sir. But we can take you there and bring you back.'

'Not necessary, I prefer to drive myself.' Oliver Barry heaved himself to his feet. All systems seemed to be closed down, now; the heavy-set face betrayed nothing of what he could be thinking.

Veronica Barry rose as well. 'I'll come with you, darling. We can call in on your mother on the way back. She ought to be told Jessica's dead.'

'No.' The word exploded out of him, then, with a visible effort, Oliver Barry put a hand on his wife's shoulder. 'I don't want you involved. You stay with Araminta, it'll only take a few hours.' He looked across at Phil Crawford. 'Do you tell me where to go or do I need an escort?'

'No, sir. I've got all the details for you.'

'Written down? No?' He jerked a piece of paper out of a drawer and flung it on the desk in front of the sergeant. 'Get them down on that. I'll just go and finish dressing. Veronica, see the sergeant out when he's finished.' He strode from the room without saying goodbye.

Phil Crawford turned to the right page in his notebook and started copying down the details onto the piece of paper. He was conscious of Veronica Barry hovering beside him.

'I'm sorry,' she said softly after a moment. 'He's very upset.'

'I can understand that, madam. Not a nice thing to have happened.'

She made a helpless little gesture with her hands and he saw they were trembling. He looked up; her face was distressed. She swallowed a couple of times then said, 'I probably shouldn't tell you this but I don't see why not. Oliver and his sister hated Jessica. But their father was an awful man. I think he deserved everything he got. Jessica was sweet when they got married. I thought she was really fond of my father-in-law. And, and he seemed crazy about her. I thought maybe everything was going to work out all right.' She stopped, her pale blue eyes soft and concerned. Phil Crawford waited. 'When, when it didn't,' she stammered, 'I honestly don't think it was Jessica's fault.' There was a long pause, then she added, 'But Oliver hates it if I say so.'

There were a lot of questions Phil Crawford would have liked to ask her but he didn't get the opportunity. Oliver Barry must have finished dressing with the speed of a whirlwind for he was back in the study wearing beige cotton slacks, a checked open-necked shirt and a cashmere cardigan. He grabbed up the directions, ran a quick eye down them then stuffed them in his pocket. 'Right, Sergeant, we can leave together. I'll call you later, darling, and let you know when I'll be back.'

Phil wasn't exactly frog-marched out of the house but he was outside the St John's Wood villa more quickly than he would have thought possible. Oliver Barry stopped beside a dark-green Jaguar and fished out his keys. 'You can tell your people I'll be there in about two hours. Shouldn't take me longer than that.' He waited, making no attempt to open the car door.

Phil gave a small nod then walked up the road to

where he'd parked his Ford. He looked back as he got out his key. Oliver Barry was still watching him, and in the front window of the villa he thought he saw the pale figure of Veronica Barry.

Chapter Thirteen

'I still can't believe it,' Ann Stocks said for what seemed like the hundredth time. 'That nice little girl, who would want her dead?'

'Not everybody seemed to think she was nice,' commented Darina dryly.

'And for you and William to have found the body! How awful for you both.' This, too, had been said a number of times.

Superintendent Roger Marks had addressed all the guests as they breakfasted in the dining room that morning. Darina knew that he had already spoken to the staff.

By the time he appeared in the dining room, word had spread. Those who had woken in the night told others the little they knew. Rumours spread faster than salmonella in undercooked chicken. Someone had been electrocuted on the slendertone, said one person; no, they'd been fried on the sunbed, said someone else. That was contradicted in turn with the news that two people had drowned in the swimming pool, one while trying to rescue the other. Who knew how these stories had started? No one had got hold of a name for the victim or victims; the rumours were satisfactorily anonymous.

It came, therefore, as a shock to have the actual details announced. All at once people were faced with the fact that someone they had talked with, spent time with, was dead. Not only dead but murdered. Suddenly something that had given an almost agreeable sense of disaster became horrifyingly real.

'I'm sure you realise that we need to eliminate as many people from our enquiries as possible,' Roger Marks continued. He'd refastened the collar of his shirt and his tie had been tightened again. It sat askew over his crumpled shirt. His abundant brown hair stood on end and the big, thick fingers played with a teaspoon he'd picked up from somewhere. In many ways he was an unimpressive figure. But there was no doubting his air of authority. He seemed to flaunt his dishevelled corpulence, and ignored the no smoking signs by lighting a powerful cheroot as his gravelly voice gave his stunned audience the bad news. 'We have a team of police ready to take statements from everybody. I ask you all to stay at the health farm until your statement has been taken. Then everyone must leave so that we can conduct our enquiries.'

There was a shocked outburst of whispering to that.

The superintendent lit another cheroot and strode out. Carolyn took his place. She looked pale but composed. Beside her stood an equally pale and composed Maria Russell.

'We do realise that this will be a very great inconvenience to some of you, not to say a disappointment. But I am sure you understand the police have given us no alternative.'

There was a rustle of indignation, now directed against the victim. Poor Jessica; her memorial the chagrin of pampered women denied their full complement of figure-trimming treatment.

'We're drawing up everyone's bill, together with a credit voucher to compensate you for having to cut short your stay here. Even those due to leave this morning will receive a voucher. Maria Russell, our health manager,' Carolyn gestured towards the tall, pale girl standing at her side, 'will weigh you, discuss your state of health and what we hope will have been the benefits of your stay. If anyone has any particular problem, I shall be here.'

Someone asked if lunch would be served.

Darina reflected with grim amusement how the demands of the stomach were never to be denied, even at a health farm and even at a time like this.

Carolyn regretted that lunch would not be possible. 'However, there will be sandwiches available at one o'clock for those who have been unable to depart by then.' She hesitated then added, 'I would just like to say how very shocked we all are by what happened last night. I am sure you all feel the same and that you will co-operate fully with the police so that whoever killed poor Jessica Barry will be caught as soon as possible.'

There was a moment's complete silence when she'd finished speaking. It was as though not only Jessica's death but the fact that someone had been responsible for it had sunk in for the first time. When conversation started again it was oddly muted.

Darina and her mother retired to sit in the garden. The sky was overcast and it wasn't as warm as it had been but they found a sheltered terrace out of sight of the large area roped off by the police. 'Oughtn't we to be packing?' asked Ann.

'The superintendent has agreed that we can stay if we'd like to,' Darina said. It had been a hard-won concession, negotiated by William. His rapport with Roger Marks Darina found irritating; there was little she could see about the superintendent to justify friendship.

'Stay in this place, where there's been a murder?' Ann Stocks glanced around the pleasant garden and shivered slightly.

'I thought you might feel like that. If you want, I'll drive you home. I think, though, that I'll return here.'

'And leave me on my own?'

Darina felt guilty. Then decided that it was time her mother started standing on her own two feet again. If the support system wasn't gently removed, her mother might never regain her independence. 'Ma, I'm sorry, but William is here and we've been apart so much recently. Then there's Carolyn also. She's asked if I can't stay and give her some moral support. She's been through a very tough time since Robert died and I'd like to help her if I can.'

'She's more important to you than your mother, I suppose,' Ann said bitterly.

'If you really need me, of course I'll stay with you, at least for a couple of days,' Darina said gently. 'You know I care about you, we both do. That's why we suggested this week here, we hoped it would help cheer you up. Instead it's all ended in tragedy!' She gave a small, hopeless gesture.

There was silence.

Ann Stocks picked at the crease in her linen trousers, her mouth set in an obstinate pout. 'You remind me so much of your father,' she said finally. 'He could always manage to make me feel I was being selfish and unreasonable.'

'But he adored you!' Darina was astonished.

'He thought I was a silly nitwit.' Her mother produced a ghost of a smile. 'And I suppose, in so many ways, I was. He should have married someone as intelligent as he was, someone he could discuss life with. Instead he had to fall in love with me, who could never carry a serious conversation and thought life was for living.'

Darina stared at her mother. Never had they talked like this before. 'I've always felt a deep disappointment to you,' she said softly.

'You, a disappointment? Why?'

'I'm so large, not petite and pretty like you. I can't socialise the way you can, get a party going, make people gravitate to me. I used to watch Daddy when we had a party, he was always so proud of you.'

Ann Stocks's eyes brimmed; she fished in her bag for

a handkerchief. 'It's my only talent. When I was growing up it seemed so important. I was never expected to work, only to make a man happy. It was all starting to change then but my father was old-fashioned. He had hardly any money but he managed to give me a season and I know he hoped I'd make a great marriage. He thought his name and my looks would be enough. Instead I fell in love with your father, the locum who treated me for a sprained ankle when I fell off my horse hunting.' She smiled, the tears gone now. 'He was so attractive. Big and strong, he made me feel I was something small and precious that had to be carefully looked after. I really didn't mind that he didn't want to become a consultant and there would never be much money.'

Darina gave a reminiscent smile. 'That's how I remember him with you.'

Then her mother's face twisted again. 'Until he found I hadn't any mind, until I bored him to extinction. And all I could do was continue to flutter, like a stupid moth getting its wings burned on a bright, bright flame.' She pulled at the little square of linen, tugging at the monogrammed corner.

Darina didn't know what to say.

'Do you know, it wasn't until Gerry came along that I found a relationship in which I felt an equal? Even my brother, your Uncle George, has always treated me as his baby sister who needed protecting from the big wicked world.'

'It's just the way he was brought up,' Darina said gently. Her Uncle George succeeded to the barony on his father's death but had renounced it in order to remain in the House of Commons. After all, he said, with the estate sold to pay debts and no money, what was the point in being a lord? Member of Parliament was a much more important title.

'Then I met Gerry. I knew he was intelligent too, but he loved just chatting to me, talking about people the way I liked to talk about them. Playing bridge. He made me feel I was a valued companion, not just somebody decorative who could throw a good party.'

This was a woman Darina had never met before. All at once she could see beneath the social ease, the sophisticated, bright chatter, to a lonely woman who'd made a busy social life and a myriad of easy friendships compensation for the lack of a deep relationship. And then, when she'd found someone she could be really happy with, he'd been taken from her.

'Oh, Ma, I'm so sorry!'

Ann Stocks gave her a smile that was only slightly tearful. 'Don't be, darling! It's not your fault. It's nobody's fault, I suppose. I couldn't turn myself into something I wasn't, any more than your father could, or you can.'

Ah, they were back where they'd started.

'I know you have to have your career, even though you're now married. I know you want to interest yourself in what William's doing, it's only right that you should. Though why you continue to call yourself Lisle instead of being known as Pigram beats me. But,' Ann added thoughtfully, 'I have to admit Lisle sounds better.'

'It's what I'm known by, it would be too difficult to start again as something else.'

'And you don't want to try,' said Ann shrewdly. 'All I ask is that you don't forget to be a woman and don't forget your old ma.'

'I couldn't ever do that,' said Darina and reached across for her mother's hand.

'I've been very naughty,' Ann Stocks said cheerfully, gripping her daughter's hand tightly. 'I've played you like a violin and now you're all ready to take me home and stay with me and cosset me and make me feel wanted. And it's very dear of you but I know it won't do me any good. I've got to pick up my old life again.' She put the handkerchief back in her handbag, shutting it with a decisive click. 'I tell you what I'm going to do; I'm going to ring Molly Creighton, tell her what's happened and see if I can't stay with her for a few days. On Friday night she was trying to persuade me to get you to drop me off with them at the end of our stay here.' Ann looked at her daughter and gave a girlish giggle. 'I hope she won't be too surprised at my taking up her offer so quickly.'

Darina felt enormous relief and a surge of love. 'Ma, don't let anyone ever tell you you're not smart and brave and fun.'

'Haven't you been able to get away yet, either?' Maureen Channing asked. She'd come through the rose garden unnoticed. 'Most of the others have already gone. I'm waiting for Len but I don't suppose he'll get here until after lunch. He said he was going to call in on a friend on the way. I tried to ring and ask him to make it earlier but he must have started already. The attractions of the friend, I suppose.' She sat down on the edge of a lounger as if poised for instant take-off.

'Have you given your statement to the police?' asked Darina politely.

Maureen nodded, fair curls dancing. She'd had her hair cut and set the previous afternoon in a much younger fashion that flattered her round face. 'It was a tiny bit frightening to start with, the young woman was so official and I thought I must be careful not to make any mistakes.' Her voice came in little spurts, giving an impression of breathlessness.

'They just want you to tell them everything you were doing last night.' Darina tried to sound reassuring.

Maureen nodded. 'That's what she said and after a bit it all came back to me. Not that it was very much, really. I mean, I went in to dinner, ate with Esme as usual, then she asked if I wanted a stroll in the garden, it was such a lovely night. But I thought I'd really had enough exercise, so I went upstairs and watched television in my room, had an early night. And that was it!' She sounded slightly disappointed. 'I never even woke when there was

124

all that commotion. Tell me, your husband's one of the police isn't he?'

Darina nodded. 'William Pigram, the tall, dark one.'

'Ooh, he's gorgeous, you lucky thing, you. Anyway, perhaps you can tell me, will they want to speak to me again, do you think?' Maureen looked anxious.

'I really can't say.'

'Only I don't think Len's going to like it at all.' Maureen gripped the pouch bag she was carrying. She was dressed in a linen suit, smartly cut with a skirt that just skimmed her knees. 'He's got a thing about the police.'

Len Channing was, Maureen had solemnly told Darina earlier, a dealer in 'pre-owned luxury cars'. If either she or her husband ever wanted a not-quite-new Rolls Royce or Maserati, Len would be able to supply them ever such a good buy. 'In other words, he's a second-hand car salesman,' Ann Stocks had whispered after Maureen had gone off to a treatment.

'If you didn't see or hear anything, I should think it's most unlikely that the police will want to talk to you again,' Darina said comfortingly. 'They take all these statements so they can build up a picture of where everyone was at the critical time.'

'I suppose I shall have to go and give mine,' sighed Ann Stocks. 'In fact, I think that policeman said it would probably be about now. I'll go and see if I'm wanted yet.' She rose gracefully from her chair. 'It's been so nice to meet you, Maureen. I hope maybe we'll be able to get together after all this nasty business has been sorted out.'

Maureen's face brightened. 'Oh, I do hope so, Lady Stocks, I mean, Ann. Remember, if you're ever in the Midlands, you must look us up.' Darina's mother smiled warmly and promised she would do just that then walked slowly off towards the house looking much older than her years.

'Will you come again to Conifers Spa?' Darina asked Maureen curiously.

Maureen looked doubtfully at her pouch bag, as though she suspected it might suddenly turn into something unpleasant. 'I, I don't know. I've loved it, of course, but, you know . . . this Jessica business, well, I'm not sure I'd ever forget it, you see?'

Darina did see.

'And it's not as though she was a nice girl!' Maureen burst out with no logic at all.

'Tell me, what set you against her?'

'What do you mean?'

'That first afternoon, when I was in the sauna with you, Gina and Esme, Jessica came in and it was obvious none of you liked her. Why, what had she done? I mean, she'd only just arrived, hadn't she?'

'The previous day,' Maureen said briefly. 'You get to know people here so quickly, don't you think? Rather like being on board ship, isn't it?'

'But even so, doesn't one tend to like people when one first meets them, unless they do something odd?'

Maureen nodded doubtfully.

'So what did Jessica Barry do?'

Maureen continued to look like a child presented with a difficult problem at school, then her face cleared. 'I remember now, Esme told us about her.'

'Esme knew her previously?' Darina was surprised.

Maureen grew doubtful again. 'I don't think that was it. Let me think exactly what she said. We were in the sauna; the three of us sort of fell into the habit of taking one at the same time. Gina is so funny and Esme and me, well, two women on their own, it was nice for us to share a table and chat. Mind you, I can't understand what she's on about half the time and she does seem to love bullying me. But then I'm used to that, with Len and all,' she finished elliptically.

'What did Esme say?' Darina tried to get her back on the track.

'Oh, yes, that was what I was going to tell you, wasn't

it?' Maureen looked at Darina hopefully, an obedient dog hoping for a pat. 'Well, Gina was telling us that this little creature had hardly arrived before she'd come up to Perry and said how exciting it was to meet him and that she hoped they'd be able to have a real chat at some stage. Gina said it was dreadful, that everywhere they went there was some girl wanting Perry to help her become a singer.' Maureen stopped and took a breath. 'And Esme asked if her name was Jessica Barry and when Gina said she thought it was, told her to watch it. She said Jessica would be after Perry and no mistake.'

'How did she know?' wondered Darina.

'D'you know, we didn't ask?' Maureen looked as though she wondered about that now as well.

'Could it have anything to do with Frank Borden?'

'I don't know.' Maureen looked doubtful, then brightened. 'I know Esme knew him before she came here. She told me he'd suggested she might like to come and he'd wanted her to eat with him but she preferred to keep her independence.'

'They played tennis together,' Darina observed.

'Oh, I think she's quite interested in him,' Maureen said slyly. 'I think she likes playing a little hard to get, you know?'

'But she didn't like Jessica monopolising Frank?'

'Oooh, you think that's what it was? Jealousy?'

'What do you think?'

Maureen considered. 'Well,' she said finally, 'Esme certainly likes men and I think she could be quite possessive. But I don't think she'd ever say anything that wasn't true.'

'So you and Gina believed what she said about Jessica?'

'Of course!'

'Do you know what Frank Borden's line of business is?'

'Something to do with antiques. I think he has a shop

in Mayfair, he was telling us about it one night. What did he say it was called?' Maureen frowned and fiddled with the latch of a heavy gold bracelet. Then her face cleared. 'Got it, Lost Horizons.'

'What a curious name for an antiques shop.'

'He specialises in ancient cultures, he said.'

Somehow ancient cultures didn't seem to connect up in Darina's mind with Frank Borden. He was too – too what? Too streetwise, she thought suddenly, too slick smart for a trade that surely called for sustained study of an intellectual kind. And anyway, what sort of connection would Esme Lee QC, specialist in criminal law, have with antiques, ancient or not? A hobby, perhaps? A way of investing her no doubt horrendously high fees? Yes, that was probably it.

'Well, anyway,' Darina continued, 'Esme told you and Gina that Jessica was a scheming bitch.'

'I didn't say that!' Maureen was shocked.

'That's what it amounted to, and she suggested that Gina should keep an eye on her husband.' No wonder the atmosphere in the sauna had grown frigid when Jessica walked in, thought Darina. Even more interesting, what did Esme know about her?

'Did you tell the police about this?'

Maureen looked frightened. 'No, should I have done?'

'Yes, I think you should. Why don't you go and tell them there's something you've just remembered and think they might like to know?'

'Won't they think me stupid?' Maureen complained, her hands grasped tightly over her bag, her eyes frightened.

'No, people never remember everything in one go, that's why the police sometimes go back and talk to them again.' Darina paused and looked at Maureen. 'If you tell them now it might mean they don't have to come and talk to you at home,' she added cunningly.

'Would they do that?'

'If Gina or Esme mentions in her statement talking to you about Jessica, the police will want to know what you remember about it,' Darina assured her.

'But mightn't it get Esme into trouble? I mean, it would sound as though I was saying she had it in for Jessica or something.'

'Just because someone says something unpleasant about someone, it doesn't follow they then murder them. Quite the contrary, I would have thought.' Darina wondered, though, just how true that was.

Maureen took time smoothing down her yellow linen skirt, then she stood up. 'All right, if you say so.' She still didn't look any too confident.

'Tell you what,' Darina hauled herself off her lounger. 'Why don't I come with you, bit of moral support.'

Maureen's face lit up. 'Oh, would you?'

Darina tucked her hand into the woman's arm and thought that, though this wasn't why she had suggested it to Maureen, it was a first-class way to find out what was going on with the investigation.

Chapter Fourteen

'So how's the investigation going?' Darina gasped, sliding first one leg forward and then the other on the langlauf, a Norwegian cross-country ski simulator. She and William were taking advantage of the equipment in the Conifers Spa exercise room.

Darina's mother had made her telephone call to the Creightons, who, she said, had sounded absolutely delighted that she could come for a few days. 'Molly said Baz has to go to Brussels for some Nato meetings, he'll be away a couple of days and she'd love to have me. Save her from getting bored, she said. She even offered to come and pick me up but I said you'd take me over. I'm sure you'd like to see them again.'

So Darina had driven her mother to the official army residence, a gracious house set in a large and attractive garden that appeared to be well staffed and run with unassuming efficiency. It was a relief to see the sincere affection with which her mother was greeted by both Molly and Baz and, after a short chat over a cup of tea, to leave her in what was obviously a milieu that would suit her down to the ground. In a way, thought Darina, starting up her car and waving goodbye, it was a pity her mother hadn't married an army officer instead of a doctor. She would have been marvellous at easing the social side of his life, so necessary to a high-flying service officer.

Returning to the health farm, Darina discovered the news of Jessica's murder had broken. She had to fight her way through newspaper and television reporters, eager to question anyone with any connection to the murder. Firmly refusing to comment, she finally broke through the cordon and made it back to the main house. There she found the forensic experts clearing up their equipment and Carolyn in the last stages of exhaustion. 'I've had it!' she exclaimed to Darina. 'Practically an entire day trying to soothe the parting guests while Maria rang those due to arrive today and over the next few days. Plus having to calm down the few we couldn't catch before they turned up here.' She drew a tired hand across her eyes. 'They were all asking when we're going to reopen but I don't suppose they'll ever come again. Then I had to give an interview to some of those news-hungry sharks out there.' She looked washed out and depressed.

Maria Russell came into the office where Carolyn and Darina were sitting. She looked equally shattered. 'That's the last of them. I've put off everybody up until Saturday. Do you think we can reopen then?'

'Heaven and the police are the only ones who can answer that, Maria. Even if we can, I doubt anybody will want to come. Not after they've heard about the murder.'

'I don't know, people react in strange ways. You know what they say about no publicity being bad publicity. There'll be lots of people with a macabre interest in seeing the scene of a murder.' Maria spoke with a briskness that was almost comforting.

Carolyn gave a shiver. 'Do we really want them?'

'We can't afford not to,' Maria said firmly. 'Things will settle down. After a week or two they'll have forgotten all about it.'

'We won't,' Carolyn said, her face bleak.

'No,' Maria agreed quietly.

'Who could have done it?' Carolyn burst out. Neither Maria nor Darina offered any answer. After a moment, Carolyn added, 'It must have been someone from outside. Someone who knew Jessica was staying here. I can't believe anyone at Conifers Spa would have been involved.'

It was the easy solution. Someone they didn't know was the murderer. Someone who wouldn't challenge their assumptions about colleagues, clients or friends.

'Except,' Carolyn hesitated, her nose wrinkling nervously.

'Except what?' asked Darina.

'I just thought that Frank Borden could be capable of killing someone. I'm not suggesting he did,' she hurried on, her eyelids blinking rapidly. 'Just that of all the people who were here on Saturday night, he's the only one I can say that of.'

She echoed Darina's thoughts. Except that Darina knew outside appearances had little to do with what went on inside a murderer's mind. The most unlikely seeming people had planned and executed the most grisly of murders.

'What about food for you and William?' asked Carolyn suddenly. 'Rick never comes in on a Sunday and I sent the other kitchen staff home after they'd cleared up the sandwiches, but there's bound to be something to eat somewhere.' She looked distractedly around the office as though plates of beef could be resting on the filing cabinets.

'Don't worry! We'll go down to the pub or I'll make us an omelette. William never seems much interested in food when he's in the middle of a case.'

What William had wanted at the end of the day was to stretch his muscles. The morning's cloudy skies had turned to a light summer drizzle so they'd investigated the health farm's exercise equipment. Now Darina was working up a fine head of steam imagining herself crossing the snowy wastes of Norway whilst William was clocking up miles on the electric bicycle, having announced he wore the Tour de France leader's yellow jersey.

'Where have we got to?' he puffed, repeating Darina's

enquiry. He adjusted the pedal gauge for more effort. Fine sweat glistened on his forehead and the dark curly hair was damp around the nape of his neck. 'Frustration alley, that's where we are. We thought it was going to be an easy case to crack. Now every line of enquiry either ends up a dead end or reveals so many possibilities it's going to take an age to check them out.' He blew through his cheeks then took in several deep breaths. 'OK, quick résumé: until you and I woke up the shop, no one seems to have heard anything untoward. Maria Russell claims she left the pool area locked up but there's a key kept in the reception area and anyone could have had access to it.'

'Did the clients know about it?' Darina slowed to allow a family of bears to lumber across her path; she had to have some excuse for catching her breath and already her hips were beginning to feel as though their sockets needed oiling.

'Maureen Channing mentioned she'd seen some keys hanging on a hook in a little cupboard that happened to be open when she reported for a treatment one day. Nobody else admitted to knowing anything about a pool key.'

'But if they were the murderer, they wouldn't, would they?' puffed Darina.

'Exactly,' William said breathlessly. 'So, it looks as though anybody could have had the opportunity.'

'What about alibis?'

William's handsome face grew agonised as he pounded at the pedals. 'There seems to have been a general exodus to bed around ten o'clock. A hypnotist had given a talk earlier and people seem to have been put half to sleep. Jessica had been noticed by several people chatting to Perry Cazalet around nine thirty. There wasn't a sighting of her after that. Nor of anyone drifting off towards the pool area. It looks likely Jessica went there some time around eleven, when the house was all quiet. But we can't rule out the possibility it was earlier.'

'Particularly since the doctor said she could have died any time after nine. But surely lots of people can alibi each other?'

William gasped, stopped pedalling and lay panting across the handlebars. 'All the married and other couples claim they spent the evening together. All, that is, except the Cazalets.'

'Ah, the Cazalets!' Darina abandoned her attempt to imagine a clear expanse of glistening snow in front of her just waiting for skis to glide cleanly over the surface and sagged between the hand poles, catching her breath and feeling the ache in various little-used muscles.

'According to Perry Cazalet, around nine o'clock he felt the need for exercise, came in here and spent an hour trying various machines. According to several of the other clients, he and his wife appeared to have had a row and weren't speaking to each other. In her statement, Gina Cazalet said her husband joined her in their room just before ten. Perry Cazalet stated it was about twenty past when he came up.'

'A slight discrepancy in their stories, then?'

William nodded. 'It may mean something or nothing. One may be trying cackhandedly to protect the other or genuinely not know what the time was. Then there are the people who came here on their own. Apart from Jessica herself, three people had single rooms, Esme Lee, Maureen Channing and Frank Borden. There are gaps in all their statements. Esme Lee went out for a walk, says she came back about nine thirty. Maureen claims to have gone up to her room about nine o'clock and didn't move out. Frank says he went up to bed just before ten, with the rest. Everyone says that they didn't move out of their rooms after retiring.'

'And nobody saw anything?'

William shook his head and sat up straight again, his breathing almost back to normal.

'What about the staff?'

'Your pal Carolyn says she was on duty that evening, mostly working in her office. The kitchen staff clocked off when supper had been cleared up, which was by nine o'clock. Carolyn said she waited for Esme Lee to come back from her walk, which was about twenty-five to ten, then left for her cottage, locking the front door behind her.'

'She didn't check the pool area?'

William shook his head. 'She said that was Maria Russell's responsibility. Apparently she occasionally does check up but not last night.'

'Doesn't a member of staff sleep on the premises?'

William got off the bicycle and wiped his hands down the sides of his tracksuit. 'Yup, the housekeeper. She claims to have spent the entire evening in her room watching television and writing letters and didn't hear a thing.'

Darina straightened up. She forgot about aching muscles as she felt a pleasant glow spread through her body, it was as though she'd been plugged into some energising source. 'Let's have a shower, then I'll see what I can find in the kitchen.'

They supped off a risotto made from a quantity of fresh brown button mushrooms Darina had found in the larder, together with some dried wild ones from the store cupboard, plus genuine Italian arborio rice. She finished the risotto with a generous quantity of chopped fresh herbs rather than calorific Parmesan cheese. The complex carbohydrates of the rice plus the fibre plus the Mediterranean extra-virgin olive oil Darina had used as the cooking medium added up to a meal that Carolyn would have declared ideal. William found a bottle of Muscadet in the bar, made a note that he'd taken it and brought it over to the corner of the quiet dining room where Darina had laid a table for them.

'So, in essence,' Darina summed up, 'nobody really has an alibi that's any use?'

William shook his head then stopped eating long enough to say, 'Not if you accept that the couples could be alibi-ing each other. But most of them seem unlikely suspects as there's no evidence they knew Jessica Barry before they arrived here. Nor did they connect with her in the way that the Cazalets, for instance, appear to have.' He returned to the risotto with gusto.

'And nobody heard anything that could help pinpoint the time?'

'Nothing,' William said through a mouthful of food.

'And forensics haven't come up with anything particularly helpful.' It was a statement, not a question, but William answered it anyway.

'The only clue, if you can call it that, is the pink ribbon you found floating in the spa pool. And that was probably from Jessica's hair. Several people saw her with her hair tied back soon after she arrived, though they say she used a black silk ruffle type of thing, not a ribbon. We've found masses of fingerprints, as you would expect. There hasn't been time yet to check and compare them with the clientele and staff. I don't think they're going to tell us anything, though; too many people had access. Quite apart from the staff and clients, apparently the place runs a non-residential health club with a large number of outside members who use the facilities on an ad hoc basis.'

'Do you think Jessica could have been murdered by someone from outside?'

William shrugged and looked down at his empty plate. 'That was deelicious. Any more?'

Darina fetched the pot and scraped out the last bit.

'If this is healthy food, you can give it to me every day.'

'Well?' prompted Darina after she'd watched him demolish the remains of the dish.

'I'm just getting my thoughts in order,' protested William.

'I thought that was what you and Roger were doing down at the pub this evening.'

He slanted a look at her across the table. 'Miffed you weren't asked to join us?'

If Darina never saw Roger Marks again it would be too soon. Something about the way he treated her, the mixture of dismissiveness and patronage, really got under her skin. Male chauvinist pig of the worst sort! But he was William's friend. 'Not at all.' She started clearing away their plates. 'I realise boys have to play together. It was just a shame you couldn't have opened up the pool before you left. I could have done with a swim.'

His look acknowledged everything she hadn't said.

Darina fetched a bowl of fresh fruit. 'So, come on, what theories have you arrived at? Who's prime suspect among the Conifers Spa clients?'

William gave a small sigh of frustration. 'I told you, we're almost spoiled for choice.'

'That bad, eh?' Darina inspected the bowl and found a peach that looked marvellously ripe. 'Well, start somewhere.'

William twisted the stem of his half-full wine glass. 'OK. There's the Cazalets. They seem to have had rows on both Friday and Saturday and several people have said they thought Jessica was at the bottom of it. She apparently made a dead set at Perry Cazalet.'

Darina speared her peach with the prongs of a mother-of-pearl-handled fruit knife. 'I think Gina was definitely jealous of her. She's very nervous of this proposed comeback, very worried about Perry's insistence she gets down her weight. And Perry suddenly encouraging Jessica's singing I think was the last straw. But all that's a long way from actually murdering the girl, and

137

Gina really doesn't strike me as murderer material.' She held up the peach on the fork and started to peel it with a fruit knife.

William gave a small guffaw. 'Who ever does, darling? Surely you've learned that by now!'

Darina continued with her peeling, unmoved.

After a moment William said, 'It could have been an accident.'

'Accident?' Darina's knife paused in its activity. 'You mean Jessica could have slipped and hit her head?'

William smiled at her lazily, he always liked it when he proved to be one step ahead. 'Apparently if you spend a long time in one of those hot jacuzzi-type pools, your veins distend. Then, if you're not careful, you can faint when you get out.'

'So if she'd gone there on her own, spent too long and, after getting out and putting on her kimono, she fell and hit her head, there would have been no one to rescue her?' Darina had a wild surge of relief that perhaps they weren't dealing with a murder case after all. 'No wonder they don't want people playing around in there on their own!' Then she remembered. 'But what about the bruises on her neck?'

William sighed. 'Yes, we can't forget those. I'm afraid they definitely prove someone tried to strangle her. We won't know until after the autopsy whether they succeeded or whether she fell into the pool and drowned.'

Once again Darina forgot her peach as she stared at him. 'You mean someone might just have left her unconscious in the pool; left her to drown?'

William gave a little nod. 'I'm afraid it's a possibility, especially considering how much blood there was in the pool.'

'Oh, darling, that's terrible!'

'On the other hand, they might have tried to get her out, then realised she was dead and panicked. I don't remember the tiling round the pool being wet before we went in but it could have dried off after the killer left.'

Darina put down the half-peeled peach. Talking about suspects had deflected her mind from the horrible reality of what had happened to Jessica. Now she saw again the thin body in its soaked silk kimono and felt a savage anger against the person who had been responsible for her death, however it had happened. The rose-gold flesh of the peach on her plate reminded her of Jessica's golden tan. The words 'sun-kissed' reverberated in her mind. Darina remembered the livid fingermarks on the slim neck, thought of the strength there had to have been in the attacker's hands and shivered.

William helped himself to a shiny red Worcester apple and bit into it without bothering with peeling or coring.

Darina picked up the peach and peeled off the final pieces of skin whilst mentally assessing the candidates she had assembled as possible suspects. 'What have you found out about Frank Borden?' There was strength there, all right, and control. If Frank Borden had attacked Jessica, Darina would bet he'd meant to kill her.

'The antiques dealer? He's an interesting possibility; admitted he'd known the victim for many years. Told us they'd been very close at one time.' William put a wealth of meaning into the words 'very close' that set Darina's teeth on edge.

'You mean they'd been lovers,' she said shortly.

William nodded.

'Why not just say so, then?'

'I thought I did,' he said in injured tones. 'Borden certainly said Jessica had come to Conifers Spa at his invitation. He was paying for her.'

'But they no longer had a relationship?'

'That's what he claimed. Said in the most open way that they were just good friends. They arrived on the same day, incidentally. Esme Lee had already been here several days. She and Borden say they have known each other some five months. Her story was that she mentioned visiting another health farm, apparently she goes regularly, and Frank said he was coming here and why didn't she try it.' William grinned suddenly. 'I certainly saw what Roger meant about Ms Lee. What a mountain of a woman!'

'Whereas Roger isn't classed as a mountain of a man?' enquired Darina acidly.

'Oh, he's just big,' said William blithely. 'But Ms Lee! Fancy having her in your bed!'

'I can imagine a number of men finding her eminently fanciable,' said Darina through gritted teeth. She would not, *would not*, she repeated to herself, say that finding yourself in bed with Roger Marks would be a fate worse than death.

William looked politely sceptical, finished chomping his way round the apple and dropped a thin thread of core onto his plate. 'Anyway, while Borden and Lee intended leaving today, Barry was booked for another three days.'

'She seemed to be getting very friendly with Rick Harris, the chef, on Friday.' Darina cut the peeled peach in half and couldn't help wondering if Rick had ever sampled a Spanish dessert that filled halves of poached pears with chopped dates mixed with butter, and topped them with meringue. Too rich for Conifers Spa, no doubt, but what a superb dish!

'If Borden was picking up the tab for this place,' William gave an automatic glance around the splendid dining room, 'I suppose he could have felt jealous. But it seems a bit of a long shot to me.'

But what about Carolyn Pierce? Could she have been driven mad by jealousy of Jessica? Darina dismissed the idea as soon as it occurred. Carolyn might well have resented the chef showing interest in another girl but Darina couldn't see her attacking Jessica.

Then Darina remembered the remark Maureen Channing had claimed Esme Lee had made about Jessica and she asked William if the police had heard whether the barrister had known Jessica Barry before her arrival at the health farm.

'She said she'd met her once before, with Frank Borden, as if you hadn't guessed. According to her statement, Frank had told her Jessica was an old friend down on her luck that he was helping out. She sounded pretty cool about both her relationship with Borden and his with Jessica.'

'Did you get the impression she was jealous of Jessica?'

William shrugged his shoulders. 'Impossible to say. Every barrister is something of an actor. She didn't tell us much but it was as though she was daring us to think the worst.'

Darina gave a strangled laugh. 'I can see her admitting to being jealous, telling you it was entirely natural and then asking what you were going to do about it.' She ate a first segment of peach, relishing the sweet, smooth succulence. Pure gold: looks, texture, taste.

William picked out a ripe pear from the bowl. 'Jessica Barry certainly seems to have been a right little bimbo.'

Darina felt sudden resentment. 'You know, she didn't come over to me as someone who went round pinching other women's men. She, she seemed much more keen on being friends. Someone desperate for approval but without the first idea how to make themselves truly agreeable. Perhaps her sexuality was the only advantage she had.'

'You're the first person to say anything nice about her,' commented William with interest. 'Apart from Borden, that is. He seemed genuinely upset at her death.'

'What about Perry Cazalet? I thought he liked her.'

William started to peel his pear, juice running over his hand. 'I wish I had your knack with fruit, how do you manage without a finger bowl?' He wiped his hand on a napkin. 'Cazalet? He told us he wished he'd never laid

141

eyes on her, that she was nothing but trouble. Said she'd had quite a sweet little voice but it would never have taken her anywhere. The message was that he was relieved she wasn't going to complicate his life any further.'

'That's really sad! What a lost little soul she was. Who, incidentally, did Oliver Barry turn out to be?'

'Stepson, and he wouldn't have recognised Jessica from your description.'

'He didn't produce the wicked stepmother bit?'

'I don't think she came even that close. He identified her body without a flicker of emotion. She could have been a piece of rubbish he was consigning to the scrap heap.'

'You didn't like him.' Darina finished the last piece of peach and decided another would be sheer greed. It was amazing how satisfied the simple meal had left her.

'Arrogant, supercilious and far too self-important. If his father was anything like him, Jessica Barry must have rued her choice.'

'Still thinking of her as the manhunting bimbo?'

'Just what was it about her that makes you think she was anything else?'

Darina watched William pour the last of the wine into her glass. 'It's just an impression I had. I have nothing to back it up, I hardly knew her. But neither did you or Roger Marks. It just irks me that you make such snap judgements about her. Aren't you supposed to keep an open mind?'

'I promise you my mind is completely open. It's just waiting for someone to tell me something about Jessica Barry that doesn't suggest she was a victim waiting to be murdered.' William paused then added, 'It's very sweet of you to want to stay here with me but I have to warn you that I'm going to be pretty involved in this investigation.'

Which was his way of telling her not to expect to see

too much of him, and asking what the hell she was going to be up to while he was otherwise engaged.

'Darling, don't worry about me, I'm going to have a wonderful time getting fit. And giving Carolyn moral support which I think she desperately needs. I also have an article to write for my newspaper column. You needn't worry that I expect to be part of your murder hunt.'

A look of guilty relief passed over William's face. 'I know we made a wonderful team over that ghastly business in France,' he said, referring to the murder they'd been involved with on their honeymoon earlier that year. 'But you do understand that this is quite different?'

'Oh, I do,' murmured Darina, looking as innocent as she could manage. 'Quite, quite different.'

'That's all right then. And don't think I haven't mentioned how astute you are to Roger. I've told him that any comments you have to offer on the matter will be well worth listening to.'

'How very kind of you. I'm sure he's dying to hear my views.'

'Now, don't get sarky! If you think of anything that could be relevant, you can be sure we want to hear it.'

Darina sat back and looked at her husband of little more than five months. Then decided not to pursue the matter further. 'Just what did the stepson say?' she asked.

'Not a lot, actually,' William confessed, finishing the pear and wiping his hands on his now badly soiled napkin. 'He told us she'd visited him last week and tried to borrow money. More than that, she tried to blackmail him by threatening to sell the story of her life with his father to the newspapers.'

'How odd! All those reports of her as a fortune hunter and then there's no fortune. What happened to it?'

'She ran through the lot?'

'In a couple of years of marriage and a few months of widowhood? If there was anything approaching a fortune, her lifestyle must have been pretty wild. You shouldn't have any difficulty checking up on it. But you said she tried to blackmail Oliver Barry? Surely that makes him a prime suspect? Or has he produced an unshakable alibi?' Darina began to get excited. Oliver Barry could be the convenient outsider Carolyn had wanted to exist. Could he have been a wicked stepson? Could he have had a secret rendezvous with Jessica at the pool – then killed her?

William was dismissive. 'Who worries much about blackmail these days? Haven't we all become inured to the worst that could possibly be revealed? I can't see Oliver Barry feeling particularly threatened by anything his stepmother could tell the newspapers. Upset maybe, but not threatened to the point of murder.' He then shuffled the pear peelings around on his plate before adding, 'As for an alibi, he says he spent the evening visiting his mother.' He glanced up at Darina, an odd gleam in his eye. 'However, there is the fact that she lives only about twenty miles from here.'

Chapter Fifteen

Gina Cazalet hauled herself out of the bath and picked up her towel with a feeling of deep depression. She might be clean on the outside but inside she felt there was an Augean stables.

The trouble had started when she and Perry had arrived back at their house in Barnes. Four days of 'sensible eating' had been more than enough. The little worms of appetite that were never far away were sending out frantic signals. Something sweet, they said; some carbohydrate spiked with sugar, something they could really get their teeth into. Feeding her appetite was like throwing midges to piranha fish, nothing satisfied it.

Gina had poked around the store cupboard and the fridge and found a packet of her favourite biscuits, a slab of really excellent Stilton cheese and, lurking in a tin since their last party, some meringue shells. Perry had come in and found her with the sweet white crumbs all round her mouth and the empty biscuit wrapper still on the table together with the hacked-about cheese.

The awful thing was, he hadn't said anything. His nostrils had flared and gone white, he'd pressed his lips together and flung her a look full of hate. Then he'd left the room.

Gina would have preferred him to rant and rave, tell her what an idiot she was, ask her what she thought she was doing. She'd weighed out of Conifers Spa at five pounds less than when they'd arrived. Maria Russell had congratulated her and handed over a leaflet on healthy

145

eating and advice on food that wasn't going to put weight back on. The leaflet had gone straight into the bottom of her handbag and would no doubt get thrown away when she did her annual sort out.

Gina reached down with difficulty to dry between her legs. Then placed one foot on the loo and teetered on the remaining leg as she leant over her stomach and knee to deal with the difficult places between her toes.

Finally, anointed with athlete's foot powder and talc, she went through to the bedroom. There was no mirror to throw back a vision of her cellulite-pitted, trunk-like thighs or the stretch-marked flabby body. After all, who needed mirrors to throw on clothes? By the time Gina had done up her heavy-duty bra and struggled into the equally heavy-duty elastic garment that attempted to cope with her folds of flesh, she was exhausted. And, after days of enjoying the freedom and comfort of her tracksuit, the feeling of bondage outraged her.

Breathless with effort, she sat down on her bed. Perry had gone out. He'd spent the previous evening incarcerated in the music room. Chords and odd phrases had reached Gina, who prayed that this evening they would sort themselves out into a new composition. Prayed that the break had given him back the knack that had once come so easily. She opened a bottle of whisky and poured herself a large glass.

But after half an hour Perry had abandoned the piano and placed an old record on the music centre. That meant when he eventually came to bed it would be in either a towering temper or deep depression.

Gina had sat listening in the room they called the snug, drinking her whisky and wondering where all the fun had gone; all the excitement they'd had playing the gigs, the one-night stands. What had happened to the days when Perry never seemed to tire of telling her she was the sexiest of singers with the greatest voice he'd ever heard? To the times when radio, nightclubs, balls, all the smart events, needed the Perry Cazalet jazz band? When Perry had written numbers in the back of the van travelling between one engagement and the next, rehearsing her and the boys in the new material until they practically fell asleep on their feet, until they had no energy left for sex or anything else but playing and singing. But, oh my, how they had made up for it later!

When had it all gone sour? When requests for her as a solo singer had started to outweigh engagements for the band? When, even though she insisted Perry and she were a team, he realised that her career had outstripped his?

Or when Gina had stopped singing to have their baby? She had been heading for forty and said her biological clock was running out, it was now or never. She'd come off the pill and conceived almost immediately. Perry had insisted she stop singing.

Perry hadn't complained when, despite all the advice from her doctor, her weight dramatically increased. It had been such luxury not to have to racket around the country, not to require amphetamines to keep her awake or grass to ease the pressure, not to worry about what she ate. Perry had said he loved her warm and cuddly.

And Perry adored Samantha from the moment she was born; a difficult birth, said the medics, and mustn't be repeated. Perry had said Gina mustn't go back to singing until Sam was older, nor had she wanted to. Sam and Perry had been her whole world. Money hadn't seemed a problem, even without her working, even though the Cazalet band had fallen apart. There were the royalties from her recordings and Perry did orchestrations for other bands, worked on recording sessions. They had enough, he said, to last until Samantha had outgrown babyhood. Then Gina could start singing again. They bought a larger house with a nursery suite for Sam, a studio for Perry.

Then there'd been the appalling morning when Gina

had gone in to Sam's bedroom and found the world that had been heaven had crashed down into a hell.

Perry had fallen apart. For months he couldn't work. Gina had buried her sorrow with her daughter and devoted her time to supporting her husband. Food had been her comfort. Not just any food: it had to be sweet, satisfying, full of carbohydrates, fats and sugars.

And music had sustained her. Perhaps because she was no longer singing, Gina had discovered a talent for writing songs. In the long nights, unable to sleep after Perry had slaked his thirst for her, knowing her womb was empty and never again to be filled, Gina poured out her soul in Perry's music room.

Perry had found one of her songs one day, left forgotten on the piano. The studio door had been open and from the kitchen she'd heard the melody played hesitantly at first then a few chords added, then some harmony. Thrilled, she'd entered, clutching a tea towel.

He'd looked up from the piano, his face twisted. 'This rubbish yours?' he'd asked curtly.

She'd nodded, unable to speak.

He'd torn the music in half and thrown it into a wastepaper basket, already brimming with screwed-up sheets of his own discarded efforts. 'Don't waste your time, you haven't the talent.' His eyes had avoided hers as his fingers started to pick out the notes of one of his best known pieces, a tricky blues harmony with the melody side slipping from key to key, the intricate rhythm driving the piece forward with an insistent beat. It could have been designed to show exactly how simple her little melody was and Gina had slunk back to the kitchen to finish the washing up.

After that she made sure her growing folder of songs was kept hidden in a drawer beneath her bras and pants. For nothing, not even Perry's contempt, could stop her writing more. And the reception her song had received at Conifers Spa had been the greatest thrill she'd had since Sam had first been placed in her arms.

Gina had sat in the snug listening to the record of Perry's greatest hits and decided that, whatever Perry thought, she was going to try to include some of her own work on the new record he was planning for her. Then she'd gone upstairs to bed and found, for once, that sleep had come quickly. She had had no need to pretend unconsciousness when he came in. Instead she was woken by Perry as he took her, weeping silently all the while, burrowing his face into her opulent breasts, displaying a need that he hadn't shown since he'd told her she had to lose weight before he could relaunch her as a singer.

Afterwards he'd fallen asleep cradled by her soft flesh, the tears slowly seeping from under his eyelids, trickling down the mound of her stomach while Gina felt guilt and suspicion creep from her mind.

She'd woken that morning to find Perry already in the shower. He'd dressed in total silence in the cupboard area between their bedroom and the bathroom.

As he'd crossed the room towards the door, she'd asked what his plans were for the day.

A meeting with his accountants and then lunch with his publicist. 'It's not going to help us to be dragged into a murder case,' he'd said shortly.

'I wasn't the one who got pally with the victim,' Gina threw at him. The words bounced off the bedroom door as it closed behind him.

Then the door had reopened. 'I've cleared the kitchen of all temptation,' Perry had said, his tone pleasant, his face blank of all emotion. 'And phoned Harrods. You'll have plenty to eat.'

Gina knew exactly what the smart green van with gold lettering would deliver: fruit, salad, vegetables and brown rice.

Sitting on her bed, waiting for her breathing to return to normal, Gina tried to make plans. If Perry had really gone out for the day, she could use the music room for her own creative efforts.

Except . . . except Gina knew that Jessica would come between her and any effort to make music.

She suddenly tore off her bra and struggled out of her corset then went and found the floatiest of her summer dresses and slipped her feet into strappy sandals. Dressed, she scrabbled in her handbag, found the bit of paper she wanted and went to the phone.

When Gina arrived at the Savoy Grill, Esme Lee was waiting for her. She looked wonderful in a scarlet silk dress, her skin golden with the tan she'd achieved at Conifers Spa, her hair drawn back in a glossy chignon. She came towards Gina and embraced her.

Everywhere Gina could feel the gaze of eyes. Eyes taking in and condemning the meeting of two fat women in a luxury restaurant. For once she didn't care. For the first time since Saturday night she felt secure and safe. 'Thank you for this,' she said, flopping into a chair, not caring that her hips overflowed its seat.

'My dear, what are friends for?' Esme settled herself opposite. 'Now, I think a little aperitif? What's your choice?'

No suggestion that it should be dry white wine, or that tonic water with a dash of Angostura Bitters made a delicious and refreshing drink; no unspoken message that alcohol carried a sinful load of calories.

'Dry white wine,' Gina said cheerfully. 'I need to keep my wits about me.'

'And I.' Esme ordered two glasses of Tattinger brut. Menus were produced and there was a pleasant five minutes whilst they studied the temptations on offer.

Freed from any sense of judgement awaiting her, Gina had no difficulty in deciding on two fish courses.

'There's something so light and yet so rich about

white fish,' agreed Esme, making the same choice. 'I always think of sole, halibut and turbot as the silks and satins of the food world. The texture of the flesh is sybaritic, the taste so subtle, so teasing.'

'And shellfish, they sing out in clear tones that have such substance, such resonance.' Gina and Esme smiled at each other in perfect accord.

'Now,' said Esme once their starters had arrived with the bottle of Pouilly Fumé she had ordered. 'You said you wanted to talk about something. Should we dive straight in or segue nonchalantly into the matter after we've soothed our spirits with sustenance?' Her eyes laughed, her tone was light, but underneath there was a stillness, a waiting that Gina recognised as apprehension.

The knowledge both terrified and reassured her. Maybe she needn't be quite so afraid herself.

'Let's leave it until after we've enjoyed this delicious food,' she suggested.

Esme had no quarrel with that.

They talked about music, about the theatre, books, an art exhibition both had enjoyed. The health farm and their stay there was never mentioned.

Gradually Gina relaxed and could feel Esme, too, loosening slightly the strict control maintained underneath the lighthearted exterior. Together they recognised a leading actor lunching over on the other side of the restaurant and spent an amusing five minutes reading his body language as he refused potatoes and roll but welcomed the filling of his glass with more wine. Together they gently refused the blandishments of the waiter offering dessert.

'I couldn't,' said Gina cheerfully, feeling no conflict between appetite and duty. 'That sole with lobster was just divine but very filling.'

'I know what would be perfect,' said Esme. 'Half a bottle of Sauternes and some almond tuiles. Any chance?' she asked the waiter hopefully.

He inclined his head, delight written over his face. 'Of course, madam. I'll bring the wine list.'

'I'm happy to leave the choice to you,' said Esme.

Gina looked at her in shocked delight. 'But suppose he brings something terribly expensive?' she asked, mentally reviewing her overdraft.

Esme shook her head. 'I'm a regular customer. They know what I like to spend. And don't worry about the cost, this lunch is on me. And don't say anything.' She held up her hand as Gina started to protest. 'I know you rang me but I suggested here. It's so convenient and I earn far more than is good for me. I hope we're going to be friends; next time it's your treat and you choose the restaurant. Now, let's enjoy the wine and get down to business.'

It was impossible to object. The sweet wine accompanied by the little biscuits with their subtle almond flavour and tantalising texture, crisp yet with the slightest hint of toothsome depth, provided the perfect end to their meal. Yet never in a million years would it have occurred to Gina to choose them. 'You really know about food and wine,' she said humbly.

'I adore both,' Esme said robustly. 'I don't over-indulge but I see no reason why I shouldn't enjoy consuming the fuel that keeps my body going. But come on, let's not avoid the issue any longer. You want to discuss something to do with Jessica's murder, don't you?'

Involuntarily Gina cast a glance around, only slightly reassured by noticing the distance between the tables and the unlikelihood of the pitch of their voices carrying to their neighbours.

'I, I wasn't quite frank with the police,' she confessed in a sudden rush.

Esme raised an enquiring eyebrow but otherwise seemed unsurprised. 'I find very few witnesses are completely open,' she observed. 'They tend to hide things for any one of a number of reasons. Sometimes simply because they didn't realise something could be important, or had just forgotten a detail or two. It's rarely something that causes a problem.' Her tone was full of reassurance. There was a slight pause. Then she asked, 'What exactly are you worried about?'

Gina looked at the intelligent, watchful face. How far dare she trust Esme? But if she didn't, who else could she turn to? And her need was overwhelming. 'I found Perry in Jessica's bedroom,' she said baldly.

Once again she could sense a relaxation in the other woman. Had Esme expected her to say something different?

'Indeed?' Esme murmured, raising an eyebrow. 'When was this?'

'Saturday afternoon,' Gina burst out. Now that she had brought herself to tell someone, it was as though a traffic jam of words had been released. 'I'd just had reflexology and I felt so wonderful.' She screwed up her eyes in remembered ecstasy. 'Totally relaxed and my legs had never been so slim. I thought I'd go and sit in a quiet place in the garden, enjoy the sun and work on a song. So I went to get my notebook from our room. As I reached the top of the stairs, I could hear Jessica's laugh and then I heard Perry's. I knew which her room was.' Her voice was scornful; the scorn was for the fact that she'd thought it important to find out. 'Just on the left of the landing, while ours was right down the corridor. So I knew they had to be in her room.'

Esme gave a little nod, as much as to say she, too, knew exactly where Jessica's room had been.

'I had to know,' Gina gave a small gulp, still horrified at herself. 'No one else seemed to be around so I went and stood outside, listening.' A small hiccup of scandalised laughter broke from her lips. 'Can you imagine? Standing there, trying to hear what was going on inside? Desperate in case someone came along, trying to think what I'd say if anyone did?'

'And did you hear anything?' Esme asked gently.

Gina closed her eyes. 'Jessica was doing all the talking. I couldn't make out what she was saying but you didn't have to hear the words. It was enough to hear the tone, all sweet and full of passion. The way she said his name, you didn't have to see what they were up to.'

Esme sat very still. 'What did you do?' she asked unemotionally.

Gina shrugged. 'Nothing! I was a coward!'

'You think if you'd burst in there and confronted them that would have been brave?'

'Don't you?'

'I think if you'd been prepared to give your husband an ultimatum, you wouldn't have hesitated.'

Gina helped herself to another little almond biscuit. The golden sweetness of the wine was warming her, caressing her inner parts, while the dry sweetness of the tuiles was taking her back to childhood, to the comforting sensation of being awarded a biscuit if she'd been a good girl. Oh, the joy of a custard cream! Or two or three or four! What matter if Mother complained because the biscuit tin was always empty when there was such satisfaction in going back and back for just one more.

'You see, I don't think I could bear it if Perry left me,' Gina said simply.

'So you stood outside that door and listened – and then went away? Determined to say nothing about it?'

'I can see how effective you are in court.'

Esme smiled grimly. 'If I suggested that in court, opposing counsel would object on the grounds I was leading the witness, putting words into her mouth. Well, let me lead you again. You are telling me this because you are afraid the police might suspect you killed Jessica to keep your husband?'

To hear it said out loud made even the idea seem ridiculous. Like the almond biscuits, it was immensely comforting. Who could suggest anyone would go to such extreme lengths? Men had strayed from their marital vows since the invention of monogamy; if they'd been murdered every time they'd been found out, the jails would be full and there'd be precious few husbands still around.

Gina smiled at Esme.

Esme continued, 'Or, of course, you could be afraid Perry had murdered Jessica to stop her ruining his marriage.'

Gina stopped smiling.

Surely, though, that sounded an even more ridiculous suggestion than that she had murdered Jessica.

'Did you spend the evening together?'

Gina reached for another tuile. 'We had an argument just before supper, about Jessica. I said he was making a fool of himself, that she was only running after him because he could help her make it as a singer. And that it wasn't fair to her to suggest she could make it anyway.'

'Could she not?' Esme smiled at the waiter who was pouring the last of the Sauternes into their glasses. 'Shall we have another of these?' she asked Gina.

Gina found no difficulty in saying, 'That was perfect, more would blunt the pleasure.' The waiter went away. 'You have no idea how hard it is to make it in the music world. You don't only need a good voice, you need immense stamina, an ability to graft and graft away with very little encouragement. Then you have to have style, an image, plus an indefinable something that will capture the imagination of the public and the media.'

'I don't know about stamina and graft but Jessica certainly had something,' Esme commented dryly. 'Even Frank, who is the hardest-headed man I know, would do the silliest things if she asked him.'

Yes indeed, Frank Borden. Gina put her head on one side as she considered Esme. A curious choice of amour for Frank?

'How long have you known him?'

'Several months. I bought a rather lovely Grecian vase from his gallery. We had a most interesting discussion and he asked me out for a drink. Since then we've seen quite a lot of each other. I find him immensely stimulating.' She gave Gina a sardonic glance. 'But I was not jealous of Jessica. He told me she was part of the past and I believed him.' She reached for the last almond tuile and nibbled at it reflectively. 'Whether he is part of my future, a question you are far too polite to ask but I see are dying to know the answer to, well, I have to say I don't know. I thought maybe I'd find out at Conifers Spa but,' she spread one broad hand open over the table in a gesture of helplessness, 'it seemed we didn't have the space we needed.'

For the first time in their acquaintance, Gina realised Esme was unsure of herself. It was unsettling; she needed Esme to be strong and decisive. 'What do you think I should do?' she asked.

Esme looked at her thoughtfully. 'In all fairness to the clients who pay me vast sums of money for my advice, I can't give you a lawyer's answer without sending you a bill I'd be ashamed to post. My advice as a friend is to examine your relationship with your husband extremely carefully. Ask yourself just what it is he is demanding you do.'

'What do you mean? He hasn't demanded anything!'

'Hasn't asked you to lose weight?'

Gina was bemused. This seemed to sidestep the main issue. Was that what Esme intended?

'Apart from anything else, have you thought what it might do to your voice?' Esme continued.

Gina nodded miserably. 'I told Perry it could make a difference and he said I sounded just as good when I was an eight-stone stripling so why should there be any risk in getting back there? As though', she added desperately, 'I had any hope of getting anywhere near eight stone again.'

'Ella Fitzgerald never worried about her weight.'

'She would if she was singing today.'

'Ninety-eight per cent of people who lose weight put it all back on again plus a little extra.'

'If you told a roomful of people all but one of them were going to die the next day, each of them would be thinking how sad it was for everyone else! Besides, Perry says I have no option. If I want to go on tour, I have to regain my figure.'

'And if you don't go on tour?'

Gina looked down wretchedly at the tablecloth. 'Then I have no future as a singer. My record sales are slipping down to nothing. It may be too late anyway but I've got to try. And as Perry says, who wants to come and see a mountain of lard opening her mouth?'

Esme's eyes narrowed to slits. 'If I were you, I'd have wanted to murder Perry rather than Jessica! Look, you are an attractive woman with a marvellous voice and a serious talent for song making. That should be enough for anyone.'

Gina gazed at Esme, her mind in turmoil.

Chapter Sixteen

Darina completed her thirtieth lap of the outdoor pool and hauled herself onto the paving surround. There was a haze in the air that promised a fine day but this early in the morning she shivered in the chill.

She did some running on the spot while she dried herself. No one else was around. William had taken himself off to study the statements taken the previous day. The police team had yet to arrive. The indoor pool area was still roped off, though word was the forensic team would finish with it that morning.

Using her towel as cover, Darina slipped out of her wet bathing costume and into underclothes and a track-suit, relishing the warmth of the dry clothes. She felt incredibly virtuous and hyped with energy.

So much so, she decided to go for a brisk walk before breakfast.

The Conifers Spa house was built into the side of a hill. On the left, out of sight of the pool, were a large car park, two tennis courts and a croquet lawn. Behind these, nestling into the shelter offered by the side of the house and the hill, was the small formal garden where Darina and her mother had sought refuge the previous day. The broad front of the house faced south with a view down the valley. A sweep of drive came up from the road, some distance below the house, then ran almost parallel to the long flagstoned terrace that had been built along the front. Another strip of terrace ran alongside the west wing from the front towards the annexe with the indoor swimming pool and treatment areas. There were two secondary drives, leading off the main one just inside the gate: one went to the three terraced cottages right at the bottom of the estate, the other, for tradesmen and staff, came up round the back of the house.

Darina started walking briskly down the main drive, admiring the extensive shrub- and flowerbeds and trying to imagine what it must cost to run it all. She turned back to look at the house, its Edwardian flamboyance softened by the misty light of the morning.

Had Oliver Barry driven up this drive late on Saturday night to meet his infuriating stepmother and parked without anyone noticing him?

Or, a sudden thought struck her, had he used the back drive?

She crossed the still dewy grass, her trainers rapidly becoming sodden.

The secondary drive led up through a wooded area. Quite soon Darina came across yellow police tape sealing off a small passing place. She stood and looked at the rough ground between the tape and the start of proper undergrowth. It was scattered with dead pine needles, with small tufts of grasses growing at the edges. At the back of the passing area the ground looked slightly muddy and Darina thought she could just glimpse faint tyre marks. She remembered the rain that had fallen on the Saturday afternoon.

Her mind busy with possible implications, Darina continued up the tarmacadam drive, past the annexe and outbuildings and round to the large cobbled yard at the back of the house.

Here was where Carolyn had found Rick and Jessica, by the large, heavy back door. Darina remembered the glance she'd seen Jessica give the chef: laughing, teasing, certainly. Overtly seductive? Darina hadn't thought so but Carolyn had immediately jumped to the worst conclusion.

The kitchen door was secured with a businesslike lock. To open it would require a key or some sophisticated lock-picking device. Darina turned and looked around the courtyard. Its cobbled surface offered no chance of tyre marks.

Most of the surrounding outbuildings were as old as the house, except for the west wing extension; its matching bricks still looked brand new. Darina went over and tried the door that led into the far end. It was locked with the same type of solid mortice lock as the kitchen door. Security seemed reasonably tight. If Oliver Barry had come up to the house, had Jessica let him in? Had she helped herself to the pool key from behind the reception desk, then gone through to the men's treatment area and opened this door at a prearranged time? Hoping Oliver was going to hand her a cheque or even cash?

Had she shown him the pool? Then demanded the money? Had he said he wasn't going to pay, then, goaded beyond endurance by her threats, strangled her? And why had she only been wearing that kimono?

Darina sighed, knew she had no chance of discovering physical clues, gave up detecting and went to find breakfast.

In the dining room, counting out cutlery, was Maria Russell in a bright yellow tracksuit.

'Can I help?' asked Darina.

'Oh, hello!' Maria turned with a strained smile. 'No, thanks, I've almost finished. Carolyn wanted stocktaking done.' It was said with a note of resentment.

'All part of your managerial duties?' Darina asked, helping herself to a bowl of cereal.

Maria's lips tightened. 'Since I can't get into the treatment annexe, Carolyn said I should do this. I suggested I had my day off so I could work through after the police have finished but, no, she said she wanted this done.'

Darina sliced a banana over the muesli and said nothing.

Maria clashed a collection of knives together and flung them back into their drawer. 'Have you seen the mess they're making in there? Everything out of place, grey powder stuff everywhere. It's going to take forever to sort it all out. Jim's going to go spare.'

'Jim?'

'Jim Hughes, runs the men's side. Technically under me but you'd never get him to admit that!' Maria gave a small grimace that had a touch of humour. 'It's been his weekend off.' She pushed the drawer back into place with an exasperated thump then leant back against the sideboard, her face strained. 'Are the police making any progress?'

Darina poured milk onto her breakfast and shrugged her shoulders. 'William tells me very little.' Not quite true but she couldn't be used as an information desk on the investigation.

Maria crossed her arms. She seemed in no hurry to continue with her stocktaking. 'How long are they going to be here?'

'Sorry, no idea. But William did tell me they've got a mobile incident centre arriving this morning. That should at least get them out of Carolyn's office.'

'Something, I suppose.' Maria sounded grudging.

'And I very much hope they'll have finished with the treatment area soon, I'm dying for another sauna.'

'I expect you're missing the massage as well. Do use the exercise room, though; that doesn't seem to have been taken over by the police and it's great for muscle toning.' Maria's glance raked itself down Darina's figure. Even sitting down, she felt the health manager could see every excess bump and roll of flesh. 'When you're tall like us you can get away with putting on a certain amount of weight but even we have to be careful.'

Darina eyed the well-built figure in front of her. 'Do you have to watch what you eat?' she asked.

Maria flushed, moved across to the other side of the room and yanked open another cutlery drawer. 'Most people have a weight problem at some time in their lives,' she said.

'Really?' Darina didn't think her mother, for one, had ever had to worry about her figure.

A collection of knives, forks and spoons clattered onto a table and Maria started sorting them out. 'Excess flesh is so unattractive, isn't it?' she said irritably.

Considering the size of the person she was talking to, Darina considered the comment less than tactful. 'Perhaps I'm biased,' she said, smiling, 'but I thought Esme Lee, for instance, was enormously attractive, in every sense. Even naked in the sauna. Gina Cazalet, too, knows how to put herself over.'

Maria looked as though she could hardly contain her disgust. 'Both of them should have their jaws wired together until they're fit to be seen in public.' Then she hastily added, 'Of course, I wouldn't dream of telling them that. We do everything we can here to encourage people to eat sensibly so as to maintain their ideal weight.' It sounded like an often repeated mantra.

Darina wondered if Maria's vision of ideal weight would match her own. 'What about the theory that dieting makes you fat?'

Maria pursed her lips and gathered up the spoons she'd been counting. 'It's all just a matter of will-power. And exercise. That's my own recipe.' She paused, holding the spoons above the drawer. Then she put them carefully inside. 'I weighed almost eighteen stone once,' she said slowly.

Darina looked at the lithe body with stunned fascination. At something like five foot ten inches, Maria was no lightweight but she looked somewhere between ten and eleven well-proportioned stone. It was difficult to imagine her nearly double that. 'How did you lose it?'

'Exercise,' said Maria briskly, starting to count forks. 'You're right about the dieting, actually. In my late teens and early twenties I got down to eleven stone twice, then ballooned up again.' The busy fingers sorted the forks into groups of ten. 'It, well, it was demoralising. Then I started running. The office I was working in entered a team for the London marathon. Everyone was joking about my size and saying no point in asking if I wanted to take part.' Maria glanced up at Darina. Her eyes flashed with emotion and she seemed to forget about counting cutlery. 'I thought I'd show them. I mightn't be able to run very fast but I was sure I could train myself to run distances.'

'And you did?' Darina was mesmerised.

'I used to run late at night, when no one could see me.'

'Weren't you worried about being attacked?'

'At my size?' Maria was scornful. 'Who was going to want to rape me!'

'There are lots of men who find overweight women attractive,' protested Darina.

Maria gazed at her scornfully for a moment then said, 'Well, I never met them.'

'But you lost weight?'

Maria started gathering up the sorted forks. 'It slowly dawned on me my clothes were getting looser. I'd given up dieting as a bad job ages before and realising that even with eating what I liked, which was pretty healthy actually, I was losing weight, gave me such an incentive. That and the way I began to feel after a run.' Her face glowed as she put the forks back in the drawer and started on the knives. 'You get such a high from exercise! After constantly feeling so depressed, it was wonderful. I began not to mind people staring at me and making remarks about my size. Then the remarks became fewer and fewer. It took me several years but eventually I got down below eleven stone.'

'Did you make the marathon?'

'Not that year but the next I did. It wasn't a fast time but I finished, which was more than some of the others from the office did. No one ever called me a fatty after that,' she added fiercely.

'When did you start training for this sort of work?'

Maria rapidly counted the knives and replaced them in the drawer. 'I started aerobics and got really interested. The girl taking our class moved away and I took over and began taking some courses. One thing led to another and here I am.'

'What an amazing story. You should tell all the clients about it, it would really put heart into those of us who need to lose weight.'

Maria shook her head as she closed the drawer. 'People don't want all that hard work; they believe if they come here they can have it all without effort on their part. Sorry, must get on. Help yourself to the exercise equipment and come to me if you've got any problems.' The lean, muscled body in its yellow tracksuit moved rapidly out of the dining room.

Darina determined to set herself a proper exercise programme and get her body under control. But what would happen if she then stopped? Would all the flesh start oozing out again? Darina considered the difficulty of setting herself a daily exercise target as well as her daily word target, her daily recipe target and her keeping the house organised target. Not to mention her keeping her husband happy target.

Perhaps, though, it wouldn't hurt to fit in a couple of exercise sessions a week.

Darina took her dirty breakfast things out to the kitchen and placed them in the washing-up machine. None of the kitchen staff had yet arrived but out of the window she could see a large caravan-type vehicle being positioned in the courtyard. The incident room.

Roger Marks suddenly appeared in the kitchen. His suit today looked marginally less crumpled but his shirt was missing a button and dark chest hairs pushed their way through the gap. He placed a packet of ground coffee on one of the work surfaces. 'Just in case you have any difficulty finding more for us today,' he said to Darina.

'I'll be delighted to show one of your constables where the facilities are,' she replied, controlling her temper with difficulty and wondering just what it was about him that set her teeth on edge.

He gave her a keen glance. 'Young Bill around anywhere?'

At that moment William appeared carrying a large bundle of statements. 'Just taking these along to be entered on the computer, Roger,' he said, without so much as a nod in Darina's direction.

'Right with you, boyo!' Roger clamped a large hand on William's shoulder and the two of them went out into the courtyard.

Darina watched them thoughtfully then left the coffee sitting in the kitchen. She intended to set up her laptop and work on the cookery articles she was due to deliver that week.

But Carolyn was sitting behind the reception desk, her fingers playing with a piece of Blu-Tack and her face blank.

'Anything I can do to help?' asked Darina.

'What? Oh, Darina! I'm sorry, I can't take in anything at the moment.' Carolyn tried to smile. 'I had the largest whisky of my life last night, I thought it would help me sleep. Instead I spent most of the night lying awake worrying and now I feel dreadful.' There were blue smudges under Carolyn's eyes and she looked ten years older than she had the day Darina arrived at the health farm.

Darina leant on the high counter of the desk. 'Isn't there something I can do to help? What about lunch?' She thought of the empty kitchen.

'You are sweet but Rick's doing that.' Carolyn drew in a deep breath and produced a strained smile. 'Did I tell you he and I are doing a book together?'

'That's wonderful!' Where had all Carolyn's life and vitality gone to? 'With his cooking and your background in nutrition, it should be a smash hit. Have you got a title?'

'*Cooking for Life.*'

'Sounds great! And a publisher?'

A trace of colour crept back into Carolyn's face and her eyes started to look as though someone was there. 'I think so. I've done a detailed outline and added some of Rick's recipes. There's no contract yet but I found an agent and now they say they've got a publisher more or less lined up.'

'Why don't we have a cup of herb tea and you can tell me all about it?' suggested Darina. For a moment she thought Carolyn was going to agree, then the slight spark disappeared again.

'Sorry, I've really got to get to grips with this.' Carolyn waved a hand over a schedule of September bookings on the desk. 'There's more phoning up of clients to do and I've got to prepare a report for the directors, try and make some assessment of the damage this is going to do to the figures. All I can see at the moment is that we need that investor more than ever.'

'Are you insured against this sort of thing?' asked Darina curiously.

'The directors are looking into it. I certainly hope we are!' Carolyn's look of worry deepened.

'Can I do some telephoning for you?' suggested Darina. Carolyn was hardly jumping at her offers of assistance; maybe choosing to hang around here hadn't been the right decision after all.

'Sweet of you to offer but it's something I've got to do myself, no matter how unpleasant. Oh, there's a message for you. I couldn't find you when they rang, it was only a few minutes ago.' Carolyn fished out a note from the back of the reception desk and handed it over.

She couldn't have looked very hard, thought Darina, reading the message. It was from the newspaper that published her column, asking her to ring the features editor as soon as possible.

In her room Darina got through but the man she was connected with was not the features editor she'd come to know over the past few years. This new man had taken over at the end of the previous week, he said. 'I know it's short notice, but can you come in today?'

'Of course,' Darina said happily. She looked at her watch. 'Provided the traffic isn't too bad, I could be there by twelve.'

'Fine,' said the editor heartily. 'Don't burn up the motorway though. I'll expect you sometime before lunch.'

Darina found something reasonably smart to put on, delighted by the summons. She wondered what had happened to the previous editor. They'd become very friendly while she'd been writing for the paper. She hoped he'd been promoted; perhaps he was now a member of the board. But she couldn't think too much about him, she was too relieved that at last they wanted to discuss her articles with her. Perhaps they were going to give her more space. She'd several times mentioned it was time they gave more room to cooking. What she could do with a whole page!

Darina parked in the Hyde Park underground car park and took a taxi from there, thanking heaven the paper wasn't in an outer reach of the East End.

The new features editor greeted her perfunctorily. His protuberant, pale grey eyes blinked nervously and refused to meet hers. Good of her to come in, he said. He hadn't wanted to tell her this on the telephone but the editorial policy had changed and her articles were no longer needed. He then mentioned the name of one of the giants in the food writing world, congratulating the editor on managing to enlist such a leading talent. Feeling numb and unable to believe what she was hearing, Darina asked what had happened to the previous features editor. He too, it appeared, had lost his job.

Ten minutes after walking into the office, Darina was back outside on the pavement. Traffic blared, the sun, much hotter than in Wiltshire, bounced off the pavement, people brushed past her, all intent on business of their own.

Her business had gone, vanished.

A bus came along. Without thinking, Darina got on. She asked the conductor where they were going and bought a ticket for Piccadilly, the nearest stop to Park Lane and the car park.

Very slowly, as the bus lumbered along the crowded streets, Darina felt blood beginning to flow through her veins once again. With feeling came a sense of rage and humiliation equally mixed. It was too much for her to deal with at that moment.

She pushed away any consideration of what had happened and tried to think of a friend she could lunch with. She got off the bus, found a telephone box and rang two pals who worked in London. Neither was available.

William was also tied up and Darina decided she couldn't face driving back to Wiltshire just yet.

For several hours she had managed to forget Jessica's murder. Now, suddenly, it was back with her, more vivid than ever. Some of her rage transferred itself to the killer and she had an idea that was so obvious she couldn't understand why she hadn't thought of it before.

Chapter Seventeen

William sat in the small office at one end of the mobile incident centre and went through the recording procedure with Jim Hughes. He had a strong feeling of injustice.

William had actually wanted to accompany Roger Marks to the autopsy on Jessica Barry. But Roger had taken one of his sergeants with him. 'I'll spare you the grisly process,' he'd said cheerfully early that morning, slurping down a quick coffee and demolishing the two doughnuts he'd bought on the way in. The paper bag, stained with grease, lay in a crumpled heap and sugar spattered the desk as he bit into the first thick, yeasty bun. 'You can finish up the staff interviews. Never know, there might be some nugget that hasn't come to light yet. Save it for my return. Remember, I'm counting on you!' He'd stuffed the remaining piece of doughnut into his mouth, called for the sergeant and was gone, leaving the unmistakable impression that he felt there was as much chance of William uncovering something important as of finding buried doubloons on Brighton beach.

William broke open two fresh cassette tapes and loaded them in the recorder with renewed frustration. The post-mortem was the place to be, that was where so many cases were cracked. He'd hoped to be at the heart of this investigation; instead, he was being left behind.

From that first disastrous encounter with the body, everything about his involvement with this case seemed doomed. Even having Darina here wasn't working out the way he'd hoped it would when he'd pleaded with Roger to let her stay. It seemed weeks since they'd been able to relax together. And he'd looked forward to introducing her to his old pal, but for some reason she'd taken against Roger and this had introduced an uncomfortable note into his relationship with him.

William started to record the details of date, time and who was in the interview room, going through the routine automatically. He wished Roger hadn't mentioned that business about him wanting Darina at home more often. Sometimes, though, William did wonder exactly what it was Darina wanted from life. Was her career going to mean less and less time for him? Was it unfair of him to want her more available at those times he wasn't involved with his work?

Then, with a supreme effort, he wiped his mind clear and settled down to interviewing Jim Hughes.

The manager of the men's side was a fine figure. Only medium height but he held himself so well you could be deluded into thinking he was tall. Well-muscled but no hint of steroid excess. Thick fair hair that he had a habit of running his fingers through to push back off his face, just as he was doing now as he glanced nervously across at William. Early thirties, William guessed.

Both that raking of the hair and a darting of his tongue across his lips were at odds with the way Hughes sat easily in his chair, leaning back with one arm casually draped over the back. Unlike most of the Conifers Spa staff, he wasn't dressed in a tracksuit. Smart slacks, shirt in a large check, a sober tie and a linen jacket said he'd felt that at a police interview appearance mattered. He spoke confidently in a voice belonging to south London.

William established that Hughes had worked at the health farm since it had opened and that the job was a step up for him. During these routine preliminaries, Hughes gradually stopped pushing his hand through his hair. He confided to William he had ambitions to open his own place.

'A small gym with massage. Unisex – well, it's all the thing these days, in't it? My brother says he'll come in with me, he's a bookie and doing all right.' Then it was as though he suddenly realised this was not what the interview was about; he stopped talking and once again ran his hand through his hair.

William got him on to the subject of Jessica Barry.

Another run of the hand through the hair, another wetting of the lips. 'Yeah, shocking bit of news that was. Heard about it when I got back last night.'

'What contact had you had with her during her stay here?'

'I gave her a massage. She, well, she said she really enjoyed being massaged by a man. Said we got right down into the muscles, where it mattered.' The slightest of smirks appeared on Hughes's handsome face.

'Do women usually prefer male masseurs?' asked the sergeant interviewing him with William, a mature man with a quiet, measured approach that William was learning sometimes managed to winkle out valuable details from witnesses.

Hughes grinned. 'Some do, some don't.'

'Some of them would no doubt like, what shall we say, a more personal service?' suggested the quiet sergeant.

Hughes's smirk grew wider, then he controlled himself. 'There's never anything like that here, sir!' he said in hushed tones. 'Not that I don't get the wink every so often. But it'd be more than my job's worth if it reached Carolyn, Mrs Pierce's ears!' The righteous note rang a little false.

'Of course,' William said soothingly, then, man to man, added, 'Did you have trouble with Lady Barry?'

'Trouble? Oh, I see!' Macho pride struggled with honesty for a moment. Perhaps it was his surroundings, perhaps native caution, but honesty won. 'Can't say I did.

Very pleasant she was, very pleasant indeed. But no hint of a come on. Mind you, my taste doesn't run to flesh that scrawny.'

'You wouldn't say she was attractive, then?' William enquired with real interest. So far the message that had come through was that Jessica Barry was irresistible to men. Then he remembered that they had heard it from women. In his experience, no woman could ever accurately gauge what attracted men. Any more than men could sometimes work out whether one of their fellows was going to be a success with women. Take Roger, for instance. You couldn't really describe those craggy features as good-looking and he was definitely overweight but whenever he wanted a bit on the side, according to him he didn't have any trouble attracting the girl his eye lit on.

'Dressed, she was a bit of all right. But you should see her bones!' The look Hughes gave the policemen could only be described as a leer. 'Would've been like riding a bicycle!'

The image of the slender, dripping body he'd pulled from the spa pool rose up in William's mind and he struggled to quell his growing irritation with the witness. 'So you only saw Lady Barry in the treatment area?' he asked perfunctorily.

'Well, saw, yes,' said Hughes with a wealth of meaning in his voice.

'Would you explain?' William asked shortly but with a sense of hidden expectation. Beside him he could sense Sergeant Penrose's interest. This was one of those times, he knew it, when a witness was going to produce a piece of evidence that could bust the case wide open. Roger had been so sure this case could be wrapped up in a few days. That once they started questioning everyone involved, they would find out who the victim had been involved with and everything would fall into place. So far nothing like that had happened. Lots of innuendo, a deal

172

of suspicion but nothing that could be added to anything to produce a theory worthy of being tested. It was like manipulating flabby flesh; everything slid around under their hands, wouldn't stay in place.

Hughes adjusted his position in the chair, leant a little closer to the table, not difficult in that confined space, and dropped his voice. 'It was Thursday evening, see?' He paused and gave a look at the two policemen. 'You know where I live, right?'

'In one of the terraced cottages near the entrance to the estate,' Sergeant Penrose said amiably.

'The end, the south end,' Hughes amplified. 'Mrs Pierce has the north end and Maria's in the middle.' There was an edge to his voice as he mentioned the health manager's name that suggested relations between them left something to be desired. Again he paused, this time as though to add to the tension. 'Well, as I said, it was Thursday evening. I'd come back, like I always do, and had the grill on to do me chops. Like a nice bit of meat at the end of the day. Burn enough off doing what I do, I don't have to worry about what I eat. Lot of fancy nonsense the chef here produces. Do a good work-out and eat what you fancy, that's what I say!'

'So you'd put your chops on to grill,' William prompted him.

'Well, I'd lit it. I was just anointing them with a bit of the old Worcestershire,' he gave every syllable a full, intentionally comical emphasis, 'when I heard someone ringing at Maria's bell. You can hear everything what goes on in the next cottage, wall's like paper!' he said contemptuously. 'So I glances out of the window, like, my kitchen bit's at the front of the cottage, and sees her ladyship standing on the doorstep. Next minute, Maria's let her in and I gets back to me chops.'

Again he paused. William and Sergeant Penrose waited, allowing him to maintain his own momentum.

Hughes linked his hands together on the table and

leant even further forward. 'Well, at first all I heard was their voices murmuring. 'Er ladyship seemed to be doing most of the talking. Odd, I thought, what can she want with Maria? Then I thought maybe she 'ad some sort of complaint to make. An' that worried me 'cause I'd given 'er 'er massage that day. Like I said, there weren't no come on but you never know with some of 'em. Think they've a right to your body and soul and if you don't give 'em exactly what they want, they've got it in for you an' no mistake.' He gave them a look that said life was tough when you dealt with rich bitches.

'So I was listening 'ard, like, seeing if I could pick up anyfing.' The more bound up Hughes got in his story, the more noticeable his London accent became.

'And?' prompted William again as another pause dragged out the tension.

'And they started quarrelling!' said Hughes in a low, thrilling voice.

'Quarrelling?'

'Went at it 'ammer and tongs,' Hughes said with great satisfaction. 'Couldn't 'ear what it was all about but it sounded as though Lady Barry was asking for somefing that Maria weren't going to give 'er. I 'eard 'er say, shout more like, "no" and,' here he threw the police a triumphant glance, 'then I 'eard 'er shout, "You're not getting anything from me!" There was more arguing and it didn't seem to be anyfing to do with the treatments 'cos there was words like, "you never" and "you always", you know, like married people fling at each other.' He sat back in his chair with the expression of a man who has produced the winning numbers on the lottery.

William carefully controlled his sense of excitement. It was difficult. Here, at last, was evidence Jessica Barry had been at loggerheads with a member of the Conifers Spa staff; one moreover who was supposed to have locked up the swimming pool area and knew exactly where the key was.

Hughes looked from one officer to the other, his face reflecting his disappointment at the lack of reaction.

'What happened then?' William finally asked.

The witness shifted slightly in his chair. 'Lady Barry left, slamming the door after 'erself. I just saw 'er walking up the lane, really fast, 'er 'ead down, like she was walking through a storm and couldn't wait to get 'ome.'

Once again William let a pause develop. Hughes raked back his hair from his forehead, obviously puzzled that his story didn't seem to have been greeted with the excitement he obviously felt it deserved.

'Did you mention to Maria Russell that you'd over-heard the quarrel?'

The witness shifted in the chair and looked down at his nails. 'Reckoned she'd not want to know anyone 'ad over'eard that sort of fing,' he said finally.

'But if the walls are as thin as you say, surely she would realise she must have been overheard?' Sergeant Penrose suggested.

The witness's unease increased. He scraped his chair back from the table, dropped his gaze, studied his shoes for a long moment. 'I reckoned she didn't know I was 'ome,' he said at last. 'I'd 'eard 'er come in just before Lady Barry called. I wasn't in the kitchen then and I'm a quiet little soul, 'adn't been making no noise. So,' he glanced up at William from under his fair lashes, 'I turned off the grill, went out the back door, then made a noise coming in the front again.'

'That was very sensitive of you.' William's tone con-tained a fine edge of irony that escaped Jim Hughes.

'Well, reckoned she'd only be embarrassed,' he muttered.

'And what about Mrs Pierce, was she in her cottage while this quarrel was going on?'

'She only gets back that early when she's got the lad wiv 'er and 'e's away at the moment. I'm not often back that early meself, usually go down to the pub for a beer at the end of the day but somehow didn't feel like it that evening.'

'You get on well with Maria Russell?'

'She's OK,' Hughes said off-handedly. 'Likes to throw her weight around, show she's in charge, like. But we rub along together.' There was a grudging note in his voice.

William reckoned that Hughes's 'consideration' was to give himself time to work out what advantage he could gain from this intriguing piece of information.

The two policemen took the man back over his story, probing without success for further details, then went through everything he knew about Jessica Barry's stay at the Spa before he'd gone off on Saturday morning.

At the end, there was little to be added to what they already had.

'And where did you spend your weekend?' asked William when it seemed there was nothing more they could get out of the man.

'With me mum in Streatham,' was the answer. 'Try and see her every few months, I do.'

William passed over a notepad and asked for Mrs Hughes's address and telephone number.

After the conclusion of the interview, when they'd said goodbye to the witness, William and Sergeant Penrose looked at each other with the excitement they hadn't allowed to show in front of Jim Hughes.

'Now we're getting somewhere,' the sergeant said.

'Maria Russell had a key to the pool area,' said William. 'She's tall and strong, fully capable of throttling the victim. Though,' he corrected himself, 'we won't know if the death was actually caused by strangulation or that blow to the head until we get the autopsy report. But Maria Russell is fitting very nicely into the frame.'

'What do you think the argument was over, sir?'

'Who knows? Time to speak to Ms Russell again.' William sat tapping the table with his pen. 'If Hughes was telling us the truth, and on the face of it there seems little reason for him to lie, Jessica Barry and Maria Russell knew each other before the victim turned up here. Now, why hasn't Russell told us this? Why hasn't anyone else? Didn't they know?' William doodled as his mind raced with possible implications. 'Things is getting interesting, Sergeant. Let's go and find Ms Russell.'

One of the men entering the statement details into the computer put his head round the door. 'There's a Mr Quinlan here. He says he's the victim's father and wants a word with whoever's in charge. With Superintendent Marks not here, that's you, sir. Can you see him now?'

Chapter Eighteen

'Thanks, Frank, I'll let you know about the amphorae. They're exactly what I need for the orangery, but the price, man, the price!' The elderly man shook Frank Borden's hand and left Lost Horizons.

Frank Borden followed him out onto the pavement and stood for a moment, enjoying the sensation of the warm sun on his head. The only advantage of thinning hair was that you could feel your scalp benefiting from such moments. He turned and surveyed the front of his Mayfair gallery with satisfaction. The massive Roman figure looked every bit as impressive as he'd expected. And he'd been right to resist his manager's suggestion that some of the Roman pottery that had recently come in could provide an interesting counterpoint. Frank wondered for a moment whether he had made a mistake in appointing the man. But his other qualifications had been so impressive, he'd allowed himself to ignore the fact that the man's aesthetic judgement could be at fault.

On the other hand, if certain officials started to wonder why such a comparative philistine was running London's foremost primitive and classical art gallery, Lost Horizons could attract even more unwelcome attention than he was having to deal with at the moment. Still, such judgement was subjective at the best of times. There could, Frank supposed, be people who regarded as desirable the overabundant approach to art.

He allowed his eye to approve the line of the statue's hip and thigh. What an athlete the man must have been!

The fullness of the mouth and the soft roundness of the face suggested, though, that the model had enjoyed other physical pursuits as well. Frank then indulged one of his greatest pleasures; that of mentally replacing the lost parts of classical figures, in this case the whole of the left arm and the lower part of the right. The posture suggested the athlete had probably been throwing a discus. Frank enjoyed the tension in the legs, the solidity of the pose, and allowed himself to imagine where the missing arm might have thrown the discus.

Which took his gaze down the street, where, to his surprise, he saw the tall figure of the girl who wrote cookery who'd been staying at Conifers Spa and had, if rumour was correct, found poor Jessica's body. Rumour had also said that one of the policemen involved in the investigation was her husband; had indeed been with her when the body had been discovered.

The girl caught his glance and smiled in recognition. At the back of Frank's mind alarm bells started to ring.

'Hello,' she said gaily. 'How nice to see you! Is this your gallery?'

'What an unexpected pleasure, Miss Lisle.' Frank's memory supplied her name just in time. 'Won't you allow me to show you around? And perhaps offer you', he was about to suggest coffee then realised it was nearly lunchtime, 'a glass of wine? I usually indulge around this time.'

'What a lovely suggestion.' The girl did indeed look delighted, deepening Frank's suspicion that her main purpose in coming to town had been to visit him. Well, now he'd made it easy for her and he'd perhaps learn what all this was about.

'Actually,' the girl said, 'it's Mrs Pigram, not Miss Lisle.'

'Of course, aren't you married to a detective?'

She nodded.

So rumour was true. Frank ushered her into the

gallery and received a jolt of pleasure as her arm brushed his. God but this woman was gorgeous!

She was as tall as he was, despite her low-heeled shoes, but that didn't worry Frank. He'd long ago learned how to handle any woman. You gotta like them, he'd have said if asked. Not difficult, he'd have added, they're all so interesting. All different, all with their own attractions. You just have to let them know you appreciate them.

So now he watched Darina with considerable pleasure as she studied the Mayan stone mask he had displayed on a square column in the centre of the gallery. She was wearing a navy-blue linen shift dress topped with a matching short jacket; no tights or stockings on long, tanned legs shod in strap sandals a subtle shade of ochre. Her toenails, long and well formed, he noted, were painted to match, and the woven leather bag on a long gold chain slung over her left shoulder was the same colour. The abundant, creamy hair that at the health farm had been worn loose or caught with a simple tie at the nape of her neck, was today arranged in a French plait that started at the crown of her head and ended looped up under itself and finished with a large navy bow. The effect was certainly sophisticated but it made her look older and, well, sharper, somehow.

'Doesn't it look fierce?' she commented on the mask. 'Look at those huge, protuberant eyes and the way he's poking out his tongue at us. Pity he's lost part of his nose. Who is he?'

'It's a Mayan god, from Mexico, probably around 300 AD,' Frank said. 'See these little wiggles running down each side of his face?' His finger traced the snake-like ridges. 'Scholars attribute them to the planet Venus, feared by the Mayans as the bringer of famine.'

'How interesting.' She wandered over to the corner where a tiny torso was displayed on a similar column. Her interest in his gallery appeared to be genuine. Frank wondered if he'd been worrying unnecessarily. 'Here's someone who doesn't need to frighten famine away.' The little statuette had no head, arms or lower legs and the power of the full, round breasts with their prominent nipples was emphasised by the size of the thick thighs and hips that sloped gracefully up into the waist. 'Is this Mayan as well?'

Frank shook his head. 'Much older, dates from around 2000 BC, a Quetta goddess from Afghanistan.' He glanced up at the figure standing beside him, all pulsing flesh alive with alarming possibility. 'In ancient cultures, size was a sign of fertility and riches. If you were fat it showed you had more than enough to eat; highly desirable.'

Darina gave him an amused smile. 'What was it the Duchess of Windsor said? You can never be too rich or too thin? Perhaps we in the West are too rich.'

'Because we worship slimness, you mean?' Frank was delighted with her, forgot his suspicions. 'Come and have that glass of wine; or is there something else I can show you?'

His visitor glanced around at the varied selection of statues, urns and amphorae that were displayed. 'Perhaps I could look some more later?' she murmured.

In his comfortable office furnished with high-quality Georgian antiques (it gave clients confidence in his judgement), Frank produced a bottle of French Chablis from his fridge, placed two long-stemmed tulip glasses on a silver tray, opened the wine and poured it.

Darina sat in a modern armchair (punters found it easier to write cheques if the seating was comfortable), and commented admiringly on the wine.

Frank smiled pleasantly. 'I took a vow a long time ago not to settle for second best in life.'

Her cool grey eyes surveyed him over the glass. 'In cooking I always say it's better to buy the best of cheaper ingredients than go for bottom-of-the-range expensive ones. Really good smoked mackerel is heavenly, cheap smoked salmon is dreadful.'

'But how nice when you can afford the best of the best,' Frank murmured. It was a long time since he'd had to settle for anything less than top of the range whether it was an art gallery, a car or a bottle of wine. Quite an achievement for a lad who'd clawed his way up from a North London comprehensive where the education in drug use was more thorough than any of the academic subjects.

'How difficult is it for you to find Mayan masks and Quetta statuettes these days? Don't most governments forbid the export of ancient treasures?'

Oh, how guileless were those grey eyes! How innocent the swing of her elegant foot!

'That's why the supply is small, the prices are high, and anyone seeking to buy, or who has something special to sell, contacts a specialist such as myself.' He paused for a moment then added, 'Because the supply is so limited, Lost Horizons also offers reproductions. I travel the world seeking out the finest craftsmen in ancient traditions. Their products aren't cheap but they cost a fraction of the price an original would command.'

'So if I wanted a Roman statue but couldn't afford the one in your window (there isn't a price but I'm sure it must be horrendously expensive), you'd tell me I could have one carved by a descendant, maybe, of an artist who worked for one of the Caesars?'

He was amused, took an enjoyable swig of wine. 'Well, yes, that is one way of putting it.'

'Is Esme interested in ancient art?'

'Esme?' Just for a moment he was taken by surprise.

'Esme Lee, the barrister.' Darina glanced at the anodyne Dutch still life he had hanging behind his chair. 'I can see her appreciating the cultural implications of the things you have here. I mean, they have more than just aesthetic qualities, don't they?' Her eyes dismissed the Dutch painting. 'With something like that Quetta statuette, you're acquiring a key to the past, something that embodies a whole philosophy of life. If she was mine, every time I looked at her I'd wonder about the artist that created her, the society that worshipped her. What sort of food they ate and how they prepared it. Famine for us today means television pictures of starving people in Somalia and Ethiopia, doesn't it? We think of it as a political obscenity, the result of poor or corrupt administration in a world with sufficient scientific knowledge to ensure everybody has enough to eat. For starving Ethiopians, though, I suppose famine is still as natural a disaster as it was for ancient societies. Something you sacrifice to gods to guard against.' Darina leant forward and placed her glass on the desk. 'It makes our worries seem insignificant, doesn't it?' The seemingly inexhaustible flow of words suddenly dried up.

'Something's upset you, hasn't it?' Frank looked at his guest more keenly. He'd missed the distress in her eyes before. Been too concerned with his own troubles, too suspicious of her motives.

Darina gave a wobbly laugh. 'Nothing much.' Then she added in a rush, as if she couldn't stop the words coming out, 'Just don't expect to see my cookery column in the paper again.'

'Ah!' He looked at her with compassion. 'The bastards! Making too many changes, they are. You let me know which paper manages to snatch you up and I'll change to it.' They both knew it wouldn't be that easy for her to find another job but you had to sound encouraging.

'Right!' she said with quick enthusiasm. 'But that's enough of that. I was asking you about Esme.'

'So you were,' Frank said thoughtfully. 'Yes, Esme is a client. She comes into the gallery quite often,' he added smoothly. 'She's bought several things. You should see her apartment, almost nothing there beyond the bare essentials. She calls her interior decorating style Japanese simplicity. I call it empty warehouse!'

'And Jessica, was she interested in possessions and

classical art?' The question was almost flung at him but it wouldn't be true to say it came from nowhere. Now that it had been asked, Frank realised he should have known all along that was why Darina was here. He forgot his delight in her appearance.

'You don't pussyfoot around, do you? The police not satisfied with my statement? Your husband sent you round here to do a little spying?' He let the anger show in both his voice and face.

She blinked unhappily. 'Honestly, it's nothing like that! William doesn't even know I'm here and he certainly wouldn't ask me to spy for him. I'm not allowed anywhere near an official investigation!' That sounded as though it irked, thought Frank with grim satisfaction.

'So why are you here?'

'Well, I was in town anyway.'

Frank suddenly realised that the newspaper must have fired her that morning. So, her visit to the gallery hadn't been planned, or at least hadn't been a top priority.

'And, it's just that I liked what I saw of Jessica and so many other people seem to have disliked her so much; everyone, it seemed, except you. So I thought I'd see if you could tell me why.'

She sat uneasily, her shoulders slightly hunched over, as though minimising her height. He realised she knew she had handled things badly and wasn't sure how he was going to react.

'Why didn't you just come straight out with it instead of trying to give me a kick-start like the fuzz hoping to startle a hostile witness?' Then curiosity got the better of him. 'What was it about Jessica that attracted you?' For, if true, it was an unusual reaction. He knew enough men who'd fallen for her sweet face and lively chatter; not many women.

Darina straightened her back and seemed to forget her awkwardness. 'I thought she was so open to life, and there was something dignified about the way she dealt with widowhood. Then she had such an unfortunate trick of coming out with the truth regardless of its effect; she never used polite evasion, it was as if she was socially tone deaf.'

'In other words, you felt she needed protecting. That's how she struck me, too.' Frank poured some more wine into both their glasses and decided that at least a show of openness was called for. 'I met her just over ten years ago. She was an air hostess.'

'Oh, yes, she told me she'd given that up when she got married.'

Frank gave a grim smile of remembrance. 'She spilt steaming coffee over me on a flight to Greece. It could have been really nasty and she was so upset! Had to cheer her up, didn't I? Took her out to dinner that evening in Athens, a taverna by the seashore. We had grilled fish and she told me her life history.' Frank sat back in his chair, nursing the glass of wine, and allowed himself to recall the girl with the breathless laugh, dressed in white trousers and top, her dark hair no longer tightly tied back but a cloud around her pretty face, heightening the effect of those amazing green eyes. What had started as just an amusing way of passing an evening had quickly deepened into something more important.

When he continued talking, it was to himself as much as to Darina. 'Jessica loved the good things of life. She was a delight to give things to, a child at Christmas, wide-eyed and astonished at the desirability of whatever it was.'

'You make it sound an exciting quality.' Darina's eyes narrowed slightly.

'Oh, believe me, it was! And don't get me wrong, there was nothing grasping about Jessica.' Even as he said it, Frank wondered if it was true. He twirled the stem of his glass, watching how the sunlight deepened the wine's golden glow. He'd been thinking about Jessica almost constantly since he'd left Conifers Spa. In a way it was a relief to be able to talk about her now.

'What Jessica needed above everything was love and that was the one thing I couldn't give her.' He moved round in his chair so that he addressed the window rather than Darina. The window looked out on the mews, enabled him to check the arrival of delivery vans.

'She'd just finished with a complete mistake for a marriage. Jessica was never made to be a serviceman's wife, especially a sailor constantly away from home for long stretches. Ending the marriage had bruised her mind and spirit but she was still full of gusto for life, so ambitious, wanting everything. And desperate to be needed, wanted, loved.' Frank sipped his wine. He tasted none of its cool depth or subtle flavour. He was seeing Jessica two months after he'd first met her, so excited at being taken to Monte Carlo; remembering her delight at the Hotel de Paris, her stunned response to the *fin de siècle* luxury of the casino, her bubbling appreciation when they went shopping, the way she couldn't decide between two outfits and her genuine astonishment when he'd bought her both. 'She moved in with me. I told her marriage wasn't on the cards.' He wasn't going to go into the reason for that, Darina would just have to accept the statement. 'But that as long as we pleased each other it was more fun to live together than apart. It lasted three years.'

Three years Jessica had shared his life. Oh, she'd continued working as an air hostess, he'd encouraged her to; it suited him for her to have her own career, especially when it was one that could take her off for several days. Even so, she'd become deeply involved in his life. How was it he hadn't realised just how deeply involved until this last week? He remembered his dismay at hearing Jessica chattering on to Esme, telling her about the occasion she'd accompanied him on one of his buying trips to Greece, complaining about the amount of time he'd spent arranging shipments instead of taking her out to restaurants and nightclubs. Esme's expression had been bored, almost contemptuous, but he'd be willing to bet no detail had escaped her razor-sharp mind.

Darina was looking at him with an expectant expression. What interpretation was she placing on his pause? Frank pulled himself together. 'Then, somehow, after three years or so, the magic went. For both of us. We split up by mutual consent. It didn't take her long to find someone else.' That still hurt, Jessica's breathless delight as she told him about her new lover, so guileless in her expectation that he'd be pleased for her. And he supposed he had been, except it had irked that she'd never had quite that look on her face for him.

'You too, I should think, found someone else without much trouble,' Darina said, her tone sardonic.

He smiled dryly. 'I'm not easy to please. I require more than just a bedworthy partner. I appreciate physical beauty in a woman but it doesn't have to be the conventional kind. Esme Lee, for example, I find very exciting, both physically and mentally. Does that surprise you?'

She shook her head, a hint of amusement in the grey eyes. 'I don't think I could be surprised at anything about you, Frank.'

'Ah, you are an intelligent woman. And an interesting mind attracts me even more than physical beauty.'

'I don't know Jessica well enough to judge how interesting her mind was.' Darina's expression said she doubted it was anywhere near as interesting as Esme's.

Frank smiled again. 'Jessica was no egghead. She wasn't even particularly intelligent, but her reactions were so often a surprise it kept our relationship fresh.'

Darina lifted an enquiring eyebrow.

'She'd work hard at achieving something she wanted from someone then, on some quixotic instinct, would throw it all away. She didn't like the way the man she'd wanted talked to a waitress, or she thought his wife needed a holiday more than she did. She was such a mixture of opportunism and generosity. And curiously innocent. Most men were enchanted by her but women always felt her to be a threat.'

'Did you know her husband?'

'Sir Paul Barry?' An ironic note in his voice underlined the title. 'I met him once. Poor Jessica, she had a talent for choosing bad husbands.'

'Was he a bad man?'

What should he tell this cool, careful girl about Paul Barry? 'How bad is bad? I don't really know what he was like but I knew Jessica wasn't happy, even though she insisted she was.'

'When did you start seeing each other again?'

'Do you know, you really do sound like the police!' he said lightly.

Darina flushed, warm colour flooding her fair skin, but she didn't apologise.

'We never stopped being friends,' he said after a moment; antagonising her would be a bad move. 'When she was first married we stopped meeting; she said Paul wouldn't understand and I didn't want to make things difficult for her. But we bumped into each other one day and after that we fell into the habit of meeting for a drink every few months or so. Then after he died, well, we met more regularly.'

'So it was natural to suggest she visit Conifers Spa with you?'

'She needed a break, she'd been through a tough time. It was the least I could do.'

'Do you often go to health farms?'

Frank shrugged his shoulders. It wasn't a question he felt like answering. Jessica had thrown all his plans into turmoil, now he had to rebuild them.

'Who do you think killed her?' Darina asked suddenly.

The question shook Frank. He'd avoided thinking of the act of murder. He, Frank Borden, the cold-blooded realist, had pushed away the image of Jessica stumbling on the edge of the spa pool, drowning in its shallow depths, the water bubbling up around the poor, abused body. No, even now he couldn't bring himself to face the facts of her death.

'I really have no idea,' he said calmly. 'It's your husband you should be asking that question.'

'It's such a dreadful thing, you see.' She put her glass of wine, still more than half full, on the desk, and leaned earnestly towards him. 'To know that someone one has spent time with is a murderer.'

'Does it have to be someone who was at the farm?' he challenged. 'Couldn't it have been someone from outside? She told lots of her friends she was going to Conifers Spa; maybe she told an enemy as well.'

'Perhaps a friend turned into an enemy?' suggested Darina. 'Do you know of anyone who could have wanted her dead?'

A large, cream-coloured van turned into the mews and stopped outside Frank's window. He rose. 'I'm sorry, Darina, I've got to attend to a delivery.'

She gathered her bag and got up; so natural were her good manners, it was impossible to tell if she'd wanted to ask him more questions or felt she'd got what she came for. Frank hoped without much conviction it was the latter.

'Of course. Thank you so much for the wine. I hope I haven't interfered too much with your day?'

'Please! Come back next time you're in town. Lunch, perhaps?' Frank gently shepherded Darina out of the gallery. 'And, to answer your last question, no, I don't know of anyone who'd want her dead.'

She gave him a look that said she didn't entirely believe him. 'I've enjoyed our chat. I'd love to talk some more about Jessica some time.'

He inclined his head politely as she left.

Gesturing to Alfred Cummings, his manager, to

accompany him, Frank made his way to the gallery's back entrance, greeted the driver and watched him open up the van's locked doors.

Working together, the three of them had removed half of the consignment and placed it in the storeroom before police cars arrived at both ends of the mews.

Chapter Nineteen

Darina left Lost Horizons wondering just how fond of Jessica Frank Borden had been. She'd needed love, he'd said, and he hadn't been able to give it to her. Why not? Jessica had been attractive enough. But Frank Borden had made it plain that conventional standards of beauty meant little to him and that he needed more than good looks.

How fond had Jessica been of him? Frank Borden wasn't conventionally good-looking; his face was too thin, too sharp, his nose beaky, the skin open-pored with new growth already shadowing his chin and jowls at noon. But it had a certain animal magnetism and his compact body held a pleasing suggestion of trained muscle. His eyes, too, were alive with interest and he was certainly a most stimulating companion.

Since she had known William Pigram, Darina's confidence had grown but she had no illusions she was any sort of a femme fatale. Yet Frank Borden had managed to make her feel there was no one he would rather have been talking to than herself. It was an enormously seductive quality.

And he had sounded genuinely fond of Jessica.

He had even sounded as though he wanted her to have found happiness with Paul Barry.

Instead he believed the marriage had been a mistake.

An assessment with which Paul Barry's son obviously agreed.

According to William, Oliver Barry had accused

Jessica of threatening to offer her life story with his father to the newspapers. Could it have been lurid enough to command serious money? If newspapers were to be believed, members of parliament had more weak spots than a worn bicycle tyre.

Darina passed a newsagent's, looked at the rack of daily papers hanging by the door, and the terrible shock of losing her column rushed back to her.

For the last forty minutes she had been able to push it to the back of her mind and that is where she wanted it to stay. So she continued puzzling over Jessica's murder. Could Oliver Barry have killed her? Just what was it Jessica had been threatening to reveal about his father?

Darina, walking in the direction of Park Lane and the underground car park, stopped suddenly, causing the man behind to collide with her back and mutter something about stupid women who didn't know where they were going. She ignored him as she wondered why she hadn't realised before what an easy source of information about Paul Barry there was not far away. One that would welcome a chat with her.

Darina rummaged in her handbag for her diary and headed for the nearest telephone box, resolving to equip herself with a mobile without delay.

Ten minutes later she paid off a taxi outside a pillared portico in a quiet square behind Victoria Station. She walked up the wide steps and rang the bell marked 'Howard'.

A buzzer released the heavy door. By the time Darina had walked into the generous hall, her uncle had opened the door into the flat that occupied the ground and basement floors.

'Lovely that you're here. Don't see nearly enough of you,' he said, kissing her on the cheek. 'Alice!' he shouted. 'Darina's arrived! Go through,' he said to his niece, 'she'll be here in a minute.'

Darina went into what had once been the main reception room of the old house. It was huge, high-ceilinged, dark and cool, the daylight filtered by trees in the square outside. The furniture failed to match the faded splendour of the architecture, being a ragbag of chairs, tables and bookshelves that looked as though they had been picked up at jumble sales and bric-à-brac shops. Papers were piled on every available surface and pillars of books placed against the walls looked in extreme danger of toppling over were even the slimmest of paperbacks to be added to the pile.

'Take a seat, don't know what's holding up Alice. Alice!' George Howard roared again over his shoulder. He was a man in proportion with the room: huge. Dressed in a faded checked shirt and baggy cotton twill trousers that seemed in imminent danger of slipping off his massive girth, an imposing Roman nose dominating a face composed mainly of a series of fleshy folds out of which peered remarkably clear hazel eyes, he made Darina feel almost fragile.

He waved her to a sofa covered in faded linen and sat himself in a large and battered Parker Knoll chair covered in some kind of leatherette, its seat sporting a split through which stuffing had started to escape. 'Now, what's brought you here, eh?'

Darina sat back with a small sigh of relief. After all the tensions of the morning, it was incredibly peaceful to be here. Almost she was reluctant to bring up the reason for her visit.

She had always enjoyed a close relationship with her uncle. He was unjudgemental, interested in everything, his conversation quirky and liable to veer off down unexpected byways. He always said his sister, Darina's mother, drove him mad with what he called her incurable socialising and relentless gregariousness but, provided they didn't meet too often, remained remarkably patient with her.

Now he seemed in no hurry to get Darina to tell him

what had prompted this unexpected visit. He placed a bookmark in a volume of political memoirs and recommended it as a good read. 'Gives you an insight into a most unusual mind. Don't worry about the distorted viewpoint, feel the width of the opinions.'

Darina rose as her aunt came into the room. She was kissed warmly. 'I know George's been looking after you. I couldn't come right up, I was making us all a salad for lunch so you will stay, won't you, dear?'

Alice Howard's broad but gaunt frame would have appeared large beside anyone but her husband. Her iron-grey hair was drawn back into a bun and her fine, fair skin wore no make up; her lips had the soft pinkness of a mouth that had never known lipstick and a faint, fair down ran along her jawbone and across her upper lip. She was wearing a cotton seersucker dress in large squares of pink and green with a matching jacket; an outfit which managed to look both oddly ingénue and laughably formal. Darina wondered whether Alice had found it at a charity shop or a jumble sale, her preferred places for fashion shopping.

'I've got one of my meetings to attend this afternoon,' Alice said. 'So would you mind if we ate now?'

'What is it today?' asked George. 'Protecting the consumer against his own appetites, school governors for the mentally challenged, or women against overindulgence of the male ego?'

She gave him an affectionate glance. 'As you well know, George, it's the action group for positive discrimination.'

'Well, you look very smart, dear. Doesn't she look smart, Darina? So much more beautiful than in her usual old jeans and T-shirt.'

'My summer committee dress,' Alice said to Darina, seeming unconcerned by her husband's comments. She moved a derisive hand down the dirndl skirt. 'If it weren't for this, I'd almost forget my legs aren't half bad.'

And indeed they weren't. Long and shapely, they ended in neat ankles and slender feet, shod in brown leather sandals. 'Come on down to the kitchen. You can chat to George after I've gone. I want to hear whether you and that nice William are still speaking to each other and if you've got a recipe that will feed a dozen people without my having to spend more than five minutes in the kitchen.'

'That's the sort of thing we all want!' laughed Darina as she followed her aunt down to the basement.

The kitchen had been modernised shortly after the Second World War, just before the Howards had acquired the flat. Little had been done to it since and now, with its green painted dresser, white china sink, mottled grey enamelled gas stove and free-standing cupboards, it had acquired a certain style of its own.

Lunch was round the large scrubbed pine table in the centre of the room. A salad of lettuce, tomato, cucumber and hard-boiled eggs accompanied slices of ham still bearing the imprint of their packaging. A crusty cottage loaf stood waiting to be cut; beside it a large plastic container of dry farmhouse cider. Also on the table was a bottle of Heinz salad cream and a jar of Branston pickle.

'Have you come up from Somerset?' asked Alice when they were all seated at the table.

That, of course, led into Conifers Spa. And of course George knew all about the murder. 'Just been reading about it in the paper. No mention of you, though.'

'We can be grateful,' Alice said placidly, hacking the bread into thick slices and handing them round. 'What was she like, this poor girl who died?'

'Jessica? She seemed to me something of a lost soul desperately seeking a role in life.'

'A bit of a drama queen?' George took a piece of bread.

'No, not really. But in a couple of days she managed to alienate most of the women and enthrall half the men. Exactly how, I'm not at all sure.' Darina refused Alice's offer of butter and noticed that George, too, ate his bread plain, French style.

'Little fatty, was she?' he asked, drawing the outline of a curvaceous lovely with his knife on the table. 'Plump little partridge?'

Darina shook her head. 'Far from it. By anyone's standards she was scrawny.'

'I like women with flesh on their bones,' he announced with satisfaction, seemingly oblivious to the fact that his wife could never qualify for this description.

Alice spread a thick layer of butter on her bread. 'It's not fair,' she said. 'I slather fat all over my food and never gain an ounce. George's diet is so sensible it's positively monastic, and the doctor now says he won't operate on his prostate until he's lost weight.'

'I've told him what an idiot he is,' George said cheerfully, dabbing tiny bits of salad cream over his lettuce. 'He refuses to believe all the evidence that indicates obesity is no health risk unless accompanied by stress, smoking, over-indulgence in drink or other such hazards.'

'Is that really so?' asked Darina in surprise.

George nodded, his eyes twinkling at her. 'You see, you've been brainwashed as well. You can't be fat and healthy, says everyone. Bollocks to that! There are some people who are genetically or chemically predisposed to be large.'

'You mean fat, dear,' said Alice helpfully. 'Now, can't we get off this obsession with weight? I want to hear how Ann is.' Conversation switched to Darina's mother.

Just after two o'clock, Alice Howard served coffee in the living room, collected a battered and heavy-looking briefcase from underneath a side table, kissed Darina and told her not to make it so long before she visited them again, and departed.

George settled Darina in a chair that faced the window, and sat opposite her. 'Right, now what's this

196

"picking of my brains" you mentioned on the phone?
Anything to do with the murder at that health farm?'

'How did you guess?'

'Ever since your poor cousin was murdered at that
historical gastronomy weekend you haven't been able to
resist meddling with matters that properly belong to the
police.'

'Don't give me that, Uncle George! You're the first
one to question official viewpoints in parliament, demand
that the establishment be held answerable to the public.
How many times have I heard you call it democracy in
action? All I ever do is tease out details that the so-called
"official investigation" appears to overlook or consider
unimportant.'

George grinned at his niece. 'Glad to hear it.'

'Don't say you were just testing! I sometimes think
there's much more establishment in you than you dare
to admit and you're a Tory manqué at heart. After all,
being brought up in the same society as my mother must
have left some effect.'

'A lifelong hatred of snobbism, elitism and patronage,'
George said promptly. 'Now we've got that out of the way,
just what is it you're poking that nice, straight little nose
of yours into this time?'

'What can you tell me about Sir Paul Barry?' asked
Darina abruptly.

'Ah!'

The soft, sad exclamation told Darina a great deal.
'You knew all along!' she accused her uncle.

'Ann rang me last night, you see, and counterpointed
a long and detailed description of the delights of staying
with a full-blown general with the horrors of becoming
involved in a murder. The fact that you and William
had found the body featured large, though none of the
newspaper reports I've read so far mentions the fact.'
George looked sardonically at Darina. 'She also said what
a relief it was that William and his police chums appeared

to have the matter well in hand and that for once you had no excuse to get involved.'

Uncle and niece looked at each other in perfect understanding.

'So why are you so reluctant to tell me about Paul Barry?'

George heaved himself out of his chair and went over to the coffee tray. Darina shook her head when he offered her more. He took his time refilling his cup. Darina waited patiently.

George sat down again, put his cup on a convenient surface and appeared to forget about it. 'I met Jessica a couple of times,' he said reflectively. 'Once at the House just after they were married and once at some do at Number Ten. She had a vulnerable quality that was very appealing.'

'Her stepson apparently claims she was threatening to tell the story of her life with his father to the newspapers. What I'd like to know is, did she have much of a story to tell?' Darina said bluntly. Nothing other than a full frontal approach was going to get her anywhere. 'I mean, older men falling for attractive young women is nothing these days. As I understand it, he didn't even leave his wife for her!'

'You know he resigned as an MP shortly after they were married?'

Darina nodded. 'Didn't he say it was because he wanted to spend more time with his new young wife?'

'He told me it was because he was threatened with bankruptcy,' George said abruptly.

'Really?' Darina was surprised. 'Why wasn't it reported?'

'Because at the eleventh hour his son bailed him out. I ran into Paul in the City one day. Barry was a snob, ambitious beyond his abilities and a ruthless user of people. But he did have immense charm. You know how the House is called a club? Well, you can't help hobnobbing with your fellow members, even those you'd never pass the time of day with elsewhere, and a session with Barry always had its enjoyable aspects.

'Shortly after he resigned, I was walking back to Bank tube station from a meeting with my City stockbroker when I literally bumped into Barry. Before I knew what was happening, he'd hauled me off to some bar and we were downing brandies. At three o'clock in the afternoon! He couldn't wait to tell someone that the ultimate indignity had been avoided.'

'Then you knew why he was resigning?'

'It was one of the rumours. Gossip is always flying around the house, members just love spreading titbits.' George grimaced. 'Sometimes it's worse than a hen party. And we all move in so many circles. We put odd fragments heard here together with others heard there. Sometimes the arithmetic's accurate, sometimes it isn't.'

'So why was Paul Barry on the verge of bankruptcy?'

'The general theory was, extravagance by his young wife. There'd been a new flat in Chelsea, lavish parties. She always appeared expensively dressed and Paul just couldn't afford it all.'

'The papers talked of him as an astute businessman. Didn't he sell a family firm for a large sum of money shortly after he became an MP?'

George picked up his coffee and drank it down. 'I wasn't privy to the details of his personal financial position.'

'Come off it, George, you can't tell me there weren't rumours about what happened. Anyone who goes from successful and well-heeled businessman to the edges of bankruptcy has to attract speculation.'

George sighed. 'The firm was started by his first wife's family. I should imagine most of the money went to her. And I believe he made her a generous settlement at the time of the divorce. Perhaps that's why his son came to his rescue in the end. I don't remember any scandal over his marriage breakdown, and these days the skeletons have to be buried pretty deep if some enterprising reporter isn't to dig them up.'

The chair creaked as George shifted position. He said nothing more. Darina was certain that it was no accident he had chosen to sit with his back to the window, making it difficult to read his expression.

'If bankruptcy had been avoided, why did he still resign?'

'Things had gone too far,' George said, but there was no conviction in his voice.

Darina leaned forward. 'Look, there's something you're not telling me here. Is it some sort of loyalty to the club, as you put it? Or are you worried what I'll do with the information if you give it to me?'

'I have no sense of loyalty to Barry. The man was a deep-dyed shit!' George rarely raised his voice, rarely used invective; irony and, occasionally, sarcasm were his chosen weapons. To hear the venom in his voice now was a shock. 'Nor am I worried about you; I trust your judgement and common sense. No, the main difficulty is that I have no evidence for saying anything. It's all rumour and hearsay, and scandal harms most the innocent.'

'The innocent in this case being Paul Barry's family?'

'Particularly his children but also Monica, his first wife.'

'But if it could have led to Jessica's death?'

George looked sceptically at Darina. 'You really feel it could have done?'

'Not knowing what is involved, I honestly don't know, but apparently Jessica was threatening to go to the press with her story. Would it have been scandalous enough both to have raised a considerable sum of money and made it worthwhile for someone to do anything to stop her?'

George hauled himself out of his chair and went over

to the window, his huge bulk dark against the shadowy light coming through the graceful trees. 'What I heard wasn't one of the rumours in general circulation. I was told about it well after Barry left the House and then in the strictest confidence. I was involved in disciplinary procedures against another MP.' George thrust his hands into the pockets of his trousers and jingled his change. 'If the story was true, it more than likely led to the break-up of his first marriage. I did ask my informant if he'd tried to warn the second Lady Barry what she might be taking on.' A pause, then, 'He said he didn't believe in interfering in other people's lives. Unless Barry told her himself, I think it's unlikely Jessica knew.'

'You must be talking about some sexual deviancy,' Darina insisted. 'Nothing else fits what you are implying. Surely it's unlikely that he'd give up whatever practices you won't mention? Then Jessica must have learned about them. And certain newspapers would fall over themselves to get an account of them.'

George looked over the square and said nothing.

'You must see you can't just leave it like this. If you won't tell me anything more, at least give me the name of the person who told you whatever it was so that the police can question him.'

George turned. 'I've already written it down, together with address and telephone number.' He went across the room and picked up a sealed envelope from the top of a large rolltop desk. It was addressed to Inspector William Pigram.

Chapter Twenty

Lieutenant Commander Thomas Quinlan, Jessica's father, had been put to wait in the reception hall of Conifers Spa.

It was in many ways a better place to conduct an interview with a willing witness than the cramped and overheated little room in the mobile incident centre.

William went to meet Thomas Quinlan with great anticipation. At last it seemed this case was going to get somewhere. First there had been the revelation from Jim Hughes of a quarrel between the victim and the health manager, Maria Russell, with its strong implication of a hidden relationship. Now the victim's father had appeared. And William was the officer in control.

Life was looking good.

The reception hall was deserted apart from the witness and a police constable standing quietly by the reception desk rather like the manager of a hotel.

The lieutenant commander sat pulling at his knuckles, making a series of gristly clicks.

He looked to be in his mid-fifties, a solid man with thick grey hair brushed firmly into place. He wore a lightweight summer suit, blue striped shirt and a dark blue tie. On it William recognised the Royal Naval Reserve insignia, a gold crown topped with R.

'Good morning, sir.'

Thomas Quinlan jumped to his feet. He was taller than his sitting figure had suggested and the way he held himself erect made the most of his height. 'Are you the officer in charge?' he demanded, his voice authoritative and carrying.

'Superintendent Marks is not available at the moment. I'm Inspector Pigram, one of the team investigating Lady Barry's death. Do I understand you are her father, sir?'

The man nodded. 'I've been away for the weekend. Got back last night to see the papers. It was too late to come down then.' He spoke calmly but his shoulders were rigidly set and his fingers twitched.

'Would you like coffee?'

'Thank you.' Quinlan's head jerked in a tight little nod of acknowledgement.

William turned to the young police constable. 'Coffee for two, please, Colin, and make sure we're undisturbed here. Do sit down, sir.'

William pulled up a chair opposite Thomas Quinlan and unobtrusively arranged his notebook on its arm. As his visitor settled again, William glimpsed cufflinks of rounded amethysts set in gold and caught an expensive whiff of a spicy citrus aftershave.

'May I say how sorry we are for your loss, sir. Particularly that you had to learn the news through the press. The only family contact we had for Lady Barry was her stepson.'

Thomas Quinlan returned to pulling at his knuckles. 'We quarrelled at the time of her marriage,' he said in a low voice.

William waited.

The other man raised a distressed face. 'I mean, the man was thirty years older than she was! His career was over, no matter that he was still an MP. Not that that lasted long.'

'So you didn't approve?'

Thomas Quinlan nodded vigorously. 'I told her she was an idiot. Throwing herself away.'

'But she was in love?' William would have placed a large bet against this possibility.

'Love! She wanted to get married!' Quinlan wrenched his hands apart and placed them firmly on the arms of the chair. His face worked convulsively. 'I was always on at her about her lifestyle, telling her she should settle down. But I didn't mean by marrying someone older than her father, without a future!'

'Perhaps we can start by taking a few details of yourself.' William took out his pencil. 'You are Lieutenant Commander Thomas Quinlan, retired from the Royal Navy?'

'I came here to see her,' Quinlan protested, 'not to answer a lot of damn fool questions.'

William had a brief vision of the pathologist's laboratory, of Jessica Barry's fragile body exposed on the steel table, cut from thorax to pelvis. 'I'm sorry, sir, I'm afraid that isn't possible. Later, perhaps tomorrow, we can arrange it.'

'I've come to see her now,' Quinlan repeated pugnaciously, staring at William. 'I don't care if you haven't had time to lay her out, tidy her up, I must see her.' Again the note of command.

'Lady Barry is no longer here.' William hesitated then decided truth was best. 'The autopsy is taking place.'

The fierce gaze of the narrow blue eyes fell.

'Now, if we could just go through preliminary details, it would help us greatly.' Matter-of-factly William elicited Thomas Quinlan's Gloucestershire address, and the fact that he hadn't seen his daughter for three years.

'I wrote to her when Barry died,' Quinlan added. 'Told her it was probably for the best and suggested we met. I, I didn't receive an answer.'

William remained silent but he could imagine what Darina would say when she heard this comment.

'I want to know exactly how she died and when you're going to catch the man responsible.'

'We found your daughter at the bottom of the spa pool here,' William said gently.

'I read *that* in the newspapers. Report also said she was strangled. I demand to know the full details.'

'All we know at the moment is that there was severe bruising to her neck and she had also hit her head on the side of the pool. Either injury could have caused her death, or she may have been rendered unconscious and drowned in the pool itself,' William said.

Quinlan stared with the fierce intensity of a hawk on the hunt as he absorbed the information. 'How far have you got towards discovering who did it?'

'We are pursuing various lines of inquiry.'

'Don't give me that rubbish,' Quinlan said jerkily. 'You must have some idea who you're after.'

'All I can tell you,' William said patiently, 'is that we have various suspects.'

'Read somewhere that the police either find murderers within three days or not at all.'

William sighed. 'Very often our investigations do uncover killers quite quickly, and we hope for similar success here.' He eyed Thomas Quinlan. 'What can help us considerably is a deeper knowledge of the victim. I'd like to ask you some questions about your daughter.'

The constable arrived with coffee and placed it on a small table between the two men. William poured out a cup and handed it to Thomas Quinlan.

'Fire away,' Quinlan said, refusing milk and sugar. 'I'd like to think this wasn't going to prove a totally wasted morning.'

William turned the page of his notebook. 'What was your relationship with your daughter before she announced her engagement?'

'Excellent! That is to say, she would come and stay with us at least once a year.'

'That's you and Lady Barry's mother?'

Quinlan tugged at the knot of his tie. 'No, Stephanie's

my second wife. Audrey, Jessica's mother, and I divorced when she was fourteen.'

'Perhaps you can fill me in a little on Jessica's childhood,' suggested William. 'You were in the navy?'

Quinlan nodded. 'Since the age of seventeen. My father and my grandfather were both sailors. Audrey came from a service background as well. Her father was an admiral.'

There was a note in Quinlan's voice that suggested this fact had been an added attraction to the young naval officer.

'I was in submarines. We had two daughters, Jessica was the younger, and then a son. Everything was fine until, in my early thirties, I realised my future in the navy was severely limited. I had no intention of being sidelined into some desk job then made redundant in my forties with little prospect of a worthwhile second career so I got out.' The fingers of his right hand began to beat irritably on the arm of his chair.

'I suppose it was difficult for Audrey, having me home the whole time when she'd been used to long absences. I had trouble landing the sort of job I wanted and, frankly, the tension told on me. On all of us.'

'Jessica as well?'

'I regarded the children as in need of discipline. Audrey had been far too lax with them, especially the girls.' Quinlan's voice was stern. 'Both were severely overweight but she refused to do anything about it, said it was puppyfat! Then baked more cakes!'

'But Jessica was incredibly slim.' William was surprised.

Quinlan looked smug. 'Soon got her to take a proper interest in how she looked. Gave her rewards, bought her pretty clothes, took her abroad.'

'Was this before or after your marriage broke up?'

'After. Before we separated, I could get nowhere with either of them. God, what a mess it was; Audrey and the girls were constantly in tears, I was having to send out letters, hound head-hunting agencies, attend interviews and try and control the situation at home. The only times I had any peace were when Alan, that was my son, and I took off to watch cricket.' Quinlan's hand suddenly clutched into a fist, the knuckles whitening. 'Then Alan was killed in a traffic accident. He was ten. Audrey blamed me, she said I shouldn't have told him he could ride his bicycle across the main road. But for God's sake, children have to develop independence!' The fierce gaze was back in the eyes.

'After that there was nothing left for Audrey and me. Alan had been everything to both of us. Of course we loved the girls but they're not the same as a boy, are they?'

William again refrained from commenting. 'So that's when you started to persuade your daughters to lose weight?' he suggested.

'The elder one blamed me for the break-up. She took it very hard. Our relationship broke down completely, it's years since I've seen her.' Quinlan's voice was cold. 'But Jessica was quite different. She cried and cried when I left and wanted to see me at every opportunity. I think Audrey grew quite resentful at my influence over her.' Deep satisfaction coloured his voice.

'Which extended to a successful slimming campaign?'

For a moment Thomas Quinlan hesitated. 'I have to say that it was almost too successful. Jessica became anorexic. And that was something else Audrey blamed me for!'

'It can be difficult coping with eating disorders,' William suggested diplomatically.

'Lot of nonsense,' Thomas Quinlan declared. 'It was quite monstrous the way the doctors questioned Audrey and myself. They more or less declared that the break-down of the marriage was responsible for Jessica's condition. Illness, they called it. Kept telling them, the other

girl wasn't affected like that, couldn't help wishing sometimes she was; nothing seemed to make her lose weight.
But Jessica – skin and bones! Audrey spent hours trying
to make her eat. I told her what a fool she was making
of herself, that no one would want her as a bag of bones!
Promised her a pony if she'd get a grip on herself.'

William found himself equally repelled and fascinated by this man. Was it the service background that
had developed his insensitivity to such a fine art? But
William knew both naval and army people who were
highly skilled in people management. This had to be
inbred.

William was beginning to feel some sympathy for
Jessica Barry, or Quinlan as she had been. Parents split
up, castigated for being overweight, then in hospital for
being underweight. He must talk to Darina about this
aspect of the case. 'But Jessica managed to come to terms
with her eating?'

'As I said, it was all a lot of nonsense. One of those
things teenagers go through.' Quinlan paused for a
moment, then added with a touch of unease, 'Have to
admit she had us worried for a time, though.' Then he
seemed to put the memory behind him. 'By the time
she was seventeen, she'd recovered. Didn't put on much
weight but enough. Lovely girl she was, no boy would
look at anyone else if she was in the room!'

Had Jessica developed all her girl skills because that
was the way to her father's heart?

'Did she go to university?'

Thomas Quinlan gave a bark of laughter. 'University!
Didn't even take A levels! No, her mother packed her off
to France, to finishing school. Waste of money, I thought.
The girl was obviously going to get married, what did she
need that sort of thing for?'

'Who knows when a girl will need to earn a living,'
murmured William.

'Right there, lad! Jessica hadn't been married three years before it all broke up.'

'Can you give me a few more details?'

Thomas Quinlan's forehead creased irritably. 'Far too young, of course! Married a young naval officer and when he was away, well, she was so attractive, you couldn't blame the chaps, the way they flocked round.'

William took a deep breath and set about with patient questioning to get down to specifics.

Gradually there was built up the picture of a girl who appeared to have dedicated herself to finding a man who could give her the sort of life she wanted.

The end of Jessica's first marriage had come after an affair with a successful businessman whilst her naval husband was away at sea. Trips to New York and Hong Kong had made her the talk of the naval base. Despite attempts at a patching-up operation, William gathered Jessica had become bored with naval protocol and divorce followed, but no second marriage to the businessman.

'Disappeared like snow in springtime,' Thomas Quinlan said. 'Well, can you blame him? I told Jess she'd been a fool. Her husband was a bright lad, he's a commander now and looks like he's heading for the top. Still, that's the young for you.'

No wonder Jessica's morals had seemed shaky if that was the sort of lead she had been given by her father.

After the divorce, Jessica became an air stewardess. 'Her stepfather had stood the cost of her Paris finishing school so I paid for a brush-up course on her French. Thought it an ideal job for her. Get around, meet lots of people, be appreciated for her looks and charm.'

'How long did she work as an air stewardess?' enquired William, thinking that it was hard work, and these days you didn't get the long lay-overs that used to make travelling such fun. 'Just a glorified waitress,' an old girlfriend of his had once complained. 'And all you see are air-conditioned hotels that could be anywhere!'

It turned out that Jessica had stuck it for nearly ten years, until she'd met Sir Paul Barry.

'Of course, she'd had other boyfriends,' her father boasted. 'Couldn't help it! There was one I know she was really keen on. Never met him, despite a load of promises from her. Don't know what happened, whether he was married or she just couldn't get him to the sticking point.'

But she'd got Paul Barry to the sticking point. She'd been in her early thirties by then. Had there been something about her that had put men off offering the security of marriage?

'She was so popular, I was always telling her to settle down, get married again, make some man happy. She'd just look at me with her sweet smile and say she was happy as she was. But Jessica wasn't a career type, not like her sister.'

And what about her sister? Thomas Quinlan clammed up when William asked about her. Apparently she had sided with her mother over the divorce, grown very fond of her stepfather and seen little of her real father.

'About five years ago she rang and asked if we could meet but we were just off to Australia on business. I said I'd ring her when we got back, but by then I'd forgotten all about it. And now, to tell you the truth, I wouldn't know how to contact her. Jessica hadn't any idea either. They'd never got on.'

William was shocked by how little it seemed to disturb Thomas Quinlan. He couldn't begin to think how such an attitude had affected Jessica's sister.

The interview had taken a long time. Glancing at his watch, William saw it was one o'clock. 'Thank you for being so frank with me,' he said. 'I'm nearly finished for now but we shall want to talk to you again later.'

'And when can I see my daughter?' Thomas Quinlan looked strained and tired. He took off his glasses and rubbed his eyes. The square shoulders were now rounded, adding years to his age. The dark eyes pleaded like an old dog's.

'Should be tomorrow, sir. We'll contact you.' William looked down at the details he'd written in his notebook. 'This your daytime telephone number?'

'What? Oh, no, that's home. My office is in Swindon.' He gave the number.

William asked what he did.

After the navy Thomas Quinlan had gone into industry and was now managing director of a firm manufacturing car components. 'We've been through a very, very sticky time. The signs are that we're beginning to pull out but for a time there it was touch and go.'

It was the perfect moment for William to ask his final question.

Thomas Quinlan's despair and weariness etched itself deeper into the lines that ran across his forehead and down beside his mouth. 'Yes, she came to see me last week. Begged me to lend her thirty thousand pounds. Said she had to have it if she wasn't to be declared bankrupt. Apparently the mortgage on the flat was in her name, it was badly in arrears and she couldn't afford to sell it because there was negative equity. Her husband had left her holding a joint bank account with a large overdraft. God knows how he'd managed that with no visible collateral, but that's MPs for you! And he'd started some consultancy. No limited liability and she was a director, they'd thought it was a good tax wheeze!' Disgust at the financial stupidity oozed out of his voice. 'Instead the consultancy owed large sums of money.'

Quinlan rubbed at his eyes again. 'It couldn't have come at a worse time. I and my fellow directors have all taken a whacking cut in salary and my own mortgage is in trouble. At the moment we're on interest-only payments and if I don't manage to keep them up, the bank will have it. Stephanie loves that house. If we lose it, I think that'll be the end of our marriage.'

For a moment William wondered about a woman who put property above a marriage. Then reflected that such an attitude didn't say much for the husband, either. 'So you told Jessica you couldn't lend her any money?'

Thomas spread out his hands in a gesture of helplessness. 'I offered her a couple of thousand; there just isn't anything more. We're up to our eyes in debt. We're in the negative equity trap as well and there's no way I can raise extra capital.'

'What about her mother?'

Thomas Quinlan shrugged. 'She died not long ago. She'd been widowed for about ten years. Her second husband left everything in trust for their son so she was well provided with income but there was no capital. She always spent every penny of her income when I knew her so I don't suppose there was much of a nest egg for the girls. Their stepfather left each of them fifteen thousand pounds but I know Jessica blew all hers on a car and some clothes.' He smiled bleakly. 'It was my saving that Audrey managed to remarry so well. I used to pray every night that it would last.'

'Did you have doubts?'

'Well, I heard her husband had a bit of a roving eye. I always wondered whether that was why Jessica was packed off to Paris so quickly.'

William made another note. That suggestion fitted with everything else he had learned so far about Jessica. She'd had the morals of an alley cat. He cast a quick eye over the notes then closed the book and put it in his pocket. As he looked up, he saw Thomas Quinlan's attention had been caught by something at the back of the hall. William turned.

Coming towards them was Maria Russell, her cool, blonde good looks polished and set off by a pale aquamarine linen suit. No trace now of the nervous, tearful girl they'd interviewed immediately after Jessica's body had been discovered. 'Carolyn has sent me to ask if you and your staff require any lunch,' she said to William with icy poise. Then her glance fell on his visitor. Her eyes first widened then hardened.

'Hello, Father,' she said.

Chapter Twenty-One

As Darina drove back to Wiltshire from London the full horror of losing her job took hold.

It had happened to other people, to friends with greater experience and reputation than herself. It was a hazard of the journalistic world. With hard work and careful manoeuvring she could replace the lost weekly stipend with freelance commissions, maybe even improve upon it. Gone, though, was the luxury of not having to worry about the market for the next article, and all the kudos of a regular correspondent's position. Gone too her contact with the readers. Would they miss her?

Her mother would welcome the news, treat it as a heaven-sent opportunity for Darina to concentrate on her marriage. And William, what would he say? Supportive as he always was, wouldn't he also tell her it was a chance for her to slow down?

Should she slow down? Take more time to enjoy being a wife? It wasn't the money that was so important. The trouble was, losing her column was like losing her identity. Without her work she was a lesser person.

Darina glanced at the handbag that contained the note her Uncle George had handed her. Suddenly she was pleased he hadn't told her all about Paul Barry. The note was now a gift for William from her. Nothing tempted her to open it herself.

*

No one was in the Conifers Spa reception hall and Carolyn's office was empty. Darina wandered through to the treatment area, now abandoned by the forensic team, and found that, too, unmanned.

Beginning to feel she was on the *Marie Céleste*, Darina wandered through to the empty kitchen and looked out into the courtyard. There was the police mobile incident centre and there, at least, there seemed to be activity.

But the young female sergeant who answered Darina's knock told her both William and Roger Marks were involved in interviewing and could not be disturbed.

There was an air of subdued excitement about the girl. Darina wondered what it meant; whether the investigation was approaching a breakthrough point. She found she couldn't get as excited about it. She had, she realised, been depending on William to pick her up, bolster her self-esteem, congratulate her on getting hold of a valuable lead. Instead she had to scribble a note and hand it to the girl with the envelope from her uncle, asking that they both be given to William just as soon as possible.

The door to the mobile centre closed and Darina found herself outside with nothing to do.

She went and rang her mother.

Lady Stocks spent some time telling her daughter how much she was enjoying herself and the various plans Molly Creighton had to keep her happy. 'She's got one or two local friends coming to lunch tomorrow. She said she'd love it if you could come too, but I said you were probably far too busy.' There was an expectant pause.

Why not? Darina might just as well lunch with the general's lady and her mother as hang around here.

Lady Stocks said Molly would be delighted and sounded so pleased herself that, once again, Darina found herself feeling guilty. It appeared to take so little to make her mother happy.

She replaced the telephone. Carolyn was probably

down at her cottage; she might well like a friend to chat to.

The weather was cooler than it had been in London. Darina fetched a jacket and started to walk to the staff cottages. The soft greens of the abundant trees and shrubs soothed her jangled spirits. She wished fervently that her stay there could have been uninterrupted; it would have done her mother and her so much good.

What hopes you brought with you to a health farm! Hopes for a better lifestyle, for a more attractive, healthier and better you. Even she, whose life most would consider idyllic, had hoped for an improved figure and, perhaps, more understanding of her mother.

Badly overweight, Maureen and Gina had come expecting a more drastic change. Had they been desperately disappointed at having to leave little different from when they had arrived? Or had they felt their attitudes to eating and exercise had changed sufficiently for them to achieve their ambitions on their own?

And what of Esme; what had she wanted out of Conifers Spa? A chance to relax from the pressures of her professional life – or had there been hopes of deepening her relationship with Frank Borden?

Then there'd been poor Jessica. Starvation-thin as she was, she hadn't come here to lose weight, surely? Relaxation, perhaps? To get away from the financial pressures that threatened her lifestyle? At an expensive establishment somebody else had to pay for? Had Jessica also hoped the visit would bring her closer to Frank Borden?

For the first time Darina wondered whether, if William had met Jessica alive, he would have found her as attractive as so many other men seemed to. Would Darina have joined the ranks of women jealous of Jessica? Was it only because she hadn't been threatened in any way that she felt sympathy for the girl?

Darina had almost reached the end of the drive. As she started to cut across the grass towards the little row of cottages, there came an ugly scream followed by a terrible crash.

Darina broke into a run. The noise had come from Carolyn's cottage at the far end.

'Hey!' said a man's voice, startled, angry and frightened.

Another crash and another scream.

Darina reached the door, panting, tried the handle, found the door unlocked and catapulted herself into the small living room.

Standing in front of the fireplace, holding a coffee table as a shield, was Rick Harris, wearing a T-shirt displaying rippling muscles, his ponytail slipping from its rubber band.

As Darina entered, a glass vase flew across the room. The missile was easily parried by Rick and crashed harmlessly against the table, glass shards joining a collection of broken crockery on the floor around his feet.

Carolyn, her eyes wild, picked up a heavy book from a small table and raised it.

Darina caught her arm. Carolyn twisted in her grip like a maddened animal desperate to get free. Darina, taller by at least five inches and much heavier, found great difficulty in keeping hold of her but finally managed to remove the book.

Rick slowly lowered the table. Then, with a quick, furtive movement, he picked up a pile of papers and slid towards the front door.

'You bastard!' called Carolyn, still wriggling desperately in Darina's grip. 'Don't you dare leave now! We haven't finished.'

'Oh yes we have!' Rick spat out as he eeled his way through the door and out of the house, moving towards a car parked by the front gate to Conifers Spa.

Carolyn tried to pull her arm free to follow him. Darina grabbed her other arm and held her back. 'Let him go,' she urged.

Suddenly the termagant disappeared and Carolyn sagged, all passion and fury spent. If Darina hadn't been holding her, she would surely have collapsed on the floor.

Darina helped her to sit in a chair and picked up a small table that had been upset. Then she surveyed her friend. Tears were pouring down Carolyn's face, long shudders shaking her body.

On a side table was a collection of bottles. Darina went over and poured a good slug of brandy. 'This usually helps,' she said as she gave it to Carolyn.

The girl raised a blotched face, took the glass and gulped down half the contents. 'God, what must you think of me,' she shuddered.

Darina opened cupboards in the kitchen area. She found a dustpan and brush and started to sweep up the broken china and glass.

Carolyn, watching her, drank more brandy, her eyes blinking hard. The tears had been stemmed but she made no attempt to wipe her face.

Darina finished the clearing up, emptied the dustpan, replaced it in the cupboard, then came and sat down. 'Now, tell me just what happened,' she commanded.

It took more than that to get the full story.

At the end Carolyn sagged back in the chair as though totally exhausted. 'What makes me hate myself more than anything is that I could have been such a fool,' she said bitterly. 'At the beginning I really thought I'd found someone special who thought I was pretty special too. After all Robert put me through, it was like springtime, a renewal. I thought everything was going right for me for once: this job, the chance of writing a book, Michael getting on so well at school, and . . .' She stumbled before ending with, 'and Rick.'

'Instead of which you've found getting Conifers Spa going tougher than you thought and that Rick just wanted to use you.' Darina brought her drink back and sat down opposite Carolyn again.

'That bastard! How could I have been such an idiot?'

'Didn't you suspect what sort of man he was when you saw him with Jessica outside the kitchen that day?'

Carolyn ran agitated hands through her hair, forcing the short cut to stand on end. 'He swore there was nothing in it. She was just delighted to see him again; she used to go to his restaurant. That's what he said.'

'And now he's told you that he's having a steamy affair with someone else?'

Carolyn dug out a handkerchief from a pocket and scrubbed at her eyes, some of her composure back in place. 'I thought we were going to have a good session on our book. After all the upset and tragedy of the last couple of days, I was really looking forward to a few quiet hours with him sorting out the recipes. We've had such fun discussing how to cut down animal fats; substitute yoghurt for cream, oil for butter; increase fibre and fruit and vegetable content, all the things I believe in for a healthy diet.' Carolyn paused and a small, cat's smile played around her full mouth. 'And one thing invariably led to another. That man has the most imaginative of minds!'

Darina sighed inwardly. How could Carolyn not have seen the way Rick's eyes caressed any halfway attractive woman?

'He obviously just saw me as a passport to publication, that's what bugs me more than anything,' Carolyn continued bitterly. 'He cooks like a dream but hadn't a clue how to get it down on paper. Now I've taught him all that and he's found someone who can offer him more.'

'Strange, though, not to use you for a little longer,' mused Darina. 'He surely can't think he can get a book together on his own?'

Carolyn shrugged. 'Who knows what that conceited prick thinks.'

'But why tell you now? And who's he involved with anyway?'

Carolyn's eyes narrowed. 'He was up at the Spa the night Jessica Barry was killed.'

'He told you that?'

A satisfied smile lit Carolyn's face. 'The police have found his car's tyre marks under the trees by the side of the drive leading to the back of the kitchen. They called him in to explain what it had been doing there.'

Darina remembered the police tape securing off the little passing place by the side of the drive and the marks she thought she'd seen. 'And?'

'And he said he'd blustered his way through, told them he drove up and down every day, of course his tyre marks were there.'

'But it rained Saturday afternoon, after a long dry spell. Those marks must have been made that evening. And wasn't he off duty that night?'

'God, how could I have been so stupid! He said there was an old friend he wanted to see, asked me if I minded him taking that night off instead of Monday. We didn't have any outside guests booked so I said yes. And all he wanted', she said with corrosive bitterness, 'was to shag his little friend. He must have thought he could put anything over on me.'

'But I still don't understand,' Darina started.

'He told me the police are interviewing Maria again.' Another note of satisfaction in Carolyn's voice. ' "Grilling her," he said. Apparently she's been with them for hours.'

'You mean', said Darina slowly, 'it was Maria Rick met on Saturday evening?' Maria whom Roger and William were interviewing now, who was causing all the excitement?

'Apparently they've been having it off in the men's treatment area.'

Cool, calm, controlled Maria, caught up in a passionate affair with Rick Harris!

'And why Rick actually told me today about their little

affair was because he's handed in his notice. She's offered to back him in a new restaurant.'

'And he thinks she's telling all this to the police?'

Carolyn looked complacent. 'He's terrified! He said he's going to tell them everything before they accuse him of murder.'

'But surely Maria is just as likely to be suspected?'

'More so if Rick's telling the truth when he says she let him out of the back door on the men's side around ten o'clock. So now, on top of everything else, I have to find another chef and another manager for the treatment side!' Carolyn threw the sodden lump of tissue into the wastepaper basket. 'As if I don't have enough on my plate. I had a call this morning to say that investor still hasn't made up his mind whether he's going to back us. Every day that goes by without a decision makes it more likely he's found something else to put his money into.'

'I can understand if he doesn't want to be connected with murder.'

'But he started pulling out before Jessica died.' Carolyn got to her feet and started plumping up cushions with angry fingers. 'If anything I thought her death would simplify things for him.'

'Why on earth should you think that?'

Carolyn fumbled with the cushion she was holding and a flood of dark colour rushed into her face. 'I, I don't know,' she stammered. 'I can't think straight at the moment, I'm saying anything.' She flung the cushion at the small sofa. 'I suppose I meant it should be easy for him to see that all the publicity we are getting is bound to make Conifers Spa a success.' She grabbed the not quite empty whisky glass out of Darina's hand, picked up the one she'd drunk from and plunged them purposefully in the sink.

Chapter Twenty-Two

William and Roger finished their questioning of Maria Russell just before eight o'clock that evening. They came through to where Darina was sitting reading a book in the drawing room. Both were in high good humour.

'Let's go down to the pub for steak and chips,' Roger said to Darina with a broad grin. 'Bill's dying to fill you in on all his success today.' The antagonism she'd sensed in their earlier encounters seemed to have disappeared.

They sat at a back table in the pub's restaurant area, Roger Marks taking up most of one side while Darina and William sat on the other.

'First of all, tell me about the autopsy findings,' demanded Darina.

'Shan't have the full report for a day or so yet.' Roger dug dirt from under a fingernail as he studied the menu. 'But apparently the victim was still alive when she entered the water. Half strangled, knocked out by hitting her head on the tiles, but not dead. She actually drowned.'

'So if she'd been pulled out of the water, she might have lived?' Darina was horrified.

'Possible,' agreed William.

Darina was silent as she thought about the callousness of the murderer in leaving his victim to die at the bottom of the pool.

The two men ordered steaks. Darina brought herself to ask for grilled sole.

While they waited for their food, William gave his

wife a quick résumé of their interviews with Maria and Rick.

'Maria Russell swears she saw the chef out of the men's treatment room at ten o'clock, tidied up after them then went straight back to her cottage and never saw Jessica at all.'

'Do you believe her?' Darina asked.

Roger, his large mouth now full of chips, shook his head. 'It all looks highly suspicious but until we've got more evidence the Crown Prosecutor would laugh us out of court.'

'Even though she concealed the fact that she and Jessica were sisters?'

William helped himself to another roll and added a thick layer of butter. 'She was afraid we'd suspect her motives if she told us they were related.'

'But surely she knew you would find out?'

'If you ask me,' said Roger, the tomato ketchup bottle disappearing into his massive fist as the red paste was blurped liberally over his chips in a way that set Darina's teeth on edge, 'she wasn't thinking at all. Typical woman!'

'And what about Jessica, why didn't she tell anyone she'd found a long-lost sister?' Jessica had spoken of an estranged sister to Darina; why hadn't she added that the sister was here at the health farm? Was she more devious than Darina had so far given her credit for?

'Russell said they'd never had much in common. She told us she'd suggested to her sister when she first arrived that it was embarrassing for both of them to have to admit to being sisters and Barry agreed to keep their relationship secret. Bill, you're in the chair I think.'

William went off to get another round of beers for Roger and himself, Darina having announced she was happy with the remainder of her half pint.

'It must have been a shock for both of them,' Darina mused, watching William's tall figure at the bar. She brought her attention back to the table and, with a slight shock, realised she was consciously avoiding looking at Roger Marks, now fastidiously mopping up smears of ketchup with the last of his chips. With an effort she brought her concentration to focus on the pit-marked face. 'Maria Russell, though, strikes me as equal to most occasions. She's one very cool lady.'

'Cool!' Roger gave a hoot of derisive laughter. 'According to that chef, Harris, she's anything but that. They've been going at it hammer and tongs in that treatment area for the last couple of months.'

'Why there?' Darina ignored the rest of the comment.

'Harris claimed it was Russell's idea; that they didn't have anywhere else. He's rooming with a landlady who doesn't allow "callers" and said Russell's place was out because her boss and Hughes would have known what was going on.'

Darina remembered how clearly the Mozart had come through from the next-door house when William and she were having a glass of wine with Carolyn the evening Jessica died. 'Tell me more about the argument Jim Hughes overheard between Jessica and Maria Russell.'

'Now that did shake Russell,' William said as he put two foaming glasses of the local bitter on the table. 'I thought we had her then. You saw how white she grew?' he asked Roger.

Roger nodded vigorously. 'Reckon there wasn't much love lost between those two. Sisters under the skin they weren't.'

'They didn't even look alike,' Darina commented, mentally comparing Maria Russell's athletic frame with Jessica Barry's anorexic body, the straight blonde hair with the cloud of dark, the still quality of one with the nervous energy of the other. 'And if, as their father claims, they each sided with a different parent over the break-up, it was inevitable they should grow apart. So what was the argument about?'

William slipped back into his seat beside Darina. 'According to Maria Russell, Jessica wanted to borrow money off her. When their stepfather died some ten years ago, he left each of them fifteen thousand pounds. Jessica apparently blew hers but Russell invested in a savings plan that has performed extremely well. It matured this year and Jessica came down to the cottage to ask her sister to lend her the proceeds to stave off bankruptcy proceedings. Russell says she refused.'

'Did Jessica know her sister was working here before she arrived?' Darina asked.

'Russell says no.' Roger caught the eye of the waitress and asked for another plate of chips. 'She claims they were equally surprised to see each other.'

'But Maria must have seen the name on the client list,' Darina objected.

'Thought it was the first Lady Barry, who apparently comes to Conifers Spa for the odd daily session. Lives not far away.'

'Didn't you say that her son, Oliver Barry, had visited her on Saturday night?'

'Spot on, Darina.' For once Roger sounded congratulatory. 'I had his tyre marks checked, could have sworn they would match those under the trees by the drive. Instead we came up with a match for the chef.'

'But you suspect Maria Russell rather than him?'

'Got to, given everything we've learned today,' said William.

'My personal bet, though,' leered Roger across the table, 'is that it's *cherchez l'homme*. Don't you agree, Bill?'

'Well, a widow needing money has to be looking for someone to bankroll her,' William said cheerfully. 'And from all accounts Jessica Barry was lost without a man.'

'That's pretty sweeping,' objected Darina. William in company with Roger Marks was different from her William. Less sensitive, less perceptive, particularly regarding his wife. This evening, for instance, even though they were bringing her up to date with the investigation, she felt like a bit player. It was as though her part was to feed them lines, to give them an opportunity to reinforce already formed opinions. There was no real discussion, no opening of their minds to other possibilities, no suggestion she might have something to offer. 'What about the rumours surrounding Paul Barry? If Jessica really knew something sensational about him, couldn't Oliver Barry have wanted to keep her quiet?'

'A possibility,' agreed William as though she was a small child needing encouragement. 'We're really grateful to you for producing that lead from your uncle. We've got an appointment first thing tomorrow morning with the chap whose name he gave us.' Darina's sense of frustration grew as she realised they weren't going to tell her what had been in the note. 'And we shall be delving further into the backgrounds of Maria Russell and Rick Harris. But gut instinct tells us sexual jealousy is the most likely motive in this case.'

Darina fumed silently. Gut instinct, indeed. If she'd made any such crass comment to William, he'd have jumped on her with a long spiel about success coming from careful police work that investigated every angle!

'Bill's summed up the situation perfectly,' asserted Roger Marks, beaming at the plate of freshly fried chips that was being placed in front of him. He reached for the ketchup. 'Look at the evidence. Her stay was being paid for by Frank Borden—'

'He told you that?'

'Yes, Darina, he told us that. Was quite open about it. Said they'd been friends for many years, that she needed a break and he'd suggested she visit Conifers Spa. Claimed that was all there was to it, but who knows?'

Darina averted her eyes from the blurping ketchup bottle and wondered if she should tell William and Roger about her conversation with Frank Borden that morning. So far it didn't seem to have occurred to either man that she might have had business in London other than visiting her uncle. But Frank hadn't said anything that would alter their perceptions of the case.

'You told us yourself how she was flirting with Harris in the kitchen,' continued William as Roger attacked his fresh chips. 'Other people have confirmed she made a dead set at Cazalet.'

'Would that have given either of them a motive for murder?'

'Come on, Darina!' William sounded astounded. 'Jessica was threatening established relationships in both cases. Relationships that meant not only emotional security but financial as well.'

'You mean you know about Maria Russell wanting to back Rick in his own restaurant?'

'I suppose you were going to mention that to us at some stage?' William sounded huffy. 'And how did you find out anyway?'

'Carolyn told me this afternoon. And, yes, of course I was going to tell you, when I got an opportunity!' Darina heard the exasperation in her voice without regret. How dare William suggest she was holding things back from him! She forgot about her visit to Frank Borden's gallery.

'So you appreciate Harris had a lot to lose if Jessica Barry came between him and Maria Russell.'

'And Perry Cazalet? What makes Gina so valuable to him?'

William grinned, for a moment back to the man she'd married. 'I never thought I'd hear you question a wife's value to her husband!'

That made Darina angrier than ever but she swallowed the hasty words that threatened to spill out as he continued. 'Jessica Barry is not the only one having money troubles. The Cazalets are in deep water too.'

'But Conifers Spa is expensive,' protested Darina. 'How can they afford to stay here if money is so tight?'

'The way Cazalet put it, it was a last-ditch attempt to

get his wife back into shape. A lost cause that, if you ask me; have you ever seen a woman so lacking in shape?'

Darina eyed Roger's over-generous frame. 'There are those who appreciate ample armfuls,' she said pointedly.

'Not me! Curves are one thing, heaps of lard another. Bill agrees with me.' The boiling and bubbling inside Darina threatened to spill over.

'Anyway, according to Cazalet, their visit to Conifers Spa was an investment. It was going to lead to a new career for his wife that would rescue their finances.'

'With the cost allowable against tax, I suppose?' Darina said caustically, then saw that that was exactly it.

'Just as your stay could be,' pointed out her husband. 'The tax man won't quibble provided you make it the subject of one of your columns.'

Darina couldn't put off the evil moment any longer. 'I haven't got a column any more,' she said shortly and forgot her anger in renewed despair and humiliation. She fought to remain calm. 'That's why I went up to town. I thought they wanted to discuss ideas, instead I was told I've been replaced.'

William immediately put a hand over hers. 'Poor darling, I am sorry. That's really rotten for you and dead stupid of them. Who on earth do they think could do a better job?'

Darina gave the name of the leading cookery writer who'd been hired in her place. 'It happens when editors change. They like to imprint their mark on the paper, so out go the established writers,' she said with careful casualness.

'Thought you were supposed to be so famous nobody would dare do that to you!' leered Roger at her. Darina dug her fingernails into her spare hand and managed to say nothing. 'Well, at least Bill will get fed when he gets home at the end of the day now.'

To have responded to that would have reduced Darina to a screaming termagant so she said nothing else for the rest of the meal while the two men gossiped comfortably, seemingly unaware of her silence. Or perhaps they thought she was sulking over the loss of her job.

Back in their room with her husband, Darina demanded, 'Just what did your friend Roger mean by my being able to feed you properly now that I've lost my column? What have you been saying? How dare you discuss our marriage with him! And anyway, aren't I usually there to cook your meals?'

He started to remove his trousers, apparently unmoved by her attack. 'Well, there was that time you were doing the television show in London, you spent half the week up there then.'

'And what about all the times you come back having eaten with "the boys" because of a case and don't want the meal I've prepared; what about them?'

William sat down on the bed and drew off his socks. He was maddeningly calm. 'I only said anything because Roger was going on about Tracy always complaining about his long hours. And how she'd been nagging him for ever about getting promoted because she wanted a larger house. So I just said no marriage was perfect, and that sometimes, just sometimes, mark you, I'd like a wife who was always at home when I got there. I went on to say, though,' William continued without allowing Darina to get a word in, 'that I reckoned I'd be bloody bored if that's the sort of wife I had all the time! I didn't say, which I nearly did, that Roger's trouble was that he was bloody bored with Tracy.'

The remark successfully diverted Darina. 'If that's what you really think, you know nothing about people! Roger wouldn't know what to do with a wife who had an idea in her head beyond the home and the family. He hasn't a clue how to talk to a woman with any intelligence!'

'Nonsense.' William hung his trousers in the electric

press each Conifers Spa room came equipped with. 'He likes you a lot.'

'He thinks I'm an interfering so-and-so,' Darina asserted, 'and that marrying me has ruined your life.'

'Now who's being ridiculous?' William went into the bathroom and started to clean his teeth.

Conversation being impossible, Darina finished undressing in a fine ferment of conflicting emotions. The disappointment over the loss of her column was now almost swallowed up in dismay at William's attitude.

'Anyway,' William came out of the bathroom, his face soap-shiny, 'I don't care what Roger says or thinks and nor should you. I don't want to be married to anyone else no matter how many columns you do or do not write.'

He drew her into his arms and ran his hands down her back, slipping them underneath her silk nightgown, capturing the flesh around her waist. 'Mmmm,' he murmured in her ear, 'a girl with curves, that's what I like.'

Her resentment started to leak away as her treacherous flesh responded to the touch of his hands. She made a weak attempt to resist. 'Wasn't it lumps of lard you didn't like?' she said acidly. 'Aren't I a bit too generously curved for you?'

He deftly drew the nightgown off in one swift movement and dropped it on the floor. 'Now, let's see.' One hand lifted her left breast. 'An ounce over perfection, is it? No, I really don't think so.' The hand slipped slowly down her ribcage to the roll of flesh over her waist. He placed his other hand on the other side. Together they slowly manipulated the fatty tissue and the lids of his eyes closed slightly. 'Without this, I'd feel your bones sticking into me; with it you're soft and warm and comfortable.' The hands slipped round to her buttocks and grasped them firmly, pulling her towards him. 'Something to get hold of here but definitely not an inch too much.' He buried his face in the curve of her neck and

Darina could no longer control her response. Maybe she'd been mistaken about Roger Marks's influence over him. Maybe the case would soon be over and they could go home.

Later, spooned into William, with his arm comfortably around her, Darina lay thinking of nothing very much when her husband said, 'You know what your problem is with Roger?'

Darina murmured something inconclusive.

'You're prejudiced against his size.'

That brought consciousness back with a start. 'I've never heard anything so ridiculous,' spluttered Darina.

His arm tightened. 'Just think about it,' he urged. 'You sat there tonight looking at him as though he was a pig head down in a particularly messy trough. Just because you don't think ketchup on chips is the hautest of dining choices doesn't mean he's a slob.'

'The man's an insensitive oaf.' Darina wriggled away from her husband.

'He's actually a sharp, hardworking, thoroughly decent guy.' William rolled onto his back and lay looking up at the darkened ceiling.

Darina sat up in bed. To accuse her of prejudice against anyone because of their size was an obscenity. 'When I think of the way you talked about Gina Cazalet this evening, I can't believe what you're saying!' she pushed her hair back from her face in a furious gesture and started plaiting it.

'Yup,' admitted William cheerfully, 'it wasn't pretty, I'll give you that. Your generous flesh I like, but Gina has no shape to her at all and I cannot find her attractive. See, I can admit to my prejudices.'

'So can I, when I have them,' retorted Darina. She found an elastic band on the bedside table, used it to secure the end of her plait then turned her back on him. She remained stiff and belligerent when he tried to draw her against him again. She was really quite angry. What a suggestion to make to her!

After a moment, William sighed and turned over, leaving Darina to hype herself up into a state of even greater righteous indignation. That he could call her prejudiced against the fat oaf he called a friend! And that he could call Roger Marks an intelligent detective when he hadn't even the wit to see she might be able to contribute to his investigation!

Chapter Twenty-Three

Esme Lee's chambers were panelled in oak. The sombre gleam of the polished wood was a perfect background for the antique bookcases filled with leatherbound reference books, her large desk, the darkly jewelled Turkish carpet, the red leather chairs. All was heavily traditional, like the old building itself, pickled in legal procedure.

In court Esme wore black to meld with her gown, her white lappets the only touch of lightness. Not even collar, cuffs or shirt of white did she allow. In the office, though, she wore rich silk suits or frocks in singing colours.

Today her A-line dress was peacock blue. Her glossy black hair was wound in its usual chignon, her skin glowed golden from the sunning she had given it at Conifers Spa. She looked, she knew, magnificent. She finished dictating the last sentences of the counsel's opinion she had spent the previous night preparing and told the girl she needed it transcribed by that afternoon. Thank God for word processors, they took all the pain out of producing perfectly typed documents.

The phone on her desk rang to announce her next appointment. Esme told the clerk to bring him in in five minutes. Then she swizzled her chair round so she could see out of the window. The view of green-leaved trees and several people dressed in summer clothes wandering through the grassy area in the centre of the courtyard relaxed her, enabling her to wipe out the previous business, concentrate on what was going to be put before her. The learned barrister whose pupil she had been had taught this. 'Don't ever rush at things,' he'd told her. 'No matter how keen you are, how eager or prepared you feel yourself. Take time to let go of one situation and prepare yourself for the next.'

Because she respected him – one of the few people in the world she did – Esme tried to put into practice what he'd recommended and had found that it did, indeed, help her to concentrate totally on whatever the next matter was.

Down on the grass she saw a middle-aged woman with salt-and-pepper hair. Esme's mother had once had a green and white patterned dress very similar to the one this woman was wearing. Had, in fact, looked remarkably like her.

Her mother had been dead for several years. Esme missed her in many ways, not least because now there was no one who remembered her as an awkward teenager struggling to adjust to a hostile world; too intense to mingle easily with her peers, too chubby to feel happy in a society that seemed only to admire thin people. Esme's mother had put her on a diet, encouraged her by buying her new clothes as she lost weight, applauded the two-stone lighter figure she achieved just before university. Had mourned with her when a disastrous love affair had ended in mammoth bingeing and a figure two sizes larger than she had been before.

More dieting had preceded her marriage to Jeremy, a marriage that had lasted no more than two years before Esme accepted that Jeremy was not prepared to make the concessions that would enable her to fulfil her potential and that, faced with the choice, work was more important to her than he was.

The woman in the green and white dress moved out of sight and Esme concentrated again on clearing her mind of all extraneous thought.

By the time the door opened, she was ready.

Frank Borden entered accompanied by his solicitor,

Peter Mainwaring. Esme knew Mainwaring by reputation but had only worked with him once before, when another of his well-heeled clients had fallen foul of the law. He was a tall, thin figure with carefully brushed back hair and a face that betrayed nothing but well-mannered concern with the matter in hand. His air of detachment covered, Esme knew, a fierce intelligence and an encyclopaedic knowledge of the law.

She shook hands with both men and indicated the comfortable wing chairs on the other side of her desk. Then she settled herself again behind the organised piles of papers tied with pink tape.

Peter Mainwaring opened proceedings by expressing gratitude that Miss Lee should have been able to meet with them so quickly.

'I'm delighted to be able to help a friend if I can,' she said in her well-modulated voice. The interview had, in fact, taken considerable juggling of her schedule by her clerk, who had shown his resentment at having to put off clients he felt had a greater call on her time, but she had insisted and, as always, had finally won. If it had been the male barrister nearest to her in seniority in the chambers who had asked, she knew the clerk wouldn't have questioned the request. The knowledge, as always, irked her: not least because she knew Frank Borden would have been carefully looked over and a possible relationship between them wondered about.

'I've told Peter that I've been fortunate enough to help you with several purchases of antique pieces,' Frank said now. 'And that I am sure you will be able to advise us on the best course of defence in this unfortunate matter.'

Well, that was a remarkably succinct and economical review of their relationship. Esme wondered what Peter Mainwaring made of it. But the solicitor wasn't her main concern.

She sat back and surveyed Frank. For a man who had spent a night in jail, appeared before a magistrate and just been released on bail, he looked remarkably composed and well-groomed. There couldn't have been much time for the shower and shave he had undoubtedly had in his Mayfair apartment before coming here. More remarkable, considering his situation, was the fact that she could see no tension in his face. It was as alert as usual, and the heavy-lidded eyes betrayed nothing of his ordeal. Nor did he show any of the signs she was used to in someone facing trial. No thrumming fingers on the arm of the chair, no twitching of a facial muscle, no jiggling of a foot, no nervous squirming of the body. Frank just sat there as relaxed as if they were still at the health farm.

'Perhaps, Mr Mainwaring, you could fill me in on the exact situation?' Esme suggested.

Peter Mainwaring detailed, in dry, economical language, Frank Borden's predicament. Esme made notes while he talked, using a succession of sharply pointed pencils. Not for her the prestige of a Montblanc pen; she preferred the easy utility of an HB, and her secretary kept a gleaming brass shellcase liberated by Esme's grandfather during the First World War supplied with freshly sharpened examples.

It appeared that for some time the police had had Frank's business under scrutiny. The previous day they had mounted a raid and had uncovered a consignment of heroin hidden in the depths of a couple of classical statues, plaster copies of ancient masterpieces.

'Needless to say,' Peter Mainwaring concluded in his precise voice, 'my client denies all knowledge of the drugs.'

Just that one statement. And from Frank, nothing. No protestations, no outpouring of accusations against others, no denunciation of the police. He just sat there with a look of grave politeness waiting for her counsel.

'Who do you think is responsible, Frank?'

He gave a small shrug of his shoulders. 'As you can

imagine, I spent much of my very uncomfortable night going through the possibilities, but came to no very firm conclusion.'

Esme glanced sharply at him. Frank's expression remained unchanged.

This was a man facing not only imprisonment but the destruction of his reputation and business. Yet he seemed unmoved by his predicament.

Esme began the painstaking business of eliciting the background detail that would underpin the police case: where the statues came from, whether they had been ordered for particular clients, how many others had been received in the past from the same source, what records had been kept of sales, whether it was likely the other statues were available for checking at the homes of their purchasers; the financial state of Frank's business, how this was reflected in his lifestyle, what he knew about the people who worked for him, character witnesses who might be prepared to vouch for him.

During this process, a tiny part of Esme's mind reviewed the time they'd spent together at the health farm.

'One final question,' she said, still writing. 'How much did Lady Barry know about your business?'

She looked up as she spoke and caught the expression that flitted across Frank's face. It was gone almost immediately but she had identified the first sign of unease since he'd arrived in her office.

He recovered smoothly. 'Lady Barry?' he enquired blankly.

'Frank, don't play games with me!' Esme didn't care that Peter Mainwaring was looking at them with open speculation on his well-bred face. 'The police aren't stupid. It won't take them long to pick up the fact that someone who could have been a potential witness to your business dealings has been murdered while you were both staying at Conifers Spa.'

Peter Mainwaring's expression turned to one of concern. 'Why didn't you tell me this?' he demanded.

'It never occurred to me I could be linked in the way that Esme is suggesting,' Frank retorted. 'Indeed, I think it's highly unlikely even the most suspicious of policemen would come to that conclusion.'

She remained silent and mourned the death of their unconsummated relationship.

Esme never mixed business with pleasure. Every client required the best defence she was capable of providing and an emotional involvement could cloud her judgement. Morality wasn't an issue; what mattered, the only thing that mattered, was the law. It was the job of the police to catch criminals and make a case for their prosecution. It was the job of politicians to make the laws under which criminals could be prosecuted. It was the job of lawyers to interpret and impose those laws, and it was the job of twelve jurors good and true to judge whether those laws had been transgressed. The only stage where justice and morality entered was the political. Which was why, in Esme's opinion, politicians should display a proper regard for justice and morality in their lives as well as in parliament.

When Esme had first met Frank she had been intrigued by his evident delight in her company. Men were often attracted by her body but most of them found her uncompromising intelligence too much to take. And Esme had no interest in pretending to be stupider than she was to flatter their *amour propre*. To meet someone like Frank Borden, who openly enjoyed battling with her on an intellectual level, was a rare and precious event.

So she'd fallen in with his suggestion she spend a few days' holiday with him at Conifers Spa; the prospect of regular massage, exercise, swimming and excellent food was as attractive as the idea of seeing more of Frank, and she'd booked in for a full week.

The first few days without him had been fun; she'd enjoyed trying to instil a sense of self-worth into Maureen Channing and Gina Cazalet and she'd looked forward to Frank's arrival with anticipation.

It had been a shock when Jessica Barry had appeared as well, almost flaunting the friendship between them. She'd met her once before, in Frank's gallery. Had seen her run a little finger down his jaw in a flagrantly intimate manner, and had instantly disliked her. And when, in her straightforward way, Esme had asked Frank how Jessica fitted into his life, he'd frozen her out. Forbidden territory, he'd signalled.

So when Jessica had appeared at the health farm, Esme had back-pedalled, refused to give up eating with Maureen to join his table, then watched with grim amusement how Jessica had moved in.

Now there were any number of reasons why she could no longer continue her friendship with Frank Borden.

'Esme,' Frank said with something very like appeal in his voice, 'Jessica wasn't interested in me, any more than I was in her. I admit, years ago we were close, very close. As close as anyone has come since my wife and child died.'

Esme regarded Frank levelly. He had never mentioned a wife and child before. Was this a last-ditch appeal for her sympathy?

His eyes were grim, his face a mask as set and implacable as any she'd seen in his gallery. He seemed to have forgotten the presence of his solicitor. It was as though it was just the two of them in the quiet, panelled room.

'We were very young when we married. Both our families were against it. I was a young tearaway with nothing but a dodgy police record. Her family were Italian, Catholics, and Julia was small and dark, soft and enchanting.' It didn't sound like Frank speaking, this was

239

someone vulnerable. 'But we married despite the opposition and I found a job hefting for a chap with an antiques shop. After a bit he found I had an eye and started sending me to auctions. I began to buy on my own account too, developed an interest in the classical and primitive stuff. Eventually Nigel offered me a partnership but we was too different.' Esme noticed automatically the regression into past patterns of speech. 'I opened my own place and right from the start it was a success. By then we had a daughter, Cecilia. We never had no more kids but it didn't matter, Julia and Cecilia was enough for me.' Frank switched his gaze to the window, his expression remote. 'One day Julia was collecting Cecilia from school and some drunken idiot crashed into her car. Killed instantly, both of them. That was fifteen years ago. No woman has meant anything to me after that.'

Frank brought his gaze back and looked levelly at Esme. 'Jessica was pretty, generous with her affection, fun to take around. But that was all. We had a good time then parted on the best of terms. I made sure she was all right, understand?' Esme did. She wondered briefly how much he'd given her. 'Then a few weeks ago she came to me and said her husband had left her up the Swanee.' Curiously, the more Frank reverted to his background, the more interesting he became to Esme. What a pair they could have made, she thought regretfully; both had fought through against the odds, he against his background, she against her sex and her size.

'I told her I'd done my bit for her, I wasn't going to do no more. I wasn't a well she could come to whenever she was tight for cash. Then I mentioned I was going down to Conifers Spa and she begged me to take her too. Said she knew she'd be able to sort herself out there, said she could get in touch with someone who'd give her everything she'd ever wanted.' Frank gave Esme a helpless smile. 'I couldn't refuse her, it seemed such a small thing. There wasn't a chance of warning you. Then, when I saw your face, I reckoned I'd made a big mistake. But there it was, nothing to be done. You either trusted me or didn't.'

And I didn't, thought Esme bitterly. 'Frank, who was this someone she was going to contact? Did you meet him?'

Before he could answer, Esme's private line rang. It was symptomatic of the turmoil Frank had put her in that she'd forgotten to switch on its answering machine. Apologising to her visitors, she answered curtly.

'Esme?' Gina Cazalet sounded dismayed.

Esme sighed inwardly. 'I'm sorry,' she said as warmly as she could, 'I've got a client, can I ring you back?'

'I need to see you,' Gina cried, her voice sounding wild and distressed.

Gina needed her every bit as much as Frank, Esme realised. But she couldn't split herself in two and Frank, for the moment, had the prior claim. 'I'm sorry, I'm not free at the moment. How about this evening?'

Gina sounded hysterical. 'Perry's left me! He's taken all my songs and left me! It's all because of that girl, Jessica, I know it is!'

'Calm yourself, Gina,' Esme ordered.

'But don't you understand? He killed her, I know he did!'

'What makes you think that?' Esme asked, too sharply.

Gina's voice rose in intensity. 'He didn't come back last night. There was no message and this morning I discovered my folder of songs had gone! Perry was the only one who could have taken them. He hates me, I know it. It's his revenge.'

Across the desk, Peter Mainwaring moved impatiently.

'Look, Gina, I'm sorry, I have to go. Can't we meet

this evening? All right, give me a ring after seven, I should be home by then.'

Esme rang off, apologised again for the interruption and repeated her question. 'Who was he, Frank? This man Jessica believed could solve all her problems?'

Chapter Twenty-Four

That morning Darina found herself in no hurry to get up. William had left just after dawn. He and Roger had driven up to London to pursue their investigation by interviewing the contact her uncle had given them.

It really was their investigation, Darina told herself. She had no right to feel aggrieved she wasn't being considered one of the police team. This was William's career, Roger Marks was his senior officer and if she wasn't careful she'd be jeopardising her husband's future.

Feeling depressed that she hadn't handled matters better the previous evening, Darina showered, put on the one smart outfit she'd brought, the navy dress and jacket she'd worn to London, ready for lunch with Molly Creighton and her mother, then went to find herself some breakfast.

Afterwards she wandered around. The police were busy in the incident centre, Carolyn and her staff were bustling about getting the health farm back to normal after the forensic investigation. Apart from a brief 'good morning,' Carolyn didn't seem to have time for conversation.

No one, in fact, appeared to have time for her. The day was fine and Darina finally decided to take her laptop into the garden and begin work on an outline for a new book. Without her column, she needed to get a project of some sort under way. She had nothing startling or even interesting in mind but she knew that if she could only bring herself to anchor some thoughts in print and work on them, eventually they would start to take a shape that could well turn into a viable idea.

Feeling determined but far from enthusiastic, she found a garden table where she could work in the sun.

By eleven o'clock she had become absorbed in several possibilities for a new cookbook and stopped to ease out her shoulder muscles. She wondered what the chances were of a massage after her luncheon date, then noticed a smart Mercedes coupé coming up the drive. It came to a stop in front of the house.

Out stepped Maureen Channing in the unattractive tracksuit she'd been wearing the first time Darina had seen her, lunching with Esme, on Darina and her mother's first day at Conifers Spa. A large leather handbag dragged down one shoulder. She stood looking uncertainly around her. What on earth was she doing back here? Darina wondered. Could she think the health farm had reopened already? Then Maureen caught sight of her sitting in the garden and waved.

'Oh, thank goodness you're here,' she called, hurrying along the path between the rose bushes. 'I was so afraid you'd have gone or be visiting someone or something. I should have rung but I was so upset I just got in the car and drove! All I could think of was that you'd know what to do.' She panted to a stop and dropped into a chair beside Darina.

'Are you all right, Maureen? Can I get you something to drink?' asked Darina anxiously, eyeing the woman's flushed face and listening to the heavy breathing.

Maureen waved what appeared to be a refusal but seemed unable for the moment to say anything further.

Darina pressed the keys that would save her work then shut down the computer. She had no idea why Maureen had come to see her but it must be something serious if she had driven all the way down from the Midlands. Even in that car the drive must have taken her over two hours.

Gradually Maureen's breathing returned to normal. 'Oh, I'm sorry, I worked myself up into a real state. The nearer I got to here, the sillier my journey seemed. Then, when I caught sight of you, it all rushed over me, I could hardly bring my legs to move!'

'What's happened?'

Maureen took another deep breath, opened her eyes wide, gazed at Darina and said, 'It's Len, you see.'

'Len, your husband?'

Maureen nodded, her pleasant round face screwing itself up painfully. 'Oh, it's so awful, I don't know how to tell you.'

'Nothing's happened to him, has it?'

A vigorous shake of the head. 'There's times when I wish it would! The way he treats me, as though I'm just there to look after him and do what he wants. Well, this time he's gone too far.'

'What exactly is it he's done?'

Maureen opened the big flap on her handbag, fished around in its capacious inside then brought out her hand in a triumphant gesture. 'Look!' she cried. 'Tell me what you think of this!'

Darina took the crumpled ring of elasticated black velvet spangled in silver that had been thrust at her and studied it in bewilderment. 'I'm sorry, Maureen, I don't know what to say!'

Maureen's chubby chin trembled for a moment then her look of puzzlement cleared. 'Of course, you weren't there when Jessica arrived, were you? You only joined us later.'

'Jessica?' Darina said sharply. 'You don't mean you think this was hers?'

'The first time I saw her, her hair was held back in something just like that – only it was black silk. She was complaining that she'd lost her velvet hairband and that the health farm boutique only had very expensive plain ones.'

'Every time I saw her, she had her hair loose.' Darina turned the velvet band in her fingers and remembered the pink ribbon she'd found in the spa pool. 'Where did you find it?'

'Under our bed!' Maureen blurted out.

'Under your bed?' Darina repeated in astonishment.

'Len left early this morning to go up north for the day, said he had to see a Roller someone wants to sell. He's always off somewhere, never tells me anything.' Maureen's hands clutched at her bag and her shoulders tensed as she continued. 'I got out the Hoover and started cleaning. Len hates me to do that, says he pays somebody else to clean the house. Well, I mean, what else am I to do? He's not there and at least it keeps me from eating. I thought I'd give our room a proper clean instead of the lick and promise Betty gives it. I pulled the bed away from the wall, and there it was!'

'You mean you think Jessica was having an affair with *Len*?' Darina exclaimed incredulously as she suddenly realised exactly what Maureen was implying.

'Oh, I know he has women there while I'm away. Saves money taking a hotel room somewhere.' Maureen sounded uncharacteristically vicious.

'But *Jessica*?'

'Well, they had several days while I was here before she turned up.'

'But where would they have met?' Darina tried to get her mind round the seeming unlikelihood of Midlands-based secondhand car-dealer Len Channing getting together with Jessica, Lady Barry.

'Could have been anywhere,' Maureen said fiercely. 'You don't know Len, he gets around. And gets the girls he wants.'

Darina continued studying the silver-spangled velvet as her thoughts glanced around the various possibilities offered by Maureen's extraordinary assumption. 'Why have you brought this to me?' she asked.

Maureen gulped, her eyes wide, the pupils distended. 'It's evidence, isn't it? Shouldn't I give it to the police? Only, only what will Len say?'

'Are you really thinking that Len could have killed Jessica?' This seemed on the surface an even more unlikely proposition than the one that they were having an affair.

'He's got ever such a temper, Len has,' Maureen burst out. 'I mean, when Jessica found I was here, she might have rung him and threatened to tell me unless he gave her some money, or something.'

'Blackmailed him, you mean?'

'Oh, I'm so frightened,' wailed Maureen. 'I thought you'd know what I should do. I mean, you're married to a policeman, aren't you?'

Darina turned the band over in her fingers once more, stretching the elastic, then she plucked a hair from a fold in the velvet. The two women looked at it.

'See,' said Maureen, 'it's dark, just like Jessica's was. I told you.' Her voice rose, threatening hysteria.

'It proves nothing,' Darina said calmly. 'Forensic analysis could tell us one way or the other but unless you've got something more concrete to give them, I don't think the police would be seriously interested.' A vision of Roger Marks dismissing the very idea of Jessica Barry being involved with Len Channing rose before her. 'And they'll be investigating all Jessica's movements before she arrived here. If she was in the Midlands, they'll find something, I'm sure. If someone turns up at your home asking questions, that's the time to decide whether you'll give them this,' she raised the piece of ruffled velvet, 'or not.'

Maureen sat looking at the hair accessory, her mind obviously grappling with everything Darina had said.

Darina put the pretty thing on the table beside her computer. 'Maureen, don't you think if you believe your husband could be blackmailed over an affair, that shows he really cares about you, that he doesn't want you to know?' Even as she said it, Darina wondered whether it could be true. Len sounded a pretty cavalier type of man to her, someone who cared very little for anyone but himself.

Maureen stared at Darina as though this idea was blinding in its novelty.

Darina leaned towards her. 'Why don't you discuss things with Len, tell him how upset he's making you?'

Maureen made a sound somewhere between a sob and a hiccup. 'But what if he says he's going to leave me?'

'If he wanted to do that, wouldn't he have gone by now?'

Maureen gazed blankly at Darina.

'Have you ever talked to him about his affairs?' Darina persisted.

Maureen shook her head. 'I wouldn't dare.'

Her subservient attitude shocked Darina. How could anyone sit back and take the sort of treatment Len was handing out to Maureen? Then she remembered how strongly the woman had reacted to finding the velvet band. 'Perhaps now you will?' she suggested. 'Don't you think he might be being deliberately careless? That, subconsciously, he wants you to confront him?'

'But I wouldn't know what to do without Len!' Maureen gasped, tears beginning to well up in her eyes.

'Then tell him so. Surely it's not worth carrying on the way you have been doing?'

It took some time for Maureen Channing to start believing she might have a part to play in her future happiness and that anything was better than continuing to turn a blind eye to her husband's carryings on. For an hour she alternated between tears and bravado then finally she drew herself up and braced her shoulders. 'You've done me no end of good, Darina. I'm really glad I came. I *will* go back and tell Len what for. Clear the air, I will. We've had some really good times together.

Perhaps he doesn't understand what he's been doing to me. Can I ring you if things don't work out?'

'Ring me anyway, I'll want to know what happens,' Darina assured her. Then she caught a glimpse of her watch. 'Heavens, is that the time? Maureen, I'm so sorry but I've got to leave, I've got a lunch date.'

'And here I've been keeping you chatting on about my silly little problems.' Maureen got up, clutching her handbag. 'You go and get ready, if I leave now, I can call in at my hairdresser on the way back, see if he can fit me in, then I'll look nice for Len when he gets back this evening.' She paused, looked at Darina, then lunged forward and gave her a fervent kiss on the cheek. 'You've done me ever such a lot of good and I'll keep in touch, you can be sure of that.'

Darina watched her large figure pick its way down the path towards her smart car, then picked up the laptop. She took it back to her room and collected her bag, her mind busy with renewed speculation about pink ribbons, black ruffled hairbands, exactly why Jessica had come to Conifers Spa, and who she could have been involved with.

When Darina arrived at Molly Creighton's for luncheon, a smart young man showed her into a drawing room furnished with unassuming but well-chosen antiques and informed her that Lady Creighton would be with her shortly. Waiting for her, looking triumphant, was her mother.

'Darling, how lovely to see you,' she exclaimed as Darina came over and placed a kiss on the soft, fragrant cheek. 'Now, I've got the most marvellous treat for you. Never say I don't try to help you in your detecting adventures!' She stepped back and waited expectantly.

'Ma, what are you on about?'

'Molly's asked Lady Barry to lunch with her

daughter-in-law,' Lady Stocks said, clapping her hands together in excitement. 'There, I knew you'd be pleased!'

For a moment Darina felt lost. Jessica was dead, how could she be coming to lunch? Then she realised. Of course, it was the first Lady Barry! And her daughter-in-law must be married to Oliver Barry.

'I was afraid they'd arrive before you, and I so longed to tell you myself. Now, you are pleased?'

'I think it's wonderful,' Darina assured her mother. She wondered just how one introduced the subject of a divorced husband's murdered second wife at a polite luncheon party.

In the event she didn't have to worry. Lady Barry herself plunged straight into the heart of the matter soon after the pre-luncheon drinks had been served. 'What a friend you are, Molly! We really needed to get away. Veronica's been driven mad by reporters in London. I suggested she came down to me to get away from it all, only to have them turning up on my doorstep as well. Even dead, Paul seems able to turn our lives upside down.'

Eileen Barry was a sensible-looking woman of around sixty, big-boned with short grey hair and a well-bred face. Wearing a comfortable cotton dress, she appeared the epitome of the upper-middle-class Englishwoman who cares little about appearance and everything about decency.

Veronica Barry looked like a dainty unicorn beside a carthorse. Fair hair drawn back under a tortoiseshell Alice band, a plain white long-sleeved shirt tucked into tight-fitting jeans that emphasised her narrow hips and slim legs, she looked fragile and under extreme strain. There were dark shadows under the blue eyes and a mouth that should have been soft was drawn into a tense line. Clinging to her side was Araminta, who, in a high-pitched but steady voice, announced her age to Darina as four and three-quarters. She had all her mother's daintiness; her small figure was dressed in an expensive-looking striped cotton jersey dress with a sailor collar, her blonde hair tied on top of her head, the fine wisps erupting from a pink ribbon as if she were a Yorkshire terrier prepared for the show ring.

As drinks were served, Araminta snuggled into her mother's side on the sofa as though she wanted to disappear. Then Molly Creighton produced a box of toys and suggested Araminta might like to explore what was in there. Encouraged by her mother, the little girl slid off the sofa, pulled first a doll from the box, then a teddy bear; then she found a jigsaw, sat herself on the floor and, with an intent expression, began to try and put the large pieces together.

'I can't think why the press should be that interested,' protested Molly Creighton. 'After all, Jessica Barry was a nobody!'

'She was the widow of an ex-politician and she was murdered; that's enough for them to get digging again into Paul's career,' said Eileen Barry.

'Of course,' commented Ann Stocks, 'they had a field-day when she married your ex-husband. "Whirlwind courtship" was the phrase I remember. How trite journalists are, always a cliché to hand.'

'It's a sort of shorthand,' Eileen said aggressively. 'Puts over a simple idea economically. Never expect your public to have brains, I think is the message.'

'Then there was your ex-husband's resignation from parliament,' Ann Stocks continued, using a vivacious charm to disguise her remorseless pursuit of the Barry story. 'How the press chewed over that. You'd have thought it was a criminal offence to resign a seat.' Darina noted her mother's decision to help her investigate Paul Barry's background with amazement.

'He was, after all, over sixty,' commented Eileen Barry evenly. 'Had he been in industry, no one would have thought it strange he wanted to retire.' Her hand clutched at her gin and tonic.

'Ah, yes,' Ann agreed. 'But no one expects politicians to relinquish power so easily.'

'Power!' snorted Eileen Barry. 'Paul was a back-bencher.'

'But he had been in the government,' Molly Creighton asserted.

'A junior minister in the Foreign Office,' her guest said shortly.

'I always thought it was a shame he lost office when he did,' said Molly. 'I remember admiring a broadcast he did after visiting some refugee camp. He balanced emotion with realism, acknowledged that the public were right to be concerned but pointed out all the difficulties surrounding action. I think even Baz was impressed.'

'Paul always knew how to put things over,' Eileen agreed with a caustic note in her voice.

'Didn't I hear that he was on the point of bankruptcy?' ventured Darina tentatively. 'Don't you have to resign your seat in that case?'

'Whoever told you that?' demanded Eileen.

'I'm not sure. Could I have read it in the papers?' bluffed Darina.

'Paul got all his financial problems sorted out before any press rat got hold of it,' Eileen declared. 'I don't know who your informant was.' But she didn't deny the story.

Veronica bent over and pushed a corner piece unobtrusively into place as her daughter struggled to fit the jigsaw together. When she sat up, her face was blank.

'And how is Baz?' Eileen turned to her hostess and asked decisively. 'I haven't seen him since that tattoo you kindly invited me to. He looked so tired; is he all right?'

Was that revenge for the interest in her former husband's career? wondered Darina.

'He never seems to have an opportunity to relax,' Molly complained. 'He's always on the go, spends his life in a helicopter or an aeroplane. Last Saturday he had to attend some parade or other in Scotland, today he's with Nato and later in the week he's off to Hong Kong.'

'He's done so well,' said Ann Stocks. 'You must be so proud of him!'

'Oh, I am,' murmured Molly. 'In a way, I dread his retirement. He hasn't an idea how to live without a career.'

'Is retirement on the cards?' asked Eileen. 'I thought he was in line for even greater things.'

Molly gave a graceful, deprecating wave of her hand. 'Who knows?'

'Gerald always said Baz would end up as chief of Defence Staff,' Ann announced.

Molly said nothing but it was obvious she felt it would be a natural conclusion to her husband's career.

Lunch was announced and the little party went through to the dining room and a chicken salad enlivened by a tarragon cream sauce mixed with fresh cherries. The food matched the house: good, traditional ingredients mixed with flair and a touch of imagination.

Darina noted that Veronica Barry only picked at the small portion she'd put on her plate and spent most of her time encouraging her daughter to eat, reminding her how much she liked chicken and scraping off the sauce for her.

Conversation centred around the delights and drawbacks of life as a service wife. 'I wish Gerry and I had met while he was still a serving officer,' Ann said with remarkable equanimity. 'I'd love to have acted as his hostess, the way you do for Baz,' she said to Molly. 'But how silly, his first wife was alive then!'

'I think she was quite relieved when Gerald retired. The life can be quite a strain,' Molly said quietly.

Nobody said anything for a moment, then Eileen started a long and involved story concerning the politics of running a local fête.

Dessert was chocolate mousse, which Araminta announced was her favourite.

'I envy you both staying at Conifers Spa,' said Eileen to Darina. 'Whenever I can afford it I have a day there and lunch is always a great treat.'

'Whenever I can afford it' suggested a tight budget, but Darina remembered the daily charge for Conifers Spa and reckoned anyone who could attend there on anything like a regular basis had to be very comfortably off. Which confirmed George's information.

'I'm definitely going there myself,' said Molly. 'I could really do with a top-to-toe day. Baz doesn't say anything but I sometimes suspect he would appreciate a more decorative wife.' She gave a small deprecating laugh that broke her plain, pleasant face into a map of little lines.

'What nonsense you talk, Molly!' said Eileen Barry. 'Baz has far too much good taste to go for surface glamour!' Then, with a sudden realisation she might have been more tactful, added, 'Anyway, you always look wonderful.'

'Thanks.' Molly gave another brief smile. 'But a bit of spit and polish wouldn't do any harm. Clare, my daughter, was telling me only the other day it was time I smartened my image.' She turned to Darina. 'I must try and get you together with Clare; she loves cooking and always cuts out your column. She wants to know when you're doing another television series.'

'I've put forward a couple of ideas that are under discussion,' Darina said matter-of-factly. This was no time to break the news of her lost job.

'Why don't we have coffee in the garden? The weather's warmed up nicely again,' Molly suggested as the meal finished.

Once outside, Eileen wanted to see the garden. Molly eagerly took her and Ann off on a tour, leaving Darina and Veronica drinking their coffee and keeping an eye on Araminta, now happily playing on the grass with a doll from the toy box.

If she and William had a daughter, wondered Darina, would she be a dainty thing like this or large and awkward, as Darina herself had been? She was suddenly quite certain it wouldn't matter; any child of theirs would be wonderful. 'What a sweet daughter you have,' she offered.

'Araminta can't understand why there's all this upset. I haven't been able to bring myself to explain about Jessica's death to her yet. She was so fond of her. How's she going to take it?' It was the longest speech she'd made since she'd arrived.

'Children have a remarkable ability to accept things, even death; much more so than us, sometimes,' Darina said. 'Did you like Jessica?'

Veronica's pale face lightened momentarily. 'Yes, I did. She was so sympathetic.' Darina said nothing and after a moment Veronica added, 'I can't tell you how terrible the divorce was. Oliver was devastated. He's devoted to both his parents but Paul was always his hero.' She stopped abruptly. 'Do you think Lady Creighton would mind if we helped ourselves to more coffee?'

Darina rose and replenished their cups. 'What did you think of your father-in-law?' she asked as she sat down again. 'That's probably rather a rude question when we've only just met but all through lunch I felt there was so much that wasn't being said.'

'You're so right!' Veronica closed her eyes and leant back against the cushioned wooden bench both women were sitting on. 'And it's a relief to talk. Oliver's mother refuses to discuss Paul or the past and Oliver just won't admit . . .'

'Won't admit what?' Darina asked as the sentence remained incomplete.

Veronica looked straight at Darina, her eyes full of turmoil. 'Just how awful his father was.'

Darina took a deep breath. 'How awful was that?'

Veronica got up, walked over to where Araminta was playing and picked up a teddy bear from the box of toys.

The little girl held up the doll she'd been undressing. 'Look, Mummy, she hasn't got any clothes on. She's naughty, isn't she?'

Veronica bent down and kissed her daughter. 'She's lovely, darling, but I think she'll be cold soon if you don't put something on her.' She watched as a dress was dragged over the doll's head. Then, still clutching the teddy bear, she rose and strode back to Darina. 'That's what that fiend has made me do to my daughter. Teach her that nakedness isn't right, that she must never expose her body.'

It took a moment for Darina to grasp what Veronica meant. Then, 'Paul Barry was a paedophile?' she gasped. Suddenly everything made sense. If that was made public there would indeed be scandal!

Veronica looked nervously towards the house but they were sufficiently far away to prevent any possible eavesdropping. 'Eileen went up to their London flat unexpectedly one day and found Paul on the bed with the small child who lived in the flat downstairs. Paul said it was the first time and nothing had happened. The child appeared to think it had been a game. Apparently she was looked after by an au pair she didn't like and had developed a habit of spending time with Paul. Eileen took her back downstairs, put the fear of God into the au pair, then waited to see if anything would happen.'

'You mean, she didn't tell the parents?' Darina couldn't believe it.

Veronica looked even more unhappy. 'I wouldn't have believed it of her either but she told me making an issue of it would harm the child far more than pretending nothing very much had happened.' She clutched the teddy bear to her chest. 'I think it was because her whole life was bound up in Paul. She'd always worked so hard in his constituency, going to all the boring events, doing all the boring jobs, supporting him in every way. I don't think she could bear the thought that his career might be ruined.'

'But she divorced him?'

Veronica sat down with Darina again, her eyelids fluttering rapidly. 'Not then. Paul convinced her it had been an isolated incident, that he depended on her to keep him on the straight and narrow.'

'But she couldn't?'

Veronica shook her head violently. 'Neither Oliver nor I knew anything about what had happened; Eileen hid it from everybody. But shortly afterwards I borrowed the flat for a few days while Paul and Eileen were abroad. We were living in Sussex then and trying to find a house in London. I was hanging something up in the wardrobe, one of those old-fashioned kinds, not a built-in job, and an earring came off and disappeared down a crack in the bottom. When I tried to lever it out, a whole plank came up and I found a sort of secret hiding place.' She clutched the teddy bear more tightly. 'It was filled with the most dreadful things,' she whispered.

Darina watched Araminta as she carefully drew a pair of knickers onto the doll then added a coat.

'I didn't believe anyone was allowed to publish magazines like that. All those children! All those horrible, horrible photos! Then a whole load of photographs fell out of one of the magazines. I shouldn't have looked at them. I didn't want to look at them but I couldn't stop myself.'

'Your father-in-law was in them?' Darina asked, appalled.

Veronica nodded, unable to say more.

'How absolutely dreadful!' Darina couldn't imagine what it would do to someone to discover their father-in-law was a paedophile. 'What did you do?'

'I showed them to Oliver when he came back that night. I've never seen him so upset. But he refused to accept his father was involved. He said that obviously

Paul had been amassing evidence to uncover some paedophile ring. I told him to look at the photographs.' Veronica fell silent again. 'I don't think our marriage has ever really recovered from that moment. I said we had to show Eileen. He said no. He'd speak to his father, but we must destroy everything. I said his mother had to know, it was only fair, and that if he didn't tell her, I would.'

'So he did?'

Veronica nodded. 'After they came back from holiday. I, I said I wanted to be there. I wish I hadn't. But I thought Paul might somehow persuade Oliver everything was all right, he was always such a smooth bastard!' There was a vicious note in her voice. 'But as soon as Oliver produced the magazines and the photographs, his father just crumpled. That was when Eileen said she couldn't take any more and divorced him. But I realised she had known something of what Paul was and that shook me. I mean, that she hadn't said anything. She must have known—' Veronica stopped abruptly.

'That Araminta was at risk?'

Veronica nodded, a violent movement that sent her fair hair flying out. 'I mean, he'd been alone with her countless times. I hadn't even thought! You don't, do you, not with your father-in-law!'

'You never suspected anything?'

Veronica looked towards her daughter. But Araminta had wandered off. Her little figure, humping the doll under one arm, was walking down the lawn towards where Eileen could be seen in the far distance pointing out features to her two guests. Araminta was well out of earshot. Veronica relaxed slightly. 'No, thank God. But after the divorce I came into the garden one day, we'd moved up to London by then, and he was there. Paul. With Araminta. It was the summer recess and I don't think he knew what to do with himself. He was always turning up unexpectedly. I hated it, I tried to make Oliver forbid him coming to the house but Oliver wouldn't. He said his father was reformed and we should help him not banish him.' Veronica hit the teddy bear with a clenched fist, a powerful jab that betrayed all her inner tension. 'He never understood what his father was!'

After a moment she continued. 'Well, that day was very hot and Araminta had taken off all her clothes, you know, the way children will, and was playing in her paddling pool.' She shivered. 'I can't describe the look on his face. I lost my cool. I shouted at Araminta to go inside, to go up to her room, then I lammed into Paul. I didn't care who could hear me, I just screamed at him to leave my child alone. Finally he dragged me into the house. He was quite frantic – and excited.' Her voice was high and full of disgust. 'He began pawing me, telling me how he'd always wanted me. That I mustn't blame him when I made myself so exciting. Exciting!' Her voice dropped wearily. 'I was wearing a pair of shorts and a very ordinary blouse I'd had for years.'

Darina looked at the Alice band, at the jeans and the white shirt that made Veronica look about fourteen and thought of her in the grip of a powerful older man with somewhere a frightened child in the same house. She must have been desperate. 'What happened? Did you manage to fight him off?'

The round blue eyes were suddenly bleak. 'Yes, thank God. I'm much stronger than I look and I'd taken some self-defence classes. Paul wasn't in good condition at all, so it wasn't too difficult. Then he broke down, apologising again and again and begged me not to tell Oliver what had happened.' She sighed deeply. 'In the end I didn't, not to spare Paul but because I thought Oliver couldn't have taken knowing what his father had tried to do. But I told Paul he was never to call on us like that again. That I'd only see him if Oliver was there. A few weeks later he announced his engagement to Jessica and before we had time to take it in, they were married.'

'Did you try to warn her at all?'

Veronica buried her face in the teddy bear's soft stomach. 'I wanted to.' Her voice was muffled. 'I told Oliver I was going to.' She raised a stricken face. 'He made me promise I wouldn't. He said Paul had told him this marriage was going to save him from himself.'

'And did it? Save Paul from himself?'

Veronica shrugged hopelessly. 'I don't know. When they were first married Jessica was so effervescent and bubbly and she seemed to adore Paul. And I thought maybe, just maybe, things were going to turn out all right. Then Paul resigned from parliament.'

'Why?'

'Eileen and I reckoned the government must have found out something. Paul would never have gone on his own. It had to have been that because they'd have done anything to avoid a by-election. They lost the seat, of course, and he was branded a traitor to his party.' The lines on Veronica's forehead deepened. 'But Eileen said that the scandal if everything had come out would have been even worse.'

'Poor Jessica,' said Darina.

Veronica gently caressed the teddy bear. Her brief moment of extreme anger had faded but Darina noticed a small tear in the bear's fur where she'd hit it. 'Yes, after Paul resigned she got quieter and quieter. I didn't envy her, having him home every day, without a job or anything. Oliver and Paul developed the habit of lunching together every fortnight and Jessica would come and eat with me and Araminta. That's when I really got to know her.' Veronica's finger began playing with the tear in the bear's fur. She looked at Darina, the emotion gone from her face as though it had all been more than she could handle. 'She told me one day she'd only fallen for Paul because he reminded her of someone else. Someone who'd been the great love of her life.'

Darina felt a leap of interest. Could Paul have reminded Jessica of Frank, for instance? Had he been the great love of her life? Had she been trying to get him back during their stay at Conifers Spa and proved too much of a nuisance? 'Did she tell you who he was, and why she'd lost him?'

Veronica shook her head. 'I was dying to know but she clammed right up. Jessica was like that, she'd come out with something interesting with that air of importance she so often put on, then it was as if she suddenly saw it might lead somewhere she didn't want to go and she'd freeze off any further discussion, change the subject. People who didn't know her thought her a party girl, all laughs and flirtations. But she wasn't like that at all really.'

'What was she like?'

Veronica's nose wrinkled as she thought a little. 'I think she was a romantic; she wanted to be the object of a great passion and she was prepared to work hard at making the man who adored her happy. But I don't think she knew how to love anyone properly.'

That made Darina as interested in Veronica as in Jessica. 'Do you think she knew about your father-in-law's sexual proclivities?'

Veronica sighed. 'I think she must have done. I never talked to her about it. I couldn't. But she lost so much of her bounce and bubble.' Veronica's finger worked itself further into the bear's body and a small piece of foam stuffing escaped the fur.

'And you reckoned she was having marital problems?'

Another piece of stuffing fell to the ground. 'Well, it was about then that money started being a real problem for them as well.'

'Money?'

'You see, after Paul stopped being an MP, he couldn't seem to get any kind of a job.'

Strange, so many ex-MPs made a generous living out of lucrative City directorships and consultancy posts. Had word got around that Barry 'wasn't quite sound'?

JANET LAURENCE

'What about the money he'd made from selling his firm?'

'Oh, that was all Eileen's. It had been her family firm. I think Paul got something out of it but I don't think it was much, and he bought that expensive flat and Jessica was always showing off new clothes and jewellery.'

'She liked a good lifestyle?'

'I'll say!'

If Jessica had married Sir Paul Barry for wealth and position, she'd certainly had her come-uppance. 'Did she talk to you about it?'

'A bit. I, well, I said she should leave him. He was taking everything out on her. Even hitting her! She had some awful bruises that she always said were because she'd fallen.' Veronica gave an absentminded little tug to one of her shirtsleeves.

'Did she think about leaving him?'

Veronica shook her head. 'She said she'd married him and she was sure he'd find a job soon. Said he needed to recover his dignity.' The frown lines between her eyes deepened. 'I just wish Oliver had liked her better. That he could have seen she was all that was keeping his father together. Paul was going downhill so fast, it was pathetic.'

'He had a heart attack, didn't he?'

Veronica nodded. 'In the underground of all places. They took him to hospital but he was dead before he got there. The police told Jessica and she told Oliver.' More foam stuffing floated out of the bear as Veronica's finger dug ever deeper into its insides.

Darina wondered. In many ways Jessica resembled Veronica. Had Oliver been attracted to Jessica, maybe subconsciously? He wouldn't have been the first man to find a stepmother sexually attractive. Easy to turn such a dangerous emotion into hate. Easy, also, when your father had toppled from his pedestal, to transfer your disgust and anger to someone else. What an explosive mix

262

of emotions that could be! Darina eyed the long sleeves of Veronica's shirt.

The bear was suddenly cast aside as Veronica's face broke up. 'I don't know what to do!' she wailed. 'It's as if we can't ever get rid of Paul or Jessica! The police keep coming round. Oliver won't talk to me and I'm terrified he's going to be arrested.'

'Arrested, Oliver?' Unobserved, the garden touring party had returned with Araminta trailing behind them, her hands full of daisies, the doll discarded somewhere. Eileen clutched at her throat. 'But why?'

Veronica looked at her mother-in-law, her face white and set. 'For Jessica's murder,' she whispered.

'Now, I'm sure Veronica's just upset,' said Molly, easing her guest into a chair. 'It can't be easy having both police and press hounding you.'

Araminta started to cry and ran to her mother. Darina watched the way Veronica picked her up, held her safely on her lap, told her not to worry, it was only a grown-ups' discussion, and kissed her neck, burying her face in the tender curve of the child's throat and shoulder. Did she believe her husband capable of killing Jessica?

'Anyway,' Ann Stocks said, taking round cups of cold coffee that Molly had absentmindedly poured out, 'wasn't he with you on that Saturday night?'

Darina looked at her mother with a certain admiration.

'Why don't you find your dolly,' Veronica said to her daughter, 'and show me what you've dressed her in.'

After a moment's hesitation, Araminta slipped to the ground and ran off down the garden. Veronica looked at her mother-in-law. 'Oliver visited you that evening, didn't he? When did he leave?'

'About nine thirty. What time did he get back to London?'

Veronica's eyes flickered. 'I don't know! I went to bed

263

early with a sleeping pill.' Was that really what happened? Or was she covering up for her husband?

Eileen's lips compressed firmly together and she said nothing.

'I think not having a proper alibi is reassuring,' Molly said robustly. 'Much more suspicious if he could account for every minute of his time. I'm sure everything will get sorted out quite soon.' She tried to move the conversation on to other areas but it wasn't long before Eileen announced it was time for them to leave.

Molly Creighton accompanied her guests to the parking area. Darina watched little Araminta trotting beside her mother, holding her hand, her high voice excitedly relating something she'd seen at the bottom of the garden, the little legs giving an odd skip every now and then as she kept up with the brisk pace Eileen set.

'Well!' said Ann Stocks dramatically as they moved out of earshot. 'Never say I'm no help in your investigations.'

Darina acknowledged that all sorts of interesting details had come to light. She was dying to leave so she could think about them all, but her mother quite obviously wanted her to stay a little longer.

Molly Creighton returned. 'Poor things, I do feel for them both. I never knew Paul, we only met Eileen when we were posted here, which was after the divorce. She's never said much but I don't think life has been easy for her. And sweet little Veronica, fancy having your husband suspected of murder like that. It can't help that she doesn't know when he got back that night.'

'Come on, Molly,' objected Ann. 'Who was it who said alibis are suspicious? I bet you don't have one for Saturday night?'

'Why on earth should I?' Molly was genuinely startled.

'Well, you and Baz came to Conifers Spa on Friday night. Surely the police will be checking everyone who could have met Jessica there?' Ann appealed to her daughter.

'Well,' Darina began uncertainly, 'I suppose they have to cover every possibility, however unlikely.'

'There you are!' Ann exclaimed triumphantly. 'Now, have *you* got an unbreakable alibi?'

'I have, actually,' Molly said evenly. 'As I said, Baz had gone to Scotland, he wasn't due back until late, so I went over to Clare and spent the night with her and the babies. And Baz's driver', she added firmly, 'would know exactly what time he got back.'

The smart young officer who'd shown Darina into the living room on her arrival appeared from the house. 'The police, my lady, have called to see the general. I've explained he's away until tonight and they'd like to talk to you,' he said. Everyone looked towards the house where, hovering in the french window, were Roger Marks and William.

Chapter Twenty-Five

'Police?' Molly Creighton said, her voice blank. The general's lady turned to her guests. 'I'm so sorry to have to leave you but I think I should see what they want, don't you?' Without noticeable haste, she disappeared into the house.

Ann's face was white. 'I said it as a joke!' she whispered. 'I should never have started on that business of where Oliver Barry was on Saturday night. I only wanted to help you,' she wailed to Darina. 'I never thought . . .' Whatever it was she never thought she left hanging in the air.

'Ma, it's nothing to do with anything you said. And whatever the query is, I'm sure it'll soon be sorted out. Neither Molly nor Baz could have had anything to do with Jessica's death.'

Her mother's face worked, the soft, paper-fine skin creasing into lines that grouped and regrouped themselves, adding years to her age. She reached out a hand and eased herself into one of the garden chairs. 'Are you sure?' she asked.

Darina regretted her facile words. 'How can I be?' she asked helplessly. 'I only know what you've told me about them.' She sat down beside her mother. 'But when they dined with us on Friday, they must have seen Jessica and she them. If they'd met her before, either of them, someone would have said something.'

But had they seen each other? Darina remembered back. Jessica and Frank hadn't been in the dining room, she was sure. Then she suddenly had a clear mental picture of them coming into the drawing room, just as Gina and Perry had crossed the room to say hello to Molly and Baz. They'd been directly in the sightlines of Darina and her mother's guests. So surely the Creightons must have seen them? Darina sat in silence, concentrating on that mental picture she had of the moment.

'Of course, dear.' Ann seemed somewhat reassured. 'What a nuisance of herself that girl does seem to have made.' Her hands unlaced their stiffness and smoothed down her skirt. She looked at her daughter with a smile that was still uncertain. 'Trust me to jump to the worst of conclusions! Perhaps you inherit your talent for getting involved in all these investigations from me.'

Darina looked towards the house. No sign of her husband, Roger or her hostess. 'Perhaps I should go,' she murmured, not wanting to at all but conscious her hostess would probably prefer to be alone with Ann after the police had finished.

'No!' her mother's hand shot out and grasped hers in an astonishingly strong grip. 'You can't leave me all by myself, wondering what's going on in there. And it would be rude to Molly,' she added. 'Do let me show you what she has done with the water garden.' As though she was incapable of sitting still a moment longer, Ann rose and led the way down the long lawn to where a stream ran.

Darina followed, listening with half an ear to her mother's description of water-loving plants that were a picture in April and automatically admiring leaves that were a triumph of nature's architectural talents. Her mind, though, was back with Friday night. There was something about that encounter with the Cazalets that teased at her. Something she couldn't bring into focus.

Ann exhausted the interest of the water garden and led Darina back by a different path that brought them round to the front of the house.

Roger and William were just being seen out by the aide.

'Darling!' William came towards her. 'I had no idea you were here!' No, he had been so bound up in his investigation he hadn't bothered to ask her what she would be doing that day with no column to write!

'Well, well, well! The luscious Mrs Pigram!' Roger lumbered over to them behind William. 'Can't go any-where in this case without tripping up over you, can we?' That gave Darina a surge of childish satisfaction that almost immediately left her feeling discomforted.

She introduced Roger to her mother and watched with grim amusement Ann's normal social skills almost desert her as disgust at the enormous beer gut and badly fitting suit fought with politeness.

'I trust you've finished your business here?' Ann said to her son-in-law.

The way he hesitated for a brief moment brought Darina's heart into her mouth. 'As soon as we can have a word with the general, I'm sure we will have,' he said smoothly.

'I can't think why you're bothering with all this,' Ann said fretfully. 'Baz and Molly can have had nothing to do with that awful girl's death.'

'Come on, Bill, we need to get back,' Roger said with brutal impatience.

'You take the car, Roger, I'll hitch a lift with Darina,' William said.

For a moment Darina thought the superintendent was going to object. Then he half raised a massive hand in a brief acknowledgement. 'I'll see you back at the incident centre then, Bill.' The unspoken implication was that there wouldn't be any delay.

'Be right behind you, Rog,' William said reassuringly.

The senior policeman got into their official car and left.

'I'm sorry about all this,' William said to his mother-in-law. 'I know how distressing it must be for you and Lady Creighton.'

'You have your job to do,' said Molly Creighton, arriving out of the house.

William turned to her, his manner warm but reserved. 'I'm sorry, we seem doomed to meet under the very worst of circumstances, first at Gerry's funeral and now in my official capacity.'

Molly gave him a little nod that offered nothing.

'Molly, dear, wouldn't you like me to leave with Darina?' asked Ann, slipping her arm through her hostess's.

'I'd hate it if you did. Is it asking too much for you to stay? Baz won't be back until late and I really can't stand the thought of being on my own.'

Ann squeezed her arm. 'Of course I'll stay.'

Darina knew a departure cue when she saw one, thanked Lady Creighton warmly for the lunch and opened her car door. A moment later she and William were driving away.

'Please, just what was all that about?' she asked William when they were out of sight of the house.

'We had a call from that antiques dealer, Frank Borden,' he said, settling himself comfortably into the passenger seat and turning slightly so he could see his wife's face.

'Good heavens!' A conjunction between the antiques dealer and the general was the last thing Darina had imagined.

'There was a tiny little detail, he said, that he'd omitted to tell us during the statement we took from him on Sunday.'

'And?'

'Apparently Jessica Barry told him she was particularly keen on coming to Conifers Spa because there was someone living near there she wanted to get in touch with. The way Borden put it was that it was someone she'd once been very close to.'

'General Sir Basil Creighton,' Darina said fatalistically. She eased up on the accelerator as they approached a slow-moving lorry and thought about the general's charismatic personality. Yes, she could understand him attracting Jessica. But could he really have fallen for her not-very-intelligent girlish charms? When he was married to the sterling Molly? Then she remembered her hostess's plain face as she confessed she thought her husband would appreciate a more decorative wife.

'According to Borden, Jessica claimed Basil Creighton was the person who could rescue her from the mess she was in. One call to him and everything would be all right. But Borden says that by Friday night she still hadn't managed to make contact with him. They had dinner together outside the health farm and when they came back Jessica was saying she was going to try the general again that evening, when there he was in the drawing room! With his wife, you and your mother. Apparently Jessica dug her nails so hard into Borden's arm he thought they were going to meet through the flesh. But she said nothing until your little party left the room. Then she leaned across to him with a face as white as a sheet and told him who Creighton was.'

Now Darina remembered what had been troubling her earlier. It had been the general's discomfiture as the Cazalets came over to meet him. At the time she'd put it down to something that had happened between him and the musicians when they'd performed for the army dance he'd organised all those years ago. But if that had been the moment he'd seen Jessica – she pushed the thought away.

'I can't believe Baz would get involved with someone like Jessica Barry! But he did go back into the house as they were on the point of leaving. He said he'd forgotten his diary.'

'But it could have been an excuse to have a word with Jessica, you mean?'

Darina nodded miserably.

'Ah, you've come round to our assessment of her at last,' William commented with a grunt of satisfaction.

'No,' she said sharply and realised how much she didn't want to have to agree with any opinion of Roger Marks's. 'It's not that! Frank Borden doesn't strike me as the sort of man who'd pay for a girl to stay at Conifers Spa if she was trying to get involved with someone else.'

'Too possessive, even of someone who was no longer a girlfriend?' William asked interestedly.

Darina saw an opportunity to overtake the lorry they were following and put her foot down.

'According to Borden,' William said, 'he asked Jessica to have dinner with him again on Saturday evening but she refused, said she wanted an early night. When he asked if she'd managed to speak to the general yet, she just smiled and said nothing.'

'Leaving him with the impression she was going to meet Baz?' Darina swung back onto the right side of the road, comfortably ahead of the lorry, and eased her speed, her mind busy with the implications of what she'd heard, happy that she and William appeared able to work together again. 'Jessica must have spoken to Baz on Friday evening. Molly said he spent the whole of Saturday flying up and down from Scotland so she couldn't have got in touch with him then. Do you think Baz came over to Conifers Spa after he got back on Saturday evening?' Darina hated the thought of Basil Creighton having anything to do with Jessica.

'Borden said Jessica left the drawing room shortly after you lot and that she looked flushed and happy on her return. But all she said she'd done was go to the loo.'

'And Frank Borden said nothing about this before?' Darina asked incredulously.

'Said it had completely slipped his mind.'

'That man's mind is like a strip of velcro, it only loses things it wants to,' asserted Darina, slowing down as they approached a main road.

Her husband looked at her curiously. 'I thought you hadn't had much to do with him.'

Darina said nothing as she remembered she still hadn't told him about her visit to Lost Horizons. It seemed now like a betrayal of her and William's relationship.

'Just as well, because his feat of memory could have something to do with the fact he was arrested yesterday for drug smuggling.'

'No!'

'The drug squad have apparently had him in their sights for some time and finally, at lunchtime yesterday, they swooped down on his gallery, just after a newly arrived consignment of so-called classical plaster statues had been unloaded.'

'And?' Darina found a gap in the traffic and joined the main road, thinking that must have been just after she left the gallery. Now did not seem the moment to tell William about her visit. It wasn't as if she'd learned anything positive during her conversation with Frank. Nothing that William and Roger wouldn't have found out already.

'Nestling within some of the statues, like one Chinese ball within another, was enough heroin to keep half London's drug merchants busy for the next three months.'

It shocked Darina. And yet was the news totally unexpected? Frank Borden was charming, undoubtedly, but there was that streetwise quality about him, slightly dangerous, unsettling. Still, drug dealing! Darina forced herself to concentrate on her driving but her mind ran rapidly through her various encounters with Frank, trying to see whether there was anything that could bring this development into focus.

'He appeared before a magistrate this morning, denied everything,' William went on, fishing about in the

DIET FOR DEATH

glove compartment for the box of boiled sweets Darina always kept there. 'He's now out on bail. It was a whacking one, too, but he seemed to have no difficulty putting up the necessary guarantees.' Darina refused the sweet he offered her. He popped it in his own mouth.

'You think he's guilty?'

'Drugs reckon they've put together a pretty good case.' The words came out blurred around the sweet.

A fragment of conversation came back to Darina. 'I don't know if it means anything, but I overheard him in the next-door massage cubicle one morning. He was on his mobile telephone and it sounded as though he was talking to someone about a shipment that had been impounded. Someone called Archimedes had been given money; it must have been a bribe because he obviously should have prevented this happening but hadn't. Oh, yes, and Frank asked, "Can we distance ourselves?" Sorry, it all sounds pretty vague but he didn't say much. Careful in case he was overheard, perhaps?' Darina gave William a quick glance. 'He was pretty sharp with the caller, told him to get it sorted.' She gave a slight shiver. 'I remember thinking the person on the other end of the phone must have been glad he hadn't to tell Frank whatever it was in person.'

'Hmm.' William sucked on his sweet, his face concentrated as he considered the facts he had. 'How much do you think Jessica Barry knew about Frank Borden's business? He admits they were very close at one time.'

'You mean, could she have been a witness for the prosecution?' Darina's foot automatically increased their speed as her mind moved into a higher gear. This was a totally new way of looking at the case, opened up fresh possibilities.

'Exactly. It could have suited Borden very well for her to disappear from the scene.'

'But he didn't know he was going to be arrested! And how do you know what that bit of conversation referred

273

to? It could easily have been a perfectly innocent antique piece!' Darina saw the speed indicator race towards ninety miles an hour and eased her foot up. The last thing she needed now was a summons for speeding.

'Didn't you say Borden had asked if he couldn't distance himself?' William argued. 'As for the rest of the conversation, the chap in Drugs who was filling us in on the case was seething with indignation. Apparently the Greek police, despite all the co-operation our lot thought had been established through Interpol, had taken it into their heads to start investigating the next shipment of classical reproductions, because they had information it could contain some genuine antiques that were being illegally exported. So, just when we were polishing off the final details of our swoop, Borden gets alerted to official interest in his activities! I tell you the fax lines were burning with all the messages flying back and forth before they got it sorted out and the Greeks agreed to release the shipment. That was on Sunday.'

'Who is Archimedes?'

'The police officer in charge of the Greek swoop.' William took another sweet. 'I'd better get back on to Drugs. If he's taking backhanders from Borden, he might have impounded the shipment to try and squeeze more money out of him.' William got out his mobile phone and put a call through to his contact in the London Metropolitan Drugs Division.

'He may want to take a statement from you,' William said after he'd cleared the line. 'That snippet could be very helpful.'

'So, let's get this clear. You think Frank remembered all this about Baz Creighton as a diversionary tactic? Because otherwise you might think Jessica knew enough to become a witness for the prosecution and had been killed for that reason?'

'You catch on quickly, my darling.'

'And you are devious!'

'Which would you prefer to cast as murderer? Frank Borden or General Creighton?'

'Not a contest.' Darina took the turning off the main road for Conifers Spa. 'So your and Roger's visit today was to confirm just where Baz was on Saturday evening?'

'His movements have to be investigated. At the moment, though, my money's on Frank Borden. He's engaged Esme Lee to defend him. She could well have put him up to ringing us. That's one smart lady. She's frustrated more of the Crown Prosecution's cases than I care to think about.'

'Esme?'

'Yup. Getting interesting, isn't it? Especially once you start wondering if Jessica Barry hadn't suggested to Frank Borden that if she was to keep her mouth shut about his activities, she'd need money.'

'Talking about blackmail, what about Oliver Barry? Surely he fits into the murder frame just as well as Frank, if not better? Did you learn anything from Uncle George's contact about Paul Barry?'

William fiddled with the seat control, lowering the back a little so his legs could stretch out more comfortably. The manoeuvre meant that he didn't have to look at Darina. 'I'm afraid what he had to say to us is so confidential I can't tell even you.'

'That's all right,' she said smugly, slowing down as she approached the village just before the health farm. 'I know all about it.' She repeated Veronica Barry's story.

'Bloody hell! How on earth did you find that out?' William's consternation was not entirely admiring.

'I have my sources.' She told him about her fellow luncheon guests. 'Veronica Barry is at the end of her tether. I'm sure if you speak to her she'll spill the whole story. Well, does that agree with what you learned this morning?'

'More or less. According to the politician we saw, the prime minister was sent a letter by the father of one of

275

his victims accusing Paul Barry of being unfit to be an MP. The man stated he didn't want to go to the police because he wanted to protect his son from what would follow.'

'His son?' Darina found there were still aspects of the story that could shock her.

'Son,' William repeated. 'But he wanted to make quite sure that Barry lost his career. If Barry resigned from parliament, he wouldn't take matters further. If he didn't, then, no matter what his son suffered, he'd report him to the police. Well, according to our informant, that did it for Barry. He was left no option but to resign. Everyone, of course, has been most careful not to let a hint get out to the papers. You can imagine what a field-day they'd have with it.'

'Is that why the bankruptcy rumour was started, as a smokescreen?'

'Oh, Barry was definitely in financial difficulties and it was convenient to allow fellow MPs to think that was why he was standing down.'

Darina drew to a full stop at a crossing in the centre of the village to allow pedestrians right of way. 'So both politicians and Sir Paul's family have carefully kept the wider public ignorant of his sexual proclivities, not to mention his criminal activities. And then along comes little Jessica and threatens to blow the whole gaff!'

'I imagine Oliver Barry had a lot to talk about with his mother that night!'

'And you still don't suspect him of murder?'

'I didn't say that,' protested William.

Darina let the car clutch out as the crossing cleared. 'So have you got a case against him?'

'He can't account for his movements after he left his mother's at nine thirty on Saturday night. It wouldn't have taken more than thirty minutes to drive to Conifers Spa and he could very well have made arrangements to meet Jessica.'

'Veronica's afraid of her husband,' Darina said slowly.

'Which means?'

'I don't know about murder but Oliver Barry is quite capable of hitting a woman. It was hot this afternoon but Veronica never rolled up her sleeves.'

'Hiding bruises, you mean?'

'And Araminta is very sensitive to changes in atmosphere. As soon as she heard her mother getting upset about Oliver being suspected of murder, she ran crying to her.'

'You think she's used to hearing arguments and her mother getting hit?'

Darina nodded as she turned into the Conifers Spa drive.

William got out his notebook and scribbled in it.

'So don't you think this means any case against Baz Creighton's pretty thin?' Darina pressed. 'I mean, look, perhaps he and Jessica did have an affair at some stage and perhaps she wanted to start the whole thing up again. He might even have been tempted,' she added reluctantly. 'Though any man who'd prefer a girl like Jessica to a wife like Molly needs his head examined. But that's hardly a motive for murder.'

'Jessica could have threatened to go to the press about their affair, if it was one,' said William.

Darina considered the unpalatable possibility, determined not to be blinded by prejudice. 'Would they have been interested? An affair that had been over for three years? Hardly earth-shattering scandal material. Except,' Darina remembered Eileen Barry's comment during lunch, 'apparently Baz could be in line for chief of Defence Staff.'

'There you are.' William sounded sad rather than triumphant. 'These days the press seem willing to print anything they think could titillate the public. A steamy kiss-and-tell story from Jessica could have made him look pretty silly, especially if it came out just when he was up for promotion.'

Darina felt her heart sink. 'Wouldn't she have to prove it though?' She drove past the front of the house to the little car park.

William nodded. 'We're hoping to find something to back this story up in her apartment. It's being taken apart with a fine toothcomb. Roger has been saying all along that this is a case of finding the man. Sexual involvement plus blackmail is a lethal combination and here we are with three top-notch suspects: Creighton, Barry and Borden.'

The further the investigation into this case went the nastier and dirtier were the things that were uncovered. It seemed as though Roger Marks's way of looking at things was proving to be correct. 'I'm sure you'll find that Baz got back much too late to have been able to get over to Conifers Spa in time to murder Jessica,' Darina said stoutly as she parked the car.

'Sorry,' William said with genuine regret. 'His driver has confirmed that he dropped the general off at the house just after nine thirty that evening, fifteen minutes after their estimated return time. Lady Creighton was staying with their daughter and there isn't anybody who can give him an alibi after that time.' He looked at his watch. 'It's taken us just twenty minutes to drive back in heavier traffic than would have been around on Saturday night. He would have had no trouble in getting over here after his driver dropped him.'

Chapter Twenty-Six

Darina got out of the car without a word. She didn't want to think of Baz Creighton driving over to Conifers Spa to talk to Jessica. She didn't want to think of him as having had anything to do with Jessica. She waited for William to get out, then pressed her little control to lock the doors.

He put his arm around her shoulders as they walked towards Conifers Spa. 'I think, one way or another, this case is about to burst open. With a bit of luck, we might get it all wrapped up tomorrow and you can go home.'

'Leaving you to get on with your undercover role, I suppose,' she said sadly. Whatever happened, William would have another job to move on to; he didn't have to wonder where he was going next. Nor did his job involve him in picking up the bits after a case like this. Darina thought of the three women she had met at lunch today: Molly Creighton and Eileen and Veronica Barry. How were their lives going to be affected by the outcome of William's investigation?

William squeezed Darina's shoulders. 'Can't you enjoy having some time to yourself? Don't worry about where the next job's coming from. Soon you'll have so many commissions to work on, you won't have a moment to worry about me, your mother or anyone else.'

William did understand, Darina realised. It comforted her.

Was more space what she needed? All Darina knew was that the trip back from the Creightons had brought William and her closer together than for some time. She didn't want to lose this contact so she walked with him, round the side of the house to where the mobile incident centre was parked in the back yard.

The centre was busy with policemen feeding information into computers and talking on phones. Standing beside the fax machine was Roger Marks, his large body taking up so much space the air seemed sucked away from everybody else. He looked up as William entered with Darina.

'Odd little bit Drugs have come up with,' he said, handing a flimsy fax over to William.

'Well, well, well,' said William.

Darina waited impatiently.

William glanced towards her, his eyes sparkling. 'Amongst Borden's business papers, in a file dealing with investments, Drugs have found letters relating to this place.'

'Conifers Spa?'

Roger Marks insinuated himself into the small corner between computer and table where Darina and William were standing. She felt the warmth of his body intruding on hers. 'It appears Borden was considering putting some money into the place, but at arm's length. Not one for declaring his hand at any stage, our Mr Borden.'

Darina forgot the superintendent's unwelcome proximity as several little pieces of information clicked together for her. 'Carolyn told me there was a possible investor,' she said. 'Had he finally decided whether to go in or not?' It seemed to her a vital question.

'Can't keep your nose out of anything, can you?' Roger's voice was tight and controlled but he picked up a small pile of papers and used them to swat viciously at a fly that buzzed around the small table. He missed.

Darina felt her own temper rise. 'Carolyn told me their potential investor seemed to be having second thoughts. If it was Frank Borden, whether he'd made a definite decision or not could surely be important.' There had been a noticeable slowing down of activity in the restricted space and officers were looking curiously at them.

William put a soothing hand on her arm and directed a reproving look at his superior. 'I think that's an interesting question, don't you, Roger? Why don't we give Drugs a quick ring?' He reached for the telephone as he spoke.

The superintendent leant back against the fax machine, crossed his arms and kept his gaze on his shoes, one finger beating irritably against his upper arm as William got through then waited for the answer to his question.

William's long frame remained relaxed. Finally he replaced the receiver and turned to Darina with an air of quiet triumph. 'Well, it appears you may have put us on to an interesting development.'

Roger Marks's head came up at that.

'Borden seems to have been considering an alternative investment possibility. There are other letters in the file that refer to a nightclub.' William looked expectantly at both of them. 'And guess who introduced it to Frank Borden?'

'Jessica!' the name burst out as Darina remembered the little scene in the reception hall. That was what Jessica had wanted from Frank, an opportunity to launch herself as a singer. What better way than to make sure he had his own nightclub!

'Wrong!' William said.

'Spit it out, Bill,' Roger commanded, his hostility gone, his attention now entirely concentrated on the result of the telephone call.

William smiled. 'Perry Cazalet!'

'He knew Borden?' Darina asked, surprised.

'According to the letter, the club belongs to some chum of his who was just about to put it on the open market. Cazalet was concerned because later this year his wife, Gina, has a contract with them for a three-week appearance to launch a new record and the club has run into financial difficulties.'

Just like Conifers Spa, thought Darina. Another place that had overstretched itself?

'Doesn't seem to have much to do with the victim,' grumbled Roger Marks.

'Jessica Barry wanted to be a singer,' said Darina impatiently. 'Frank Borden was a very close friend; after all, he was paying for her to stay here. If he could be persuaded to invest in a nightclub, she'd have a pretty good chance of an engagement there.'

'You mean Perry Cazalet could have seen Jessica as a threat to his wife's career?' asked William.

'But engaging Jessica needn't mean Gina lost out,' objected Darina. More pieces fell into place for her. 'Frank and Gina left the drawing room together after her recital on the Thursday night. It had gone very well, he could have wanted to discuss the nightclub engagement with her. I should have realised they must know each other. Perhaps Jessica knew the Cazalets were also going to be at Conifers Spa when she asked Frank to pay for her to come.' Darina had forgotten any sense of antagonism towards Roger Marks as her mind raced with possibilities.

'I like the idea of Jessica Barry persuading Borden to invest in the nightclub rather than this place,' said Roger ruminatively, 'but isn't it more likely that Carolyn Pierce would have seen that as a threat rather than Cazalet?'

Darina stared at him. 'That's a bit farfetched, isn't it?' she said impulsively. Then cursed her quick tongue as his eyes narrowed.

'Come through, Bill, and we'll run it round the starting block.' He glanced at Darina. 'Expect you'll have things to do, busy little career girl that you are.' He turned his back on her and walked off towards the next compartment of the mobile centre.

William grinned at Darina and gave her cheek a quick

kiss. 'Well done, darling! I'll see you later. Thanks for the lift back.'

He followed Roger through and closed the door behind them. Darina saw various heads become totally involved with their screens. She stalked out of the police centre feeling angry. What an incredibly stupid idea of Roger Marks's, that Carolyn might think eliminating Jessica would mean the health farm got the investment it needed.

Then, as she walked round the annexe towards the main house, an odd comment of Carolyn's came back to her. Something about the fact that Jessica's death should have simplified things for the anonymous possible investor. Had Carolyn realised it was Frank and known he was wavering in favour of a nightclub? A nightclub that could launch Jessica's career as a singer?

But even if she had, the idea Carolyn would murder Jessica was as ridiculous as the idea that Len Channing had been having an affair with her and Darina had already dismissed it as she reached the front door.

As she went inside the reception hall, a small bouncing bomb hurtled towards her. 'At last! I thought you weren't ever going to get back.'

'Gina!' Darina automatically fell back a pace then steadied herself. 'What are you doing here? Has the Spa reopened?' Then she saw tears streaming down Gina's blotched and swollen face. 'Hey, what's happened? Let's go and sit somewhere comfortable so you can tell me all about it. Do you want some tea, shall we try the kitchen?'

Gina shook her head, her face intense. 'I don't want anything to drink or eat, I just want to talk to you.'

Darina put her hand under the singer's elbow and shepherded her through to the drawing room. She settled her into the corner of a comfortable settee and moved the chair next to it so she could face her.

Gina shook with tension, her hands trembled as they fussed with her hair, then pulled at the skirt of her floaty dress. As soon as Darina was seated, she burst out, 'Perry's left me. He's taken all my songs and left me! I tried to tell Esme, ask her what I should do but she was too busy. So then I thought of you. I mean, your husband's investigating Jessica's death and any moment now, I know it, he's going to arrest Perry!' Gina's wide, bright eyes flickered nervously as she gazed at Darina and her hands now pulled at the fringing of the settee.

Had William been right? Was Gina saying Perry had killed Jessica to protect her career? Darina remembered how the musician had stood in the drawing-room doorway as Frank had almost promised Jessica he would help. How cross Perry had been. Had that little scene been a prelude to a later one when Frank told Perry he was going to back Jessica rather than Gina? But could it be right that Perry wanted to protect Gina? He had shown every sign of wanting to help Jessica and of persuading her she had a future as a singer. If he was thinking of switching his allegiance, he'd hardly murder his new star.

'Why don't you say something?' urged Gina, stretching out a hand and grasping Darina's knee.

'I'm sorry, I was trying to take in what you were saying.' Darina concentrated her attention on Gina. 'Exactly what makes you think Perry is going to be arrested?'

Gina clasped her hands together, a large citrine flashing as the knuckles whitened. 'I saw Perry going towards the pool room that night,' she whispered. 'The night Jessica died.'

Had she indeed! 'That doesn't necessarily mean he killed her,' Darina said gently.

'He wanted to get rid of her!' Gina burst out. 'She was a nuisance.'

'I thought he was interested in launching her as a singer.'

Gina gave a cry of frustration and banged a hand on

the arm of the settee. 'You don't understand! I'd told him that I'd leave him if he didn't get rid of her.'

Did Gina really have that sort of hold over Perry? 'Forgive me, but surely there were other ways of discouraging her?'

'Nothing discouraged that girl!' Gina sniffed. 'Didn't you see the way she went at him?'

Yes, once Jessica had decided on something she wanted, she didn't give up easily. Everything Darina had found out about her pointed to that. Including the single-minded way she had tried to repair her financial situation!

Darina wondered how best to put her next question. 'I know Perry is devoted to you,' she began.

'I was his meal-ticket,' Gina interrupted harshly. 'Perry was worked out as a composer. I earned the bulk of our income over the last fifteen years. But I haven't done a video or toured for years and royalties on my records and tapes have dropped to almost nothing. We're desperate for money. The mortgage is behind and any day now Harrods is going to give up delivering! We could hardly scrape up the credit to stay here but Perry said it was vital to get my weight down.' Gina looked at Darina with desperation in her eyes. 'Why should my size be such a problem? Why can't people just let me sing? I sound as good as ever I did. Better. Why should I have to be thin as well? Perry designed a video that was going to disguise my size but I walked out on the filming. It was so humiliating!'

Darina pressed the chubby hand that rested on the arm of the settee. 'I think you look wonderful. Your hair's a fantastic shade, you've got wonderful fine skin, and your eyes are great. I don't understand why it can't be enough, I really don't.'

'But you do understand that it isn't!' Gina mourned. 'Everywhere I go it's the same thing. I see it in people's eyes. How could I let myself go, their looks say.

Sometimes they even *ask* how I can bear to be this size! They don't seem to understand I've tried and I've tried and nothing works, I end up a balloon again.' Her eyes narrowed to slits. The effect was oddly terrifying, as though a kitten had suddenly turned into a jungle cat. 'I hated that Jessica! So smug and self-satisfied. Thought she could wind Perry round her little finger. Thought he could open all the right doors for her. These days Perry couldn't open a door into the musical world if it was automatic!' she said scornfully. 'That's all over and done with. He's finished and he knows it.'

If that was true, how demoralising for Perry it must be, thought Darina.

'He persuaded me to have one last go at losing weight. So we came here, Frank suggested it.' Gina cast a look round the luxurious room. 'I think he organised some sort of discount for us, said one of the directors was a friend of his.'

'You knew Frank Borden then?'

'Oh, Frank's been around for some time,' Gina said carelessly. 'Can't remember where we met, some big rap party or other. Perry invited him to a gig I was doing and then he asked us out to dinner, you know how these things go.'

Darina nodded but she was thinking that if Frank really was involved with drugs, he would inevitably also be involved in some way with the entertainment scene, it was such a rich market.

'So you think Perry's gone to ground, afraid he's going to be arrested?' Did that mean he really had killed Jessica? Could he have been capable of such violence? Perhaps he'd been a little excitable but Darina had put that down to his creativity. She knew nothing about him really and Gina had been married to him for years.

Gina's face screwed up. 'He's terrified, I'm sure of it.' Like quicksilver her expression changed again. 'And he hates me! He was a big name when I met him. Then he made *me* a big name and after that everything went wrong for him. People just wanted me, not him. And then our baby died, I became fat and ugly and my career died too.'

'You had a child?'

Gina nodded. 'A little girl, Samantha.' The sorrow in her eyes went down to the bottom of her soul; for a moment she was quite still. 'They say parents shouldn't blame themselves for cot death but you can't help it. If you'd gone in earlier, placed her differently, done something, anything, she might still be alive.' For a long moment she said nothing and Darina waited, sharing her agony. 'Everything went sliding downhill for Perry and me after that. I,' Gina gulped, 'I suppose I used food as my comfort. I'd put on a lot of weight when I was pregnant and after Sam's death I put on more. Perry said,' she gulped again, 'Perry said he liked me cuddly.' Once again the mercurial face changed, storm clouds gathering in the grey eyes, the freckles standing out on the pale skin. In so many ways she was like a child who reacted emotionally, unable to use reason. 'I was everything to him. He even killed for my sake! Now he's taken my songs and gone. He hates me, he hates me because he had to kill Jessica!' Little fists pounded at the settee arm.

Darina wondered if this was gut instinct speaking or if Gina had built Perry's disappearance into a great drama. 'Are you sure Perry didn't tell you he was going away? Perhaps he had to see someone?'

'No!' Gina shouted at her. She swallowed then took a deep breath. 'He had a meeting with his accountant and then he was going to have lunch with his publicist. He said he was worried about what effect being involved in a murder investigation was going to have on my career. I expected him back by the evening.' She sniffed. 'It's never any use trying to tie Perry down to definite times. But he never came back.' The words came out in a long cry. 'I went to bed,' she caught a sobbing breath, 'and when I woke up I knew immediately he hadn't come to bed. And then I found all my songs had gone!' she wailed. 'He thinks they're worthless, he's taken them to spite me! It's a message, to tell me we're finished and he doesn't want me to have anything.' Gina gave a long, heartrending cry. 'Oh, Perry, I don't mind if you're a murderer, I just want you back!' She pounded at the arm of the settee again, the ample flesh under her loose dress quivering with every hit. 'Oh, God, why am I fat? I'm so ugly it's horrible. My life is ruined!'

Darina moved to sit beside her on the settee and put her arm around Gina. It was like holding electricity; emotion seemed to be threatening to tear the singer's body apart. 'Don't, Gina. I told you, you're not ugly. People come in all shapes and sizes and beauty depends on so much more than having a model-girl figure.'

Gina banged some more on the settee arm. Tears were pouring down her face. She seemed to be letting go of something she had held bottled up for a long, long time. Suddenly she swung herself round, bursting free of Darina's arm, and flung herself full length along the settee. Darina could do nothing but wait for the hysteria to calm down.

Which it gradually did. After a little Darina managed to gather Gina into her arms, gentle her with soothing movements as though she were a baby and murmur consoling words into her ear. 'Hush, hush, you aren't ugly, you're attractive, never stop thinking that,' she said. 'Size doesn't matter a thing.'

Gina hiccuped away the last of her sobs. 'It's easy for you to say, you're tall and elegant. I'm short, dumpy and *fat*,' she mourned resignedly.

'Look at Esme; she hasn't allowed her size to stop her believing she's attractive.'

Gina pulled away a little, scrubbing at her eyes. 'She's not an entertainer,' she objected. 'And don't start trying to tell me about Ella Fitzgerald again, or Sarah Vaughan or Two-Ton Tessie O'Shea. That was yesterday.'

'Well, how about Dawn French and Jo Brand and that American comedienne?'

'But they're funny!' Gina pulled down her dress and gave a hiccup. 'You're allowed to be fat if you're funny. The only successful fat straight actors are men. It's all right if you're male; well, more all right, anyway.'

Darina thought about Roger Marks. He didn't seem to have any hangups about his size.

Gina gave a last little sniff. 'But thank you for trying to make me feel better.' She produced a small smile then scrambled off the settee and headed for a large, gilt-framed mirror on the drawing-room wall. 'What a sight! Look at my hair!' She pulled at the copper curls, teasing out the strands that had locked themselves together in the midst of her rage. Her concentration was absolute, she might have been at the hairdresser's, and Darina marvelled at how quickly she had regained her poise. Even the red and swollen eyes seemed to be returning to normal.

Gina pushed her shoulders back, adjusted the set of her dress over her breasts, then stood for a moment looking at herself, quite silent. Her fingers, light as butter-flies, traced down the shapeless line of the skirt and Darina realised that the poise that had seemed so easily assumed was very fragile. 'I think I should find William,' she said gently, 'and tell him everything. If the police can find Perry, they could sort everything out for you.'

Gina whirled round, consternation filling her face, her figure forgotten. 'But then they'll arrest him for murder!' She ran over to Darina and clutched her arms, fingers digging into the flesh. 'I couldn't bear that!'

'Look, let's go through what you saw again. Perhaps there's something you've forgotten that could tell us a little more about what Perry was up to that evening.' She led her back to the settee and sat her down again.

Gina gave a great sigh then sat up straight and crossed her ankles over each other. 'I was in my room. Perry and I had quarrelled again, over Jessica. I'd told him he had to get rid of her.' It looked as though tears were about to take over again.

'Let's go up to your room,' suggested Darina hastily. 'Then we can try to re-create what it was you saw.'

Gina leapt up at the idea of action and set off out of the drawing room, half running, half walking. With Darina following, she scampered up the stairs and then along the corridor to the room she had occupied with Perry.

The bed stood unmade, duvet neatly folded at the bottom, and the room had an unused, empty look. Without so much as a glance about her, Gina crossed to the window.

Darina followed and peered over her shoulder at the view.

The treatment annexe that included the pool room was to their right, out of sight. Below was the flagstoned path that led from the terrace at the front of the house. In front of the window stood two ancient cedars of Lebanon. The tall trees spread out their branches of dark green like a series of immense wings that obscured much of the path.

'That's where I saw him.' Gina pointed dramatically down. 'Perry was walking along that path towards the pool room.'

'What time was this?'

'Just on ten o'clock. I know because I'd been watching television. I told the police he came up just before ten but that was to give him an alibi.'

Totally ruined by Perry's statement that he hadn't come up until well after ten.

'Could you really recognise him?' asked Darina doubtfully. 'Remember it was quite a dark night and there were no outside lights.'

'It was Perry, I know it was!' Gina insisted. 'I was about to draw the curtains, something made me look down and there he was.'

Darina was by no means as sure as Gina seemed to be that it was possible, in the dark, through all those branches, to recognise anyone.

'Look, stay here. I'll go down and walk along that path. Just watch, then tell me how much you can actually see of me.'

Darina dashed down the stairs and out of the front door. She turned to the right, skirted the corner of the house then began to walk along the path to the pool room. She restrained herself from glancing up towards the window where Gina was stationed and continued until she'd passed out of sight of anyone watching from the side of the house.

When she re-entered the room Gina was sitting on one of the beds. 'I saw you!' she said triumphantly.

'But could you recognise me?' insisted Darina.

'Of course, I saw your blonde hair through the branches. Not many girls have hair like yours.'

'And Perry has white hair,' said Darina slowly.

Gina clapped her hands together and got up. 'That's it! That's why I recognised him. There wasn't anyone else staying here with white hair. It had to be him. I told you!'

'Not anybody with white hair staying here, no,' Darina said even more slowly.

Gina paused, her hands held together in front of her body. She stood before Darina, excitement throbbing through her. 'You mean it might really have been someone else, not Perry? Who? Who could it have been?'

'I can't tell you,' Darina apologised. 'And it may have been Perry after all. You may have been quite right.'

The warning went unheeded as Gina collapsed onto the bed with a seraphic smile. 'Oh, Darina, how marvellous! I don't mind if he's left me, not if he didn't kill that girl.' She started humming the little tune, 'When the man in my head is the man in my bed'. Then she lay down, curling herself into a ball, and said, 'I'm staying here tonight. I can't go back to that empty house.'

Darina looked at her for a moment, then said, 'I'll find Carolyn and see what can be arranged.'

But Carolyn wasn't in her office, nor did she answer the telephone in her house. In the treatment area Darina found Maria sitting at the reception desk, a sheet of appointments in front of her. She was staring into space, her face pale. When Darina asked if she knew where Carolyn was, she looked down at the desk. 'The police are interviewing her again,' she said, then looked up again, appeal in her eyes. 'They can't suspect her of Jessica's death, can they?'

Chapter Twenty-Seven

Darina stared at her. Carolyn being interviewed again? Had Roger and William taken up the implication of Frank Borden's involvement in Conifers Spa after all then? But it was no use discussing any of that with Maria Russell. 'Gina Cazalet is here; she wants to stay the night. Can I make up a bed for her?'

Maria's expression turned to exasperation: 'That ball of lard! What on earth does she want?'

'Her husband seems to have disappeared and she doesn't want to be on her own.'

Maria reached for the telephone. 'Disappeared, has he? Well, I can't say I blame him.' She got through to the housekeeper and arranged for her to make up the bed.

While Gina's room got sorted out with swift efficiency by a taciturn housekeeper, Darina took Gina downstairs again and out into the garden. They commandeered a couple of loungers and lay in the last of the sun while Darina listened to tales from Gina's past.

Entertaining though Gina was, Darina found herself unable to concentrate. Her mind couldn't get away from Carolyn's possible involvement in Jessica's murder.

Despite her lack of attention to Gina's tales, however, the number of times Perry Cazalet's name was mentioned made an impression. It seemed Gina's world really did revolve around her husband. It was Perry who arranged her songs, even those he hadn't composed; Perry who managed her engagements; Perry who sorted out recording details and monitored the result; Perry who was in charge of publicity. Indeed, the only aspect of Gina's life that Perry wasn't concerned with was her composing.

For Gina had passed on from tales of her singing to talking about her own songs. 'I had this idea. I suddenly saw how the songs could fit together into a story,' she was saying. 'All about a girl who wants to be a singer and is taken up by a Svengali figure. She becomes a big success, chucks him in favour of a young musician and then realises that he is, after all, the love of her life.'

'Not autobiographical at all, is it?' asked Darina dryly.

'Nothing of the Svengali about Perry,' Gina giggled. 'Far too down to earth. But, you know what they say, write about what you know – I reckoned that went for songs as much as for novels.' She got up from the lounger and danced along the path between the rosebeds, her light dress floating around her as she swayed, her arms stretched out, humming little tunes. Suddenly she swung back towards Darina. 'The songs are good, I know they are. Why couldn't Perry see that?' Her eyes brightened as though tears were not far away. 'Why did he have to take them?'

'Here's William,' said Darina hastily as her husband appeared from round the house.

'Oh, I don't want to talk to him,' Gina said. 'I'm going for a walk.' She swayed further down the path, passing out of sight behind a large macrocarpa hedge.

'Have you finished with Carolyn?' Darina asked her husband as he gave her a light kiss on her mouth, then lowered himself onto a lounger beside hers.

He nodded. 'I suppose everyone knows everything we police are up to every minute!'

'And have you got any further?'

He sat on the edge of the seat, arms hanging down between his legs, looking defeated. 'Nowhere. She told us, yes, she'd suspected Frank Borden was the possible investor and laughed to scorn any idea that she might think murdering Jessica would ensure he chose Conifers Spa to invest his capital in.'

'I should have thought the very existence of a corpse on the premises would be enough to put anyone off,' Darina said stoutly. 'So you've crossed her off your list?'

'No one gets crossed off that easily, but we've finished with her for the time being at any rate.'

'And have you finished for the day?'

He shook his head. 'Roger's got some telephoning to do so I thought I'd spend a few moments in the sun with my wife.' He held out a hand to her and they sat for a while in pleasant silence. 'Roger doesn't mean to be so dismissive,' he said after a moment.

Darina took back her hand. 'Oh no?' she said acidly.

'He just doesn't like amateur interference in what he regards as a professionals' world.'

'I don't think you're particularly happy about it either,' Darina murmured.

William sat up again. 'You can't say that,' he exclaimed. 'Look at how we worked together in France!'

'Ah, but that was France.' Darina lay back and closed her eyes.

After a moment she heard William say in surprise, 'Is that Gina Cazalet?' She opened her eyes and saw the singer had reappeared at the bottom of the rose garden and was now bending down to sniff the late flowering.

'She's worried about her husband, thinks he's done a runner, along with her songs. For some reason she thinks that proves he hates her.'

'Done a runner, has he?' William repeated thoughtfully.

'The most interesting thing she said was that she thought she saw Perry going towards the pool room on Saturday night. When I went into it with her, though, all she saw was a man about his size with white hair.'

William swung his legs off the lounger and sat up. 'Medium-sized with white hair? I only saw General

Creighton that one time, at Gerry's funeral, but doesn't that description fit him?'

Darina nodded reluctantly.

William looked thoughtful. 'If I remember their statements aright, Perry Cazalet was supposed to have been using the exercise room before he went upstairs, he says at twenty past ten but she claimed he came up shortly before ten o'clock. When exactly does she say she saw this white-haired medium-sized man walking towards the pool room?'

'Ten o'clock; she'd just turned off the television so she knew exactly what the time was, she said, and she'd only stated Perry came up to the room just before ten to give him an alibi.'

'Typical!' groaned William. 'Didn't help him at all.'

'If she did see Perry going towards the pool room at ten and he really did come up at ten twenty, that didn't give him much time to meet and kill Jessica.'

William nodded. 'Not much but enough. Or perhaps he really was pedalling that electric bicycle all the time.' Then, 'Ten o'clock!' he exclaimed striking his forehead. 'What an idiot I am! Of course!'

'What have you thought of?'

'Maria Russell! Ten's the time she claimed she let the chef, Rick Harris, out of the men's treatment area. She must have heard something.' He rose rapidly to his feet and stood for a brief moment looking down at his wife. 'Thanks, darling,' he said.

Instant warmth that had nothing to do with the sun flooded through Darina.

'Can't stop, we've got to get that girl back in the interview room. She must have the key to everything.'

Chapter Twenty-Eight

It was a very tired-looking Maria Russell who was brought into the tiny police interviewing room in the mobile incident centre. She was also angry.

'I don't understand what all this is about! I thought you'd finished interviewing me! I've got my work to do.'

'Sit down,' said Roger Marks curtly.

William reminded her about the tape procedure and asked if she wanted a lawyer present.

'Why should I, I've got nothing to hide!' she retorted, her tired eyes flashing with renewed anger and defiance.

Yes, William decided, this girl had something to hide. Perhaps, at last, they would get to the bottom of this case.

'We have received evidence', began Roger Marks, 'to suggest someone met your sister beside the pool just on ten o'clock. By your own admission you were in the men's treatment area at that time. I ask you now to tell us exactly what you heard.'

Maria's eyes shifted from side to side as she looked from one man to the other. 'I gave you my evidence before,' she said but this time the anger had leaked away and she looked scared rather than defiant.

'There are penalties for withholding evidence from the police,' William warned her.

Maria looked down and seemed to conduct some sort of inner discussion with herself. The two men waited.

'I didn't hear anyone actually come into the pool room,' she said at last, still looking down; then she brought up her tightly clasped hands and laid them on the table in front of her and looked at the policemen. Her eyes seemed larger than usual and held a resigned fatalism. 'I was tidying up the treatment area, folding up towels to take back for washing, clearing away the drinks we'd had, when I heard a voice cry out someone's name. I didn't hear exactly what, something short, I think; it could have been a nickname.' She spoke deliberately, not hurrying her words. 'At first I didn't recognise the voice, just that it was female. I was about to go out and tell them they shouldn't be in the pool room, when she said something else – "Thank heavens you've come, I thought you mightn't," or something like that, and I realised it was Jessica, up to her old tricks.'

'What do you mean by that?' Roger cut in.

'I mean Jessica was always after the men. Usually it was one belonging to someone else.' Her tone was suddenly savage and the eyes were no longer resigned. 'I thought, any moment now and she'll bring him in here! I hurried up. I didn't want anything to do with whatever was going on.'

'You didn't wonder why they were in the pool area; why she hadn't taken him to her room?' asked William.

Maria looked startled. 'No. That is to say, nothing Jessica ever did surprised me.'

'Or wonder how she'd got hold of the key to the pool?'

'No, Jessica always had eyes in the back of her head.'

'What did the man say?' asked Roger.

'Oh, I don't know, I wasn't really listening, I was too busy trying to clear up.'

'You didn't recognise his voice?' asked William, watching the way her gaze flicked between the two of them.

Maria shook her head. 'I wasn't listening to them.'

William didn't believe that. This woman was emotionally involved with the victim, there was no way she wouldn't be trying to take in every word of what was going on.

'But you heard enough to have recognised the voice if it belonged to someone staying at the health farm?' suggested Roger.

'I don't get to know everyone's voice,' Maria snapped back. 'I told you, I was trying to get out of there. I wasn't interested in listening to what they were saying.'

'Come off it,' Roger said aggressively. 'We know that layout. Everything that goes on in the pool area can be heard quite clearly in the men's treatment area, even when the door is closed.'

'Not if people are whispering.' Maria's voice sank dramatically.

'You heard something,' William reiterated.

She looked at him, her small hazel eyes frightened, like some hedgerow creature caught in headlights.

'It's a crime to obstruct the police,' pressed Roger, bending forward so that his heavy face encroached on Maria's territory.

She flinched, drew back and ran her hands nervously down her thighs. 'I, I did hear one thing.' She cleared her throat. 'I think the man, whoever he was, said, "What about my letters?" He sounded upset. Then Jessica said she needed thirty thousand pounds and she'd give them back to him for that.'

'In other words she was blackmailing him,' grated Roger Marks.

Maria's gaze fell. 'I, I suppose so. But all I could think of', she hurried on, 'was getting out of there. I wanted nothing to do with Jessica or what she was up to. I told you last time, I finished with my little sister a long time ago. We were nothing to each other.'

'What happened after that?' Roger asked.

Maria shook her head. 'I left. I'd finished clearing up and I got out. If any man was fool enough to have got himself involved with Jessica, he deserved everything coming to him.'

William marvelled that she could be so matter-of-fact.

They were talking of the murder of her sister. 'Why didn't you tell us this before?' he shot out. 'Didn't you realise this man probably killed Jessica?'

Maria swallowed hard. 'Would you have believed me if I had?' She stared challengingly at William.

'But this was your sister's murderer!' he persisted.

Something blazed deep in her eyes. 'But I don't know who he was! I don't see that telling you could have been any help at all.'

'You have to let us be the judge of that.' Roger let some of his menace fall away as he moved back in his chair. 'Now, let's go through all this again, shall we?'

They went backwards and forwards over her story. It came out the same each time.

Eventually they told Maria the interview was over for the moment but not to leave the health farm. They might want to question her again.

'Do you believe her?' demanded Roger after Maria had been escorted out of the little room.

William put the sealed copy cassette tape away and balanced their copy on one hand assessingly. 'I think I do. The mention of letters, the demand for thirty thousand pounds, it all adds up with what we already know. I think I can even understand why she didn't volunteer the information before.'

'Hmmf,' snorted Roger. 'Bet she would have been quick enough to tell us if we'd arrested her for her sister's murder.' He got up and stretched, resting his hands on the low ceiling of the room. 'Well, Bill my lad, it seems pretty clear now. The Barry girl was threatening to send the general's letters to the newspapers, thereby ditching his chances as next chief of Defence Staff. Either he couldn't afford thirty thousand pounds or he wasn't willing to cough it up. So he throttles her and takes them.'

'You think she had them with her?'

'Just the sort of damn fool thing a girl like her would do.'

'She doesn't sound like the sort who would stash the originals in a safety deposit box and carry around copies, either,' agreed William. 'Pity Russell can't identify him, though. Without that, are we much further forward?'

'We've got enough to bring him in.' Roger opened the door and called for his sergeant. 'We'll get his plane met and bring him straight here. Don't want to give him time to compose himself, do we? No matter how influential and mighty his position is.'

William realised Roger was enjoying this. He was high on the power of having a knighted general to interrogate.

Roger loomed over him. 'You got some reason why this chap shouldn't be guilty, Bill?' William felt the aggression flowing out of him like a physical force, and for the first time understood Darina's instinctive antipathy towards his friend.

'No, Rog, no reason at all. I just wonder, though, whether news of an extramarital affair could really have done much harm to the general's career.'

Roger grunted. 'Everyone at it, you mean? But this is the army, boy! You're not supposed to do things like that.'

Was that still so, William wondered?

Roger Marks had his way. Two hours later the general arrived, had his fingerprints taken and was shown into the interview room.

Appearing unflustered by what was happening, he then demanded to have his solicitor present.

Fuming, Roger had to wait another hour until the tall, thin lawyer arrived, stupefied at this unexpected turn of events.

At last they were able to start the interview.

'We would like you to give us full details of your movements on Saturday night,' said William after the preliminaries had been completed.

Baz Creighton maintained his composure as he gave them details of his return from Scotland. 'I understand you have already spoken to my driver and therefore you know he dropped me at my home shortly after nine thirty. My wife was away. I had a cup of coffee, listened to a couple of CDs whilst I read a book, then went to bed,' he said.

William was fascinated that news of their visit that afternoon had already been relayed to the general in Europe. Army efficiency for you!

'A man answering your description was seen on Saturday night approaching the pool room at around ten o'clock,' Roger Marks grated out. 'Do you still maintain you were at home?'

Baz Creighton looked politely interested. His solicitor advised him to say nothing more.

William ran a hand through his curly hair and wondered if this wasn't all too much of a cliché; the general and the bimbo.

'Sir Basil, I repeat, you were seen approaching the pool room at ten o'clock on Saturday night.'

'A man answering my description may have been; you cannot have any proof it was me,' came the reply. The general's hand, resting on the table, remained loosely curved, relaxed. 'I can only repeat, I remained at home after being dropped by my driver.'

'Gentlemen,' started the solicitor, 'I really think—' He was interrupted by a knock at the door. A sergeant asked Roger Marks to step outside for a moment.

William took over. 'Look,' he said courteously, 'we're going to get at the truth in the end. It would save a lot of time and trouble if you told us everything now.'

Not a flicker came from the general.

'Are you telling us you didn't know Jessica Barry?' William changed tack.

The speed with which the lawyer told his client not to answer confirmed William's growing conviction that the general had something to hide. 'Acquaintance with the deceased does not necessarily imply guilt in her death,' he suggested quietly.

Neither of the men on the other side of the desk said anything.

Roger came back, his face set and determined, his eyes alight. He sat down. 'We have matched your finger-prints with ones found on the patio door leading from the terrace to the pool room,' he announced with only a trace of triumph.

The solicitor leaned forward but Baz Creighton lifted his hand to forestall him. For the first time something flickered in the general's face. 'I visited Conifers Spa with my wife on Friday evening. We dined with Lady Stocks and her daughter, Darina.' He looked towards William. 'Your wife will tell you they gave us a tour of the health farm. We couldn't go into the swimming pool because it was locked but we looked through the window from the terrace.' He added levelly, 'No doubt that is when my prints got on the window.'

'Know about this, Bill?' Roger grunted out.

'Darina told me about the visit, yes.'

'Go and confirm the business about the window.'

William slipped out of the interview room.

Darina was giving Gina supper in the empty dining room: pasta with roasted peppers and olive oil. Darina had said she was trying the food-combining diet, not mixing pro-tein with carbohydrates, that Carolyn had recommended. William didn't know about the nutritional advantages, but the sight of the dish made his mouth water. All they'd had in the incident centre was sandwiches.

Darina looked up in delight as he entered. 'I'm sorry,' he explained, 'I've not finished, there's something I need from you.' He smiled at Gina. 'Can you spare her for a couple of minutes?'

'Be my guest,' she sparkled at him. 'I have my wine, I can be happy by myself for five at least.'

'What on earth's happening?' demanded Darina outside the dining room.

'We're interviewing General Sir Basil Creighton.' He paused as Darina drew in a harsh breath. 'I know you believe he must be innocent but the evidence, such as it is, suggests otherwise.'

'Which means', she said sharply, 'that Maria placed him there with Jessica. Why else would you have got him in at this time of night?'

Darina's quick understanding could be a constant delight but sometimes it led her dancing merrily down paths to nowhere. It was undisciplined, untrained, unreliable. Still, she often had a startling ability to fit odd-looking pieces together in a way that completed the picture.

'The general claims you gave him and his wife a tour of the health farm.'

Darina nodded. 'Yes, that's true.'

'And that you looked at the pool through the patio door?'

Again she nodded.

'How near did he come to the door?'

'Baz?' she wrinkled up her nose charmingly. 'We were all practically licking the glass. He commented on the shrubs, said the place must have an expert to keep them in that condition and I explained most were fakes.'

'How near was he to the handle?'

Darina thought for a moment. 'I think he was the one nearest it.'

William groaned. 'So he could have touched it?'

'I guess.' She looked questioningly at him. 'So that's it, you've found his fingerprints on the door. Well I'm sorry, but he could easily have put them there on Friday night.'

'You're not sorry, you're delighted!' William gave her a wry smile, kissed her on the tip of her nose and left, hearing her call despairingly as he vanished out of the reception hall back to the incident centre.

Back in the interview room Roger Marks had got nowhere.

William sat down. 'My wife confirms that it was possible you may have touched the handle of the patio door,' he said smoothly.

'Apart from the fingerprint, we have a witness who places you in the pool room with the victim,' Roger pounced.

The general blinked incredulously and his solicitor again advised him to say nothing.

'You were being blackmailed over the return of letters,' Roger continued.

Once again something changed in the general's face.

Once again his solicitor pressed the advisability of silence on him.

Basil Creighton opened up the hand that lay on the table and spread out his fingers. He studied the pattern they made, then looked across the table with tired eyes. 'It's time for the truth,' he said shortly.

'General,' protested his lawyer.

'I realise you have my interests at heart,' Basil Creighton told him, 'but honour and honesty require me to speak.'

The lawyer gave a defeated sigh.

The two policemen waited without a flicker of excitement.

'I met Jessica five years ago.' The general spoke to his hand in a monotone. 'She was an air hostess on a long-haul flight I was taking. In first class the staff have time to talk to the passengers. I, I thought she was very pleasant. Several days later we met by accident in Bond Street and I suggested we had a drink together. After that, well, I think you can probably fill in the picture for yourselves.'

'You are saying she became your mistress?' enquired Roger matter-of-factly.

The general slowly nodded his head. 'I was working in London at the time, at the Ministry of Defence. My wife was often in the country. Jessica was available.' He paused, thought about his statement, brought his head up and looked at the two policemen with a level gaze. 'No, that is not the truth. The truth is I fell crazily in love with her and she with me.' He smiled caustically. 'I don't expect you to believe that.'

'Did you tell her you would divorce your wife and marry her?' Roger again, still matter-of-fact.

The general shrugged. 'Probably. All I could think about at the time was my job and her. Just about in that order.' He paused then added, 'It was, I suppose, something of a mid-life crisis. I was afraid of being offered a bowler hat and she, well, she gave me back my confidence. Then came the Gulf conflict. Out there she became a dream to hold on to, a memory to lighten the dreadful task I was faced with. Once the worst was behind us, I, I saw that the dream was impossible, should never have been allowed to arise. I wrote and told her it had to finish. When I got back, she attempted to see me. I discouraged her. Effectively so.'

'You wrote her other letters,' Roger stated.

The general slowly nodded and considered the bare walls. 'It's hard to realise how I could have been so indiscreet. I wrote them from a theatre of war. The tension at the time was enormous and they were a form of release. In them I described my feelings to Jessica, for her and about the campaign, its conduct and various military decisions that had been made.' His voice was dreamy, detached. 'Had the press got hold of them at the time, there would have been a major scandal. Even now were they to be published I would have to resign and say goodbye to my dearest ambition, to lead the services.'

William was stunned both by what the man was saying and the fact that he was saying it. 'You didn't ask for the return of your letters?' he enquired.

The general bowed his head. 'I regret to say, I did. By then I'd realised the foolishness I'd indulged in, not to mention the impropriety.'

'But she didn't send them back?'

'No.' The word was, as all his other words had been, quietly uttered. 'For several years I regarded them as a ticking time bomb. Then, with the passage of time, I began to think she'd either got rid of them or never intended to use them.'

'And then you met her here?' William suggested.

Baz Creighton gave a long, long sigh. 'As you know, my wife and I dined here on Friday. Just before we left, I saw Jessica come into the room. It was a great shock. I hadn't seen her since before leaving for the Gulf. Then she sang to us. She was very good and I thought perhaps she was on the threshold of a new life. I, I didn't want to introduce her to my wife, so as soon as I could I suggested it was time to go. But I knew I had to have a word with Jessica. When we were outside, I pretended I'd left something behind and went back. Jessica was waiting in the reception hall. I was worried someone would see us so we went into the dining room. She looked as beautiful as ever, but I said we couldn't talk. She told me she knew that but asked if I was interested in having the Gulf letters back.'

The general paused and closed his eyes for a moment. 'It seemed unbelievable that the sword which had hung over my head for so long could be removed. I agreed to meet her the following evening, after I got back from Scotland. I knew my wife had planned to spend the night with our daughter. Jessica suggested we'd be undisturbed by the swimming pool; she said she knew where the key was kept.' Basil Creighton might have been describing a training exercise.

The lawyer sat, pen in hand, gently tapping on a large notepad. He had given up any attempt to persuade his client to remain silent.

'You were still attracted to her,' Roger asserted flatly.

The general sighed. 'I could only remember what a fool I had so nearly made of myself. If it hadn't been for the letters, I wouldn't have had anything more to do with her.'

William looked at this distinguished soldier and reflected how galling it must have been for him to realise how stupidly he'd behaved. How far had he been prepared to go to prevent anyone else finding out? 'So,' he said, 'you made an appointment.'

The general squared his shoulders. 'As soon as my driver left after dropping me on Saturday night, I got into my own car and came over here. I parked behind the main house and walked round to the pool house. I – I was conscious that it would be best if no one saw me.' For the first time he looked uncomfortable. He got out a handkerchief and drew it across his forehead.

William offered to get him a drink of water. It was courteously refused. 'Jessica was standing by the patio door as I came up. She opened it and let me in, closing it again behind me. She . . . she seemed relieved I had come.'

'How was she dressed?' Roger Marks's harsh voice reverberated through the room.

The general was startled, lost his train of thought. 'Dressed?' he repeated.

'What did she wear?'

'Ah, yes.' The handkerchief was drawn across his forehead again. 'A kimono, silk with flowers. She tried to kiss me, I drew back and told her I'd only come because of the letters.' He drew a deep breath. 'Then she told me she needed thirty thousand pounds and that was their price. To say I was flabbergasted would be to put it mildly.'

'You had never seen her as a blackmailer?' suggested William.

The general shook his head. 'I thought she might use them as a revenge, yes, but never that she'd ask for money.'

'You turned up thinking she was just going to hand them over?' Roger Marks said incredulously.

Basil Creighton shook his head. 'No, I thought she was going to try and start up our affair again. I was prepared for blandishments, tears, persuasion. At least, I had tried to prepare myself for them. It was a shock to find that she wanted money, and so much money!'

'You knew she'd married?' William asked.

The general nodded. 'And that she was now a widow. That's why I thought she was going to ask if we couldn't try again.' There was a brief silence before he continued. 'I told her such a sum was quite impossible but that if she really was in desperate need, I'd try and raise a few thousand. She then suggested I divorce my wife and marry her.' A bleak smile flitted across his face. 'I think she had some notion I would be able to keep her in a certain amount of luxury. I told her that, too, was out of the question.'

'So, you refused to give her thirty thousand pounds or to divorce your wife. What happened then?' asked William.

'She gave me the letters,' Basil Creighton said simply.

'What!' roared Roger.

The general's left eyelid shivered for a fraction of a second then stilled. The tic repeated itself as he said, 'I suppose I have to tell you everything. Indeed, that was my intention when I started. I, well, I accused Jessica of being a kiss-and-tell whore whose only motive was money. That I would never have believed she could stoop so low. She flung herself at me, started to cry.' The voice dropped to a pitch well below what the recording tape could register.

'Please speak up,' interposed William.

Basil Creighton cleared his throat and raised his voice to its previous level. He seemed, for the first time, embarrassed. 'She, she claimed I was the love of her life, that she would have done anything for me. She opened her kimono. Up until then, I'd hardly noticed what she was wearing. Now I realised that underneath this Chinese silk thing she had nothing on.' He drew the handkerchief across his forehead once more. 'She, she, well, she pressed herself against me and begged me to take her one last time.' He stopped and cleared his throat. There was a long pause. Nobody said anything.

'I told her I had loved her once, that she had been very important in my life but now that was over and I couldn't go back. Nor should she ask it of me.'

Could this dry-sounding man have abandoned himself to the passion his evidence had suggested? And where was the charm and quicksilver intelligence Darina had enthusiastically described to William?

Another throat-clearing. 'Jessica flung herself to the floor weeping dreadfully. I tried to pick her up. At last she sat up and took a packet from the pocket of her kimono. They were the letters. She took out the top one and started to read it. Then she bundled it back with the others and handed them to me. "Take them," she said. "I couldn't harm you, not really." '

The general stopped talking, his gaze fixed on his clenched right hand.

'What happened then?' demanded Roger Marks.

'I left.' There was no emotion in the general's voice. 'Through the patio door, no doubt leaving my fingerprints there. I drove myself home and burned the letters in the boiler, congratulating myself no one would ever know what a fool I'd once made of myself.' His voice was bitter and self-deprecating. He looked across at them. 'Gentlemen, I am not proud of any part of my behaviour but I swear to you that when I left Jessica by the swimming pool she was alive.'

Silence fell. For a long moment no one spoke.

Then Roger Marks shifted his bulk in his chair. 'Let me suggest another scenario,' he said with slow and careful emphasis. 'I suggest Jessica Barry did not give you back your letters. Rather, she insisted on either marriage or money as the price for doing nothing with them. I suggest she taunted you with the contents of those letters, reminded you just what they could cost you until, in a fit of rage, you attempted to seize them from her and killed her. I suggest you did not intend to kill her but that, driven mad by what she was threatening and by her very presence, you lost control. Manslaughter rather than murder.' He watched the general carefully.

William saw no flicker in the general's eyes to suggest that the manslaughter charge could be an attractive option to murder; only a hardening of the facial muscles. 'I repeat, she gave me the letters and I left. Jessica Barry was very much alive when I left that swimming pool.'

'I repeat, you took the letters from her by force and, in so doing, killed Jessica Barry.'

'What evidence, Superintendent, do you have for that accusation?' the lawyer leaned forward and took control. 'You have my client's statement. He has been very frank with you; franker, indeed, than I would have thought necessary or wise. I can see no reason for you to hold my client any longer. And,' he added with a strong note of warning, 'I have no need to remind you of the confidentiality of police files.'

'No need,' Roger Marks said expressionlessly. 'But finished we are not. Indeed, we are only beginning. Now, general, let's go back to the start of your story.'

Chapter Twenty-Nine

'You haven't arrested him?' Darina exclaimed in delight as William joined her in their bedroom with the news that the general had left.

William looked exhausted. He sagged onto the bed, pulling off the tie that hung open around his neck. 'No,' he said briefly.

'And you're not going to?'

'Not without evidence.'

'Which it looks unlikely you're going to get?'

He nodded, sitting with his head in his hands, elbows supported on his knees, tie trailing from his fingers.

'Oh, that's wonderful,' Darina flung her arms round him.

'Here, hold on,' he protested, righting himself. 'I haven't said we think he's innocent.'

'I can't believe he's guilty.'

'One of these days someone you believe innocent will prove to be anything but,' he said grimly.

Darina leant back on the pillows and looked at him. 'Poor darling, you have had a rough evening! Can you tell me about it? Did Maria Russell hear Baz and Jessica together by the swimming pool?'

'That woman!' William straightened his shoulders. 'She's worse than a politician prevaricating about his intentions.'

'But you got enough out of her to place Baz at the scene. What did he say?'

'He admitted he met Jessica there on Saturday evening,' William said carefully. He took off his shirt then bent down to undo his shoes.

'And?' prompted Darina.

His head remained bowed over the shoes. 'Nothing. That's all I can tell you.'

She lay back on the pillows and looked at him searchingly, then smiled lightly. 'Let me see if I can work it out for myself.'

William gave her a tired look, levered himself off the bed, removed his trousers and walked towards the bathroom.

'Jessica must have had something on him,' Darina said conversationally. There was no response, only sounds indicative of teeth-cleaning. Darina picked at the duvet, fluffing up the feathers as she thought. 'It must have been something concrete. Wild allegations wouldn't have got her anywhere without solid evidence to back them up. Letters!' she shouted triumphantly at the bathroom. 'He sent her letters. Of course! And she kept them, Jessica would.' There was a brief pause in the toothbrushing noises. She decided she'd hit the bull. 'If her attempt with Oliver Barry is anything to go by, she tried to blackmail Baz by threatening to give them to the press. Which I suppose would have been goodbye to his professional future.' She lay and thought some more as the sounds of vigorous washing came from the bathroom. 'The fact you haven't denied any of this must mean he admitted it. The fact that you haven't arrested him suggests he's either convinced you he left without touching Jessica, or you can't prove anything to the contrary.' Her brain was racing now. 'I'm sure you would have told me if any such letters had been found in Jessica's flat. Or if you'd found a key to a safe deposit box.'

'What?' William came out of the bathroom towelling his face.

'I said, you haven't found any evidence of a safe deposit box, so presumably Baz got his letters back.'

'Who said anything about letters?' William tossed the towel over his shoulder and retreated back to the bathroom.

'You didn't need to,' called Darina after him.

'Look, my clever little wife,' he said as he climbed into bed beside her a few moments later, smelling of peppermint toothpaste. 'It's more than my job's worth even to hint you might have anything like the right end of this piece of string. Understand?'

'Quite!' She grinned at him, turned off the light with a decisive click and snuggled up against him. A light snore greeted her.

Darina couldn't sleep as easily as William. For what seemed like hours she lay turning over in her mind everything she had learned about the case. Lying awake in the dark listening to her husband gently snoring beside her, resisting an urge to turn and place her arms around him and force him to respond to her needs, Darina considered her piecing together of the police progress that evening.

Maria had obviously told them she'd heard Jessica and Baz together by the swimming pool. Roger and William then appeared to have jumped to the conclusion that Baz had killed Jessica. It was this mania of theirs for believing all they had to find was the man in the case.

Well, consideration of Jessica's career would suggest that, she supposed.

They had then brought in the general for questioning. Darina, remembering the straightforward, humane man she'd met on Friday evening, had no trouble in believing that he'd decided to make a clean breast of matters. Would he have stopped short of confessing to murder if he had killed Jessica?

She rather thought that what he had had to confess would have been as difficult for him as murder. She took a moment to feel sorry for Molly. If Darina's assessment of the general was correct, he'd go straight back and tell his wife everything. How much would be news to her? Darina had a high opinion of Molly's intelligence. The general's wife could well have known a great deal and decided the situation was best dealt with by allowing her husband to come to his senses.

Yes, Darina felt that if Baz had killed Jessica he either wouldn't have said anything or would have made a complete confession. So, whatever Roger and William might believe, when Basil left the swimming pool Jessica had been alive. Which meant someone else had met her there and killed her.

So far so simple. What did the evidence suggest happened next?

For Roger and William were hooked on the necessity for evidence. As, Darina supposed, they had to be. They had to be able to support any conclusion in court, against clever lawyers working for the defence.

Careful police work was what solved cases; how many times had she heard that? Well, where had it got them with this one?

Three clues, that's all they had. There were Baz's fingerprints on the patio door handle and a set of tyre marks and there was an explanation for each that had nothing to do with murder. Then there was the pink ribbon they'd found at the bottom of the spa pool. Darina paused in her assessment of the evidence. For the first time it occurred to her that Jessica could have used the ribbon to tie round the letters. Perhaps that was its significance and nothing more. The only other useful piece of evidence was Gina's sighting of the man she thought was Perry, and there was only her word for this anyway. None of it could be said to add up to a case.

Darina moved onto her side, stared out towards the curtained window, just faintly less dark than the surrounding wall, and thought about her encounters with Jessica, with the staff and her fellow guests at the health farm, with the Creightons and with the Barry family. Somewhere amongst them had to be the killer.

OK, Baz Creighton could well have had a motive for wanting Jessica dead. Who else had? Maria Russell? She could have remained in the men's treatment area until Baz had gone, then confronted Jessica. But why would she want to kill her sister? They hadn't seen each other for years. Could Jessica have offered a threat to Maria's relationship with Rick Harris, the chef? When she was leaving in a few days? It was unlikely. She'd asked Maria to lend her money but Maria had refused. Could there be some secret in their past that Jessica was threatening to reveal? After all this time? Possible but unlikely.

Carolyn, though, also had access to the swimming pool. If she truly believed Jessica dead meant the future of Conifers Spa was protected, could she have killed her? Darina had seen her lose control on two occasions. Given the right circumstances, perhaps, yes.

Oliver Barry, though, was a much more acceptable candidate for murderer. Darina had never met him but everything she'd heard about him added up to a ruthless, unprincipled brute, rather like his father. He wanted to protect that father's reputation and his mother's peace of mind. Darina had no trouble seeing him as Jessica's killer. The trouble was there was no evidence to place him anywhere near the swimming pool. Surely someone would have seen him? But the only person who'd seen Baz was Gina and she'd thought him someone else.

Then there was Frank Borden, another potentially ruthless man. He could have feared Jessica as a witness for the prosecution if, as seemed likely, his smuggling operations were about to be exposed. And he was on the spot. Again, no evidence.

Perry Cazalet might have tried to discourage Jessica and ended up throttling her through desperation. His wife, after all, believed she'd seen him going towards the swimming pool.

Yes, his wife! Darina lay very still.

Could Gina have killed Jessica?

She had said she'd seen Perry go towards the pool room around ten o'clock. According to Baz Creighton's evidence, it must have been him she'd seen; nevertheless, Gina had believed it to be Perry. Suppose, just suppose, when she thought she'd seen him, he hadn't been going *towards* the indoor swimming pool but coming *back* and not at ten o'clock but around quarter past? Had she suspected Perry might have had a rendezvous with Jessica, slipped downstairs, gone to the swimming pool and there found Jessica after Baz had left her? A Jessica spurned by her ex-lover and maybe delighted to suggest to Gina that Perry and she were an item?

Gina was passionate, reacted to emotion. She wasn't tall, but then neither had Jessica been and Gina had size on her side. Against Gina in a rage, Jessica wouldn't have stood a chance. And Gina had a lot to be angry about. The possibility of losing Perry, the impossibility of losing weight.

Darina remembered Gina's hysteria that afternoon. How powerful it had been! In the evening Gina had seemed to recover her equilibrium; she had even sung for Darina before drifting off to bed half drunk, declaring that tomorrow she would find Perry – somewhere. It was hard to remember she had been so distraught that afternoon.

People thought most of the overweight were cheerful and happy. Darina felt she now knew better. The cheerfulness was a front; behind it most of them were riddled with self-hate and self-doubt. Like Gina.

Put a fat person beside someone like Jessica, anorexically slim with a figure envied by the majority of society, and expose them to her discipline, the power she exercised over her body, her inability to see much outside herself and her absorption with her own needs, then let

Jessica become a threat – it could indeed be a lethal combination.

Had it tipped Gina over the edge?

Darina felt a familiar stirring of excitement. She was near the heart of Jessica's murder, she knew it.

Darina then had a sudden moment of doubt. So much of the circumstantial evidence surrounded Jessica's need for money. Could she really have been so quixotic as to give Baz back his letters? Darina could understand William and Roger finding that hard to accept. But then they hadn't heard Frank Borden describing how Jessica could fling away an achievement she'd worked hard towards all for a moment of altruism. And if she really had loved Baz . . .

A picture of Baz with his silver hair dissolved into one of Perry as Darina found herself sliding into sleep. People slipped out of their allotted places, facts started shifting around. She dreamt she was in court. The judge was Esme with pink ribbon wound in her hair handing down sentence of death on those who couldn't accept the overweight for what they were, while Carolyn cooked steak and kidney pie beneath the judge's bench chanting 'never count the calories', Maureen Channing played with a model Rolls-Royce on the courtroom floor and a jury of slim little pigs in pink tutus danced around the witness box. And in the box stood Roger Marks, twice his normal size, stuck, immovable, announcing they could never convict him of an open mind.

Darina woke early the next morning. William was still asleep beside her. She slipped out of bed, had a quick shower then went downstairs, decided it was too cool for the outside, and let herself into the indoor swimming pool, taking the key from its hiding place behind the treatment reception desk. With slow, powerful strokes she swam up and down the pool, reflecting once again on the thoughts she'd had before sleep had muddled everything. And found that somehow, in the night, various bits and pieces had come together in her mind to form a picture that made sense of everything. It had all been there the previous evening; she just hadn't put the various elements together in the right way.

Now it made sense.

She dragged herself out of the swimming pool and stood looking at the small spa pool. Once again she saw Jessica lying on the bottom, the butterfly silk kimono fluttering liquidly around her body.

Sighing deeply, feeling depressed despite the exhilarating effect of the exercise, she wrapped a bathrobe around herself and went back to the bedroom.

It was empty. William had dressed and gone. Too often these days they were missing each other. She had a momentary sense of panic; were they moving apart? Was the fact that he hadn't told her about his interview with Baz Creighton last night really discretion or hadn't he wanted her interfering in his life? Darina had a quick shower, slipped into a tracksuit and went to find her husband.

William wasn't in the dining room having breakfast, or in the kitchen. Carolyn was there, though, banging saucepans bad-temperedly. No, she hadn't seen William. 'How about you taking over here?' she asked Darina. 'Save me looking for a new chef.'

'Sorry, Caro, not in my line, not these days,' Darina said firmly and escaped out into the back yard conscious she was going to have to make a decision about her future but deciding it wasn't going to be now.

The incident centre was already full of officers looking busy with clipboards, telephones and papers.

William and Roger were there, talking heatedly. They stopped the moment they saw Darina.

'Hello, darling, what do you want?' asked William. It was nicely said but the implication was obvious.

Roger Marks looked through her.

Darina took a deep breath. 'I've been thinking,' she said.

'Brilliant!' growled Roger. 'A girl that thinks! Bill, you certainly know how to pick 'em. Look, I say we've got to have him back in. He'll have relaxed, think he's made it, be congratulating himself on how successfully he handled us. Get him back in now and he'll crumble.'

'A man used to handling pressure, Rog.'

'On the battlefield, Bill, not in the interview room.'

'It's all the same, Rog.'

They were taking no notice of her at all. Even William seemed to have forgotten she was there.

Darina turned and left the incident room. After all, without evidence, why should they listen to her?

But she was right, she knew it.

She thrust her hands deep into the pockets of her tracksuit and started to walk round the annexe to the front of the house, head down, thinking.

'Hi!'

She looked up and saw Gina at the window of her room, blinking blearily at the day. 'Who's an early bird, then? I shan't be up for hours yet.' The head disappeared. Darina wondered if thoughts of Perry had disturbed her night.

She reached the front of the house and stood on the terrace, looking down the sweep of lawn, towards the terrace of staff cottages where Carolyn lived side by side with Maria and Jim Hughes. Then she saw a bright red Lamborghini powering its way up the drive.

The long, low lines of the car were brought to a gravel-crunching stop outside the front door and out stepped Esme Lee, dressed in a black silk suit. With her glossy black hair in its customary chignon and red lipstick flaming as brightly as her car, she made an impressive sight. 'Ah, Darina, just the person,' she said imperiously.

'What on earth are you doing here?' Darina asked, eyeing the Lamborghini with a certain amount of awe.

Esme dived back into the car and rescued a patent-leather clutch bag. 'On my way to Bristol Crown Court. Got a case there this afternoon.' She stuffed the bag under her arm and marched round the car to where Darina was standing. 'Conifers Spa wasn't a million miles out of my way so I thought I'd pop in on the off-chance Gina was here.' A hint of anxiety creased Esme's forehead.

'I don't know how you guessed but, yes, she is. Would you like a cup of tea?'

Esme grinned suddenly. 'Wild cherry would be great. Quite a little zinger that one.'

Darina led the way into the dining room where there was a hot water dispenser with a box of herb teas. While Darina placed two tea bags in mugs and poured on the water, Esme said, 'Gina rang me yesterday when I was in conference. I couldn't talk but she sounded pretty desperate. I said I'd call her in the evening but there was only the answering machine. I tried several times; I even rang first thing this morning.'

'Not a very good idea with Gina,' Darina said sardonically, handing over a wild cherry tea.

She got another quick grin. 'Probably right! Well, she didn't seem to have many friends, otherwise why would she have latched on to me so quickly? I thought of our sessions in the sauna. Maureen seemed an unlikely bolt hole but you and this place had to be an option.'

'You knew I was still here?' Darina asked curiously, as they moved back into the reception hall with their drinks and settled in adjacent chairs.

'I knew your husband was part of the investigation and I couldn't see you decamping whilst he was here,' Esme said positively. 'So, how is Gina?'

'She was desperately upset when she arrived but seems to have settled down now.'

'Hmm, it's that husband of hers I blame for most of

it.' Esme sipped at the tea, her dark eyes searching Darina's face.

What had brought Esme to Conifers Spa? Had she really come just on the off-chance that Gina had fled here? Darina's pieces that had fitted together so nicely started to float apart.

'Did I hear Frank Borden has enlisted you as his defence lawyer?' Darina asked boldly.

Esme gave her a straight look. 'News travels fast!'

'It was quite a shock to hear of his arrest. But, somehow, I couldn't be all that surprised.'

'Really.' Esme was obviously not going to be drawn.

'I thought you two were getting on famously when you were staying here,' Darina added disingenuously. 'It must have been a shock to you.'

'Gina still in the same room?' Esme enquired, rising majestically from her chair.

Darina nodded.

'I'll go and have a word. I haven't got long.' Still holding her cup of wild cherry tea, Esme went up the stairs.

Darina sighed. It had been foolish of her to think she would get anything out of the barrister. She finished her tea, testing in her mind the validity of the picture she had formed in the swimming pool that morning. Esme did not seem to be in that much of a hurry because she remained upstairs.

Darina went through to the kitchen; she needed to talk to Carolyn. But Carolyn was no longer there. Lugubrious Pete was scrubbing out the larder. No, he had no idea where Mrs Pierce was but he thought she might have gone to the treatment area. 'Lotta problems there, ain't there?' he said with gloomy satisfaction. 'Lost a manager, ain't she?'

Yes, news spread fast and bad news the fastest of all.

In the treatment area three of the girls were cleaning out cubicles and checking equipment. But no Carolyn.

'Said something about going down to her cottage,' Theresa said cheerfully, banging shut the front of a Turkish bath.

'Is Maria Russell around?'

A broad smile split Sally's face. 'She's off! Cooked her goose, she has.'

'With the help of chef!' Theresa giggled happily. Neither seemed particularly upset at the disappearance of the health manager.

Darina left them to their work and walked briskly down the drive towards the cottages.

Chapter Thirty

The front door to the middle cottage was open, and Maria was slinging cases into the back of an estate car. She looked in a hurry. 'Is Carolyn in?' asked Darina.

Maria shook her head. Her face was flushed with the effort of heaving suitcases around.

Darina made up her mind. 'You're obviously in a hurry but there's something worrying me. You wouldn't have a moment, would you?'

Maria put her hands on her hips, her lower lip pushed out obstinately. 'Can't you wait for your friend?' Her voice was cold.

'Carolyn's a food expert. You're the one who knows all about exercise, the figure and all that,' Darina said persuasively.

Maria sighed. 'Come on then, I suppose I can spare a couple of minutes.' She marched back into the little cottage, followed by Darina, who eyed the long, straight back and powerful shoulders with a certain trepidation. She wondered whether it wouldn't be better to make some excuse and wait for Carolyn to reappear.

The small front room was sparsely furnished with inexpensive pieces bought from DIY superstores. It offered a minimum of comfort. On the floor, against one wall, was a large cardboard box almost filled with books and CDs. Maria sat on an upholstered, low, armless settee, and waited.

Darina lowered herself onto a matching chair. She waited for a moment before speaking. The only weapon she had was surprise and she needed to make the most of it.

'I thought you'd find it easier to confess to me than to the police,' she said quietly.

Maria stared, then gave a harsh little laugh. 'Confess? What have I to confess to? Hasn't your dear husband told you what I overheard by the swimming pool that night?'

'I gather Jessica met an old lover and tried to blackmail him with letters he'd sent her,' Darina said carefully. 'And that you told the police you'd left whilst they were still discussing the matter.'

Maria's face grew very still. She exuded tightly controlled power. Darina wondered if she wasn't, after all, making a serious mistake.

'If you know that, then you must know there's nothing more I can say. I don't know who killed Jessica, and quite honestly I don't really care.'

'No, you don't, do you?' Darina plunged on, quelling her unease. 'You never cared much for Jessica. She was the little sister who got everything. All the attention to try and make her eat, all the boyfriends who should have been yours, the boys who thought you were too fat to love. All the love of your father, who praised the way she'd starved herself, her discipline in refusing to eat. Then, to cap it all, she attracted the attention of your stepfather. Hadn't you hoped you were his favourite?'

Maria's lips drew back in a snarl but she said nothing. Darina continued with increasing confidence. 'What did Jessica threaten you with when you wouldn't lend her the money your stepfather left you, the money you'd invested so carefully, the money that was now available to back Rick Harris in another restaurant? Did she suggest she only had to make the right moves and Rick would be hers? That he had only been attracted to you because you could make it possible for him to have his own place again?'

Maria gave a small, derisive snort. 'Fancy yourself as

a detective, do you? Well, you'll have to do better than that. What had she to offer him other than her pathetic body? She was broke, she couldn't give him a restaurant, or even help him to write a book. Motive for murder? Don't make me laugh!'

Darina changed tack. 'How much did you resent Jessica monopolising your father?'

'Our father? Who was so very far from heaven?' Maria snorted again. Then her eyes narrowed and moved their focal point from Darina's face, fastening on something the other side of the room. 'He was a shit and a bastard,' she said coldly. 'You should have seen the way he behaved to us when he got back from the navy. Always on about our size, our behaviour, our looks. No wonder Mummy couldn't stand it. No more could I. The peace of it when he left us!'

She brought her gaze back to Darina. But Darina rose and went to pick up the photograph frame Maria had been looking at. 'But you still keep his photograph, don't you?' She held out the montage of several snaps that included a large one of a naval officer. Beside that was one of a tall man with a middle-aged woman who looked so like Jessica it had to be her mother. 'Your mother and stepfather?'

Maria nodded wordlessly, her eyes still narrowed, tension in her shoulders.

'He left you money, didn't he? What was his name?'

'Giles, Giles Rackstraw.' Maria was watchful.

'And this is him – with you?' Darina heard the disbelief in her voice as she looked at another of the snaps. Maria had said she was large, and so she had been. It was difficult, in fact, to recognise her in this picture.

Maria rose, grabbed the frame from Darina, stalked across the room in two quick strides and placed it face down in the open box with the books and CDs. 'I don't think we have anything to say to each other,' she spat at Darina.

Darina sat down again in the low chair. Her pulse was racing, her breath coming quickly. She was so near, she knew it.

'Jessica didn't resent your father the way you did, did she? She was his favourite.'

'Always clinging to him she was,' Maria turned away sullenly and leant against the window-ledge. 'After our little brother died, all he could see was her.'

'That was it, wasn't it? She made herself into what he wanted and you couldn't do that. No wonder you hated her.'

Maria shrugged and prowled over to the empty fireplace. 'She was a nothing,' she said, gazing intently at Darina like a jungle animal wondering when to pounce.

'Did she jeer at you? Taunt you with your size? Use your failure to bolster her success in getting down her weight?'

Maria's gaze flickered uneasily. A sense of triumph began to rise in Darina. She was getting to the girl. Only a bit more and she'd lose that cool, that control. Then they'd hear the truth.

'Who was it who warned your mother Jessica might be making herself a little more attractive to your step-father than any stepdaughter ought?'

Maria said nothing but her eyes narrowed to slits.

'I think it was you.'

Again, Maria said nothing.

'And whatever you said, it worked. Jessica disappeared from your life, first to France, then into marriage. Until the other day, when she turned up here.

'You must have thought you had managed to get your life together. You'd forced yourself down to a weight you felt was attractive. You'd changed your life, found a job you enjoyed, gained a lover. Then, suddenly, along comes Jessica.' Darina paused, looked at the tense girl. 'I can sympathise, you know; it must have been a hell of a blow.'

327

'You have no idea about anything!' Maria flung at her.

'But couldn't you have had a little sympathy for her? Too thin to be really attractive, saddled with debts her much older husband had bequeathed her, her loyalty in sticking to him despite everything repaid by imminent bankruptcy? Not knowing where to turn?'

'Why didn't she get a job?' demanded Maria suddenly. 'I've always had to work!'

'She worked too.'

'You can't call being an air hostess work.'

'Very hard work, I believe,' murmured Darina.

'Swanning around, giving herself airs, having it off with the captains in glamorous places! Allowing herself to be picked up by the first class passengers. Call that work!' Maria sneered.

'So, instead of looking for a job, Jessica asks you to lend her your precious money.'

'I told her, no way! I couldn't believe it when she walked into my reception and I realised who it was. She didn't recognise me at first,' Maria said proudly. 'And when she did she knew I'd said nothing deliberately. Always was a cunning little girl, Jessica, always could pick up other people's leads. Then twist them to her advantage. Like coming down here and trying to play on my sympathy. As if I had any sympathy for her! Then asking me to lend her money. I soon told her what I thought about her. And I've told all that to the police as well. I don't know what you think you're up to but I have nothing to hide,' Maria burst out. Her foot kicked at the low settee, then kicked again. The settee moved slightly along the cheap carpet.

Once again Darina changed tack. 'What did you discuss with Rick Harris on Saturday evening in the men's treatment area? His interest in Jessica? The way Carolyn was behaving as though he was her personal property? Did you ask if he'd still love you if you weren't able to put up the money for another restaurant?'

Maria kicked again at the settee, her mouth set in an obstinate line.

'What did Rick say? Nothing you wanted to hear – no professions of undying love? Did you quarrel, perhaps? Did he stalk out, leaving you to clear up after you both?'

Maria stood quite still, her powerful body tense.

'Then as you clear up, trying to manage your rage and distress, you overhear Jessica beside the swimming pool. Jessica with a man. Trying to blackmail him into giving her the money she needed. Did your hopes rise? Did you think this was going to get her off your back? Remove her from Rick's orbit? Then, instead of holding out for every penny he can raise, she gives him the letters. Gives them to him for nothing!'

Darina looked across at the girl standing now so rigid she might have been one of the statues in Lost Horizons. 'Oh, you must have been so angry!'

'Angry?' Maria repeated. Suddenly words started to gush out of her. It was as if she couldn't control them any longer. 'Angry? What do you think? He'd offered her thousands. Not what she was asking for, but something, and she might have got more later. But she flung it all away. No thought for me! I was going to be let off the hook. It was always the same, Jessica never thought about anybody but herself.'

'Perhaps you never gave her a chance to do anything else?' suggested Darina.

Maria looked at her scornfully. 'You don't know what you're talking about. I told you, you don't know anything about Jessica.'

'I know you went and confronted her, lost your temper with her. Did she taunt you then? Remind you of how fat you used to be, how fat you might soon be again?' Maria flinched, a hand involuntarily ran down the line of her hip.

Darina continued remorselessly. This was her only chance. She had to reduce Maria to the state she'd been in that Saturday night, beside the spa pool. 'You've put on weight recently, haven't you? Are your skirts getting too tight? Your waistbands uncomfortable? Don't you like the sight of yourself in trousers any more? Has Rick commented on excess flesh?'

Maria closed her eyes for a brief moment. When she opened them, Darina saw hate glaring through. 'What did you do? Grab Jessica? Grab hold of your little sister. Shake her, perhaps? Try to frighten her just a little, make her understand she couldn't go around making your life a hell whenever she wanted to? Then did you lose your temper – go further than you meant to?'

Maria swayed slightly, her eyes became unfocused. 'She kept on moving away from me,' she burst out. 'Telling me things and moving away so I couldn't get my hands on her.'

'What things did she tell you?' Darina asked softly.

Maria's control slipped completely, the words sprang from her like water from an unlocked dam. 'She said I wasn't the only one Giles had loved. He'd had it off with her, she said! How could she call it that? How could she? What Giles and I had was lovely. But Jessica jeered at me, asked me how I could imagine anyone could love me when I never loved them!' A tear sprang out of Maria's left eye. 'As though *she* knew anything about love!' A matching tear appeared from the right eye.

'Who did you love, Maria?' Darina asked, watching the tension in her posture. 'Your stepfather, of course. But who else? Your mother?'

Maria's lip curled. 'She never knew how to deal with either of her husbands. Even Giles she never gave the warmth he wanted. That's what he loved about me, my warmth.'

'And what did he love about Jessica?' demanded Darina cruelly, never taking her eyes away from the woman.

Furious eyes glared at her. 'He never loved her, never!'

'And what happened to your marriage? Why did that fail? Couldn't you give your husband love?'

Contempt filled Maria's face. 'He was a fool! I only married him because he met Jessica and saw her for what she was. Giles always said I was far too good for him.'

'So it was nothing to do with not being able to love him, then? Jessica got it all wrong?'

Maria hunched her shoulders, clenched her fists and brought them up, like a prize fighter preparing for a move.

Darina braced herself. 'When was it you started to strangle Jessica? When you forced her up the steps of the spa pool? Is that when you managed to get your hands round her neck?'

Maria hissed, 'All those years she'd laughed at me, all those years she'd jeered at my size, as though she hadn't once been fat herself! At last I had her where I wanted her.' Her eyes suddenly opened wide. 'I didn't mean to kill her, you know. She just slipped. One moment she was struggling; one moment she couldn't do anything, her eyes bulging, terrified.' The voice gloated. 'Then suddenly, she slipped and crashed into the pool. Nearly had me in as well!' An expression of surprise crossed her face. 'There was all that blood!' The tension went out of her posture and she sat down on the settee as though her legs wouldn't hold her any longer.

'So there Jessica was in the pool,' said Darina conversationally, feeling relief that the worst was over. 'And you were safe on the side. Did you try to get her out?'

Maria looked frightened. 'Of course! I jumped in, I tried to lift her but she just flopped. I tried to find a pulse but there wasn't one. She was dead. So I left her there.'

Darina didn't dare let herself think of Maria abandoning her dead sister to lie at the bottom of the spa pool.

'She wasn't dead, you know. The autopsy proved that.

You could have saved her even then.' Darina held Maria's gaze with hers, watched the eyes narrow again. 'What did you do with your wet clothes?' Darina's voice was steady; she could have been talking about everyday things. 'They must have been dripping. Did you have dry ones with you?'

Maria looked confused. 'My clothes? Yes, I suppose they were wet. Yes, I remember now, I dried my tracksuit in the centrifugal machine and put it back on. I could hardly drag the trousers over my hips, they were all damp and seemed a size too small. And they were cold, cold against my flesh.' Her eyes were without expression, dead.

'And then you came back here?'

Maria nodded like an automaton.

'And you were prepared to allow an innocent man to be charged instead of you?' Darina was incredulous.

Hate sprang back into Maria's eyes and her upper lip curled. 'He was no better than she was. He called her a kiss-and-tell whore. But he was worse, he was supposed to be honourable. He talked about his command in the Gulf. He was a senior officer. My father always said the services had a duty to Queen and country before their families. That man forgot all that.'

'And what about you? What about killing your sister and allowing an innocent man to be suspected? All because she called you fat!' Darina had forgotten her fear, had failed to notice how tension had built up in Maria again, so she was completely unprepared for Maria's cry of rage or the way she suddenly launched herself at her accuser.

Darina had counted on her extra height and weight to give her an advantage in any attack. But the force of Maria's charge took her by surprise. The chair rocked and crashed backwards, taking her with it. As she felt herself grappled to the floor, she realised she had completely underestimated Maria's strength. Slight, frail Jessica could not have stood a chance against this woman.

Rolling on the floor beneath Maria, Darina felt solid muscle weigh her into carpet, then strong fingers fixed themselves around her throat. She kicked out but her legs met air. She grabbed the hands that were attempting to strangle her and tried to dislodge them. Not a chance. She could feel the air being squeezed from her lungs, her head felt as though it would burst, the blood built up in every vein, her eyeballs bulged out of her head, her ears roared, drowning the sound of Maria's voice grinding out words through clenched teeth as she lifted Darina's head and banged it against the floor, beating it down in time to every fourth word of her repeated refrain. 'She called me fat, she called me fat, she called me fat!'

Darina tried to grab Maria's throat or gouge at her eyes. She could feel her strength ebbing away as zooming stars flashed before her and her flailing hands caught nothing but air. Then they fastened around Maria's breasts and with the last of her strength she squeezed the heavy flesh. To no effect. She could feel Maria's weight crushing her lungs. Was this how Jessica had felt as her consciousness ebbed away? Had the blow to her head as she fell into the pool come as a merciful release?

There was nothing now before Darina but a red swirl that was rapidly darkening into black and her cries had long given way to a series of strangled grunts.

Just before she slid into the dark, she heard a door open and someone cry, 'Bloody hell!'

Pain invaded Darina, pain and a glorious realisation that she was not going to die. The pressure had gone from her throat; instead it felt as though a fire from hell burned there.

Cautiously she opened her eyes.

Beside her on the floor lay Maria, still and limp. Standing over her, a poker grasped firmly in his hand, was Jim Hughes.

'You OK?' he asked. 'I'm sorry, I daren't help you in case she's not right out.' He hefted the poker a little higher in his upraised hand.

'Police,' Darina croaked, her hands slid up to her throat, so swollen and aching she doubted she'd ever be able to swallow again.

'On their way,' Jim assured her. 'Just as well I was taking a couple of hours to give my place a bit of a clean. Thought it must be daylight robbery, never heard such a racket! First thing I did was dial 999. Then, well, I've never been particularly fond of La Russell but you can't let your colleagues be murdered before your very ears, can you? So I grabbed the first weapon I could find and came over. Brave, eh?' He took a step back, still holding up the poker, his eyes never leaving Maria's still body.

'Very,' rasped Darina, hoping she sounded as grateful as she felt.

The full enormity of what he had done seemed to percolate through to Jim Hughes. The poker wobbled in his grasp and he sat down on the toppled-over chair as though his legs wouldn't hold him any longer. Darina dragged herself up till she was sitting on the floor supported by the wall. She didn't feel able to say anything else.

Maria stirred and muttered something.

Jim raised the poker again, then dropped it. 'Could have killed her!' he said in shocked surprise. 'Then who'd be for it? Eh?' He looked around the small room as though for some less lethal weapon, then back at Maria. 'Shall we sit on her? Both of us should just about do it.' He got up, rolled the girl over onto her stomach and plonked himself down on her back. She started to struggle. Darina dragged herself over and flung herself across Maria's legs, stopping them from scissoring backwards and forwards.

'Attagirl,' said Jim. 'Now we've got her.'

Darina felt Maria's struggles grow less.

'You all right?' Jim asked. 'What did you do to antagon-
ise the duchess anyway?'

'All right,' Darina managed to get out. Explanations
would have to wait.

Dimly in the distance Darina heard the wail of a
police siren. She remained conscious long enough to
wonder whether it was coming from the health farm or
somewhere else, then dropped into a dark abyss as the
car drew up with a screech of brakes.

Chapter Thirty-One

Much later Darina woke up after a long sleep to find herself in bed at Conifers Spa, her throat no more than unpleasantly sore.

For a moment she lay listening for sounds that could tell her what was going on.

Nothing appeared to be happening.

She flung back the bedclothes and discovered she had been stripped of her tracksuit but left in her underclothes. Had William done that? She could only remember a confusion of police crowding into the tiny terraced cottage, of someone trying to ask her questions, of Jim protesting. Then she'd been back at the health farm, croaking out what had happened, telling William to arrest Maria for Jessica's murder. A doctor had appeared and refused to allow her to give a statement. Carolyn had appeared from somewhere, had helped William to put her to bed. The last thing she remembered was a prick in her bottom, then it had been oblivion.

Darina looked at her watch: three o'clock in the afternoon; she had been under for hours! She swung her legs off the bed and tried standing up. It proved more difficult than she had anticipated. Gingerly she walked across to the bathroom and turned on the shower. Gradually under the stream of warm water she began to feel slightly stronger.

Twenty minutes later she was making her way downstairs.

'Darina!' Carolyn came out of the office. 'Are you all

right? We've all been so worried. William's been out of his mind. I'll ring through; he's in that funny caravan thing they've got parked outside the kitchen.' She disappeared back into her office then reappeared before Darina could do more than limp across to the reception desk. 'He'll be right over. Now, how are you? Can I get you anything – lunch, a drink?'

'A drink, please,' Darina's voice was husky and her throat was still painful.

'Sit down, I'll get you some honey and lemon.'

Darina lowered herself carefully into one of the reception chairs. 'Where were you this morning,' she croaked. 'I wanted to ask you about Maria, what you knew about her background. All I had were suppositions.'

Carolyn flushed. 'I'd gone into the village. I wanted a last word with Rick but I couldn't find him, not then.'

'Rick! Does he know about Maria?'

Carolyn nodded. She gave Darina a shamefaced smile. 'He arrived at the cottages just after you were rescued. He was really shaken by what happened. I've suggested he goes on working here and that we continue with the book.'

Darina felt depressed; hadn't Carolyn learned anything? 'You've forgiven him for Maria – and Jessica?'

'Oh, Jessica was nothing, and it was because Maria was going to make it possible for him to open another restaurant that he gave her any encouragement.' Carolyn glowed.

Darina gave up. There were some people you just couldn't help.

'And you wouldn't believe how enquiries and bookings have picked up. It must be true that there's no such thing as bad publicity. The directors are delighted! I think we're going to make it!' Carolyn gave a broad grin and disappeared.

Darina sat back in the chair and closed her eyes, then opened them again as William hurried through from the back of the house. 'Darling, how are you?' He crouched down and took her hands in his, looking anxiously into her face.

'I'm fine, really,' Darina said huskily.

His expression of concern didn't change.

'What – ' Darina's voice failed. She tried again. 'What's happened to Maria?'

William's expression hardened. 'She's under constraint. She fought like a wild thing, the doctor had to give her a sedative. Now she's in a cell awaiting interrogation. We wanted to talk to you first. We've been waiting for you to wake up.'

Darina wondered what Roger Marks had said about it all.

'We had our suspicions about her, you know?' he said painfully. 'She was so conveniently on the scene. But it was the motive; we couldn't really find any motive.' He paused, his expression a mixture of concern and bafflement. 'What convinced you it was her?'

'I could imagine just how antagonistic she felt towards her sister,' Darina croaked through her sandpaper throat. 'Jessica was so thin, you see, and Maria has never really been able to conquer her weight problem.'

William gazed at her, stupefied. 'You mean that was it? She hated her sister because she was thin?'

'And because Jessica was their father's favourite and stole their stepfather's affections. Maria always had a hard time attracting men but they flocked around her little sister.'

'Jealousy.'

Darina nodded. 'I was sure if Baz Creighton had killed Jessica, he would have told you.' Talking was gradually becoming easier. 'If he didn't kill her, the most likely person had to be her sister. I really couldn't see Maria leaving the health farm and Jessica and Baz together without knowing exactly what the outcome would be.'

Carolyn came back into the hall bearing a tray with

a gently steaming jug and a glass. She poured out some warm honey and lemon juice, handed it to Darina, then tactfully disappeared back into her office.

The drink tasted wonderful, fresh yet soothing. Darina sipped at it and waited.

William dragged a chair over and sat facing his wife. 'But what on earth possessed you to go down and confront her like that?'

'I just thought – ' The drink eased her throat. 'I thought a little chat might sort one or two things out.' She considered for a moment then added, 'If you analyse all Maria's tracksuits, you'll find one with traces of bloody water from the spa pool. She said she'd tried to get Jessica out.'

'After she'd strangled her first?'

Darina nodded.

'Why didn't you tell us?' he asked in a tight, constricted voice. 'Didn't you realise what a risk you were running? What the hell do you think our job is?' he spat out finally.

Darina winced.

William put a hand over hers. 'I'm sorry, but why didn't you say something to me?'

'I had no facts,' she croaked, her throat seizing up again.

'You could have told us your theory, allowed us to test the clothes.'

Darina closed her eyes and felt bullied. 'I didn't know about the clothes then and you wouldn't talk to me. This morning you wouldn't even listen to me.'

'My fault, I think,' said Roger Marks's voice.

Darina's eyes flew open. The superintendent stood before her, rumpled suit looking even worse than usual, his fleshy face as unembarrassed and open as always. 'But you got to fight to be heard around me. No use going off in a huff and tackling murderesses without backup. Unforgivable that,' he said brusquely. 'Still, my inability to realise you had something to contribute was unforgivable too. Quits?'

There was none of the guilt in his voice that had filled William's, making him defensively aggressive. Perversely, Darina found herself preferring the superintendent's approach.

'Quits,' she said, looking him straight in the eye.

He clasped a large hand on her shoulder. 'We'll make a colleague of you yet!'

It slowly dawned on Darina that the superintendent and Esme were the only really large people she had met who seemed genuinely unconscious of the effect their size could have on others.

Which reminded her. 'Where's Esme?'

'Esme Lee? She been here?' Roger Marks's voice was full of lively curiosity.

'She was this morning,' said Carolyn, who had been hovering outside the door. 'Came to see Gina Cazalet.' Carolyn glanced towards Darina. 'She left you a message, said you'd done as much, if not more, for Gina than she could have done. Hopes you can all meet up soon. Then she went off to Bristol, apparently she's appearing in a case there this afternoon. Disappeared just before all the ructions broke out.'

'Pity, I had something I wanted to say to that baiter of police.'

Yesterday such a comment would have set Darina's teeth on edge. Now, suddenly, she saw the exuberance of spirit in which it was uttered. With a sense of shame, she realised that her opinion of this man had been swayed by his size, just as much as anyone else's was by Gina's or Esme's or Maureen's. How insidious prejudice could be!

William sat down on the arm of her chair and put his arm around her. 'Forgive me, too?' he asked quietly.

Something inside Darina relaxed, she leant against

his shoulder. 'Of course! You were only doing your job.' His arm tightened around her.

'God, the sins that ask for pardon in those words, I was only doing my job!' boomed Roger. He looked down at Darina. 'What about your job, eh? Going to keep Bill here properly fed now?'

She looked up at her husband. 'William knows I'm not the sort to sit quietly at home, keeping house. Something will come along – but I'm not going out looking for it,' she added. 'He'll get his meat and two veg for a bit.'

'I'll bring the missus down to sample some,' Roger promised. He swung round to find Carolyn. 'Got a good bitter on tap here, then?'

Carolyn drew herself up. 'Nothing like that, I'm happy to say. But we do have a very good champagne. I think we have a bottle in the fridge.' She whisked out of the hall.

The superintendent looked disappointed. 'Nothing like a good bitter,' he mourned.

The front door opened. 'My wife here?' Perry Cazalet asked.

For a moment no one spoke.

Perry looked enormously tired yet ebullient. His lightweight suit could have been slept in it was so creased, the open-necked shirt looked as though it hadn't been changed for days and his thatch of silver hair surely hadn't seen a comb for an equal length of time. But subdued excitement pulsed in his eyes and there was authority in every line of his body.

As though summoned by some psychic bell, Gina leant over the landing. 'Perry!' She started down the stairs, her little feet dancing with incredible speed, shrieking her husband's name. 'Perry! You found my note!' He strode across the hall to meet her, then rocked back on his heels as she flung herself at him off the last couple of steps.

'Here, careful!' He steadied her, his hands running lovingly over her back.

Gina burst into tears.

'For heaven's sake,' he said in exasperation. 'What's all this about?'

'Oh, Perry, I thought you'd left me. That, that,' Gina swallowed hard, no doubt realising to confess she'd thought him capable of murder was perhaps not the best of ideas. 'Well, that you were fed up with me.'

'But I left you a note,' Perry said in astonishment. 'Didn't you read it?'

'You did not! You did not leave me a note,' Gina stamped a foot. 'I searched everywhere. Where did you put it?' she demanded suspiciously.

A ghost of doubt flickered across his face. He felt in his pockets – and drew out an envelope. 'Oh,' he said. Then held it out. 'Forgot,' he said simply.

Gina looked at him murderously. Then her expression changed and she started to laugh. She brought her hands in front of her face and tried to contain the laughter that broke out but it was too much for her. Her body rocked with mirth. The onlookers found themselves laughing with her. Perry began to laugh himself.

He tossed the envelope over his shoulder and drew his wife to him, wrapping his arms round her body as though he'd never let her go. 'Don't you want to know what I've been doing?' he asked at last as the laughter died away.

Gina drew back and clapped her hands together. 'Oh, tell, tell!' she cried.

'I think we'd all appreciate hearing that,' William said, drawing Darina close to him.

'Too right, Bill,' said Roger, leaning imperturbably against the mantelshelf, his hands in the pockets of his baggy trousers.

'Come on,' Darina urged, feeling the warmth of William's shoulder under her head, the familiarity of his body against hers. 'Do tell us.'

Perry held the floor. Darina thought that, despite his tiredness, he had a new confidence about him.

'I've been to New York,' he announced and waited for their gasps of surprise.

He was not disappointed.

'I knew I had to do something.' He looked at Gina. 'You were never going to lose weight and the effort was destroying you. And, dammit, I don't want you any different; I love you the way you are, every last ounce of you.'

Gina glowed at him.

'So I rang Marvin in New York. You remember Marvin? Produced your last record there, years ago.'

'Marvin? Of course I remember him.' But Gina looked bewildered. 'I thought he'd gone into musicals now, though.'

'Right!' Perry shouted with a note of triumph. 'And he wants you to write a musical for him. I took him your songs and that tape you recorded, remember?'

'The one I did at home, the one that you said hadn't got a future?' Gina asked sternly.

He looked a little shamefaced. 'I know. But a man can be wrong. When I saw how everyone reacted to your song here the other night, I began to think again. Maybe, just maybe, there was a market for your stuff. So I took it all to Marvin.'

Gina clasped her hands and looked as though she could hardly believe what he was saying. 'And he liked it?'

'Every single song,' Perry assured her solemnly. 'He's drawing up a contract. He says the decision on who writes the book is his but that you're to do the songs and lyrics. And he's offering you a socking great sum. Which as your manager I advise you to accept,' he added with mock solemnity.

Gina looked hysterical with delight and flung herself into his arms again.

'Congratulations.' Darina was back to croaking. Carolyn appeared carrying a tray of glasses and a napkin-wrapped bottle of champagne.

'What timing!' cried Gina. 'Open, quick, open!'

William rose, reached for the bottle and twisted off the wire from the cork.

Roger straightened himself. 'Not a champagne man myself. I think I'll go and start organising statements,' he announced.

Gina took a foaming glass. 'You mustn't go now!' she insisted. 'The fat lady's going to sing!' She walked briskly through to the drawing room and a moment later they heard the sound of the piano.

'When the man in my head is the man in my bed,' came lilting through to the hall.

'The party's over,' murmured Darina.